D1356054

House of Silence

Also by Patricia Marques

The Colours of Death

Patricia Marques

House of Silence

First published in Great Britain in 2022 by Hodder & Stoughton
An Hachette UK company

1

A CIP catalogue record for this title is available from the British Library

Hardback ISBN 978 1 529 33671 9
Trade Paperback ISBN 978 1 529 33672 6
eBook ISBN 978 1 529 33674 0

Typeset in Sabon MT by Hewer Text UK Ltd, Edinburgh
Printed and bound in Great Britain by Clays Ltd, Elcograf S.p.A.

Hodder & Stoughton policy is to use papers that are natural, renewable and recyclable products and made from wood grown in sustainable forests. The logging and manufacturing processes are expected to conform to the environmental regulations of the country of origin.

Hodder & Stoughton Ltd
Carmelite House
50 Victoria Embankment
London EC4Y 0DZ

www.hodder.co.uk

CASCAIS
(WHERE THE BODY IS FOUND)

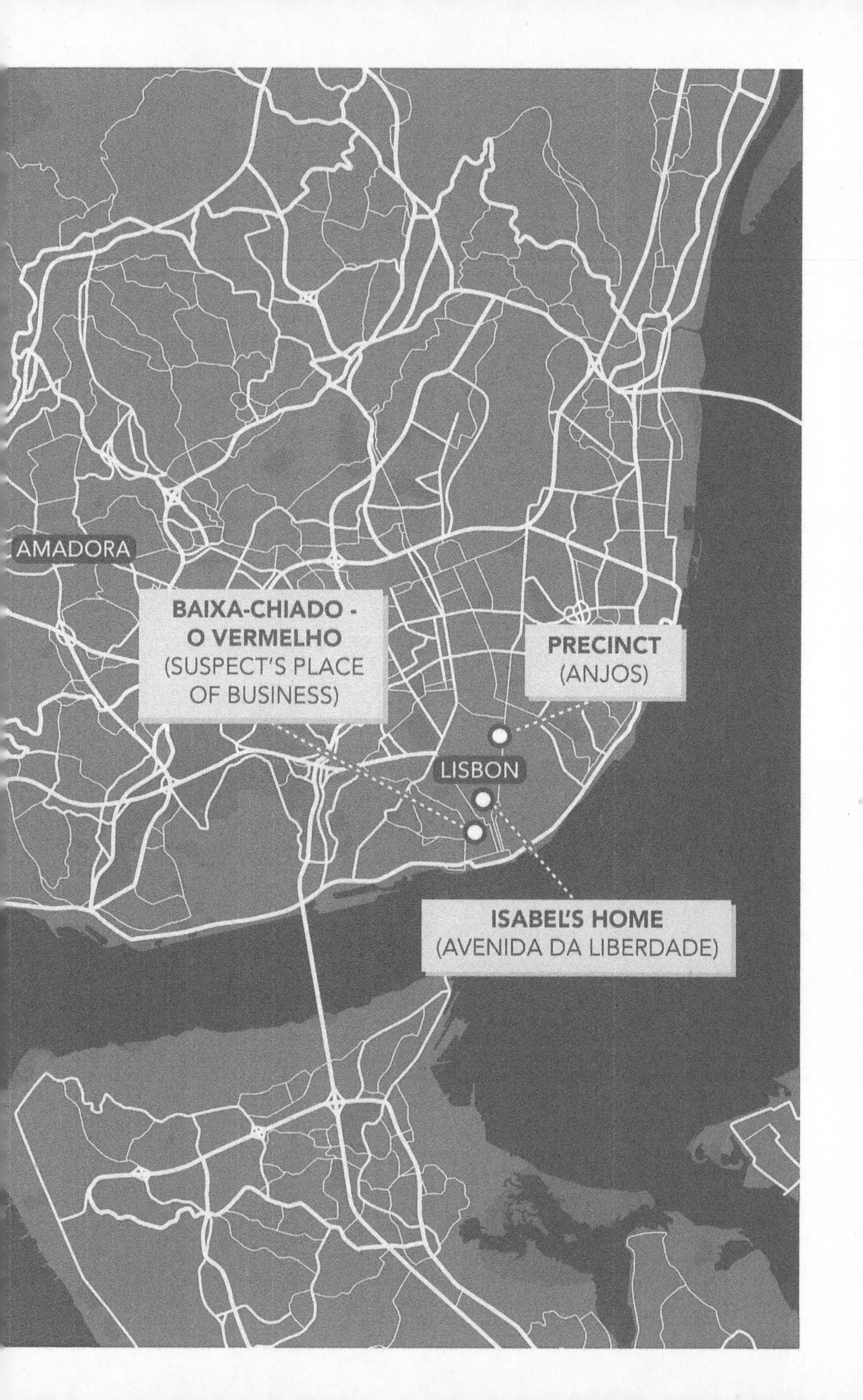
AMADORA
BAIXA-CHIADO - O VERMELHO
(SUSPECT'S PLACE OF BUSINESS)
PRECINCT
(ANJOS)
LISBON
ISABEL'S HOME
(AVENIDA DA LIBERDADE)

1

Isabel hovers outside her car, thumb smoothing over the small, rumpled piece of paper with a neatly scribbled address and number written on it. She's touched it so many times that the paper is soft now, the blue ink taking on a purple hue and bleeding into the creases.

She's had it for weeks and today she'd woken up determined to do something about it.

Well. At least she's got herself here.

The breeze is warm and soft, tugging at her curls. They catch on her face, and she brushes them aside.

The house is at ground-level, and cheerful looking. Not very big but painted in a soft yellow that makes Isabel think of spring. It's ringed by a black iron fence and there's a paved path leading up to the dark wooden door. The grass on either side of it is a vibrant green, as are the plants lining the outside of the house in heavy stone pots. She can see some chillies from where she stands, gleaming berry red.

The windows have white shutters, giving the house a touch of the fairy-tale. Warm. Inviting.

Standing here is a waste of her time.

Teeth locked together and unable to shake off the tension, she straightens away from the car and slams the driver's door shut.

In the pocket of her light jacket, her phone goes off, the vibrations tickling against her hip.

She curses under her breath and steps back, hurries a little way down the road so she's not standing directly in front of the house.

Voronov's name is on her screen and she slides her thumb across it to take the call. 'Isabel here.'

'Hey,' Voronov, her partner, says, 'I went by your place so we could get breakfast.'

Isabel eyes the house and turns her back on it. 'I had something to do. Sorry.'

'All right. I'm heading in, want me to get you anything or are you good?'

Ever since their last case caught the media's attention, it's safe to say that Isabel and Voronov have had little to no action. The Chief had wanted them to fly under the radar, which has led to them being saddled with a shitload of administrative work and dealing with petty crime.

And though Isabel is grateful for not having to deal with a major case while trying to manage the escalation of her powers, it's got to the point where she would rather have a tough case on her hands, so she doesn't have to focus on how it's starting to feel more and more as if she's losing her mind.

'Actually—' but before she can finish, her phone buzzes again and she pulls it away from her face to see who is trying to reach her now. It's the Chief. 'Aleks,' she says, 'the Chief is trying to call me.' Even as she says it, a message lights up the screen.

'Yes. I just got something now.'

She checks the message.

I need you and Voronov in Cascais ASAP. Call me on your way there.

The message is followed by the location.

Isabel sighs and puts the phone back up to her ear. 'Did you see that?'

On Voronov's end, Isabel hears voices and the sound of heavy steps. 'I did. I'll head out now.'

'Traffic shouldn't be too bad right now.' She flicks a glance at her watch. 'I can make it in an hour. Less if I break a few rules.'

'Please don't,' Voronov says, 'I'll get started while I wait for you.'

'See you there.'

Isabel casts one last look at the house and heads back to her car. She tosses the crumpled paper into the glove compartment and sits back in the driver's seat, letting her head rest for a moment, her eyes closed.

Another day.

Just one day at a time, Isabel. That's all she has to focus on right now.

One day at a time.

She dials Chief Bautista's number and starts the car.

The abandoned fishing port in Cascais sits on the river's edge.

It's a large squat building overlooking the small port. The windows are covered in so much dust that the glass has turned a muddied grey, barely reflecting the light. Some of them have been smashed in and left only with jagged points, giving the impression that they're yawning open when you peer at them. The brightness of the early morning sun waters the creepiness down.

Still, Isabel wouldn't want to be around here at night-time.

There's a tiny pier leading out to the water. It's low tide and the pier stands about four or five feet above the waterline. A small boat is tethered to it, partially embedded in the visible soft sand, water lapping gently at it from the other side. A slim sandbank stretches out either side of the pier and into the distance. Boats dot the calm surface of the water here and there and continue beyond where Isabel can see.

It should have been a tranquil image, but police cars line the side of the building, and the place is a hub of activity. Isabel can make out two crime scene investigators she recognises but isn't familiar with. She spots two more officers, in uniform, standing near two people in jogging gear. The woman has her arms around herself and is pacing back and forth in the small space while the man talks to the officers.

Voronov is standing with one of the suited-up investigators. At their feet, Isabel sees the body of a naked black woman, laid out on the black sheet.

As Isabel approaches, Voronov glances up from the discussion and, with a last word to the man, makes his way over to her.

Her partnership with Voronov is still pretty new but Isabel feels as if they've been working together for years. Voronov had previously been an inspector with Vice and had switched over to homicide last year after testifying against his partner, Seles, who had been Gifted, like Isabel; word had spread through the force that Voronov had turned on him because Voronov himself was anti-Gifted. Not too hard to believe considering that historically, Regulars, people with no Gifts, weren't too keen on Gifted individuals.

The divide started at a young age, from the moment children went into the National Testing Institute as equals. There, they would undergo the testing process to determine if they were Gifted and, if so, their affinity. Their Gifts always fell under either the telekinesis or telepathy category. By the time they walk out of the NTI, that equality is gone.

In Voronov's case, the truth was that Seles had just been a dirty cop.

It had taken Isabel a while to figure out that she could trust him and that he wasn't there to throw her under the bus. For someone who was used to working her cases predominantly alone, Isabel couldn't say it had been all bad being partnered up with someone. Even if this is the Polícia Judiciária's way of toeing the line and ensuring every Gifted officer has an eye kept on them at all times.

Isabel stops just off the pier. Something in her stills as awareness spreads through her, her skin rippling out in goosebumps.

It feels as if someone is standing behind her, breathing with her. The sound of their breathing echoes in her head and she feels everything in her lock up.

Slowly, she turns, knowing that, like every other time, she won't find anything, but unable to help herself.

All she sees is the path she took from her car to here. Not for the first time, she wonders if this sudden feeling is a side effect of having stopped her medication.

As someone classified as Gifted – and more importantly, as a telepathic Gifted who constantly has to guard against others' thoughts and emotions – Isabel had spent a large chunk of her adult life attempting to protect herself against her own Gift through self-medicating. Illegally. It had worked for a long time, despite the debilitating headaches she'd had to live with as a result of consistent use of the S3 pill, which was designed to tamp down a Gifted's power before the pill was recalled by the government.

The pills eventually ceased working for her, and just standing here without their protection has her on edge.

It's her new way of existing. Always on edge.

The scrape of Voronov's trainers on the rough ground draws her attention back to her surroundings. He stops at her side, slides his hands into his pockets and turns to face the proceedings.

She's glad she's left her jacket in the car. Despite it being only early spring, the air is warm, and she knows from experience that the day is going to get warmer as it shifts toward noon. Isabel is fine in her loose-fitting white T-shirt and an old pair of stretchy blue jeans. She's got her running trainers on too, which, if she's going to be trekking all over sand, means she won't be ruining yet another pair of work shoes.

She takes a deep breath, pushing the foreign feeling to the back of her mind and breathing in the smell of open water. There are a lot of thoughts here, busy, clinical, cataloguing the scene. Those are easier for her to rise above, monotone in colour and feeling – just the crime scene specialists doing their job.

There are two others that Isabel can pinpoint; they reverberate with shock and the blue of hysteria. Isabel carefully pushes her walls up against them before they can weaken her defences.

They'll come back, she knows. Insistent, and louder, as soon as she steps closer to the source.

'A couple were jogging past and spotted her,' Voronov says by way of greeting.

Isabel scoops her curls from around her face and takes the hairband from her wrist to tie her hair back in a loose knot at her nape. From where she's standing, she can make out a line that cuts deeply from one side of the woman's throat to the other, revealing flesh the same ruby red as pomegranates. She swallows convulsively.

'Dumped here?' She looks up at Voronov.

Either Voronov hadn't had time this morning or he'd been feeling a little lazy, because he's left his stubble alone. He's a tall guy, tall enough that people always do a double-take when he walks by. Isabel isn't used to seeing his face anything else other than perfectly clean-shaven, so the dark stubble is different. It makes the blue of his eyes stand out more. Like her, he's dressed casually, in a navy-blue T-shirt and dark blue jeans.

But there is something that feels – not off, exactly, but an unsettled feeling peeling away from him. It's unusual. For a Regular, Voronov's natural shields are impressive. He's one of the people Isabel doesn't have to shield too strongly against. Some people just have an instinct for protecting their thoughts – maybe it's something to do with personality and being naturally protective of oneself. Voronov is one of them.

'No actually, they found her half in and out of the water.'

Isabel is startled for a moment, before she realises. 'She washed up here?'

Voronov nods. 'Probably would've kept being dragged by the current except her arm caught on the rope tethering the boat.' He tilts his chin in the direction of it. 'Lucky.'

'Yeah,' Isabel says, eyes drifting back to the body, 'for us. Is that them?' she asks, looking at the man and woman in jogging gear.

'Yes, we took their details and statements but I asked them to stay on in case you thought you could get anything more out of them.'

They've been partners for a little over two months. It still surprises her when he refers to her Gift with this kind of ease. It's

refreshing after a lifetime of people, even those she worked well with, tiptoeing around it.

'Did they see anything else?' Isabel asks and starts towards the body, Voronov alongside her.

'No. Just passing by.'

'How come we don't have Jacinta today?' Jacinta is their head crime scene specialist and looking around, Isabel doesn't see her among the small number of police on scene.

'She was on call all night and still processing another case. She sent some of her people ahead.'

Isabel glances at him, frowning when the sunlight hits her right in the eyes. She wonders briefly where she's left her sunglasses. 'So, she'll still be with us on this case?'

'I don't think the Chief will be inflicting you on anyone new any time soon.'

Isabel cuts him a look but doesn't do anything but shake her head lightly.

As they make their way over, the forensics specialist glances up from where he's kneeling beside the body.

'Bom dia,' Isabel says.

'Inspector.' He stands to attention a little too fast, snapping his shoulders back like he's about to salute her, and Isabel blinks a little at him. She doesn't recognise him. 'I'm Angelo Pinho, I'm the head crime scene officer on site today. We've almost finished here; the body is ready to be moved. Our team is still combing the sandbank, but I don't think we'll find much.'

'Inspector Voronov told me the body wasn't dumped in this location, that she washed up here,' Isabel murmurs and kneels. It will be hard to pin down where she was dumped. It could have been anywhere along the Tagus. They really are lucky she didn't flush out into the Atlantic.

The woman hasn't been in the water long enough for it to completely degrade the state of her body. She's maybe about Isabel's age, early thirties or thereabouts, and clearly very physically fit. Her physique makes Isabel think of a ballet dancer, all strength and

grace. Her hair spills beneath her in a multitude of neat braids. Up close, the cut across her neck is even deeper than Isabel had thought, and she has to glance away from the split muscle and skin for a moment. As she takes in the rest of her, she notes that not only is the woman not wearing any clothing; there's also no jewellery. No earrings, no rings or bracelets, no necklace or watch.

The woman's eyebrows are perfectly shaped and her mouth, dry and cracked from the water, is wide and full. The kind that would have made a lot of people look twice.

There's nothing on her to indicate anything of who she is apart from her skin. Isabel notes the smaller lines and scrapes marring her body.

Young, beautiful and at the peak of health.

Isabel should be used to seeing dead bodies. But there's something that always gets to her about seeing someone like this. Their life thread severed; their body treated as if it were nothing more than garbage. No respect or honour for the life that had been.

Despite having spent the last few months itching to get back out there and on cases, Isabel has not missed this part of her duties.

'We had to be careful when moving her,' Angelo says, looking at the woman with a touch of pity, 'the cut was vicious, all the way down to the cervical spine.'

Isabel winces and can't help running a hand over her own throat. She rubs away the phantom sensation his words conjure. 'What kind of damage has she taken from the water? The small cuts and the scrapes?'

'Rigor mortis hasn't completely set in but with the body having been submerged in the water it's likely that onset has been significantly slowed. It'll be hard to determine how long she's been in there. The smaller wounds could be from being dragged along by the current. But it's too soon to say and it's something we might not be able to determine.'

'I'm going to take a wild guess and say we have no weapon either.'

'Apart from her,' Angelo says, 'we don't have anything. We've been combing the sand just in case but so far we haven't found anything.'

Makes sense, Isabel thinks. The odds were slim that evidence would have washed up alongside her.

Isabel sighs and rubs at her head. Close up, Angelo's thoughts are playing in the back of her head, an ongoing murmur listing things off as he frowns back down at his clipboard of notes. Isabel puts some physical distance between them.

'Let us know as soon as you're done here,' she says, 'we'll need the results of the post-mortem as soon as possible and if anything else does turn up, call us right away.'

Angelo nods his head a little too fast, a little too eager. She wonders how long he's been with Jacinta's team. He must be good. Jacinta would have kicked up a fuss and made sure he was out of there if he wasn't.

'Did the witnesses see anything else?' she asks Voronov.

He shakes his head. 'No, nothing else.'

'Okay, I guess there isn't much else they can give us right now.' Isabel pulls out her phone, turns away and starts walking off. 'We can let the witnesses go, we won't be needing anything else for now,' she calls out to the officers standing with the couple. She pulls up a search engine page and a map of the city.

Voronov stays behind for a moment, speaking to forensics, before rejoining her.

'For her to get caught here . . .' she looks out at the water and the sandbanks, 'there aren't a lot of places she could have been thrown in.'

'Estoril, maybe,' Voronov says.

'Maybe.' She eyes the map and bites into her lower lip. 'Or maybe Carcavelos.' No way to be sure really. She pushes her hair back from her face. 'We'll have to wait for the post-mortem results.' A glance at her watch shows her it's nearly ten. 'Get back, pick up some breakfast on the way?' She glances back at the team and watches as they shift the victim into a body bag and start to

zip it up. 'Once we have her prints . . .' Well, it won't do them any good if she's not on the system. 'We'll trawl through missing persons.' Just thinking about it has her rubbing her eyes in sympathy for her future self's eyes.

Voronov gives her that half-smile. 'At least we're off minor offences.'

Isabel sighs. 'Yeah, at least there's that.'

2

Walking into the precinct is something that Isabel needs to brace herself for.

She heads straight for the bathroom, calling out greetings as she speeds there. It's blissfully empty and she walks into a cubicle and locks the door behind her.

She slumps back against the flimsy wall that divides the cubicles and lets out her breath slowly as she takes a moment to recalibrate.

Even with walls between her and the rest of the people in the building, she can hear them. Thoughts and emotions crowding each other in a myriad of colours that makes Isabel's head spin and tests her stomach.

It's a new addition to her daily routine. Crowded places were difficult to manage before, but she could pull it off. Now they are much worse. She builds up the walls in her head, tall as she can, to keep the thoughts out, but eventually they reach over them, fingers like tree roots trying to sink deep into her and bind her to the ground.

She's in there for maybe ten minutes, maybe fifteen, until eventually her heart isn't trying to pound out of her body and the sense of being overwhelmed begins to fade.

It's a reset, that's all. As long as she can find a quiet place to reset every time, she can manage.

'Merda,' she mutters, rubs at her eyes as she gathers herself. As steady as she's going to be, she unlocks the door and steps out.

She startles, almost jerking back into the cubicle in the second it takes her to realise that Voronov is waiting there, leaning against one of the sinks.

Instantly she narrows her eyes. 'Could've at least said you were out here,' she says.

He shrugs his large shoulders, eyes as sharp as ever, taking in the pallor of her face as she walks to the sink next to the one he is leaning against. 'Sorry.'

Isabel scoffs and side-eyes him as she switches on the tap and rinses out her mouth. 'I wouldn't lean on that if I were you. What are you trying to do? Break it?'

Voronov's lips tilt up at the corners, but the small smile is gone as quickly as it appeared as his eyes roam her face. 'Are you all right?'

Isabel rinses her mouth one more time and splashes water on her face, the cold a sharp, stark grounding that she needs.

Her head is quieter now.

She can still hear all their voices coming from behind the door, as if everyone is standing there, waiting for her to let them all back in again, to let them wrap their thoughts around her like chains until it chokes all the air out of her body and sinks her into a pit that she can't drag herself out of.

Isabel straightens and clenches her hands around the porcelain edges of the sink, and closes her eyes. It takes her a moment, maybe two, to find that place within herself, that little island in her mind's eye, and to check to make sure her wall will hold when she walks back out there.

She's not lying to herself. She knows the moment she leaves here their thoughts will be slamming against her. It's exhausting. She can feel it slowly, slowly, eroding at her sanity. But for now, she's still in control enough to function.

Only when she's home can she breathe a little easier, settle into her own space and let her guard down. Even then she'll still catch the thoughts of people in the surrounding apartments, but it takes less effort to block out. It isn't like right now, where so many people in one space like this turn the mass of thoughts into one single monster trying to drown her.

Isabel opens her eyes and looks at Voronov, the curl to her mouth wry. 'I'm fine,' she says and walks around him to get some paper towels, patting them over her face. She balls them up and tosses them into the bin. 'Following colleagues into toilets now. A kink I should know about?' she asks, dry.

He shakes his head slightly and straightens away from the sink. He's got used to her humour by now, so she knows he won't think anything of it. He has definitely stopped being surprised by it. Although to be honest, she doesn't remember if anything she's done up until now has ever truly surprised him.

That's not true, she thinks, *he wasn't expecting to see you talking to him out of someone else's body.*

She shies away from thinking about it. Has avoided thinking about it ever since it happened, and she doesn't really want to think about it now either – especially not now.

'Come on,' he says.

Isabel cuts him a look as he holds the door open for her to leave and then ignores the side-eyes they get as he follows her out. Voronov doesn't so much as bat an eyelash.

They don't get far.

Chief Bautista is standing outside her office, hand on the door frame. She has a cigarette poking out above her ear. Her hair is down, curls cut at a precise chin-length. She's had that hairstyle as long as Isabel's been at the force; Isabel has never seen it any other way. She's always had dark hair peppered liberally with white; even that, Isabel thinks, hasn't changed.

The Chief gestures them both over and goes into her office without waiting to see if they'll follow.

All the windows in the Chief's office are open and the blinds are gathered along the tops of the windows, their dangling strings swinging gently from side to side from the breeze filtering in alongside the sunshine.

The windows being wide open has less to do with the nice weather and more to do with the cigarette Chief Bautista is tucking between her lips as she sits down with a grunt. She lights up.

Isabel takes a seat and the Chief waits until Voronov has closed the door and sat down before saying anything.

She blows a stream of smoke in the direction of the windows, not that it does much to keep the smoke from permeating the room. Sharp hazel eyes assess them both.

'I know sending you both out like that was sudden.' The Chief has that whisky voice, the rasp in it always makes Isabel want to soothe her own throat, 'but I'd say you've both had enough of being on minor crimes. And this one looks ugly. Tell me what we have.'

Isabel shares a look with Voronov before turning back to Chief Bautista. 'She was dumped in the water, Chief. Her throat was cut badly, almost severed through to the spinal cord. CSS team are on it and we're hoping to receive preliminary reports at some point today.'

Chief Bautista sighs and runs a hand through her hair but it just swings straight back into place. 'Keep me updated. Brief your team. I've assigned two junior inspectors to you both. Hand over anything that needs to be wrapped up for minor crimes to them and start working this ASAP. Anything looks like it'll blow up, come to me. From now on, we've got eyes on us however we move.'

This is what happens when you make enemies in the political sphere. They don't forget and they don't let it go. And all of them have friends in high places. Last year, Isabel and her team had done just that with a leader of a right-wing political party. Despite them finding his son's killer, he's had eyes on them ever since.

'Daniel and Carla will join you tomorrow,' the Chief says, 'get them up to speed. Maybe that will finally make Daniel stop complaining to anyone who will listen about being benched,' she mutters, rubbing at her temple.

Inspectors Daniel Verde and his partner, Junior Inspector Carla Muniz, had also been on the case with Isabel and Voronov that had led to them all being put on minor offences. Isabel had heard all of Daniel's bitching. She doesn't blame the Chief for wanting a break from it all. Isabel had just about managed to keep from throttling him herself.

'Yes, Chief,' Isabel says.

The juniors are already waiting for them by their desks. Their IDs hang around their necks, hair in place and presentable clothes. Isabel can practically smell the new on them. Nerves and determination roll off them both. Next to them, Isabel and Voronov look like they've just rolled out of bed.

They introduce themselves as Felipe and Sansão, both Regulars from what Isabel gleans from their IDs. Sansão sports a very neatly trimmed goatee, and his hair is jet black and pulled into a tiny ponytail at his nape. He's actually in proper white shirt and black suit trousers, patent shoes so shiny Isabel can see her reflection in them. Felipe is a little more relaxed-looking, wearing a white shirt but blue jeans and trainers. He has an easy smile and short, light-brown hair.

Isabel appreciates that they just get on with it, taking notes and not looking as if they're resentful for having to finish off someone else's less than exciting work. If anything, all she can sense is a fresh green eagerness that makes her think of newly cut grass.

They're just wrapping up the handover when her phone pings in her pocket. There's a message from Angelo in CSS telling her the crime scene photos are on the system and that Jacinta will be following up with them soon.

Isabel glances up at the two junior inspectors, who had been leaning over Voronov's shoulder and listening intently as he'd taken them through the last bits of the handover. 'You can both take it from here? We'll be in one of the case rooms if you need us for anything.'

They both straighten up.

'Yes, boss,' Felipe says, 'think we're good to go.'

Boss? Isabel arches a brow. Really eager to please.

She doesn't have to look at Voronov to feel his amusement. 'Right. Thanks.' She knocks Voronov's chest with her knuckles. 'Come on, CSS have uploaded the photos.'

She's ready to get back to her real job.

3

They've just finished setting up their new case room when Isabel's phone rings.

'Inspector Reis.'

'Hi,' Jacinta says, 'busy?' As well as being their department's head of CSS, Jacinta is also a friend. Like Isabel, she hadn't taken too kindly to being put on the backbench after their last case. The Chief has only recently been sending her back out to scenes.

Isabel tilts back in her seat and locks her eyes on the ceiling. 'I haven't been but it's looking like that's about to change,' she says.

'Yeah, I can imagine. Sorry I couldn't be there this morning. I've had to pull Angelo onto a different case too but will have the crime scene report over to you in the next hour or so.'

'All right, sounds good . . .' She is distracted by Voronov striding over. He's gesturing to catch her attention and has his mobile phone pressed to his ear. 'Jacinta, I'll call you back once we've looked over everything.'

'Okay, talk later.'

Isabel hangs up and stands. 'What is it?'

Voronov grabs his jacket from the back of his seat. 'Coroner wants us to see something.'

Isabel's eyebrows fly up.

Well. Something is better than nothing.

One thing that Isabel appreciates about the morgue is the utter dead silence.

Emphasis on dead. It's rarely packed with people, not living ones anyway.

Luckily, this small branch is here mostly for the benefit of the PJ, working on bodies that are linked to ongoing investigations. There are usually only about two to three people working this morgue at any one time.

The last time Isabel had been in here, the coroner had been manning the front while waiting for Isabel and Voronov to arrive because they had been short-staffed that day. It is what it is.

They make quick work of signing in and the person at the front desk rushes them through, exuding the same impatience a sales assistant does when a customer walks in as they are about to close.

Their victim's body is still on the examination table when they enter, covered with a sheet.

Isabel curls her shoulders in and wraps her arms around herself as they're enveloped in the cold of the room, trying to preserve warmth. As usual, Voronov barely seems to feel the cold.

'That was fast,' the coroner says, and gestures them over. 'The cause of death is exactly what it looks like,' she goes on. 'There's no fluid collection, so she was dead when she hit the water and all the lacerations and abrasions were post mortem. Most likely a result of the body colliding with other things in the river.'

Okay, that fits with Angelo's initial observations at the scene.

'Quick run-down,' she continues, 'there's a little maceration.' She carefully picks up one of the victim's hands in hers and flips it over. There's a small, thumb-size stylised arrow inked on the inside of her wrist, but Isabel's attention is quickly drawn to the wrinkled and thickened skin of the palm of the hand. It's got an unusual soft, white look to it. It reminds Isabel of an extreme version of pruned fingers after soaking in the bath too long. 'Given the temperature of the water, I'd say she was in the water for about four hours, maybe five. It's hard to say exactly.'

Isabel and Voronov share a look. Does this mean that she was killed as early as last night?

'But there's something you should see.' And it's then that Isabel realises there's an organ tray still laid out, and she swallows convulsively as she recognises the brain. She hasn't seen many, something she's grateful for. This particular one, she can tell, isn't right.

Catching Isabel's frown, the coroner's eyes crinkle at the corners above the line of her mask.

'Yeah. That's what I wanted you to see. Cause of death' – she pulls the sheet back and gestures at the cut, which is now neatly sewn – 'she bled out from the cut to the throat. If they had gone just a bit further, they would have severed her head completely. I'll detail it in my report but this—,' she taps the edge of the tray. The organ gleams under the harsh lights of the room and Isabel tries to pinpoint what it is that looks wrong about it.

'That's . . . significantly smaller, isn't it?' Voronov says beside Isabel, and he is frowning too.

The coroner nods. 'To put it bluntly, there are extreme signs of cognitive fatigue – it is, to all intents and purposes "fried".'

What? 'What do you mean?' Isabel asks. 'Like "burnout"?' Is that a thing?

The coroner sighs and readjusts her glasses. 'It's hard to explain, I've never actually seen this in person but definitely in some case studies of post-mortems carried out on Gifted after their death.' She points to the organ. 'There were examples of brains that had shorted out, if you will. They couldn't keep up with the output of an affinity. They looked like this.'

She beckons them closer, taking them through an explanation riddled with scientific terms that hurt Isabel's head.

'Like I said,' the coroner says, 'the cause of death is definitely from the neck wound. She bled out. But she was young, mid-thirties at most. The state of her brain is extremely unusual, Gifted or not. We won't be able to get much else without further examination. Knowing if she had any previous medical conditions would be a big help.'

Isabel chews on her lip, mulling it over. She glances at Voronov. 'Not great news but at least we know she was most likely Gifted. That should help with narrowing down the search.'

Still. Even if she was Gifted, that doesn't explain why her brain is in that state.

'You said that her brain is like this because it couldn't keep up with . . . the level of power of her Gift?' Isabel asks.

'Not exactly. That does exist, people in the field refer to it as erosion. It's quite frequent in cases of higher-level Gifted. Say level eight and up. In a lot of cases because that Gift level is so hard to control, it overloads the organ and begins to erode. Most often it's the frontal lobe that suffers the worst damage.'

Isabel glances away, tries to ignore the chill that spears through her chest at those words. She breathes out through her nose and turns back to the coroner.

'This doesn't quite look like that,' the coroner is saying. She picks up the organ and Isabel finds herself leaning away without meaning to. 'Like I said, I think she's too young. We'd expect to see the start of the erosion but not something full-blown like this.'

Voronov frowns. 'Then what?'

'Maybe a full-blown output of her Gift? All at once? This is all conjecture,' she says, 'there's no way to tell. Once we've properly examined it, I may have more for you.' She sets it back in its tray.

A full-blown output?

No Gifted would go that far unless it was a severe loss of control that they just couldn't claw back, or it had been intentional. An act of desperation maybe – like trying to fight for their life.

'There's something else that may help,' the coroner says and, with practised ease, manoeuvres the body so it tilts onto its side. The sheet covering the corpse whispers over the skin as it slides but stays mostly in place, draped over her front and back. 'Take a look.'

The coroner points at the back of the victim's neck.

Isabel and Voronov step closer to take a better look.

On the back of the victim's neck is the Greek letter psi.

4

It's not until Isabel gets home and isn't greeted by the click-clack of small claws on the floor and loud panting breaths that she remembers she'd asked her brother, Sebastião, to stop by and pick up Branco and Tigre after she'd been called to the crime scene that morning. She'd been worried she would have to work overtime and wanted him to go and make sure they were okay.

She sighs, for a moment just feeling the weight of the day on her. Closing the door behind her, she toes off her trainers. Already, she's aware of them. Voices that aren't voices on the other side of her walls.

She walks into her small living room, pulling her top up and over her head as she goes. It is nearing half past six and the light from the sun paints the walls of the room through the open windows, turning everything red. Isabel has to squint as she walks over to lower the shutters and eyes her plants critically. One of them is looking a little thirsty and she makes a note to water them all before she goes out for her run.

She doesn't lower the shutters all the way down, leaves a little of the natural light to spill into the room. Without the warm light of the sun on her, the skin on her chest and arms pebbles in the cool air of the room.

She switches on the TV to replace the usual sounds of her dogs following her around the house and wanders into the kitchen, flipping the light on as she does. She stops and a soft smile steals over her mouth when she notes the dishes have been done and left to dry on the drainer. There's a note on the kitchen table with writing she recognises as Sebastião's:

Don't work too hard, Tia Simone sent food, check the fridge and message me when you get home, beijos maninha.

Sebastião and their Tia Simone have always kept an eye on her. Sebastião in particular has always been protective of Isabel. He's her half-brother, from her dad's first marriage, and had been raised mostly by Tia Simone, their dad's sister, after his mum had passed away when he was young. Isabel's always thought that he's always watched her back more than Rita's because in a way, Isabel was just like him. Isabel's mum might be alive and well, but she might as well not have one.

In the fridge, as promised, is a clear container. When she peels back the bright blue lid, the smell of feijoada makes her stomach grumble and she wants to shove it in the microwave and scoff it all down right away – except she knows if she has anything now, she will just end up bringing it all back up, and having done that once today already is enough for her.

That makes her pause.

She puts the container back in the fridge and fills a glass with water before heading to her room to change into her running gear.

It displays the evidence of her new routine. A giant cushion is tucked into the corner of the room by the window, topped with holey old blankets and a squeaky toy. Her own bed is a mess, pillows at risk of falling off the edge of the mattress and her sheets scrunched towards the end from where she'd shoved them off with her feet when her alarm had gone off that morning.

Her laptop is balanced precariously on the edge of the nightstand, a clear yellow plastic folder on top of it. It is stuffed with sheets of printed paper and a handful of envelopes that Isabel hasn't ever opened. The pen that was on there is now on the floor. Red. Tia always tells her it's bad luck to write in red and tells her off when she sees her doing it. Isabel doesn't know why it's always the first colour she reaches for. If someone asked Isabel's mother, she would most likely spout some bullshit that it's because Isabel is a descendant of hell or some such thing.

She rights the bedsheets and picks up the folder. The printer has made a line that cuts straight through the image, a photo of a woman. Isabel had bought the thing cheap a month ago and had screwed up the set-up, so it prints with that line marring every page.

The woman on the page had been Gifted. A level 10.

She's the latest one Isabel has discovered. She found out about her in one of her search sessions the previous week and added her to her pile. Another face and another name for Isabel to try to dig up information on.

Anti-Gifted sentiment has always been rife in society. People have been especially hostile toward higher-level Gifted. Higher-level Gifted like Isabel herself. There have always been stories, rumours, of them disappearing without a trace, something the government always scoffs at. Conspiracy theorists, they say, amateur wannabe-sleuths grasping at nothing. Regular people are only too happy to believe the reassurances.

Gifted people, not so much.

With Isabel's own Gift evolving, it's something she can't afford to just wonder about any more.

One would think, with how much information gets leaked onto the web, that she would be having an easier time of finding what she's looking for. But it seems Portugal is not the only country that has been treating its higher-level Gifted with caution.

She puts everything back and links her hands behind her neck. It's a lot harder to get on with her normal end-of-day ritual when her dogs aren't here.

She should really stay in after her run and put in another research session.

But her house and this silence . . .

She stands there, listening to the irritating peppy music of a commercial coming from the living room. She moves her laptop a bit further up on the bedside table to prevent an accident from happening and then gets changed.

A group of people are walking by, passing below her bedroom window, joking and talking about dinner. Their thoughts bubble up to her, mingling with their voices, nothing keeping their leaking emotions at bay.

No. She doesn't want to stay here when it's this quiet. She'll hear everything.

Might as well put her time to good use.

It's approaching ten in the evening when Isabel walks back into the precinct. Belly full of the feijoada, muscles worn out from her run. Her mind is quieter too, her Gift calmed for now. More and more, lately, it's felt as if she has something alien beneath her skin, barely controllable and ready to lash out when she least expects it.

She says hello to the night shift on reception and takes the stairs up to their floor slowly, rolling her shoulders to work out the muscles that feel a bit too tight there. It'll only get worse with lack of sleep.

Their floor, when she gets there, is mostly empty, only one of the side offices with its light on and three other people in the open section, overhead lights acting like spotlights and leaving pockets of darkness between them.

It's a contrast to that morning and she breathes easier. She walks past the Chief's office. The door is closed, and the lights are off. Looks like the Chief is having a rare early night.

The row of rooms that stretch down past the Chief's office are all closed too. Those are usually used for interrogation and as case rooms. Mostly, everyone works in the space outside where all the desks are clustered together in twos or threes.

Around the corner from the open space is one of their bigger rooms, usually reserved for large meetings or used as a backup when they can't use the floor downstairs for a conference room.

There is a light on in one of the offices at the end of the hall. The name plate on it has been changed, a new case and a number scrawled in black, block letters. She can hear voices from behind it and for a disconcerting second the voices and thoughts tangle together, and she can't pull them apart.

Voronov's empty desk sits next to hers. She'd messaged him before leaving the house, letting him know she was going back in.

Her trainers squeak on the floor as she heads over. The darkness suits her mood.

She doesn't bother taking off her zip-up fleece. With spring coming soon, the temperature has been steadily rising, but the nights are still cool. Without the usual number of people packed into their desks heating up the space, sitting still is going to chill her pretty quickly, so she has dressed warmer than normal, a thermal long-sleeve top beneath her fleece, and worn blue jeans for comfort.

While the computer boots up, she goes to the meagre kitchenette, puts on a pot of coffee and leans back against the counter, eyes closed and enjoying the quiet of the moment. The gurgle of the pot is the only noise in the small space and the scent of hot coffee blooms in the air. She evens out her breath, taking satisfaction from the aches in her muscles.

Maybe she won't stay too long – a few hours – and then she might actually be able to get some sleep without her dogs at home.

With a hot mug in her hands, she flexes her shoulders. The light from the computer is jarring and she blinks at it a few times. She needs to remember to get some eye drops or something. She always hates how her eyes feel after a session spent staring at a screen for too long, but she never does anything to prevent it happening again.

She opens the photos from the site in Cascais where their Jane Doe's body was found.

Isabel stares at the image of the woman lying on her back as she had been when Isabel had arrived on site. Her eyes are drawn to the wide line across her neck. The way the skin is split open and the flesh revealed beneath it looks almost like a grotesque smile. Isabel pushes herself to move past it and fixes on the face, thinks again about how striking it looks. The kind of face that would have drawn gazes filled with appreciation.

The coroner had said she had bled out.

Had someone stood there? Stood over her, watching her struggle to breathe, blood bubbling up from her wound and her mouth? Then, once it was over, tossed her into the river? What did it take for you to be able to watch someone die like this and not do anything to prevent it?

Isabel tracks the swathe of the woman's braids with her eyes, a soft sadness tugging at the corners of her mouth for the life that had been.

She closes the image and begins looking at the ones documenting how she'd been found.

In those initial pictures, the victim's arm is caught on the rope tethering the boat to the pier. Her torso is a limp heavy weight digging her other shoulder into the wet sand. Her waist-length hair is draped over her face, covering it from view. The rest of her is submerged in the water from the waist down. The tide had been a little higher then.

Isabel squints and zooms in. The picture quality is good and the tattoo on the back of her neck can clearly be seen. Under the sunlight, the black letter psi stands out on her skin.

Isabel flicks through the rest of the on-scene photos but it's half-hearted; she doubts she will find anything in a handful of photos that the CSS officers on scene didn't.

She clicks back out of them and opens the coroner's report.

The coroner places her age between late twenties and mid-thirties, makes a strong suggestion that the victim was Gifted, based on the severe atrophy of the brain, which points to possible extreme overuse of a Gifted ability. Physically, their Jade Doe had been in her prime, but they still have a day or so to go before the toxicology report comes in. A search of her prints hasn't brought up any results. Which doesn't mean much. All it says is that she was never in trouble with the law.

Isabel pushes up her sleeves and shakes her hair out of her face. She really needs to book an appointment to get it cut. The thought makes her wince. The hairdresser isn't the best of places for her right now either. They're always filled with buzzing thoughts and conversation and in her current state, it would be too much. Maybe she'll be able to convince Tia Simone to do it for her.

The problem with searching missing persons is that their Jane Doe's death is recent. To people she knows, she might not be missing at all. Not yet. Isabel doesn't want to have to resort to making a public appeal to find out who this woman is though. Facing off with the press isn't really one of her strong points.

Given that just her name is guaranteed to get the press salivating, she'd rather not have to be in that position. But if they don't find out who she is and fast, she may not have a choice.

They have a starting point for now though. The tattoo, and the thing that has been bothering Isabel since they spoke to the coroner: the state of the brain at the time of death.

She wants more on that. A lot more about what could have caused such a devastating and fast-acting deterioration, the kinds of things that could trigger it. Maybe there would be something in that.

If the woman really had been Gifted, had she depleted her Gift and herself fighting off her attacker? Had she been a telekinetic Gifted? And depending on her level, if she'd got into that state fighting for her life with her Gift, then maybe she'd left a mark somewhere. A mark they could find.

She looks at the photo of their victim one more time, trapped there in the water, lifeless.

'I'll find you,' she says, 'I promise.'

Isabel takes a sip of her coffee and gets to work.

5

Something cold presses against Isabel's cheek. She jerks up straight and slaps away the hand. A piece of paper unsticks itself from her face, and she squints up at Voronov, who is looking down his nose at her, holding a can of Coca-Cola and wearing a smirk.

'Estúpido,' she mutters. The iciness from the cold can lingers on her skin. She wipes her hand over her mouth and is grateful that she won't have to live down any embarrassment involving her drooling on her papers.

When she glances up at her screen, she sees it has gone black. 'What time is it?' She blinks away the sleep from her eyes, cursing under her breath. Good thing it hadn't been the Chief who had caught her out.

A peek out of the windows shows that it is still dark outside. The previously occupied office is now empty, lights switched off. Their floor is a wall of silence.

Her watch says it's only 12:13.

'Great,' she huffs out a breath and digs the mounds of her palms into her eyes and, after a bit, rubs roughly.

'Take it,' Voronov says and sets the can on her desk, 'we can order in if we're having a long night.'

Isabel pops the tab on the can, the hiss and the bubbles loud for a few seconds before she takes a gulp of caffeine and sugar. 'Thank you. Wasn't actually expecting you to show up, by the way.'

'And give you reason to ask the Chief to get rid of me?'

Isabel scoffs. 'That would imply that the Chief actually listens to me.' That Isabel may have done that at the start of their working partnership goes unsaid. They both know that is not the case any longer.

'How is it going?' he asks, nodding at the computer.

'Well.' She sighs and sets the Coke down. She turns her notebook so Voronov can take a look at the notes she'd been making before she'd fallen asleep on them.

He rests a hand on the back of her chair. Isabel catches a hint of his aftershave as he leans past her to have a look and finds herself breathing more of it in. It smells good, sharp and clean.

Voronov runs his thumb over the words she has got down on the paper, a line of concentration etching itself between his brows. 'These are the only things that could cause that level of damage to the brain?' he asks.

Isabel nods. 'Through the use of a Gift, yes.' She rubs at her eyes.

She'd been digging for a couple of hours before she'd found a few snippets of text that referred to the effect of a Gift on the brain beyond what was common knowledge. Everyone knew that high-level Gifted were at risk of damage, that over time their Gifts would lead to erosion, primarily in the frontal lobe. Isabel had looked into that plenty in her own time. To her, it was a personal threat, something looming over her head that she prays will never come to pass. Not that anyone will be on the lookout for that with her.

No one knew about the results of her latest test but her.

What she'd found in her search, though, went a little beyond that. Enough to make her wish she hadn't looked.

According to some of the medical journals she'd looked through on the subject, when the erosion was extreme to the point where the brain suffered mass erosion like this, it was as the coroner had said, but not quite in the way she had explained it. The results of Isabel's search had made her feel sick, and when she'd first understood what it was that she was reading she'd had to stop for a moment.

The information had been obtained as a result of an investigation into incidents of the same phenomenon occurring in Gifted children. It had happened a total of nine times worldwide. That had been made public at least. They found all the children had been born as high-level Gifted.

Usually this isn't the case. Typically, higher-level Gifted reached their final level between the ages of thirteen and sixteen. In these cases, these children had been born already at the highest setting, so to speak.

Isabel can't make herself look at the notebook as Voronov continues to read, doesn't even realise she's cracking the knuckles of her right hand one by one until Voronov looks over at her, blue eyes sombre.

For children born that way, with their Gift level on full blast, without the ability to control it or guidance on it, most of them were in a vegetative state by the time they reached seven years of age. In the cases mentioned, only two of those children had made it past that age and their bodies had shut down a couple of years later.

Sometimes Isabel wonders if nature itself is against them all.

'I didn't know this,' Voronov says. He reaches for a chair, drags it over and sits down with a heavy sigh.

'Neither did I,' Isabel says and when she smiles it's bitter-edged, 'wish I still didn't, to be honest.'

Voronov glances at the open pages. 'Is that all that came up?'

Isabel breathes out and shakes her head. Grabbing the can of Coke again, she takes enough gulps that her eyes start smarting from the way the fizz feels as if it's burning its way down her throat.

'No, but it's mostly along the same lines. A sudden and consistent use of their Gift, where they're unable to shut it off.' She flicks her nail over the top rim of the can a couple of times. Tries not to think about how that sounds a little too close to home. 'The consistent high output eventually leads to the same result. But in theory,' she nods at the computer, 'in theory it could happen in a much shorter time, depending on their level.'

One of the hypotheses is that if a Gifted who is high-level but has never used their Gift at full capacity, suddenly turns the volume all the way up and maintains that, then that could also have the same effect.

It's almost like bleeding out, Isabel thinks.

Voronov closes the notebook and slides it back over to her. 'What are you thinking?'

Isabel folds her arms and shrugs a shoulder. 'I'm wondering if maybe she burned up fighting for her life.'

And lost. She'd lost.

'We already know her prints aren't on the system,' he says, 'what about missing persons? Anything there?'

'I started,' Isabel says, 'but I needed a break from it so I switched to this. I was hoping it might be helpful.'

'We don't know it won't be.'

'I suppose.'

'I looked up the symbol,' he says.

'The tattoo?'

'I don't think I found anything that useful, but a few things were still interesting.'

Isabel sits up and scoots her chair forward. 'Like what?'

'It's usually associated with the idea of the soul and divine power. It's also a common tattoo among telepathic Gifted,' he says.

Isabel is surprised. 'Really? Why?'

'Something about it symbolising a better grasp of mind and soul and navigating between the two.'

Huh. She's not sure how true that is, but to each their own. 'Fair enough.'

Voronov doesn't respond and is quiet for a moment, eyes staring off at a point over Isabel's shoulder.

She lifts an eyebrow. 'What?'

His eyes snap back to her face and when he frowns, a line carves itself between his dark eyebrows. 'I'm not sure. Something about it feels familiar.'

'You could have just seen it somewhere if it's as popular as they say,' she says slowly.

'Maybe.' But he doesn't sound convinced. 'I'll keep looking into it. Where are we now?' He rolls his chair back away from her. 'I'll pick up where you left off from the missing reports.'

Isabel finishes off her Coke. She needs to go splash some cold water on her face, refocus properly. 'I was thinking it's worth looking in the system, check for any similar attacks in the area.' Anything that will help better position the investigation once they discover her identity. 'And food. We need food.'

Voronov stops in the act of shrugging off his jacket and then gives a short shake of his head. 'This is the real reason why you want me here,' he scoffs, 'because I feed you. All right, but I don't want to hear complaints about it.'

She groans and gets up to go to the bathroom. 'You're going to order sushi, aren't you?'

It is nearing three in the morning and Isabel has moved onto missing reports as well. She's long since kicked off her trainers, her curls pulled into a messy bunch atop her head as she clicks through reports and blinks her eyes furiously to keep the worst of the dryness at bay. She has a tempura roll caught precariously in chopsticks halfway to her mouth when Voronov pushes back from his desk.

'Isabel.'

'What?' she asks around the mouthful and rolls her chair over to his side.

'Take a look.' He makes space so she can get closer to the screen.

The report is relatively recent. Isabel glances at the picture and when her eyes settle on the woman's face, she feels a lick of excitement mixed with dread.

There is enough likeness there.

The picture in the report looks like a really bad ID photo. In it, the woman's hair is pulled back from her face, smoothed back into a tight ponytail. The shape of her face is similar. Despite how unflattering the picture is, it doesn't fail to hide her high cheekbones.

Isabel's heart speeds up with hopeful anticipation even as she tries to tamp it down. The report names her as Marta Nunes, thirty-two and from Setúbal.

Yes. This could be her, she thinks.

She checks the report again. It says that Marta Nunes went missing in December. The report itself wasn't filed until February. 'Missing for over a month,' Isabel murmurs, 'she's been gone a while. Why wait so long to file it?'

She looks over the rest of the details in the report. Height and build, other noted identifiers.

Right there in the report is the detail of a Greek letter tattooed on the back of the missing person's neck. Excitement spills over. 'It mentions the tattoo,' she says, 'it's her.'

She glances over at Voronov and locks eyes with him, sees the satisfaction in the narrowing of his eyes and the uptilt of his mouth.

Voronov glances back at the screen. 'Report was filed by a Madalena Nunes, but it doesn't state who she is to the victim.' Same surname. Could be a mother or a sister, maybe.

'Let's hope this is her. And if it is, then tomorrow is going to be rough.'

6

It's early the next day when Isabel and Voronov open the door to the interview room where Madalena Nunes awaits them. Laura, who mans the front desk at their precinct, had said she'd walked in at 8.00 a.m. sharp.

Isabel and Voronov had squeezed in some sleep in the case room before making a quick trip home to wash up before coming back. Not their smartest idea, and Isabel can feel a knot in her lower back from having slept curled over a desk for a few hours.

The weather has carried over from the previous day, the sun eye-wateringly bright and flooding the room through the window. The sound of birds singing adds a touch of the surreal to the situation.

The first thing Isabel notices is that Madalena Nunes looks awfully young.

She has grey eyes and cheekbones that belong on a runway, but she sits in the chair shrunken in on herself, her hair pulled back off her face, short tight ringlets escaping here and there, behind her ear, at her temple, like someone who has rushed through getting ready. There are bags under her eyes, making them seem deeply set. She's swamped by an oversized light-brown bombazine jacket, thin baggy white jumper and blue jeans. She looks ready to jump out of her skin.

As they step inside, Isabel represses a wince, forcing her expression to remain smooth because the agony radiating from the tiny, tiny woman in front of them is like an anchor wrapping around Isabel's neck, trying to drag her all the way to the bottom.

Isabel throws up her walls in self-defence. The last thing she needs is to make a spectacle of herself so early in the morning.

There is enough gossip about her at the precinct without her giving her colleagues anything else to talk about. The Chief has done her best to stamp it out, but these things aren't something that a boss can really control. Isabel will just have to ride it out.

Voronov, as if tuned in to her, throws a sharp glance Isabel's way as he gently shuts the door behind him. His other hand holds a steaming paper cup of tea. Isabel gives him a subtle nod to say she is okay. She doesn't know what she did to give herself away but, even if it's just Voronov, she needs to do better. Next time it might be someone who won't be as willing to keep whatever they see to themselves.

'Good morning, Miss Nunes,' Isabel says as she takes a seat across from her.

Voronov slides the cup across the table's surface and Madalena reaches for it like it is a lifeline.

'Thank you,' she murmurs, 'thank you so much for,' her voice cracks down the middle, 'for calling me in. I hadn't heard anything for weeks and I was starting to—' She sets the tea down and twists in her seat, fumbling for her bag, fingers clumsy like she's forgotten how they work, and it's such a frantic thing that Isabel can't help but feel for her.

'Miss Nunes, before we go any further,' Isabel says, gesturing for her to slow down, 'I need to make sure you've been informed that I am a Gifted inspector.'

That doesn't slow the woman down; nervous energy spikes from her and scrapes at Isabel's wards, leaving lines cleaved into the protection. Isabel inhales deeply, counting in her head and mentally smoothing them over.

'Yes, yes, they told me—' Madalena keeps tearing at her bag and finally manages to unsnap the buckle and yank it open. 'It doesn't matter. I don't care. Just, please, this is Marta—' She pulls out two slightly bent photographs and hurriedly pushes them across the table at them.

Voronov drags them the rest of the way over.

Isabel feels a bit of a disconnect happening as she takes in the face in the picture. The woman in the photograph is so clearly full of life, but familiar. It's always eerie, comprehending that the version of her that Isabel has seen is so stark with its absence of life.

'Miss Nunes, who is this woman to you?' Voronov asks.

'Marta. My sister. She's my sister.'

They don't look much alike. Different bone structures; the woman in the picture is fuller in the face and body, hair a crazy cloud of curls. The eyes are the same though, grey. Except the ones in the picture are vivid with life. Isabel imagines that maybe this is what Madalena's eyes usually look like too.

'Can you tell us about her? The report you made says she's been missing since December, but it was only recently filed,' Isabel says.

Madalena wraps her hands around the cup again and hunches over it. She opens her mouth, shuts it again. She runs a shaking hand gently over her hair before breathing out slowly, as if steadying herself.

'We're not close to the rest of our family. And I work on cruise ships. I'm gone months at a time and I can't always check in.'

'What do you do?' Voronov asks.

'I waitress. It's not crazy amounts of money but I get food and board, so you save some,' Madalena says. 'Sometime around November I noticed she hadn't replied to my emails for a while. It happens, but then a few more went unanswered and I tried calling between shifts when I could get reception. It's so spotty out there. You don't always manage to get through.'

'You didn't get through to her?'

Madalena shakes her head and takes another sip of the tea. 'Couldn't reach her at all.' She shrugs, helpless. 'It's not the first time this has happened, so I didn't worry, I thought she'd just gone off again, you know?'

Isabel shares a look with Voronov.

'What do you mean, Miss Nunes?'

'Marta is Gifted. She started branching off quite early on in her teens . . . I think I was the only non-Gifted person she interacted with.' She makes an impatient noise and waves that away, 'but she started hanging out with certain groups of people on these causes. Eventually she stopped telling me about what she was up to, but she'd come home looking different.' She gestures at her eyes. 'Sometimes it was as if she was somewhere else completely, just tuning out in the middle of a conversation. When I took up this post on the ships, I wasn't here to keep an eye on the situation. She'd drop contact with me occasionally, but I never thought anything of it because a few weeks later she would always get back in touch and update me. And she was always here when I came back.'

Except this time, she hadn't been.

'When I got back to Lisbon, I went to her place, but no one answered. I don't have the number for her landlord and her car wasn't there either,' she says, and in a tight voice gives them a description of Marta's car and what she can remember of the licence plate.

In one of the pictures, Marta Nunes sits at the bottom of a graffitied staircase shoulder to shoulder with someone who doesn't make the cut of the picture. Her smile curls around a stream of smoke, short cigarette pinched between her fingers with the ease of a lifelong smoker, and she is in shorts and an oversized T-shirt. Her trainers are scuffed, and her braided hair is caught at the base of her nape.

So young.

In the other she is tucked into the corner of the sofa, legs curled to the side in pyjamas, a present on her lap, smiling right up at the camera, big and bright. She has a crooked tooth that gives her a mischievous look.

'She's gone,' Madalena says, her eyes glued to the picture. They have taken on a wet gleam. She tucks her hands into her lap, away from view. 'She's gone,' she says again, 'isn't she?'

Isabel glances at Voronov. He's looking at Madalena, sympathy etched into the angles of his face. 'We can't confirm that, Madalena,' Isabel says, softening her voice, 'we need to get you down to the morgue for identification.' Isabel almost doesn't want to carry on, but she doesn't want to make the situation worse by giving the woman false hope. 'But it looks to us to be a very close likeness.'

Madalena chokes. Her shoulders heave and her back curves until her forehead touches the table. Her rasping breaths fill the silence.

The intensity of her emotions surges, a build-up with no way out. Isabel feels it swell, pushing at her wards.

Isabel has to force herself to keep breathing, can feel a trembling in her brow as she tries to keep everything pouring off Madalena from crushing her. She can feel cold sweat start to dampen the fabric under her arms. She can't let this thing win and affect her ability to do her job.

She focuses and once she feels more in control, her walls persevering, she gets up to round the table and kneels down at Madalena's side. She doesn't touch her. Doesn't dare because she's not sure she won't be knocked flat by the deepening of contact between them.

'Madalena, can we call anyone for you?'

For a moment, Madalena can't reply; all she can do is lift her head and try to get her sobs under control. Her cheeks are wet, and her nose is a mess. She lifts her hands and presses her eyes to her wrists and goes suddenly quiet. Only her shoulders still move with the hitches of her breaths as she tries to calm herself.

Finally, she quiets and drops her hands. Her eyes are swollen and the redness in them is so bad it almost makes Isabel's own eyes water.

'No. It's just us.' She doesn't seem to realise that she is still using the present tense. Madalena turns her head to look at her. 'I want to see her. I need to know.'

Isabel is leaning against the car as she waits for Madalena and Voronov, grateful for the low foot traffic outside the morgue.

Madalena's emotions inside the interviewing room had been

like great waves, battering relentlessly against Isabel's wards, so Isabel had stepped back from going in with them. When she'd explained to Madalena that Voronov would be going in and that Isabel would wait outside, Voronov had only given her a quick startled look – they'd gone in together not too long ago – before understanding had settled.

Isabel tilts her head back and closes her eyes. It worries her, how fast that one interaction had worn her down. The old habit that she hasn't quite unlearned makes her want to dig out a couple of blue pills, then wait for them to do their work and keep other voices out. Even if she had to spend the rest of the day fighting through headaches that would have her gritting her teeth with every small movement.

Except those pills don't work on her any more.

She breathes out, listening to the city around her; two neighbours talking to each other as they lean out of their windows, hanging their washing in the building opposite. An older man walking past, cane digging into the spaces in the cobblestones, back hunched, newspaper tucked beneath his arm and a tiny dog trotting at his side. The cars driving past heading toward the main road.

Easing away from the car, she digs into the pocket of her jeans and tugs out the creased paper she'd had with her for a while now, and that she'd carried with her yesterday too. The address and number on it belong to her old Guide, Rosario. She'd been assigned to Isabel after she'd been designated as Gifted. Guides were there to help Gifted learn to use and live with their Gift. She'd had to do a lot of digging to get it but now that she finally has it, she hasn't been able to make herself use it.

Isabel knows one thing though. She can't sustain this. She needs help and maybe if her dad had been here, things would have been different; but there's no one else for her to turn to with this.

Rubbing her thumb over the mobile number, she pulls out her phone and unlocks the screen.

She feels the moment that Voronov and Madalena step out of

the morgue. The slam of emotion is vicious and feels like it cuts through Isabel's chest all the way to her gut. It's so visceral that she flinches and almost doubles over. She manages to stop herself, just, but her hand is pressed between her breasts where the grief is trying to dig its way through.

Isabel straightens up, shoves the phone and the paper into her back pocket and fixes her eyes on them.

Voronov, standing a good deal taller than Madalena, is guiding her toward Isabel with a gentle hand on her arm. His mouth is pressed into a grim line and when he meets Isabel's gaze, she knows they have the identity of their murder victim.

Isabel forces herself to push past the slam of devastation and opens the back door of the car for Madalena.

Despite the emotions screaming from inside her, Madalena stares straight ahead, expression without animation of any kind. Her eyes have a flat look to them, as if there's nothing in front of her.

It looks as if she's not with them at all.

Isabel stands to the side and watches as Voronov hands her into the back seat with care. He lowers to his haunches beside the car, voice kind. 'The family support worker is on their way; you won't be alone.'

Madalena gives a slow, almost absent nod. She's staring straight ahead. Her feet are tucked into the footwell, and her hands are on her lap. That's when Isabel notices that she's holding what look like photos. She's gripping onto them so tight that they are crumpling in her hands.

Voronov straightens away from the car and steps back up onto the kerb, turning to Isabel and keeping his voice low. 'She confirmed the ID,' he says. His eyes take in Isabel's face and he follows up with, 'but I guess you figured that out for yourself.'

Isabel scrubs a hand down her face. 'You could say that.' The intensity of emotions is harder to take this close up but she refuses to step away from it, even as she feels her stomach roiling with them. She's not going to let this Gift keep her from doing what she's supposed to do.

'I've called one of the juniors,' he says and looks back over his shoulder at where Madalena sits, eyes still straight forward, body rigid. 'I asked them to get the family support worker and for them to take her home from here.'

Isabel blows out a long breath. 'Good. I'm worried about her being alone and it doesn't sound like there's anyone that we can reach out to on her behalf.' She looks at him, then turns back to Madalena, mimicking Voronov's movements of a moment ago and lowering herself so that she's looking up at the woman.

With Madalena's emotions tearing at her, Isabel reaches inside the car. She catches the edges of the photos between her fingers – she sees now they *are* photos – and eases them from Madalena's grip. Setting them on the edge of the seat, she smooths out the bent paper, careful not to smudge the gloss with her fingers as she flattens the creases. When all of them are as straight as they're going to be, Isabel glances up.

Madalena's watching her. Her gaze still has that same dead quality to it and Isabel feels a chill go through her. It takes her back to the fishing port, staring down at Marta's lifeless eyes.

Isabel holds the photos out.

In the beats of silence, she stays steady through sheer will, doesn't let a sliver of the battering she's taking slip through to show on her face.

Madalena takes them back from her, arranges them in a neat pile and holds onto them, hands cupped beneath them as if she's cradling a wounded bird. But the ache in Isabel's chest subsides a bit and she breathes easier.

The shock isn't gone, not by any means, but something has penetrated through Madalena's fog of pain.

'Madalena, I know you've had a shock. But can you tell us about Marta? Did she live or work in Cascais or in that area?'

'No,' Madalena's voice rasps and she clears her throat, rubs a hand over the spot like she can fix the hurt from the inside,

'No. Marta lives in Setubal, and she worked there too, at a youth centre. They focus on Gifted teens.' Then her face crumples and her words come weighted with sobs and tears not yet shed. Her breaths hiccup as she tries to stay in control. 'I went there. To her work. I asked them if they'd s-seen her, but they said she'd resigned, and I was s-so *confused*. Marta loved her job.'

Resigns, disappears, and then turns up dead.

Isabel glances at Voronov and finds him looking her way too.

'What about friends, maybe? Do you know of anything or anyone Marta could have known in Cascais? Someone she could be visiting or any other business?'

Madalena drags in a shuddery breath. When she speaks again, her voice is a whisper. Her eyes stay on the photos in her hands. 'I'm sorry,' she says, 'I wish I did.'

7

Isabel feels as if she's been put through a meat grinder, her mind tender and oversensitive, flinching at the smallest touch of anything against her shields.

As Voronov rolls his chair closer to hers, notebook in hand, Isabel digs through her drawers for painkillers and any snacks she hasn't already eaten her way through. She finds the box of pills, but no food. Before she can truly feel the disappointment, a shiny bar of chocolate in red wrapping is tossed onto her desk and she almost groans in thanks before tearing into it.

'Thanks, I forgot to top up my supplies,' she says, shoving half of the bar into her mouth and relaxing almost as soon as the sweetness of the chocolate melts across her tongue. Using her Gift burns up energy and usually Isabel is careful to keep energy bars and other quick bites stashed in her desk or her car. When they're in the middle of a case she can't always fit in a proper meal, so it helps to keep her going. She pops a painkiller.

'It's been a busy morning.'

Isabel caps the water. 'That's one way of putting it.' She rubs her hands over her face. 'So, Marta Nunes. That's our Jane Doe.'

She flips her notebook open to reveal the two pictures that Madalena had brought with her.

Marta Nunes had been thirty-two years old and taught art at a local Gifted youth centre. Single, with no partners that her sister had been aware of. The two were estranged from the rest of their family. Another case of family turning their backs on Gifted individuals and casting them out to fend for themselves. Their parents had died in a freak pile-up when the Nunes sisters were sixteen and seventeen. They had been staying with their grandmother in

Belgium at the time, having emigrated there when they were toddlers. Their grandmother had returned with them after the accident, but had since passed away, leaving the two girls cut off from any blood relatives.

Isabel thinks of how small and alone Madalena had looked in that chair. It makes her think of her brother Sebastião and her tia, her sister Rita and her mum.

It hits a little too close to home.

The pictures in front of her are miles away from the pictures in the case file they have on her. No knife wounds here.

A rap of knuckles on the door has them lifting their heads to watch as Daniel walks into the room, closely followed by Carla.

Both Daniel and Carla, along with Jacinta from CSS, had worked with Isabel and Voronov on their last major case.

As far as Isabel's concerned, the Chief's decision to keep them together as a unit is a welcome one, and she's pretty sure she's not the only one who feels that way.

Isabel raises her eyebrows, though, at the new look Daniel's sporting. He's in a bright blue T-shirt and jeans, police ID dangling from his neck, and with trainers beat-up enough to rival Isabel's.

'When did that happen?' Isabel asks, nodding at his head.

He grins at her – it lifts his expression despite the ever-present bags under his eyes – and rubs a hand over his newly shaved head. 'You know it looks good.'

At his side, Carla folds her arms and shakes her head. She walks around him, always a sharp contrast to her partner in every way. It's a rare day that they see Carla with a hair out of place. She's a small woman with a strong nose and jaw and eyes that make Isabel think of Bambi. Her hair has been cut into a short, straight black bob that swings around her face as she walks. She's dressed neatly in black jeans, a buttoned white shirt and a black cardigan.

More importantly, she's carrying a brown paper bag spotted with grease stains and its opening rolled closed. Isabel doesn't even need to ask what's in it; the smell of fresh bread and chouriço has her mouth watering in seconds.

'Carla,' she says, making pleading eyes, 'please tell me that's to share.'

Carla smiles and holds the bag out to her. 'Thank your partner for putting in the request.'

Isabel looks over her shoulder and blinks at Voronov, surprised. He just lifts a shoulder in response.

'We wanted to come and catch up yesterday,' Carla says, 'but we still had a few loose ends to tie up on our end.'

Isabel holds the bag open, and they wait until everyone is holding a still-warm pão com chouriço. She takes a bite out of hers as she heads over to shut the door to the case room, humming in appreciation at the soft bite of fresh and slightly sweet bread in contrast with the spiced saltiness of the meat.

'Well, it's not pretty,' Isabel says as Voronov gets up the information they have so far. 'She was found in Cascais by a couple who were out on their jog.'

They take Daniel and Carla through what few details they've gathered so far. The location with its lack of cameras, the state of Marta's brain and what it could mean, the tattoo, the loss of communication between the sisters, the resignation. 'Madalena also said Marta's car wasn't at her house either.'

Daniel is frowning and chewing on his lip, looking over one of the crime scene photos that had been left on the screen. 'The sister – Madalena? – says that dropping off the radar is something that happened often?' he asks.

'She said it wasn't unusual,' Voronov says.

'Okay,' Carla says and puts her pen down. 'What are our next steps?'

'Focus on what we have,' Isabel says, 'if you guys can start looking into the car. Let's track that down and if you can get a hold of the landlord too, tell them we need to get into Marta's place today. We'll head over to the youth centre. Madalena says her sister loved that place and she was surprised she had left.' Isabel glances at Voronov. 'Let's find out why she did.'

8

According to Madalena, the youth centre deals with a mix of teenagers. Some runaways, some just wanting to escape to a place that accepts them and supports their needs, all of them vulnerable. They work closely with other services, some of them government-sanctioned although apparently they don't get much funding and often have to raise money themselves to keep running. It is a cherished gem in the local Gifted community.

Marta had started working there six years ago. Madalena had said she was involved in all the locally run fundraising events and helped organise trips but, most importantly, her role was as a counsellor to the kids. She was their check-in, the one they went to share their worries and challenges with. According to Madalena, Marta had loved those kids. Madalena had been there a couple of times and seen her sister at work, witnessed the joy she got from making a difference. When Madalena wasn't away on the ships she'd sometimes volunteer and help too.

'No boyfriend or friends to speak of,' Isabel mutters. That had been something else Madalena had said. It wasn't that surprising.

Isabel thinks back to the Salão de Jogos that she had gone to with Dr Alves, just a common games bar with some darts, pool, and a few other things. Nothing out of the ordinary. At least not for Regulars. But for those who are Gifted, places like that, and like this one, are few. Safe havens.

Gifted people had learned over the years to keep themselves to themselves. There is always the risk of backlash or mistreatment, or discrimination taking place if some random arsehole overhears that so-and-so is Gifted.

That's how the rumour mill works in this country. *Oh, did you hear? So-and-so's daughter tested as Gifted, I hear they're sending her off to her aunty's*, or, *heard it from the neighbour next door, said the butcher's wife has been hiding her classification for years, you never know where these people are hiding.* Isabel has heard it all.

It makes it hard to put yourself out there and form bonds with people, form friendships and romantic relationships. Often, it's hard enough just keeping the relationships you have with your own family.

Isabel scoffs softly to herself and shakes her head. She should know that better than most.

From what Madalena had said to them, for Marta it had been the same thing.

Only Madalena and her grandmother had stood by her.

Isabel touches a finger to the picture of Marta's smiling face. She tries not to think about how much she has in common with this woman who is no longer alive.

A double tap on the door drags her attention and Isabel twists in her chair.

Voronov is leaning against the door frame. 'You ready? Marta's landlord will meet us in the afternoon, we can stop by the youth centre now.'

Isabel tucks everything away and grabs her jacket.

'Let's get started then.'

They've settled into a routine over the past few months. If they're leaving the precinct, it's usually Voronov driving. It may have been something that would have irritated Isabel before, but when she's spending the majority of her energy trying to keep herself sane it's a welcome thing, especially on days like this where she's had little-to-no sleep.

On the way Isabel rests her eyes, lulled by the radio and Voronov's quiet presence. She's starting to realise that he's one of those capable people. Which to some might come across as boring, but she finds it soothing.

It had taken a long time for Isabel to stop expecting for him to turn round and stab her in the back – not because of what had happened with his partner, but because he'd found out more about her than she had meant to share. It had left her feeling vulnerable.

She still feels vulnerable. She just has a little more trust now.

Slowly, the tension that had filled her every time she'd been in his presence had seeped away. Voronov must have known what she'd been thinking because as soon as she'd stopped waiting for him to turn her in, he'd seemed to become more relaxed too. He hadn't said anything, hadn't changed his behaviour around her, but there had been this wariness there that had been palpable and hard to ignore.

Last year, they'd arrested Gabriel Bernardo, a high-level Gifted, for the murder of two very well-known and respected people. During the course of their investigation, Isabel and Voronov had discovered that Gabriel possessed two affinities; he could use telekinesis as well as telepathy, something that had previously been unheard of.

The problem was that Gabriel had realised Isabel's level matched his and had taken a liking to her.

Try as she might, she hasn't managed to forget the touch of hurt she'd sensed from him when he'd realised she had every intention of standing against him. She hasn't been able to get rid of the guilt either – of turning on one of her own. She doesn't think about the letters she's received since, with a prison stamp on them. Ones she's put away without reading.

That entire investigation had left a mark on her.

They cross the bridge in no time and the ride to Setúbal passes quickly and in quiet. The Setúbal Municipality is a roughly 40-minute drive from Lisbon, and traffic isn't bad at this time.

It's not a slick place; there's a rustic honesty to it that Isabel has always enjoyed whenever she's made the trip. When she'd been younger, she'd gone every now and then with her small group of friends, catching the ferry once they got to Setúbal to cross over to the Tróia peninsula and to enjoy the long stretches of beach under the burning sun of summer. She'll always remember the first time they did it and spotting the dolphins swimming in the waters, so close to the ferry.

Her best memory of this place, though, was from before she'd been classified as Gifted. They'd come here as a family, her, her mum and dad, Rita and Sebastião. Spend the day at the beach and at the end of the day when the ferry had pulled in, instead of heading straight home they'd walk along the water, her mum carrying bags filled with their buckets and beach towels, her dad carrying the cooler box, the parasol resting on his shoulder. Their feet would be dusted with sand that hadn't quite come off. They'd stop at a little café by the water and stay there until evening, eating mussels and chips and little crystal taças de mousse de chocolate. They'd sleep the rest of the way home, with the windows of the car down and her mum and dad quietly talking, tired but content, in the front of the car.

She has good memories of this place. But for all its charm, it has its dark corners.

The youth centre is a squat square building situated down the road from a secondary school. It's a bright building with colourful graffiti proclaiming its title against a white background, its hot pink and bubble-gum blue making it pop and catch the eye of anyone walking by.

Its front door is open and sitting on giant tyres and the picnic table out at the front are teenagers, someone's phone blaring out music that none of them seem to be listening to because they're all just talking and laughing instead.

Isabel and Voronov park across the road and cross quickly at a break in traffic.

The teenagers go quiet when they see Isabel and Voronov heading their way, eyes wary.

More music inside, the sound of people playing on a ping-pong table and young laughter.

Isabel pauses just inside the door; she can feel the stares of the teenagers outside on her back and wonders if they can sense that she's one of them. Maybe not. Probably all that they can see is someone who doesn't belong intruding on what is probably their only safe space.

It looks fun, geared completely towards its target audience. The walls and the low ceiling are painted white but the graffiti that decorates the walls inside too pops in vibrant colours that cheer the place up. There are three stands next to one another, filled with leaflets and information on all sorts of things, from safe sex to career advice.

There are what seem to be four offices lining the walls to Isabel's right, separated from the hallway by glass, their doors shut, and then to her left, just a few steps ahead of her, the hallway opens into a wide-open space that she can only get a glimpse of from where they're standing.

The office at the end of the hallway has its door open and Isabel can hear people talking inside. Despite the thoughts drifting to her, she can easily separate the voiced words from them; the thoughts are drowned out by the ease and calm of the centre. The people who come here are clearly very much at home.

'Can I help you?'

A woman, maybe in her mid-fifties, approaches them. Her blue eyes are bright and fringed by a shock of black lashes. Her hair is a loose wave of white that makes the contrast to her eyes all the more startling. She's dressed in a soft cream cardigan that falls to her knees, worn blue jeans and black flats. Her nails are short and painted an eye-popping red.

'Yes, we're here to speak to Sofia Fontes. We've been told she's the manager here.' Isabel pulls out her ID and steps closer so that the woman can see it without any nosy eyes being able to see what she's doing. 'This is my partner,' Isabel says, gesturing to Voronov.

The woman's demeanour, which had been friendly and polite when she had approached them, suddenly changes. She draws herself up taller and apprehension lines her mouth and widens her eyes as they flick between Isabel and Voronov. 'If someone has made a complaint about one of our kids—' The defensiveness fills the woman's shoulders, squaring them up and tilting her chin back.

Isabel waves a hand to cut her off before she can get going. She wonders how often the kids here are reported for something. She wonders, too, how often those reports are due to what these kids are, rather than what they've done.

'We're not here about any of the kids. We can't disclose anything, however. Is the manager here today?' Isabel presses again.

The woman, still eyeing them warily, says yes and then walks to the office, from where they can still hear the conversation. She knocks on the door.

When they'd approached the woman, they had come into full view of what Isabel can now see is a rec room. There are about ten or so teens in it at the moment. None of them bother to pretend they aren't blatantly watching the exchange taking place.

Isabel arches a brow at them and some of them have the decency to duck their heads and look away and go back to what they were doing; others just stare back, defiant.

Isabel snorts and shakes her head. Kids.

Although, from the woman's reaction, maybe they have good reason to be acting that way at the sight of strangers on their turf.

The woman comes back. 'This way, please,' she says and walks them over to the office door.

As they approach, two people slip out of the room, a black man and a white woman; they both give Isabel and Voronov an unfriendly look.

If this is a hint about how this conversation is going to go, then she's not sure how useful this visit is going to be for them.

Another woman appears at the door. She's dressed a bit more formally; her suit trousers are a hot orange that is almost red, and her white shirt is crisp, buttoned all the way up to her neck, cuffs neatly done at her wrists. Her make-up is simple, barely there, and her hair is pulled up in a soft ponytail. She's just as wary as the woman who had approached them first, who hovers outside the door.

'Sofia Fontes?' Voronov checks first, reaching out a hand.

'Yes,' she says, takes his hand almost absently. 'Clara tells me you are inspectors?' She has a surprisingly low deep voice and her words are unhurried, adding an odd soothing quality to her speech. She steps back and motions for them to follow.

Isabel and Voronov go in and Isabel notes that Clara joins them too.

'Clara is deputy manager here at the centre,' Sofia says and leads them to the desk that's tucked at the back of the room, backed up to a solid wall. The rest of the walls are glass, with a view out of the centre into the skate park and playground outside.

She settles on the edge of her desk and gestures to the more casual seats a little further away from it before folding her arms across her chest. Clara moves to stand by her.

Isabel takes out her ID again and identifies herself. Voronov does the same.

There's a small change in Sofia when she notices Isabel's classification on her ID. Her eyes flick up to Isabel's face and curiosity lurks there for a second.

'How can I help you, Inspectors?' She directs the question only at Isabel.

Isabel checks again that the door is properly closed behind her and then takes one of the offered seats. Voronov moves to stand at her side, and she wonders if he realises how that kind of makes him look like a protective bulldog, and feels a brief touch of amusement because of it.

She gets straight to the point. 'Marta Nunes. She used to work for you.'

Sofia straightens. 'Yes. She was one of the favourites here at the centre.'

'How long did she work here for?'

'Almost since we opened. I'd say maybe five, six years?' She folds her arms over her chest. 'But she's no longer a part of our team. She resigned a couple of months ago. Is everything okay?'

Worry is clear to see on her face, but oddly enough Isabel isn't being bombarded by emotions here.

She realises that, since stepping inside, although she's been catching snatches of emotions and thoughts they're not as intense as what she's been experiencing since her control disappeared. And then she remembers that this is a youth centre for Gifted teens and it occurs to her that the kids and the staff here are probably all taught how to keep their thoughts and emotions from being constantly telegraphed.

After all, Rosario who had been assigned to Isabel as her Guide after she'd been classed as Gifted, had taught Isabel how to build her walls. Isabel had always naturally kept those up, not only to protect herself from other people and what she might pick up from them, but also to protect her own thoughts and emotions.

Isabel has been missing that guidance now more than ever.

In the back of her mind, the memory of standing on slippery rocks and staring Gabriel dead in the eye rises.

She hadn't always been successful at protecting herself.

Isabel blinks her thoughts away and focuses her attention on the woman in front of her. 'This is confidential and needs to stay in this room,' she says. 'Marta Nunes was found dead yesterday.'

Clara's hand flies up to her mouth and her eyes snap to Sofia, who freezes and stares at them, eyes wide.

'What?'

'I'm sorry,' Isabel says, 'were you all close?'

Clara drags her chair out and drops heavily into her seat, rubbing at her mouth. 'I— I . . . we do have a close team, yes. Marta, too.' She starts tapping at the floor with her right foot, knee bouncing with it.

'Her sister told us she came here looking for her and that she was told Marta had resigned.'

Sofia shifts in her seat and grabs onto the handles of her chair. Her grip is tight enough that the skin of them turns white, but she remains composed. 'Yes. She did.'

'When did she resign?'

'December, she came in December,' Sofia says, and her eyes are unfocused, like she's thinking back to the day.

'Yes,' Clara says softly, nodding her head in quick bobs, 'I remember being surprised because Marta had overseen the Christmas party committee and she'd done so much work with the kids on it. When she resigned, I remember thinking the kids were going to be devastated. Marta was their favourite.' She drops her head and smooths an imaginary wrinkle from the leg of her jeans, over and over. 'She still is,' she murmurs.

Sofia sighs, shoulders slumping with it. 'I can get you the exact date if you need it.'

'It sounds like her resignation came as a surprise,' Voronov says, and his voice seems to startle the two women, like they'd forgotten he was there.

'It did,' Sofia says, 'like I said, Marta was here almost from the beginning. She helped build this youth centre into what it is today, and Clara is right, she really was the kids' favourite. She connected with them the best.'

'Did she say why?'

'She said she'd made the decision to move for personal reasons and had found a job in Porto that was starting in the new year. She worked her one-month notice and then went. I remember being surprised because she forgot to leave a forwarding address for us to stay in touch about the kids. That wasn't like her at all.'

'And after that you didn't see her again?'

'No, we were meant to have a goodbye dinner for her the weekend following her last day,' Sofia says, 'but she messaged saying she wouldn't be able to make it. We cancelled it, thinking we could reschedule, but I didn't hear from her again after that.'

'Any calls or emails requesting references or anything like that?'

'No.'

'Was anything else happening around that time?'

'Nothing of note,' Sofia says. Then she seems to think again, and frowns. 'Actually, yes. A week after Marta resigned, one of our regular kids stopped showing up. They tend to come and go as they please – we're just here as a support for them – but it's unusual for them to stop coming by all together.'

Voronov tugs out his notebook. 'What was their name?'

'Alma Pontes.'

'Did anyone go to check on her at all?' he asks.

'We did check,' Sofia says, 'one of our other staff members went to check at the address we have on file. Her father hadn't seen her, and it wasn't exactly a cause for concern for him. She's also legally an adult so there's nothing much that we could do.'

'Was Alma one of the kids here who were close to Marta?' Isabel asks.

Sofia looks to Clara. 'Yes, she wasn't close with many of the staff but she spent a lot of time with Marta. We thought that since Marta had left, maybe she just didn't see a reason to return here, but she does have friends who still come. They haven't seen her either.'

'I see.' Isabel glances at Voronov and, when he shakes his head, she stands up. 'Thank you for your time. We might have some more questions for you.' She tugs her mostly unused notebook out and scrawls her number and her work email down – she has no idea where she's put her cards – and walks over to place the torn page on Sofia's desk. 'This is my number. If you remember anything or learn anything new, please give me a call. If you could send the dates of Marta's resignation and Alma's details to this email address that would be helpful. We'll have some officers come over and speak to the rest of your staff if that's okay. We may have to talk to the students but if any of them want to come and talk to us on their own, please give them my number.'

Sofia gives a slow nod. 'I'd prefer it, however, if any officers sent over to speak to the kids are Gifted,' she says, and spears Isabel with a look, 'and you'll have to get permission from their parents for anyone under eighteen.'

Isabel nods. 'That's fine. The number will put them straight through to me. Thank you again.' She doesn't offer to shake hands, she never does any more, but Voronov does. She wonders if they think she's being rude or if they understand. If anything, worry aside, their attention on her just seems curious.

The kids who were in the recreational area of the building are blatantly watching them as they come out of the room. The two staff members who had been in with Sofia before Isabel and Voronov's arrival are also standing by, arms crossed, watching as they head toward the exit. Isabel tilts her head and wishes them a good day.

The music that had been playing outside when they'd arrived is still blasting out and the kids watch them walk away.

Isabel waits for Voronov to unlock the car and then slides inside. She waits until he's in his seat and the door has slammed behind him to look over at him.

'That wasn't what I was expecting.'

Voronov's expression is grim. 'Me neither.'

9

The GPS guides Isabel and Voronov past boxed-together houses the colour of granite, some a little rougher than others. The car bumps over the cobbled road and a train sounds not too far off. They eventually stop at a series of pastel-coloured buildings that have seen better days.

Marta's building is much like the others – a block of apartments in a closed square with a recreational area in the middle. A tree dots each corner of the park and there is a sectioned-off children's playground on one side, benches and tables and a basketball court on the other.

Isabel's steps echo on the staircase. There are no elevators; it is one of those old-school buildings, five floors if you count the ground level. A resident holds the door open for them, with a murmured greeting. The landlord should have been waiting for them to let them through but there is no sign of him. Inside, the foyer's black and white chequered floor is spotless, and there's a clean lemony smell that has Isabel breathing in deeper to get more of it. The wall just in front of the stairs is all floor-to-ceiling postboxes. They have no names on them but Isabel easily spots the one that corresponds with the address they have for Marta's apartment.

Postbox 13's slot is jammed with what mainly looks to be promotional leaflets. They'll have to get the key for that from the landlord too.

They'd stopped on the way to eat and Isabel's feeling fortified, steadier in herself. There are thoughts and emotions lingering on each floor that they pass; she can feel them, as if they're standing on her doorstep just waiting to be let in. Ready to force their way in if she shows any weakness. She thinks she'll be all right if she's not immediately faced with someone else swamped by intense emotion.

'First floor, right?' she asks.

'Yes,' Voronov says, glancing down at her as she follows him up the stairs, 'why? Too tired?'

Isabel rolls her eyes.

The landlord is waiting by the apartment door. A bald man, with a stomach that spills over his belt and strains his white button up, his puffy coat is open and a gold ring on his finger flashes in the light. He's pacing back and forth outside number 13.

The door is flanked by two dead plants in their pots and has a scratchy doormat.

When he hears their footsteps, he stops. 'Are you the inspectors?' he asks, and eyes them like they're about to rob him.

Isabel just gives him a flat look and shows him her identification, aware that at her side and just as unimpressed – but better at not showing it – Voronov is doing the same.

The landlord's eyes widen a little when he takes note of Isabel's classification, and he jerks away too fast before seeming to catch himself. His neck flushes red and he clears his throat. He introduces himself as Pedro, the owner of the property. When they ask, he reveals that he owns two more in this block, on the upper floors.

'I'll just get this open for you, Inspectors,' he says, and turns to the door, suddenly very intent on being helpful.

'Please do,' Isabel says, dryly. She side-eyes Voronov and catches a small smirk that he is quick to wipe off his face.

The landlord opens the door and instantly an unpleasant smell hits them. Isabel flinches away.

Thankfully, it's not the smell of a dead body. That would have been ten times worse, and it's a complication Isabel would rather do without.

'Do you know if anyone else has the keys to the apartment?' she asks.

Pedro stays by the door. Clearly, his curiosity about what exactly is happening inside the apartment is not greater than his revulsion at the smell spilling out of it. 'Maybe a family member, I'm not sure. Marta could have made copies. I didn't deal with her outside of collecting the rent.'

'Hmm.' Isabel stares into the apartment with distaste and then does a double-take at the number of locks on the inside of the door. 'Aleks,' she says, stepping inside and gesturing for him to follow. Covering her nose and mouth to stave off the stink, she half shuts the door so he can see. 'Look at this.'

Voronov's eyebrows shoot up in surprise and he turns to the landlord. 'Were these here when the property was rented out?'

Pedro comes inside and examines the locks, frowning. 'No, just the main lock and the chain.'

So, Marta had had those added herself. 'Thank you,' Isabel says, 'you can wait outside.'

Pedro is only too happy to do that.

It's a decent-sized place, a larger T1 apartment. The short corridor is marked by a door into a small bathroom and opens into a large living space with a white-tiled floor. Isabel can see straight into a nice big kitchen and a bedroom. The living room is bright, light pouring in through the wide windows that look out onto the balcony. The curtains are gauzy white and are open so they can see the bare trees dotting the street outside.

It's decorated with mismatched furniture that somehow all seems to fit together, a quirky mix of bright colours. Plants fill the space; they have wilted from lack of care. The sight of them makes something twist in Isabel's chest and she's not sure why.

Voronov is right behind her, also attempting to shield himself from the smell with his hand as his eyes scope out their surroundings.

The smell, which has deepened into a sweet rot, is coming from the kitchen and when Isabel goes to stand in the short archway leading into it, she tries to breathe in as little of it as possible.

It looks like someone left in a hurry. There are bags set on the kitchen table and a few cups and cutlery in the sink. The fridge is studded with alphabet magnets in different colours and other bits and pieces. A taxi company's card, a short shopping list, a little piece of torn lined paper with an arrow and a smiley doodled on it. There is a photo too, pinned to the grey surface with an M and an S: a picture of Marta and Madalena, laughing together. Madalena's face is half covered by her hand, eyes crinkled with mirth and so different from the woman they spoke to today. Marta is grinning into the camera, hand up in a peace sign. There is a postcard pinned by a yellow O and a red X, picture side out, depicting a cruise in open water. Isabel unpins it from the fridge and flips it over. On the back, in purple marker, is a short message from Madalena that talks of being tired, wanting to come home and missing her sister. Isabel thinks of how there's no coming home for Marta now. Madalena's going to be missing her sister for the rest of her life. Isabel carefully replaces the postcard, feeling a little protective about what is now a memento.

Next to the shopping bags are pots filled with used paintbrushes and a few pencils. There is a closed sketchbook, and a scatter of landscape images, some that have clearly been torn from magazines, others printed out in black and white. No sign of any paint, although the surface of the furthest edge of the table is splattered with it. Isabel flicks through the sketchbook and sees random watercolours; slices and snatches of storm-grey seas and the bright green of what looks like Parque das Nações.

The bin is full and is probably where the majority of the stink is coming from. The inside of the fridge is a mess of rotten food and spoilt milk.

Wandering back to the living room, she sees Voronov coming out from the corridor where the bathroom is.

'Anything?' she asks.

'Nothing. Looks like someone got up and got ready for their day and that's it.'

Together they go into the bedroom. There are two bedside tables, one on each side of the double bed. It's unmade, blankets and sheets kicked off. The pillows on the left still have an imprint on them.

The shutters on the windows are up and the light spilling from it gives the room an eerie feel, dust bunnies dancing in the stream. There's a digital alarm clock on one bedside table and on the other, books stacked on top of each other; one is lying open. Clothes are tossed over a chair in the corner of the room, some draped neatly over its back, others a whirl of fabric that would take some time to untangle. Shoes are tossed carelessly beneath the bed, hidden behind the drag of the blanket where it's drooped onto the floor.

Behind her Voronov is opening the wardrobe, pushing clothes aside and checking the back. Nothing on top of it. He moves to the bedside table drawers and Isabel zeroes in on the open shelves tucked into a corner of the room. The mirror that is balanced on top of it reflects her image back at her.

The first shelf houses bits and pieces of jewellery, thin necklaces tangled with rings and earrings in little trinket boxes, some candles, and dried rose petals, scattered for the aesthetic, Isabel guesses. There are handbags on the lower shelves, pushed up together.

No sign of a laptop or other computer.

'Isabel.'

'Yeah?'

Voronov has the door to the balcony open and is standing outside. She goes over.

'What is it?'

'Balcony door was unlocked,' he says and then he points.

At the far end of the balcony there's another cluster of plant pots. There are even some hanging from the ceiling above them. All of them are starting to droop.

But in one corner, the pots have been shoved together and one is on its side, soil spilled on the floor. And when Isabel looks closely, there's a clear shoe print on it. But there's no soil trailing back to the door.

She breathes out. 'Okay. Let's get the scene investigators in here,' she rubs at the back of her neck, 'and start trying to make some sense of all of this.'

10

Daniel and Carla have pulled a table closer to the whiteboard at the other end of the room. They're dragging over chairs when Isabel and Voronov go in.

'Jacinta will be in for a briefing later,' Isabel says, closing the door behind her and heading over to join them, 'she's with forensics at the victim's house now.' Isabel drags over a chair so they're all sitting around the same table.

'Nothing in the house?' Daniel says.

'No, not that we could see. Jacinta's people might find out something we haven't though. Shoe print on the balcony,' Isabel says, and Voronov pulls out his phone to show them all the picture he snapped before they left Marta's apartment. 'Door to the balcony locks from the inside but it was unlocked when we got there. Only other person that we know for sure has a key is the landlord. We'll check his whereabouts just in case.'

'Not the sister?' Daniel asks.

Isabel shakes her head. 'No. No point. She spends most of the year away, so Marta never gave her one. Even if it had been the sister or the landlord, would they not have locked the door and cleaned up the mess? And told us about it?' Isabel points at how the pots are clustered together and knocked over. 'Why would someone have shoved them all like that? The other plants are all neatly lined up on the balcony.'

'There were multiple locks on the door that the landlord claims he knew nothing about,' Voronov says. 'We have a victim who was either extremely paranoid or expecting some unwanted company.'

Isabel nods. 'Unpacked shopping on the table ... she would've put that away if she'd just headed out of her own volition. That shoe print and flowerpots – maybe that was her making a run for it.'

Carla chews on her bottom lip. 'Maybe she was surprised at home . . .'

'We asked the landlord about CCTV and there's only one camera, which is in the foyer, nothing else in the rest of the building. We're expecting the tapes by the end of the day,' Isabel says. 'That's a lot of hours of viewing.'

Voronov leans forward on the table, resting his arms on the table. 'Her old boss says she resigned in December, which means it's been a little over a month. We'll have to retrace whatever steps we can. And there's also the girl.'

Carla glances up from the notes that she's taking down. 'A girl?'

'A teenager. Her name is Alma Pontes. She used to frequent the youth club but went missing a week after Marta left.'

'Okay, so,' Daniel gives Isabel an expectant look, 'tell us what you want us covering and we'll get started. You guys have been going since last night, right? You should take a few hours.'

'Yeah.' Isabel does need to recharge. Maybe a few months ago she could have powered through, but now – well. She can't afford a slip-up, so she's going to have to suck it up, leave this in someone else's hands for now and get as much rest as she can squeeze in. She looks at Voronov. 'You too, right?'

He nods.

'Right.' She turns to Daniel. 'Get some people over to Marta's building, door-to-door. I want them to talk to the whole building. Anything is good. If the CCTV isn't here by the end of the day, get on their ass, but after that I'll need you with Carla.' She looks at Carla, who is waiting expectantly. 'The youth centre doesn't want their staff or the kids being spoken to by someone who isn't Gifted. So I need you down there. Start speaking to them, but not just about Marta – see what they have to say about the young girl, Alma. Please stop in and speak to Alma's dad as well. The youth centre has already sent us what we requested.' Thank God.

Voronov stirs. 'Phone records too. We don't have her phone, but we have her number and her sister provided us with possible phone companies.'

'I'll work on getting her bank records as well. All right.' Carla shuts her laptop and stands. 'Buzz us when you're back in?'

'Yeah. And if you get anything, let us know.'

11

When Isabel gets home, she hears her brother's voice from inside. As soon as the door swings open, sharp nails scratch her shins through her trousers and she curses. Branco and Tigre. They scrabble up her legs and bark with excitement.

It gets a tired laugh out of her. 'Shh, shh, you'll piss off the neighbours!' She steps inside and drops down to the floor to let them clamber onto her lap, licking at her face again and again. Isabel can't stop laughing and it feels good. Something in her eases a little and she feels her body become heavier, tiredness settling in but a sort of peacefulness as well.

'Yeah, yeah,' she busses kisses over their heads when they let her, stroking them as much as the frenzy allows, 'missed you guys too. It was only one night!'

Sebastião is standing in the hallway, leaning against the wall, arms folded, as he watches, his expression a mixture of amusement and worry. It makes his dimples wink into existence, the ones that both he and their younger sister, Rita, share with their dad. Isabel didn't get those. She has her dad's eyes instead, big, and soft brown. But overall, Sebastião is the one who takes after their dad's side of the family the most, with his darker brown skin and short, tight curls.

When they were younger, for a time Sebastião's hair had been long enough for twists and Isabel remembers sitting with Tia Simone, fingers glossed with sweet-smelling cream, both of them working small sections of his hair into twists. He almost always dozed off.

'You look like crap, maninha.'

She waves his concern away and then groans as she forces herself back to her feet. 'Thank you for taking them yesterday.'

He shrugs. 'You know I don't mind. And the parishioners love them.'

'They better not be feeding my dogs all the time,' she says. She knows the three elderly ladies who always arrive early to help Sebastião before evening mass have a fondness for biscuits. They have a fondness for bribing Isabel's dogs with biscuits too. 'How are you?' She drops a kiss on his cheek as she heads for the kitchen, following her nose.

Something smells good.

'Look at you being the best brother,' she says.

'Yeah, yeah, it's just tortilha,' he says.

Even better.

She uncovers the plate on the counter. She can smell the fried onions. Washing her hands quickly, she cuts herself a slice and by the time she's sitting at the small table, Branco and Tigre are at her feet, big eyes eager. But they don't get her as often as they used to with the puppy eyes. If they did, they'd be waddling rather than walking. They're like hoovers.

Sebastião sits down on the other chair with his own plate.

'What were you planning on eating if I wasn't here? Your fridge is empty, Isa,' he says, voice softly chiding. He's watching her as she decimates the chunk of tortilha on her plate.

'I was meant to have done some shopping today,' she says after she's slowed down, 'but when I got home yesterday, and they weren't here . . .' Her eyes drift down to the dogs now lying at her feet. As soon as they notice she's looking at them, their tails start swinging gently. 'The house was too quiet and there was still some work to do so . . . I went back. Ended up working all night.'

'So come home earlier.'

Isabel smiles. 'I couldn't. We had an unexpected breakthrough.' She sighs and pats his hand. 'I know you've been worried. I'm sorry. I've honestly been pretty good lately. You just caught me on a bad day.'

'All right. So, do you get to actually get some sleep tonight or do you have to rush back?'

'No,' she gets up, gets another slice of tortilha, and sits back down, 'no, my plan for tonight is a shower and then bed.' She'll probably give the run a miss too. Looks like the all-nighter has done the job. Even the neighbours seem quieter.

Unbidden, the coroner's words come to mind, and she remembers the state of Marta's brain. Suddenly, the pink of the ham peeking through the layers of potato and egg isn't as appetising as it was. Isabel swallows back the sick feeling and finishes off the rest of it, going slower this time.

'Rita and Tia Maria stopped by for the morning service today,' he says.

Isabel wipes her mouth and lets herself melt into her chair. Not even the mention of her mother and sister can ruin the feeling of a satisfied stomach and she slips a little further down in her seat. 'Oh yeah?'

'Rita says you two have been talking a bit more . . .' He leaves it open, arching an eyebrow. Isabel is sure she got that habit from him. He was always doing it when he was in his teens and Isabel had been impressionable then.

'She said that in front of Mum?' Isabel says, disbelief lacing her words.

'You think so?'

Isabel lets out a bitter laugh. 'No.'

'It was while Tia Maria was speaking to someone else. Rita sounded . . . happy, though. That you guys are talking again.'

Isabel sighs. 'Well . . . yeah. She's been making more of an effort ever since . . . well. Always when Mum isn't around of course. I wonder if she even realises she's doing it.' Keeping her attempts at mending her relationship a secret from their mother.

Isabel wonders if Rita realised that doing this, hiding Isabel away like this, is also something that she needs to change. Isabel doesn't think that's really occurred to her. But Rita has made it abundantly clear, especially with recent events, that Isabel isn't really a primary concern. A concern, sure. But not to be put above her own needs and wishes.

'Are you really going wedding dress shopping with her?'

Isabel groans. 'I told her I probably wouldn't be able to.'

'That's not what she heard.'

'That's the problem. Rita only ever hears what she wants to hear.' She'd accepted that Isabel is still refusing to attend her wedding, learned the hard way not to push for that again after her last attempt, when Isabel had stopped answering her calls and messages and Rita had shown up at her door, eyes like a kicked dog, with two bottles of wine and a box of sample wedding invitations. Isabel had reluctantly let her in. By the second bottle, she was helping her little sister pick out the invitations she'd be sending out for her wedding to Isabel's ex-boyfriend and former aider and abetter in procuring the pills that are useless to her now.

Isabel's relationship with her sister has always been shaky.

Their mother had doted on Rita and brought her up almost as if she were her only daughter. She has never made any secret of the fact that she can't stand her eldest daughter, not after Isabel was classified as Gifted.

There's always been an element of discomfort to Isabel and Rita's interactions because of that, maybe even guilt on Rita's part for always siding with their mother. Isabel's not sure how her sister thought that going out for a year in secret with Michael, who Isabel had had a long and serious relationship with, and then dropping a surprise engagement on her, was going to work out okay.

It had taken them a long time to get through the awkwardness of that and Isabel still feels a lick of betrayal when their relationship is mentioned.

So, helping her sister plan her wedding to her ex isn't really something Isabel is keen on doing.

'True. It's because she's the youngest.'

Isabel shakes her head. 'And you? Are you doing okay?'

Sebastião looks at her, not saying anything for a moment. 'I'm worried about *you*,' he eventually says quietly, and doesn't give her the opportunity to brush off his words, just stays steady and calm. 'It's been a while and I've been letting it slide because I don't think I have the right to be in your business, but . . . I know things have changed for you since that case. I know something changed then and I know you've been keeping it to yourself.'

Isabel can't lie, so she doesn't. She drops her gaze to her hands and doesn't say anything.

'I appreciate that at least you're not telling me I'm wrong.'

She shrugs. 'I don't like lying to you.'

'I know that. But we're here to take care of each other. I can't help if I don't know what's wrong.'

Isabel realises that there's a hangnail on her finger and rubs a thumb over it, wincing a little at the sharp little pain that blooms. It fades just as quickly.

'Isabel?'

Finally, she meets his gaze. 'Maybe I haven't told you because there's nothing that you can do to help. And if that's the case, why would I worry you?'

'I'd still rather share the burden.'

The smile Isabel gives him isn't quite a steady one. 'Give me some time. I'm not ready to tell just yet.'

He doesn't argue with her. 'Okay.' He sighs. 'Go shower. I'll make some tea and then let you sleep.'

Isabel nods and gets up, then hugs him tight. 'Thank you, mano.'

12

THEN

'This is our last session.'

Isabel stops tracking the plane, tiny in the distance where it's leaving a trail across the clean blue of the sky, and turns her attention back to the room.

Rosario hasn't changed much in the years since she became Isabel's Guide, helping ease Isabel into her Gift and teaching her to navigate it.

She's seventeen now and her birthday is next week. When Gifted turn eighteen, they no longer need their Guide.

'Isabel?' Rosario leans forward in her chair, head dipping so she can peer into Isabel's face. Her wispy hair is loose today, the waves framing her face and tangling in her hoop earrings. They're a shocking pink. Over all the years they've been together, Isabel has come to think of Rosario's earrings as her trademark. Without exception, she always has them in, and they're always eye-poppingly bright. Isabel has wondered on more than one occasion where Rosario is able to find them in so many different colours.

She's in a chunky poppy-red jumper and slim-fitting black trousers, at ease in what Isabel has come to think of as Rosario's chair, which is big and soft and a faded lilac-grey colour. They've been using this room for their sessions since Isabel was thirteen.

It's seen a few licks of paint in the last couple of years, but the colours are always soothing: the calm peaceful blue of the walls, the grey wooden floorboards, and the fluffy white carpet. The door and the window frames are painted white too.

In this room, Isabel is safe and everything can be worked out. She doesn't know what she'll do when she no longer has it.

'Sorry,' Isabel says and gives Rosario a small smile as she picks at the curls trying to escape from the ends of her braid where it rests on her chest. Her hair is long and Tia Simone says they should cut it soon – too many split ends.

Rosario nods, slow. There's a hint of a smile to the corners of her mouth but Isabel thinks her eyes look sad. 'How are you feeling about it?'

Isabel drops her braid and readjusts herself in her chair, scrapes her nail over the velvety feel of the arms as she tries to put her thoughts into words.

She's learned over time to keep things in. It's easier that way. Less chance of her saying something that will get her verbally eviscerated or evicted from some new part of the house.

Turning eighteen will be good. She'll be able to leave home permanently. She's been working towards it, putting money away even though Tia Simone and her brother have said they'll help. Yes, it will be good. Even if it means losing this safety net.

'It scares me.' Isabel shrugs a shoulder and turns her face away, can't quite make herself say it while looking at Rosario. The plane in the sky is no longer there. She chews on her lip. 'Not sure who I'll be able to ask questions if something goes wrong.' With her Gift. There's no one in her life apart from the woman in front of her who can help her with this.

Rosario clasps her hands together and the silver rings on her fingers catch the light. 'That's understandable and I think it makes sense. We're always going to come across situations we're unprepared for, and for us, as Gifted and in a place where we're not always understood,' she says, 'it's wise to be as ready for those things as we can. But Isabel, no one will ever be ready for absolutely everything.'

Isabel huffs a laugh because she understands that a lot better than most people. 'Right.'

'Isabel, look at me.'

Jaw set, Isabel does as she's asked and finds Rosario looking at her, a determined expression on her face. 'You're smart. You pick up things very quickly and you're a strong level five – strong enough that if you weren't already at the peak age of Gift maturation, I'd say you'd probably tip over into a 6 at a retesting a few years from now. Your shielding is impeccable, and you've got an amazing control over your Gift as well as a healthy dose of respect for what it can do. You've got nothing to fear.'

She seems so certain, her eyes asserting her belief as she looks at Isabel that Isabel feels the pressure on her chest ease. She lets herself relax in her seat and smooths the pads of her fingers over the texture of the chair as she lets Rosario's words settle her.

'Have confidence in yourself, Isabel.'

Slowly Isabel nods. 'Okay.'

The stern set to Rosario's face melts away then and the look she gives Isabel is undeniably fond. 'You've done well. Your dad would be very proud.'

In response to that, all Isabel can do is nod again, ignoring the stinging in her eyes. She doesn't hide it though.

Here, she doesn't have to.

She'll miss this.

13

Miraculously, Isabel had fallen asleep with no problem. She finds herself blinking in surprise at the light creeping under the gap of her bedroom shutters.

She fits in her run, Branco and Tigre easily keeping pace with her, and takes the time to have a proper breakfast before heading in.

The Chief calls out to her as she's heading over to her desk and Voronov, who is already in, lifts his head at the sound of her name. Isabel holds up a hand in his direction and backtracks.

'Morning Chief,' she says.

The Chief flicks a look over Isabel's shoulder and motions her in. 'Close the door.'

'Something wrong?'

The Chief gets up and rounds the desk, sitting on the edge. She's pissed off already and it's not even nine in the morning yet.

'Monitoring are here.'

For a moment, Isabel can't react. This is how her worst nightmares start. 'Okay . . .' she says.

'They want to talk to you again, regarding what happened the night of Gabriel Bernardo's death.'

She stays calm. 'If it's about the case then shouldn't the prosecution be here to talk to us?'

Chief Bautista pushes away from her desk. 'That's what I asked them. But I can't tell Monitoring no. And we have nothing to hide. Tell them what they need to know and send them on their way. I've told them I don't want them here wasting police time.'

If anyone gets wind of the fact that Monitoring have shown up to speak specifically to Isabel, then it will spread through the whole precinct like wildfire. Isabel doesn't need to deal with additional rumours. Best to just get downstairs and find out what they want from her. She draws in a deep breath and nods. 'Okay.'

'They're downstairs waiting for you.'

'All right. I'll head down now.'

'Good.'

Isabel doesn't bother to knock on the door. They're on her turf, they've intruded on her place of work; she doesn't owe them anything. Still. She's taken aback when one of the people who turns to greet her is a face that is very well known to her. Nazaré Alves.

'Dr Alves,' Isabel says.

Dr Alves smiles at her, dimples popping up and lending her face youth and charm.

Nazaré Alves had been the expert they'd requested from Monitoring to weigh in on certain aspects of their previous investigation. Isabel had had some questions at the time about the extent of a particular level's capabilities. They'd spent a little time together outside of the investigation too and Isabel had enjoyed her company. Had *liked* her.

'Hi Isabel, it's nice to see you again.'

Isabel notes the familiarity with which she addresses her. Pointed familiarity? She sidesteps what would have been considered the polite response and comes into the room, making sure the door is closed behind her. 'Sorry, I've just arrived and the Chief said Monitoring was here to see me about the Gabriel Bernardo case.' She glances at the man in the room. 'I'm surprised. Will the prosecution be joining us?'

Dr Alves keeps her smile, at ease. She takes a seat and shuffles the chair closer to the table. 'No, it's just us.' She gestures at who Isabel is guessing is her colleague. 'This is Manuel Coval, he's a case evaluator with Monitoring.' Coval has the kind of face that a person would find hard to remember after looking away. A little bland. His brown shirt is neatly buttoned, collar edges perfectly ironed triangles and tucked into his black trousers, and his ID hangs from his neck. His hair is slicked to the side in a side parting.

'Right, how can I help you?'

'It's like Chief Bautista explained to you. We wanted to go over the events of that night with you. I'm sure you know that Mr Bernardo's case will be going to trial soon and both Monitoring and the prosecution have been going over the details in preparation. It's just given rise to some questions.'

'Inspector Voronov and I have already provided our statements of that night and answered any subsequent questions regarding what took place.'

The smile fades from Dr Alves' face and she tucks a lock of hair behind her ear. 'I know. We just want to make sure we have everything straight and then we can all move on from this.'

'Okay,' Isabel says, 'ask what you need to ask.'

Dr Alves smiles again, but this time it's smaller and more serious. 'Thank you, we appreciate you cooperating.'

Cooperating. Interesting choice of words. Also, interesting that they hadn't asked to speak to Voronov. Only her. Isabel's sure that hasn't escaped the Chief's notice either.

Coval places a folder on the table and flips it open. He leafs through pages of text before pulling one out and setting it on top. 'Miss Reis—'

'Inspector,' Isabel corrects, eyebrow shooting up. If they're trying to claim they're here in relation to Gabriel Bernardo's case, then they're both doing a poor job of it.

Coval's eyes flick up and his thin mouth twitches like he's just tasted something unpleasant. His irritation is a quick spike in the room that leaves Isabel feeling a touch of satisfaction.

'*Inspector* Reis.'

Dick.

'In the statement provided by yourself, for the night of Gabriel Bernardo's apprehension by the Polícia Judiciária, you say you spoke to his girlfriend, Luisa Delgado, and that after speaking to her you were able to locate Gabriel's whereabouts.'

'That's correct.'

'And how were you able to do that?' he asks.

Isabel looks from Coval to Dr Alves. She's watching Isabel with a sober expression. 'As is *also* in my statement, his girlfriend was the one to supply the location.' Gabriel Bernardo had had complete control over his girlfriend. He had managed to use his Gift to manipulate and control her. Luisa hadn't even been aware of just how exactly he'd used her. Not until Isabel had done something she wasn't supposed to be able to do – she'd looked inside Luisa's mind, using her own Gift to track Gabriel through her. Luckily for Isabel, Gabriel's interference with Luisa's memories meant that that hadn't made it into the report. Voronov had corroborated Isabel's account of events.

Coval narrows his eyes. 'His girlfriend was unaware of his location at the time' – he glances down, sliding another paper out from the pile – 'as subsequent interviews with her have found, she had severe memory lapses during this time and had major knowledge gaps as a result of his control.'

'I'm aware of that, yes. That night you could say was the night his girlfriend woke up,' Isabel says.

'And how exactly did she do that?'

Isabel smiles. Here for the case her arse.

'I wouldn't know, Mr Coval. I'm not a Gifted specialist.'

Aggravating him probably won't do her any favours but she's not going to have this smug prick sitting opposite her, trying to bait her into saying something that will land her in the fire. Isabel doesn't have time for this, she wants them to lay all their cards on the table.

'Isabel,' Dr Alves says, 'it's just that there seem to be some details missing when we look at that night as a whole.' Her tone is more reasonable, no arrogance. But she's watching Isabel like she knows.

Except she can't know. She wasn't there. Unless someone has blabbed, she doesn't know shit. The only people who could give her away are Gabriel and Voronov. No one else was there that night.

No one else had witnessed her taking over someone's mind and forcing them under her command.

'I did everything by the book. I asked his girlfriend for permission before searching her memories. I didn't find anything. As far as I know, the specialist said she thinks that by poking around I may have disturbed Gabriel's . . . work. If you want more information on that, as I said, I'm not a specialist.' She looks from one to the other. 'Again, this is all in my statement.'

'All right,' Coval says, 'you were the one who found Mr Bernardo and the victim. Your partner was with you when you received the information regarding their whereabouts. Why was he not with you? Why was the exact location not relayed to the rest of your team?'

'It wasn't the exact location. She said Sesimbra, she mentioned a highly recognisable spot on that strip of the beach. We knew where to start looking, but we didn't know the exact spot that we'd find them.'

'Then how did you find them?'

'The victim,' Isabel says. 'I was closer to them when we started searching. I heard her call out and found her. As per my statement,' she says pointedly, 'the victim had her arm caught on the rocks and was very weak. She passed out when I reached her.'

'And then Mr Bernardo found you.'

'And then he found me, yes.'

'And just handed himself over?' Coval asks. His tone and his smirk make it clear that he doesn't believe her. It turns his plain face unpleasant, a look of mean smugness to it that makes Isabel wish she could plant a fist in it.

'Well. He didn't throw himself at my feet and beg me to arrest him, no.' She turns in her seat to face him more directly. 'He was surrounded and he'd only hurt those who had hurt him, and were a threat to him. Neither myself nor my partner caused him harm. He was never hostile towards me.'

'You're saying he didn't think of *you* as a threat?'

'I said, he was surrounded. Hurting me wouldn't have done anything but add another nail to his coffin. And I think we can all agree, Mr Bernardo is not a stupid man. Look.' She spreads her hands and leans back in her chair, ignoring how her heart is thundering in her chest. 'If you're asking me to explain to you why Mr Bernardo didn't harm me, I can't do that for you. I am not him. The only person who can explain that to you is Gabriel Bernardo. My statement, my partner's statement and that of our team, and the entire documentation for that case lay out what was done in minute detail. You're clearly not here for his prosecution.' She looks at Dr Alves. 'Why are you here?'

'Isabel—'

'Inspector.' It doesn't matter that this is someone Isabel had felt a small connection to in the past, someone she had pictured herself possibly growing to have a friendship with. The woman in front of her does not have her best interests at heart.

Dr Alves pauses then and there's a change in her posture. A subtle straightening of her shoulders. That familiarity that has been there since their first encounter, that was there still when Isabel had walked into this room not so long ago, disappears. Isabel feels it, and she sees it too, the shift of Dr Alves' emotions – she's used to seeing them emanate from the woman in warm tones. Now they disappear, leaving behind a frosted blue that makes Isabel think of ice burns.

'Monitoring has taken a look at your records,' Dr Alves says, 'we have had a look at your tests. You've consistently tested as a level five.'

'That's correct.'

'And all evidence at hand suggests that your Gift is operating as it should.'

'It is.'

'We're requesting a full disclosure from your personal doctor.'

Isabel narrows her eyes. 'For what reason?'

Dr Alves folds her hands together on the table. 'Why are you in correspondence with Gabriel Bernardo?' she asks.

'Excuse me?' Isabel asks.

'Records from the institution in which Gabriel is being held show that he has been sending you letters. Why?'

'I don't know. I didn't read them,' Isabel says. And it's true; she hasn't read a single one.

'What if they contain evidence?'

'I'm not required to declare the letters,' Isabel says, 'nor do I want to further involve myself in this case. I've done my job and now it's up to you and the prosecution to do the rest. You should also watch how you word things. "Correspondence" implies that I've reached out to Gabriel as well. I haven't. I got his letters, yes. I also binned them. I haven't written back to him and I haven't called. I've had no contact. So please strike the word correspondence from whatever papers you've brought in with you.'

Dr Alves stares at her. Isabel stares right back.

'There are things here that don't add up here, Inspector.'

Isabel plants her hands on the table and leans in. 'I have two people from Monitoring showing up at my place of work under the pretext of getting further information but in fact asking me things that don't impact the trial. I also see two people from Monitoring who have just told me they're going to push for confidential documents without an actual reason for it, considering I have complied with all retesting requirements ever since I was registered as Gifted. All *I* know is that two Regular representatives appear to be trying to fuck over yet another Gifted individual without cause. That's what *I* know, Dr Alves.'

Dr Alves opens her mouth but the knock on the door interrupts whatever she was going to say.

Coval's entire face morphs into a scowl when the person on the other side fails to wait for an invite and pushes the door open.

Voronov steps in and looks from Dr Alves to Coval and then to Isabel.

'Sorry to interrupt.' He turns to Isabel. 'Chief sent me to get you. Daniel and Carla found something. We need to go.'

Isabel rises.

'Inspector Reis, we're—'

'Apply for a consent form to see my medical files, Dr Alves.' Isabel throws a hard look over her shoulder. 'If Monitoring go over my head for them, I promise you I'll make sure you have your name dragged through the mud as badly as the Registry had theirs. I'll also be filing a misconduct complaint – you had me here under false pretences and with no representation.' Isabel pins Dr Alves with a disgusted glare. 'You should know better.'

Voronov ushers her out of the room. 'Good to see you again, Dr Alves.' He closes the door in their faces.

His hand stays on the small of Isabel's back the whole way back up the stairs.

It's the only thing that keeps her moving.

14

Isabel doesn't complain when Voronov drags her into one of the bathrooms and locks the door behind them. Her legs are trembling. She buries her face in her hands and tries to breathe slowly.

'Isabel.' Voronov's hands are huge on her shoulders. 'Isabel.'

'I'm okay,' she says into her hands, 'I'm okay.' Her voice is muffled and her whole body is flushing from hot to cold.

Voronov doesn't say anything else, but he doesn't leave her either. He keeps his hands on her and, at some point, she notices that his thumbs are smoothing over the line of her shoulders, over and over again.

She doesn't know how long she's standing there, hearing people walk by outside, phones ringing, someone calling out someone else's name. Everyone just going about their day-to-day. And here she is, losing her absolute shit in the bathroom, fear digging in so deep that she can feel her top sticking to her lower belly and her shoulder blades.

It feels like they're so close, so *close*, to finding out the truth. That she isn't a level 5. That she hasn't been a level 5 Gifted for a long time. That her Gift is much more powerful than they think. Powerful enough that they'd strip of her of her life, bury her in the same place that they take every other high-level Gifted. The ones no one ever looks for, the ones who they make disappear and no one ever bats an eyelash.

She doesn't want that. Doesn't want to disappear. Doesn't want to cease to exist.

Isabel drops her hands and leans her head back against the door, eyes still closed. 'Thanks.'

Voronov gives her shoulders a squeeze and steps back. 'I wasn't lying though; Daniel and Carla are waiting for us.'

'Right, right.' Isabel goes to splash water over her face. 'What did the Chief say?'

'To go check if you were still in there.'

Isabel looks up and finds a handful of paper towels right in her face. She takes them from him and pats at her skin. 'Wait . . . she didn't tell you to . . .?'

'She didn't tell me I couldn't interrupt,' he says.

Isabel laughs.

Isabel sends Voronov on ahead and steps outside onto the street briefly to make a call.

'Hey, it's me.'

'Isabel?' Michael's voice is surprised.

Isabel shoves her hand into her pocket and stares out at the pedestrians going about their day. She's a few feet down from the entrance to the precinct and from where she's standing, she can see old man Días' café is packed with people.

The tree next to her is mostly bare but she can clearly see the buds on the branches, just waiting for one more little nudge from the weather before they try to open.

'Yeah, sorry to call,' she says.

She's spoken to Michael once since she found out he was sleeping with her sister. Well. Marrying her sister.

It had been a blow.

They'd dated for about two years – it had been serious and at one point Isabel had thought that if marriage was on the cards for her, then it would be to Michael. Except, her Gift had given her too much of an intimate window into his thoughts, and being with someone who worked the hours her job demanded wasn't for everyone. Michael hadn't handled it in the best way and the more Isabel had tried to get some space and breathe, the tighter he'd clung on.

It hadn't been an ugly ending, but neither of them had been left unscathed either.

And then, months ago, in the middle of the hardest case of her career, she'd found out not only that he'd started seeing her sister, but that they were in love and planning on getting married.

To say Isabel hadn't been happy would be an understatement.

Maybe it wouldn't have hit her as hard if she hadn't spent a good portion of their time apart still having to rely on him for help with her Gift. Up until recently, Isabel had been suppressing the strength of her Gift with a steady supply of S3 pills that Michael, as a doctor and one of the only people who had known about the changes to her Gift at the time, had procured for her. Though that had come at a price. In exchange for not having to hear the thoughts of everyone in the city, Isabel had suffered debilitating headaches.

Over time, the pills became less and less effective until they did nothing. So Isabel didn't have the problem of the headaches any more; but if she had to choose, she would go back to them in a heartbeat.

'No,' he says, and suddenly the voices in the background she'd been hearing from his end die down, followed by the clear sound of a door being shut, 'No. I'm between appointments and' – he sighs – 'it's been a while since I've heard from you.'

That's what happens when you decide to marry your ex's sister.

Except she doesn't say that.

'How are you?' he asks.

Isabel watches a mother nearby lowering herself to speak to her child, who has her head thrown back and is wailing at the top of her lungs. The mother speaks in soothing tones and wipes carefully at tear-streaked cheeks. 'Good. Thanks.'

She's surprised when he laughs softly. 'Is that really true?' he asks.

Isabel frowns. 'What do you mean?'

'You don't call me when nothing is wrong. Not any more. You only call me when you have to.'

The words simultaneously make her feel like shit and get her back up. Because he's not wrong. She wouldn't be calling at all if she could help it. 'Yeah. Well. It is what it is.'

The affectionate amusement disappears from his voice. 'Right. So, what's wrong?'

She glances around her to make sure she's more or less alone. 'Monitoring came to see me this morning.'

'What? About what?' Hearing him worried like this gets to her.

'It's a long story and some of it is confidential, so I can't talk about it too much. But they threatened to put in a request for my medical history, go over my head. I don't know how much you can do about that without getting yourself in trouble – maybe nothing. I don't even know what my records look like from a medical perspective so—'

'Isabel. You don't have to worry. I've always been careful whenever you've booked something. If they do that, you'll be fine.'

She closes her eyes in relief. 'Okay. Okay. Thanks. I know – I just needed to check.'

'I keep telling you.'

She opens her eyes again. The little girl has stopped crying and is hopping along next to her mother as they make their way down the street, holding tight to her hand. 'Telling me what?'

'That you're safe with me.'

Isabel lets out a long breath and digs her teeth into her bottom lip. 'Anyway, thanks.'

'Wait, wait.'

'What is it?' She pushes away from the wall, already heading back in.

'Rita was telling me you agreed to come to the engagement party.'

Except, she grits her teeth, *I fucking didn't*. 'What about it?'

'Thanks. It means a lot to her that you're trying.'

That pushes her to the edge of pissed off. 'Yeah. Sure. Thanks again and sorry for calling. I have to go.' She hangs up before he can spout any more bullshit that will make her throw her phone across the street, and goes inside.

* * *

'There is an unusual rise in calls from Marta's phone to a particular number around the time of her resignation,' Carla says. She tucks her hair behind her ear and half-rises off her chair, pushing the records at Isabel and Voronov, red pen leaving a little crimson mark as she uses it to indicate the relevant points. 'I've highlighted the ones we're looking at. This number isn't seen at all until a week or so before the day she resigned.'

The numbers will mean nothing to them. They don't even tell them where in Portugal the caller is from. Although it's something, at least, that they know they *are* based in Portugal. The calls themselves, from the looks of it, are for the most part missed calls, but the first one is about an hour in length. Followed by another one that same evening that's about thirty minutes. There are six more calls after that, about ten to fifteen minutes each.

Isabel notes that all the calls are outgoing. She leafs through the pages Carla has given them, seeking out the same number as incoming, but nothing. All the calls involving that number are *from* Marta's phone.

'Do we have any idea who this number belongs to?' Isabel asks.

'Without her actual phone and her contacts, no. We tried calling it but seems like it's been disconnected.'

They're going to have to go to Madalena with it. She'd been hoping to avoid that. 'Merda,' she sighs and pushes her hair out of her face, leaves her hand there as she continues to go through the list.

'What about the neighbours? Anything?'

Daniel is tapping the butt of a cigarette on the palm of his hand, foot tapping on the floor. 'Not yet. Our officers are still going door to door, haven't heard anything significant yet, no one on her floor has seen anything so we've branched out to the rest of the building.'

'Good.'

'There is something else though,' Daniel says. He tucks the cigarette behind his ear, drags his laptop over and gestures at the whiteboard on the wall. A whirring sound distracts Isabel, and she realises it's a projector. An image flickers onto the board and she squints at it.

'Her bank was fast at getting us her statements,' Daniel says.

Voronov shoves his sleeves up and walks closer to the board, crossing his arms as he looks at the transactions. 'How far back have they given us?'

'I asked them to go back eighteen months,' Daniel says, 'just in case.'

'Have we had a chance to look through it all?' Isabel asks.

'Not yet,' Carla says, 'I'm still going. There are a couple of transactions that are popping up though that I think may be connected to the phone calls.'

Carla walks over, grabs a black marker and underlines two transactions, one for €1,250 and another for €750. 'These are just the most recent ones. But see these dates?' She circles them with a squeak of the pen on the board. 'There was one on the twenty-eighth of December last year and then again on the ninth of January. Now check out the dates for the last two calls on that list.'

Isabel flips back to the most recent calls. 'Sent on the same day as the last calls,' she murmurs. She looks back at the statement on the board. The account named on it as the recipient of the funds is L.J. Pinto.

'So, who is this person and does that phone number belong to them?' Isabel muses.

Voronov turns away from the board. 'We'll have to go back to Madalena.'

15

When Isabel and Voronov arrive, Madalena offers tea and sits them at the kitchen table.

It's a smaller kitchen than her sister's had been and has a more modern look, everything white and spotless. Too spotless. Unlike how she'd been at the precinct, Madalena is steady as a rock. Only her eyes give her away, the skin around them shiny and swollen, more delicate than before. Her hair is wrapped in a protective silk scarf and she's wearing worn cream jogging pants and jumper.

The kitchen table is the only thing that one could call messy. Isabel glances over the papers spread out in front of her. Funeral arrangements.

'A friend of mine,' Madalena says as she sets coasters in front of them and mugs on each, 'his uncle owns a funeral company. He brought me some things. Just need to set the date for the funeral . . . I haven't ever done this before. Not by myself.' She starts pouring and the scent of chamomile drifts up into the air.

Drawing out a chair for herself at the table, she crosses her arms, fingers tight around her own forearms. Her nails had been neat and pretty when she'd gone to see them the day before but now the polish is flaked, the broken pattern on their surface an indicator that she has been gnawing at them.

Madalena notices Isabel looking. 'I used to chew them when I was younger,' she says and puts a hand out in front of her, examining it herself, 'my grandmother used to put this special polish on it that made them taste bad and I stopped.' She laughs, the sound sad and wounded. 'It didn't quite go away.' She gets a faraway look in her eyes then, seeing beyond Isabel and Voronov like she's vacated the room, and it worries Isabel.

The second she'd opened the door to them, Isabel had seen it, felt it. There was a grief as dark as a pit surrounding Madalena, thick and choking. For a moment Isabel had frozen, half expecting that grief to open wide and swallow Madalena completely, and make her disappear right in front of their eyes.

It hadn't and when Isabel had refocused, Madalena was stepping back inside and gesturing for them to go in. She hadn't been surprised to see them. Isabel had made a note then to remember to check in with the grief counsellor, see when she'd be calling in again. Madalena had said herself that the two of them were cut off from the rest of their family. That meant no support to speak of. No one to actually make sure that she was okay and talk this through with her. Isabel feels a little better knowing there are at least some friends on the scene helping her.

'Madalena, we were wondering if we could show you some of the information that came back to us yesterday about Marta,' Voronov says and waits.

Madalena takes a sip from her mug, then sets it aside and links her fingers together. She breathes in deep. 'Of course. Is it anything that I— Will it be hard to look at?'

'No, we want you to take a look at some records for us,' he says.

The hum of the refrigerator fills the silence as he takes out the folder containing the highlighted phone numbers and the bank statements.

When he sets them out on the table, Madalena scoots her chair closer to the table and rubs at her eyes before taking a closer look.

'We haven't recovered Marta's phone,' Voronov says, and Isabel has to subdue a wince at the spike of pain, a sharp steel point jabbing through her chest, at the mention of Marta's name. Her hand is halfway to the spot between her breasts to soothe it away the pain before she catches herself. She forces herself to wrap her hand around the mug in front of her instead and focuses on the heat that scalds her palm.

When Isabel is able to focus back on the conversation, Voronov is nudging the pages forward and pointing at the number in question. She realises she's missed half of his explanation.

'Does this number seem familiar to you at all?'

That finally seems to make a difference and Marta's face loses the mask of blankness that has been in place since she opened the door. It doesn't change the inky grief surrounding her though.

'I do,' she says and her brows furrow. She pulls the page closer to her, eyes flicking as she takes in the dates and duration of those calls. 'I—but—' She looks back at them, confused. 'That's my uncle's number.'

From the family that cut her and her sister off? Well.

'What's your uncle's name?' Isabel releases the mug and rubs the sore skin of her palm over her thigh, the denim a little too rough against her hand but the change in temperature welcome.

'Lucas Pinto,' she says, and she sounds lost, like nothing is making sense, which it probably isn't to her. Her sister's been found dead, she's been told there's foul play and now she's finding out that her sister has been in contact with some of the family who cut them off.

Isabel remembers the name that came up again and again on Marta's bank statements: L.J. Pinto. 'But Marta hated that side of the family,' she says, 'there's no way she would have been talking to him.'

'Maybe something came up that prompted her to get in touch?' Isabel suggests and hearing how evenly her voice comes out relaxes her, helps her feel in control.

'No, if anything like that happened then . . . he would probably have just spoken to me. He— Inspectors,' she looks from Isabel to Voronov, 'when I told you our family cut us off because of Marta being Gifted, maybe I didn't explain how bad it was. They wanted absolutely nothing to do with her. I can't imagine why he would even take her call, I just—' Madalena stops then. She bites into her lower lip, frowning, and her gaze drifts off to the side as she mulls something over.

'Madalena?' Voronov prompts, trying to regain her attention.

'The only thing is . . . my grandmother's inheritance. It's been tied up in a legal battle for the longest time.'

'Inheritance?'

'Yes. Grandma didn't have much, but she and our grandfather owned a house and a small bit of land in Porto where there's a small property. The property was specifically left to Marta and me. They've been fighting us on it from day one, for years.

'But we were finally awarded the house around summer last year. Our aunts and uncles weren't happy about it, Tio Lucas especially, but they didn't reach out to us regarding it. Apparently one of our cousins is living there with a family of his own.' She shrugs. 'We'll have to pay to get them out of there too but . . . we needed to save to start that process. Marta and I didn't want a personal confrontation.'

Madalena sets the pages down and Isabel feels that first lick of anger. It tightens up Madalena's cheeks and for some reason, in that second she looks more like her sister, the expression outlining her cheekbones and jaw and lending her a regal air. 'You think they did something to Marta?'

'No,' Voronov says, 'not at this point in time. But we have to look into any peculiarities surrounding the circumstances of your sister's death to help us build a bigger picture.'

That doesn't appease her, but she gives them a short, sharp nod and drops her gaze back down. There's a muscle working at her cheek and that anger pulsates beneath the skin, clearly something she's ready and willing to latch on to. Isabel supposes feeling something is less scary than the numbness of shock that had been coating her from head to toe.

'Madalena,' Isabel says, voice quiet but firm. She waits until Madalena meets her gaze. 'You need to let us do our job and handle this. Please don't get yourself into trouble right now. You're hurting. No making snap decisions, understand?' Despite her words, her voice is kind. She needs Madalena to understand that doing anything, even reaching out to her uncle while she's in this state, will do more harm than good, whether it's related to the investigation or not.

'You don't want me to contact him,' Madalena says.

'That's right. Not about this.'

Madalena says nothing. Just sits and watches her, eyes staring into Isabel's as if trying to find something. Sincerity, maybe. Isabel's not sure.

'Trust me,' Isabel says. 'We want to do right by your sister.'

At that, Madalena's eyes flutter shut and she looks away, expression crumpling.

But she nods.

As they leave the building, Isabel breathes easier. It's like a weighted blanket is removed and her lungs are no longer being suffocated by the emotion and thoughts filling Madalena's home to the brim. She has to fight off the compulsion to throw herself into the shower and wash the emotions off herself. It feels like each time she comes into contact with someone else's strong emotions, they're able to dig deeper into her. She wonders if it'll continue this way, little by little, everyone else's essence seeping into her until one day—

Until one day. She doesn't even know. Whatever that day is, she hopes it will never come.

As they descend, she feels Voronov's eyes on her. 'What is it?' she asks, keeping her eyes straight forward, hand trailing along the cool metal of the rail as they go.

As they come out of the stairwell and out onto the main street a little girl with pigtails on a bike almost decimates Isabel's toes as she rushes past, her mother's yell echoing and drawing attention from others. The mother utters a quick apology as she hurries off after her daughter and Isabel scales back the scowl on her face.

She sticks her hands in her pockets as they head to the car. 'Porto,' she says, 'what are the odds that we can get him here to talk?' Madalena had given them Lucas's address.

Voronov's car is next to what looks like a newly created recreational area spanning the length of the block. More cars are parked alongside it, most likely belonging to the residents of the bairro.

Voronov stops and sits on the bonnet of his car and Isabel leans against the driver's window, facing him.

'We can call,' he says, squinting up at the top of the building, 'but then we lose the benefit of you being able to glean anything from him.'

Isabel wouldn't mind missing out on that. But it'd be stupid not to use it. It's what gives them an edge. Because if Lucas lies to them, she'll be able to tell. Merda.

'If you'd rather not, then I won't push it.'

Her eyes snap to his. 'What?'

He doesn't so much as blink. 'I think you know me well enough by now to know I'm not stupid. You're more sensitive than usual,' he says, 'have been for a long time now.' He doesn't say it, but even without listening in to his thoughts, she knows he's thinking it. That she's been this way since the last case. 'I know it's bad, Isabel,' he says, 'the only thing I don't know is how bad.'

Isabel scoffs and shakes her head. 'Thought I was supposed to be the mind reader.'

'I'm not trying to steal your title if that's what you're worried about.'

She rolls her eyes and resists telling him to fuck off.

'Well?'

'Well, what?'

'How bad is it?'

She sighs and turns so she's leaning back against the car. She tilts her head back and breathes in deep.

There's a café towards the end of the block that Madalena lives in. She can hear the chinking of spoons on saucers, and glasses clinking. She can also hear the buzz of words not said aloud. A car drives past, pop song blaring and then fading with it.

'Bad,' she says eventually.

'What did Dr Alves want?'

Isabel still feels vaguely sick at the thought of the meeting with Dr Alves. She's surprised neither Daniel nor Jacinta said anything about how she looked afterwards, because she'd caught her reflection in that bathroom mirror, and it hadn't been pretty. Carla is too polite to say anything, but Daniel and Jacinta usually have no filter.

'Officially? They were there to double-check a few things in relation to Gabriel and the upcoming trial.'

'And unofficially?'

'They suspect I did something.'

For a time, Voronov is quiet. 'You think Gabriel said something?'

'No.'

It's not that she trusts Gabriel – although she does feel that he wouldn't have thrown her under the bus like that. She can't say why. He owes her no loyalty. He's trapped because of her. It would make sense for him to try to drag her down with him. But if it were him, then Dr Alves would have had more to confront Isabel with than just a few questions. She's surprised they even approached her with so little. But then again, the system isn't exactly geared towards helping Gifted. Maybe a few suspicions are all that they need to drag someone in.

No. If Gabriel had told them anything about what really happened on the rocks that day, Isabel wouldn't have been able to walk out of that room so easily. She looks at Voronov. 'You never asked me.'

He takes his eyes off the passers-by. 'Asked you about what?'

'About what happened. After I retested the last time.'

'Do you want to tell me?'

That's what she thought he would say. 'Nah. I'm okay, thanks.'

She's not sure what she expects him to say but they both stand there for a moment, watching everyone else carry on around them. The pace is slower right now; most of the bairro's residents are out at work. It's the older residents who are sitting in the cafés that dot the ground floors of the buildings. In the playground section of the recreational area out front is a group of children, and three women mill around, wearing matching pale green work aprons over their clothes. They're probably from a nearby crèche.

'What do you think, head straight to Porto or stop by the precinct first?'

Voronov shrugs. 'We're still waiting to hear from the neighbours,' he says.

True. Daniel is still working on the CCTV too and they need the toxicology report, the only thing that's still outstanding from the coroner. They've put a search out for Marta's car too. There's nothing urgent waiting for them here.

'All right. Let's make a trip.'

16

They get permission from the Chief and let Carla and Daniel know before they set off.

It's a long journey by train. Luckily, Marta and Madalena's family live in central Porto, so it shouldn't take them too long to locate the house once they arrive in the city. And the local police have agreed to drive them from the station.

Isabel keeps her back firmly to the packed station. She is holding a shot of bica, which feels tiny in her hand. It's always served in a minuscule cup that you have to keep pinched between your thumb and index finger and the coffee hits strong and bitter, with a trace of sweet smoothness at the end. Service announcements sound overhead, briefly drowning out the chorus of thoughts. Voronov stands beside her, a small frown on his face as he checks his phone. Both of them are parked firmly at the counter of one of the many little cafés in the terminal.

Gare do Oriente is a wonder of a station, an architectural gem that has tourists staring around in awe. Last year it had been the crime scene at the centre of the National Testing Institute case. Isabel hasn't been here since.

The atmosphere is completely different from how it was on that day. Now, people are going about their day, groups of teenagers passing through on their way to the shopping centre or to reach the river to walk along its banks. It's that kind of weather, the kind that means people are staying out later not just at their local café but walking around the city, sitting on benches with a friend until the sun starts to set, couples taking their time as they walk hand in hand.

Isabel sips at the bica, eyes fixed on the little granules of spilt sugar on the stainless-steel counter. The man who'd served them stands tucked into the small space behind it, arms crossed and attention on the small TV higher up. Isabel isn't paying attention to what exactly he's watching but it keeps the man's attention off them and his thoughts occupied, so she's grateful for that at least. Their train leaves in twenty minutes.

It happens then – that ghost sensation of being watched that's been haunting her for a while now. The sounds around her fade and she becomes aware of a presence at her back, like a stirring at her nape. She stills, slowing her breathing.

It's the same feeling that you get as a child, hurrying up onto the mattress before an imaginary hand could sneak out from beneath the bed and snatch your ankle.

Voronov's hand on her shoulder startles her and she yanks away before she can catch herself. He stands there for a moment, hand hovering where her shoulder had been, then lets it fall to his side.

'That's our train.'

Isabel smooths her hair back from her face, but it spills back over her eyes. 'Right,' she says, digging into her pocket for loose change and paying for the bicas with a *thank-you*. The man scrapes the money off the counter and wishes them a good day, barely glancing away from the TV.

Before she was startled back into the present, her thoughts had been lingering on the way her day had started off.

Voronov had got her out of that meeting with Dr Alves quickly, but Isabel doubts that that's the end of it.

Fuck. She needs a holiday.

They find a carriage that is mostly empty. Voronov motions for her to take the seat near the window and she gives him a look, which he returns blankly. She should be used to this. The walking ahead and opening of the doors, the making space for her to go first; for the most part she just accepts it with a roll of her eyes, but it still throws her when he does it. 'So you can lean against the window and get some rest,' he says.

Huffing out a breath, she squeezes past him to the window seat. She's not sure when it happens, but at some point the movement of the train has her closing her eyes. She sinks into sleep.

A police car is waiting for them at the São Bento station, and the officer introduces himself as Nelson Gustavo. Rather than taking them out to Lucas Pinto's house, though, he drives them to the local police station.

It turns out that after they'd received a call from the Chief to request a lift, the officers had gone one step further and called Lucas in.

'We thought it would save you both some time,' Nelson says as he gets into the driver's side. His accent comes through thick, his a's flat and his v's pronounced closer to b's. His partner greets them both with a smile and a nod of her head. The fact that Nelson hadn't so much as blinked at the clearly stated classification on Isabel's ID, just smiling brightly at them both, had made her like him. He has an honest warmth radiating from him. 'Got a call just as your train was pulling in to say Mr Pinto has arrived at the station,' he adds.

Isabel and Voronov get into the back, Voronov taking up a significant amount of space. She's used to being in a car with him, but it feels like he takes up more room when there's no space between them. His aftershave is sharper this close up too.

'That saves us a chunk of time,' Isabel says, 'thank you.'

'Eh,' he waves aside her thanks as he pulls out onto the road, 'it's good to help each other out.'

For a moment, Isabel forgets about having to constantly keep her walls up as she looks out of the window, Voronov's conversation with the officers in the front making for pleasant background noise as she stares out at the unfamiliar scenery.

She's never actually been to Porto. To be honest, she rarely leaves Lisbon.

It's funny how you can live somewhere all your life and only know a small slice of it.

Like in Lisbon, the buildings they pass have an old-town feel, tall and narrow, exteriors in bright colours or traditional tiles. The city is crowded, with roads and houses packed in, but vibrant and picturesque. The people walking the cobbled pavements here seem to move to a different beat, the pace not quite the same as Lisbon. It makes Isabel think of indulgent naps on the sofa with sunlight streaming in. It's that kind of feel.

For a moment, she wonders what it would be like to get out of the car and lose herself in the middle of all these people. Would the thoughts and emotions here be different?

'It looks different, doesn't it?' Voronov says from beside her.

Isabel tears her eyes away from the view and glances at him. She hadn't realised the conversation had come to a stop. 'To Lisbon, you mean? It's nice,' she says, 'you been here before?'

He shrugs a shoulder. 'I spent a weekend here a while ago.'

'Like it?'

'It gave me what I needed,' he says.

'What was that?'

'Quiet.'

Quiet. Yeah.

Isabel could use a lot of that.

When they get to the precinct, curious eyes follow their progress through the building. It's a little slicker than their headquarters in Lisbon and Isabel eyes the gleaming air-con equipment with no little amount of envy. In summer their building turns into a heat trap, and the Chief has told them on more than one occasion to stop complaining.

'Lucas Pinto is in through there. Not too happy to have to come in,' the officer is saying, 'but he said he preferred that to having us on his doorstep where his neighbours are happy to have a good listen.'

That gets a smile from Isabel. 'Not much of a surprise,' she says. If a neighbour gets wind of it, next thing you know the whole street knows about it too. Usually with a few added embellishments.

The man inside the room has clearly come straight from work. In overalls and work boots, Lucas Pinto has white sawdust up his arms that stands out in stark contrast to his dark skin. He's wearing a black cap and sporting a short white beard that covers the entire lower half of his face.

His eyes are the same colour as his nieces', a startling grey. On the surface, he looks calm, but just a step closer and Isabel knows for certain that he isn't. The emotion is strong – of being wronged, of resentment and an instant dislike towards her and Voronov. She's impressed by how none of it translates to his expression.

'Boa tarde,' Isabel says as she heads for the opposite side of the table, 'Mr Lucas Pinto, yes?'

Voronov shuts the door behind them and follows Isabel, stopping to offer his hand in greeting. Mr Pinto takes it reluctantly and Voronov sits down beside Isabel, all business as he pulls out his notebook and pen.

'Yes, that's me,' Mr Pinto says. His voice has a bit of an accent; it reminds Isabel of her Tia Simone's. 'Can I ask what this is about? I've had the police show up at my door right after my shift at work and not tell me why.'

'Of course,' Isabel says, 'my name is Inspector Reis, this is my partner, Inspector Voronov. We're from the PJ unit in Lisbon. In the interests of transparency, I also have to disclose that I am classified as a telepathic Gifted officer.'

It's such an odd thing, to see someone looking at you so placidly but feel the way their very soul seems to twist in disgust under their skin.

As a telepathic Gifted herself, Marta would have felt that for sure.

'Unfortunately, we have upsetting news,' she says, keeping her voice carefully neutral. It's Isabel's job to remain impartial, going only on evidence. Despite Madalena's explanation of what had taken place in terms of their family dynamics, despite having been fairly certain that Madalena hadn't exaggerated the severity of the fall-out, Isabel has readied herself to put that aside and listen to Lucas Pinto's side of the story.

Clearly, Madalena had been right on the money about the way their family felt about her sister. Isabel wonders if the man across from her will be at all that upset at the news that his niece is dead.

Is this how mãe would feel if someone showed up and told her I was dead? Isabel feels a sick twist of humour at the intruding thought. She doesn't think there would be much sorrow.

'A recent victim of a violent crime has been identified as Marta Nunes, who we believe to be your niece' – as she's speaking, Pinto's eyes widen – 'the PJ is currently conducting an investigation into her death which is why myself and my partner have travelled here to speak to you.'

'We're deeply sorry for your loss,' Voronov offers.

The shock is real. Isabel feels it, like ice water to the face.

'Marta?' he says, and there's a touch of disbelief on his face. That's genuine too.

Isabel's surprised. Maybe he's not completely heartless.

'Yes. Madalena Nunes has confirmed that the young woman who was found is Marta,' Isabel says.

'When?'

'Marta was found two days ago. She was seen by a couple jogging past and they alerted authorities. Evidence was found that indicates foul play.'

At that he looks affronted. 'Why didn't she call us? Why am I hearing this from the police?'

'Miss Nunes spoke to us about the nature of your relationship. We got the impression that you aren't particularly close.' Isabel leans back in her chair. 'Perhaps that played into her initial reluctance to reach out.'

'Mr Pinto,' Voronov cuts in at the sour expression that has finally risen to the surface on Pinto's face, 'we were informed that the relationship between yourself and your nieces, Marta Nunes in particular, was not an amiable one.'

In his seat, Pinto shifts and the hands on the table twitch as if about to curl into fists, but then he folds one over the other. He fixes his stare on Voronov, as if daring him to continue.

Inside though, he's seething. Is it because he's been caught off guard? Because his dirty laundry has been aired?

'Given how the situation has been described to us, we wanted to ask about the nature of the calls that took place between your niece and yourself in the last couple of months.' Voronov flicks open his notebook and lays it on the table so that Pinto can see. On the page, in Voronov's neat handwriting, are the dates and duration of the calls between Marta and her uncle.

'This is something you had to come all this way for? You couldn't have simply called?' He darts a look at Isabel. 'You think I don't know why one of your kind is in here?'

'I appreciate you being honest about your concern,' Isabel says, 'but please rest assured that I can't use my Gift without explicit consent on your part, Mr Pinto.'

Voronov ignores Pinto's words completely but, although his tone remains even, any suggestion of pleasantness is gone. 'There are also a number of bank transfers from Marta's account to yours. Again, given the nature of your relationship, these things seem out of place. We just want to clear this up so we can continue with our investigation.' His voice brooks no refusal.

Beneath the surface, anger overrides the shock, rusted flecks rising in the air that Isabel can't help inhaling.

The shock had been brief and she couldn't sense any remorse coming through. Nothing but indignation and resentment over being questioned by someone like her.

'Mr Pinto?' Voronov prompts when he doesn't say anything.

Lucas Pinto holds the stare off for a bit longer but then flicks his gaze to Isabel before speaking. '*She* got in touch with *me*,' he bites out.

'Yes. We know. What we want to know is why.'

'My mother left Marta and Madalena a plot of land before she passed. My mother and father had built on that land. My son is living there at the moment with his wife and child. She wanted to use it.'

'But why call you? The house belongs to Marta and Madalena, doesn't it?'

His mouth works and he's tapping his fingers on the table now. 'It's complicated. She was in a rush to get them to vacate.'

'So what was the money for?' Voronov takes out the bank statements and places them on the table too. 'We know she sent you money. Around the same time as those phone calls. What was it for?'

He responds but it's as if the words are being dragged out of him. He forces them through his teeth. 'She wanted them out. They have nowhere to go.'

'That doesn't answer our question,' Voronov says.

Isabel leans on the table, her arms crossed. 'Was the money an incentive?' she says. 'Get them to leave a little faster?'

'Yes. So what? Did you want them to end up on the streets? Unlike Marta, my son has a family. A child. You think that they should end up homeless just because that one had gone and got herself in trouble?'

Oh.

Isabel narrows her eyes. 'Hardly homeless. You could have housed them, no?' she says. 'What makes you say she was in trouble?'

He scoffs. 'Those two have never had any problem minding their own business and all of a sudden she's calling all the time and wanting to come up here. Wouldn't leave me alone, trying to call me at all hours of the day. I'm a working man. Besides, she's not from around here, she never liked it even when her and her sister were younger. And being so quick to send the money? Of course, she was in trouble. She was desperate.'

Definitely no love lost here. And it doesn't sound like he had any problem taking the money either, despite his obvious disdain for whatever situation he thinks Marta was in and for Marta herself. But the longer Isabel sits across from this man, the quicker she feels her objectiveness start to slip away.

'Did your son and his wife leave the house then?' she asks.

That startles him out of his smug certainty. 'What?'

Isabel taps the pages on the desk. 'Didn't she send the money so they could move out? So? Did they move out?'

He shifts in his seat and turns his gaze to Voronov instead. Maybe just looking at 'one of her kind' is painful for him.

'It's hard at the moment. They hadn't found a place to go yet.'

'And now she's dead,' Isabel says. 'Convenient.' She ignores the sharp look Voronov sends her way. She hates this type of thing the most. A disgruntled family member, money and property involved. 'You understand this doesn't look good, don't you?' she says.

'What are you trying to say?'

Isabel drags all the papers back and puts them in a neat pile together and leaves them there, linking her hands together and keeping her face straight. 'Nothing.'

'We need to know your whereabouts for the last couple of days, Mr Pinto,' Voronov says.

'I've been here, working,' he says, and Isabel can feel the anger in him building, tapping at the lid holding it all down, 'you can check with my boss. Asking me all these questions – what a joke. If you think I did something, just say so.'

Isabel makes sure her voice is calm and pleasant – insultingly so. 'This is all just procedure. Is there anything else you'd like to share with us?' she asks.

He looks at Voronov, dismissing her entirely. 'I can go?'

'You're not under arrest, Mr Pinto,' Voronov says.

He leaves without saying anything else, not bothering to close the door behind him.

Isabel stares at the spot where he'd been sitting just a few seconds ago, feeling the red trail of his pulsing anger getting weaker and weaker until it leaves her sphere of awareness completely.

When she refocuses, Voronov is watching her. 'What?' she says and pushes the papers at him.

He tucks them away calmly. 'Did you want to provoke him?'

Isabel can't say anything. She knows he's right and that she'd been starting to lose hold of her temper. She wants to ask him if he knows what it's like to sit across from people who think she's scum and have to just take it with a smile all the time. She wants to ask him if he knows how tiring it is. She doesn't do any of that.

'Sorry.' She blows out a long breath and pushes up from her chair. 'I'll rein it in next time. Let's go see if we can get them to send some of their officers to check if he's made any trips to Lisbon recently. We can't be sure of much until we know his approximate movements when she died. Need to check in with the coroner, see if there's any update on that. Hopefully they have a Gifted telepath they can send to speak to that son of his and his wife. It'd be good to get a read on them when they approach them.'

Voronov is quiet for a moment longer. Then he puts the papers away, eyes on what he's doing. 'Let's do that.' He comes over to stand next to her and sits on the table. 'But you don't think he's involved, do you?'

Isabel runs a hand through her hair. 'I'd love for it to be that cut and dried,' she says. 'I don't know.' She thinks about all the locks on Marta's door and the knocked-over pots. The food left to rot in her kitchen. 'He thinks she was running from something.'

'Aren't we thinking the same thing?'

She sighs. 'I think we are.'

He puts a hand on her shoulder and turns her toward the door. 'Let's go talk to them, see if they have any officers available to do the follow-up down here.'

Isabel is so used to always being a little more protected from Voronov's thoughts that she's caught by surprise when they drift through the touch and whisper over her own, gossamer soft. They send a chill through her because what she hears is *don't slip up, or I won't be the only one who notices.*

She slides her shoulder out from beneath his hand and ducks her head, leaving the room ahead of him.

Neither of them says anything else.

17

Isabel can hear Branco and Tigre's claws scraping at the door as she slides the key in. Just hearing that, she feels the change in herself. For a moment she just stands at her door, forehead pressed to the surface, so completely exhausted and – open. She feels too open.

When she steps inside, the dogs are on her in an instant, wriggling with excitement and soft under her hands. She shuts the door and sinks to the floor right there, their happy panting for a moment all she can hear, and it's comforting. They step all over her lap, Branco jumping up to put his paws on her shoulder, his claws leaving scratches, and Tigre trying to wriggle under Isabel's arm.

She lets out a tired laugh. 'Tio brought you guys home for me, hmm?' She strokes them until they're less energetic and then pushes up to her feet. She feels guilty sometimes – she's practically forced Sebastião into co-ownership – but he's assured her more than once that he likes having them around too. They break up his day. Break up the quiet.

Funny how they both find comfort in Branco and Tigre but in a completely different way.

She fires off a quick message to her brother saying thank you and notices two missed calls from Michael. She swipes them from the screen and pushes herself up off the floor to get changed. She forces herself to squeeze in her run, Branco and Tigre only too happy to go along with her, and then spends a solid hour in the shower, letting the hot water run over her and sluice the day away.

It helps but doesn't entirely do the job. The pressure on her chest doesn't budge. It's been there since she walked into that room at the station to find Dr Alves and Coval waiting for her.

Hair wrapped in a towel and changed into sweats and a T-shirt, Isabel plops down on the sofa with a reheated bowl of caldo verde soup, a bottle of water and the bulging brown folder.

The living room is cool; not quite the bone-chilled cold of winter, but the temperature has dropped with the evening, and she has to drag the blanket off the back of the sofa and cover herself up with it. She switches on the TV and makes space for Tigre and Branco, who end up using her legs as a convenient place to rest.

It's late, nearing nine in the evening, and the familiar voice of the anchorwoman fills the room as the news programme starts. Isabel takes a deep breath, insulating her mind until everything other than the small sounds inside her apartment, and the cars driving past outside, won't intrude. No thoughts, no words other than the ones coming from the TV. At least not for a little bit.

Isabel takes the envelopes that are stashed in the folder where she keeps all the findings she's made to date on other high-level Gifted. Her name and address are written in blue ink on the front in a crisp, neat hand. A faded blue franking mark in the corner gives the name of the government institution they were sent from. These are the letters Gabriel Bernardo has sent Isabel from prison.

There aren't many. Four in total.

She should've got rid of them.

Sorting through them, she rips through the top of the first one with her thumbnail and pulls out a few sheets of folded paper. She'd expected to see lined letter paper and more of that neat writing, but what she pulls out is clearly printed. Frowning, she takes out the pages.

She stills.

She's conscious of her heart thundering in her chest and a vaguely sick feeling sinking to the bottom of her stomach. Carefully she lays the three pages out on the sofa cushion.

Three pages. One of them is a portrait shot of a woman, like the kind you'd take for your passport. Her face is serious, and her hair is scraped back from her face into a bun. These kinds of photos are never flattering but the look in her eyes makes Isabel stare at her for a long time. It's like the person inside has vacated the premises.

There's a watermark over the information printed there. Isabel sits up and does a double-take. It's the emblem for the National Testing Institute.

Her heart is beating fast. She grabs up the folder again, the suddenness of her movement making Tigre and Branco sit up, alert. She sifts through the results of her own research, muttering under her breath as she tries to find one piece of paper in particular.

She hasn't told anyone about how she's been dedicating her free time to finding more people like herself. How would she explain? That she's searching for these people so she can get a glimpse of what her own future will look like? To find out that it's not all that bad and maybe she has nothing to worry about? And how did Gabriel know to send her this?

She pulls out the sheet she'd printed just weeks earlier. It's the most recent one she has found. A Portuguese national classed as a level 10. This one had been on a thread that went on about conspiracy theories a little too much for her liking, but she'd printed off the information nonetheless. The thread goes on to provide a name, Elisabete Tavares, and what looks like a small cut-out of a column Isabel hasn't been able to find anywhere else online. There's a blurry picture too that is supposed to be of the woman in question. Screenshots of the blog claim the family appealed for help, said that she'd been taken by Monitoring and they never saw her again. Isabel hasn't been able to find the post itself, or any other mention of this.

Still, Elisabete Tavares' name is in Isabel's notebook, along with the others that she's come across in her research.

Quickly, fingers fumbling as she tries to understand what she's seeing, Isabel opens up the other three letters from Gabriel.

More photos, all with the NTI emblem. Isabel recognises their names and faces too. She spreads them all out and has to nudge

Branco back when he steps on one of the printed pages, the paper crumpling under his weight. 'Branco, stop,' she says, distracted. 'How . . .?' She frowns as she stares down at the pictures, and shakes her head.

She double-checks the envelopes but there's nothing else there. Not a note or any other kind of personal touch.

Each picture in the letters matches with one of the high-level Gifted names Isabel has come across in her research. And from the looks of it, they've been taken from the NTI system.

How did Gabriel Bernardo get hold of these? And why has he sent them to her?

What the hell is going on?

18

Surprisingly, Isabel makes it in before Voronov the next day.

Caffeine is the order of the day. After opening Gabriel's letters, she'd spent most of the rest of the night on her laptop, trying to find out more and figure out what the hell it all means.

The contents of the letters had detailed the known monitoring details of the four women, the observation results. A lot of it had been in specialist language. Some of it Isabel had been able to piece together, the rest of it had left her confused. She'd gone to bed at 3 a.m. and spent the better part of the night staring at her wall, listening to her neighbour's nightmare reach a crescendo that woke the woman up, a chorus of *oh God, oh God, oh God, I'm losing my mind* seeping through the walls and making Isabel close her eyes tighter and try to focus on the soft snores coming from Branco and Tigre lying peacefully at her feet. Eventually, she'd fallen asleep.

Isabel drags out her desk chair and dumps her bag on her desk.

The third room along is occupied and has a light on. From her desk, Isabel can glimpse a section of the room. She sees a young man sitting at the table, looking around nervously. There doesn't seem to be anyone else in with him.

She shrugs off her jacket.

'Morning.'

She glances up at Voronov, who's stopped in front of her desk. Despite the tense way they'd parted the day before, she can't help but give a small teasing smile. 'Running late this morning, are we?' He's always the first to arrive.

His answering smile makes her feel a little better. 'I was about to ask you what made you come in early.'

Isabel scoffs and shakes her head. Before she can say much else, though, Daniel joins them both. The bags under his eyes are terrible.

'Hey,' he says.

'Hey,' Isabel says, 'you worked overnight?'

Daniel leans on the partition and rubs at his eyes. 'Yeah. Carla and I started going through the CCTV footage that's been turned in, but then there was a pile up on the 25 de Abril and it was all hands on deck.'

For Isabel, those words bring with them flashes of memory – herself, on their old family sofa, staring up at her father's Chief telling her sobbing mother that there had been a car accident on the 25 de Abril and Isabel's father hadn't made it.

She dips her head and rubs a hand over her mouth, and pays attention to what Daniel is saying.

'Carla found something for you guys, said for you to take a look. She said that she didn't have the chance to go through it properly but thought you'd want to know ASAP. I sent her home. She was dead on her feet.'

'Okay,' Isabel says, 'thanks. You go rest.'

'One more thing.' Daniel gestures at Room 3, where Isabel spied the young man. 'Was waiting for you to come in, hope you don't mind. He got here about an hour ago. Carla and I were going to take him, but he said he wanted to speak to the Gifted officer that went to the youth centre. His name is Mario, wanted to talk to you about the missing girl, Alma.'

Isabel looks back at the small bit of him that she can see. 'Okay. Sure, we've got it from here. We can debrief when you guys are back in later.' She pats him on the shoulder but keeps the contact brief. 'Go, get some rest.'

Daniel nods at them both and heads to his desk to pick up his things.

'Give me a second,' Voronov says and stops at his desk to shrug off his jacket and dump his gym bag, then they head over to Room 3.

The young man glances up when they walk in, eyes wide. His hands drop to the sides of his chair and grip it tight, and he swallows convulsively.

'Hi,' Isabel says. She doesn't remember his face from the youth centre but that doesn't mean anything; he could easily have been one of the kids milling about who had seen them. 'I'm Inspector Reis and this is Inspector Voronov. We were told you wanted to speak to us?'

The kid's foot starts bouncing up and down and he clears his throat, seeming unsure about what to do. He seems to be avoiding looking Voronov's way, though, and when he finally does settle on something, it's Isabel. He peers up at her from beneath his eyelashes before quickly dropping his gaze again.

Standing, he's probably taller than Isabel and eye-to-eye with Voronov, which is – something. He's got a shaved head and is wearing a *Star Wars* T-shirt and joggers.

'What's your name?' Isabel pulls out a chair and drags it around to his side, making sure to sit comfortably, stretching out her legs, body language open.

Huh. She can't hear his thoughts and can only sense a smidge of emotion from him.

Voronov, clearly reading the boy's discomfort right, takes a seat opposite him but leaves a little extra distance between them.

'Um. I'm Mario.' His eyes flick up to Isabel and then away again.

'Hi Mario.' She smiles, gentle, encouraging. 'My colleague said you wanted to speak to me about Alma. Are you two friends?'

Mario takes a deep breath and seems to make up his mind. He meets Isabel's eyes. There's a moment of recognition. Not like when you know someone, or you're familiar with them, but more like recognising like. 'Yes. We live in the same neighbourhood. We've known each other since we were babies.' He grips onto his other arm, scratching absently along the length of it. His knees bounce as his feet tap, tap, tap on the floor. He glances nervously at Voronov. 'You *are* Gifted, aren't you?' he asks Isabel.

'I am,' she says and takes out her ID for good measure so he can see.

The second he sees her classification he visibly relaxes, shoulders slumping into a teenage slump. 'Oh, cool, thank you.' He hands it back to her and gives her a shy smile. 'My affinity is different,' he says. He casts another wary look at Voronov but goes on, 'I'm a telekinetic.'

'How old are you, Mario?'

'I'm seventeen,' he says, 'but don't worry, my parents are here. They're waiting downstairs. Sofia said we should tell them and ask for permission if we wanted to speak to you guys, said we had to have them with us.'

'That's right. I just wanted to make sure. You said telekinesis?' Isabel asks, smiling. 'I saw a Gifted use their telekinesis to play darts a couple of months ago.'

His eyes widen. 'Really?'

Isabel grins at him. 'Yeah. I was impressed. It was pretty cool.'

Mario laughs. 'I can't do that! I mean, I've never tried but . . . my level is kind of low so I'm not sure.'

Isabel shrugs. 'With practice, you never know. Maybe just don't try it around anyone else. Just in case.' She doesn't want his mum calling the precinct to yell her ear off because her kid lost control and accidentally stabbed someone's arse-cheek with a dart. 'So, Mario. What did you have to tell us?'

At that his smile dims and his gaze drops to his hands. 'Um. Sofia and Clara said you wanted to know about Alma.'

'That's right. We were told she's been missing so we're a bit worried. We were also told she was quite close with Marta, so we were concerned that she may have been upset and taken that a little harder than the rest of you.'

Mario's face scrunches up a bit. 'She really did like Marta a lot. And she was sad when she found out she was leaving. Alma's like, a telepath like you.' He peers up at them. 'She's quite strong too. She talked to Marta a lot, because she was worried. I know she was worried because her Guide told her she might need a Monitor.'

She'd still had a Guide? Guides rarely ever continued with their subjects after they reached eighteen, unless there were special circumstances. Alma is nineteen. Is Alma a higher-level Gifted? That would be the only explanation for her still having a Guide beyond the usual cut-off age.

'The thing is, she went missing for a while,' Mario says.

'Who did?'

'Alma. Before Marta told everyone she was leaving. Like a couple of months before that. I think maybe summertime last year. She went missing for about a week. We used to go biking every evening – her dad is . . . so Alma didn't like being at home at night too much. But she was gone for a week.'

'But she came back,' Isabel says.

'Yeah. I was hoping this time it might be the same but . . . I haven't heard from her at all.'

'Did she tell you where she'd been that week?'

Mario shook his head. 'No. But when she came back, she was . . . quieter. Didn't want to go biking any more. She stuck to Marta more than before. Oh, and she had like, at first I thought she was hurt.' He lifts his hand and gestures at the back of his neck. 'But then after, I noticed it. It was one of those really warm days in September and she had her hair up. And it made a bit of sense I guess because she'd had it bandaged up, but turns out it was just a tattoo.'

'A tattoo?'

'Yeah. I asked her about it, and she snapped at me. Told me to shut up and that she hated it. She told me not to tell anyone about it. It was, um . . . She didn't talk to me for a while after that.'

'That's odd,' Isabel agrees. 'Did she ever show it to anyone else or . . .?'

'No. And I noticed she was extra careful to keep it covered up.'

What in the . . .

'When I saw it I kind of thought it was because Marta had it. That she'd wanted the same one, you know? But after I saw how upset she was I didn't want to ask her any more.' He scratches at his head, the sounds loud as his nails scrape over the black stubble. 'I really didn't want her upset at me any more. And I'm really worried. I miss her a lot.'

Voronov eases forward in his seat and his voice is extra gentle as he looks at Mario. 'Mario, what do you mean the same one?'

Mario turns to Isabel for reassurance and when she nods to gives him the go-ahead, he turns back to Voronov and answers his question.

'Marta had a tattoo on the nape of her neck. Alma got the same one, the psi symbol.'

19

When they reach the room, Isabel notices their case number has been added to the door and is surprised to see Jacinta sat at the table, papers spread around her.

'Hey,' Isabel says.

Jacinta glances up and gives her a tired wave. 'Hi.'

As Voronov comes in behind Isabel, Jacinta gives him a nod in greeting. Like Daniel, she is looking a little worse for wear.

'Did you work overnight too?' Isabel asks.

Jacinta groans and rubs at her neck with both hands, digging her thumbs into the muscles. 'Sadly, yes, but I wanted to see you both first before I took a break.' Despite the obvious tiredness, she looks sharp; the frost-blue blouse she has on pops against her black skin and her long nails are perfectly manicured and painted glossy white. She's even found the time to add a nude gloss to her lips.

'Something from Marta's place?' Isabel glances at the board, which now has Carla's writing on it. But she pays attention to Jacinta.

'Yes,' Jacinta concedes, 'we didn't find much but there's something we think might be useful. There weren't any personal electronics, no computers or tablets or phones.'

Great.

Jacinta pushes her chair away from the table and shuffles it around so that she's facing them. 'No obvious signs of a struggle inside her home, no blood. The footprint we thought might be a possible sign of a struggle. But the size of the footprint is different to Marta's.'

She flips open the folder in front of her, slides out an A4 print of the shoe print against the ruler. The ruler and the notes scrawled on the bottom mark it as a size 37.

'Marta's shoes are all a thirty-nine,' Jacinta says, 'and although we could attribute the dirt spill to a struggle, we don't think it's likely. The damage would have been greater. It looks like the pots were carefully pushed away first. Whatever happened, it might not necessarily be related.'

Isabel blows out a breath. 'I thought you were giving me good news?'

'I never said good.'

Isabel groans.

'But,' Jacinta holds up a clear, labelled evidence bag with a piece of paper inside.

'Arsehole,' Isabel mutters as she takes it from her.

It's a grocery shopping receipt. For the second of February.

Isabel reads the small print that names the shop and the address.

'It corresponds with what was on the table inside the bag.'

Isabel glances up at them. 'This was two nights before we found her,' she says, 'her sister filed that report two weeks ago. Madalena said she'd gone by to check on her multiple times. Called her. Nothing. No response. But . . .' She glances at the receipt.

Unless it wasn't Marta who had gone shopping that day. Unless it wasn't Marta who had gone to her home that day.

But that's her name on the receipt.

Could someone have stolen her card?

'We can check the shop, in case they have any CCTV up,' Voronov says.

'Thanks,' she says to Jacinta, 'and the receipt gives us a point of reference. Someone was definitely in her apartment recently. Let's assume they went in through the front of the building. Maybe we can spot who it is.'

'Yeah,' Jacinta says and pushes up to her feet, moving like every bone in her body hurts. 'Oh. And Carla logged some information onto the system for you, said for you to take a look at it. Thinks it could be important.'

'Daniel told us. We'll check it out.'

'All right, then I'm out of here.' She looks dead on her feet.

Voronov frowns. 'Are you driving?'

Jacinta waves his hand away. 'I'll be fine. I'm not too far away.'

They ask her if she's sure, but she's stubborn about it. Isabel makes her promise to let them know when she gets home, then sighs and looks at what Jacinta has left them with. She pulls her hair up into a short bun at the nape of her neck and wraps it in a hairband. 'All right, let me get my laptop in here.'

'I'll see about the shop and whether they've got anything on camera,' Voronov says, 'and then I'll pick up where Daniel left off with the CCTV.'

After going over the new information Carla has added to the board, Isabel gets settled in. Nothing more than dates, names. She's already added the information from Jacinta.

It only takes a few seconds for her to log in and she heads straight for the new items entered in Carla's notes, which are time-stamped earlier that day.

Marta Nunes, previously a person of interest in relation to Operation Fado.
Case currently listed as open but inactive.
Investigation centring on Ezequiel Venâncio. Can't get access to the full files, might need to talk to the Chief.

Isabel clicks on the hyperlink, waits for it to load up the different section of the Polícia Judiciária's intranet.

The files are locked. Almost all of them. Isabel can only view the subfolders under the persons of interest. The name of the operation itself isn't on the section; instead it has a case number assigned to it.

She can see Marta's full name followed by her date of birth, and her postcode, all of which match what they have on file. For the rest of the file itself there is nothing. Not unless Isabel can somehow get access to it.

'Coffee machine is broken,' Voronov says as he comes in. 'We can grab something when we take a quick break.' He's got two bottles of water and his own laptop with him.

Isabel spins her chair around, still thinking over this new information, and reaches for the bottle he's handing her. 'Thanks,' she says, 'just took a read of what Carla left us.'

Voronov looks taken aback. 'That fast? From what Daniel said I'd thought it was something that would take a little longer.'

'I wish there were more.' She chews on the inside of her lip and unscrews the bottle. 'It's a locked case file. Something from a couple of years ago. It seems Marta was a person of interest. But it's all password protected.'

Voronov pauses in taking a drink and tilts his head, curious. 'That's only done with highly sensitive investigations, usually in relation to a criminal organisation.'

'Your old beat, isn't it? Vice?' Voronov had worked Narcotics before.

He caps his water and sets it aside, then opens his laptop and gets ready to start in on the CCTV. 'Kind of.' He logs in and then turns back to her, considering. 'But if she was involved in something like that it might explain all those locks on her door . . . and maybe the short disappearances her sister mentioned. Do we know the name of the case?'

Isabel gives him the number. 'Carla's note says they refer to it as OF. She says it stands for Operation Fado.'

Voronov's head snaps around to her. 'Ezequiel Venâncio?'

It must be a shock, because she feels the way it ripples through him, temporarily shaking the calm that always coats him. At least outwardly.

'Yeah . . .' she rolls out the word slowly, not having expected that kind of reaction, 'why, who is he?'

Voronov shifts in his seat and then rubs a hand over the back of his neck. 'They call him O Fadista.'

That's a new one. 'Is he one?'

Voronov's lips quirk into a smile and the lines of his shoulders ease a bit. 'No, but he owns a fado house in Baixa-Chiado, called O Vermelho.'

The name rings a bell and an image flirts at the edge of Isabel's mind. She can't quite fully touch it, but she gets the impression of narrow streets and a tight corner by a set of stone steps and surrounding cafés, and the throaty notes of a fadista belting out a sorrowful melody. Fadista is what singers of fado, a mournful form of music that Portugal is well known for, are called. Fado houses are usually informal restaurants serving traditional Portuguese food, usually with a fadista singing in house. Lisbon is littered with them, but they are particularly numerous in the Chiado area.

But the name really does seem familiar to her.

'The business is legitimate, frequented by a lot of people in the upper circles of society. It has a reputation for being hard to get into. If you're not on the list it doesn't matter how much money you throw at them, they don't let you in – it has a good reputation among the locals, funnily enough,' Voronov says. 'The operatives on the case were sure the neighbours saw a lot of things, but no one ever said a word against him.'

Isabel rests her elbow on the table and her head on her hand. 'Someone always says something,' she says.

'True, but in this case, not the neighbours.' He scratches at his chin. 'Part of the issue with Venâncio is that he has friends in high places. Maybe even, or especially, in the force. No proof of that either, but there were rumours relating to special parties. That Venâncio was supplying entertainment in more ways than one.' He looks at Isabel. 'Apparently he was said to cater to people who had a taste for Gifted individuals.'

Okay. Isabel wasn't expecting that. 'For what? Did they expect them to do magic tricks?' She's honestly baffled. Physically, there's no difference. Sex with a Gifted individual is like sex with a Regular. It's not as if they have different anatomy. Unless it was some kind of superiority complex, something about control and exerting dominance over someone who otherwise they may consider stronger than themselves?

What is the angle here?

'I'm not sure,' Voronov says, 'I wasn't involved in this case, but I dealt with informants who I know also worked with the team overseeing that operation. I crossed paths with Venâncio a couple of times. A lot of business happens in and around his place.'

There's something there, a murky thought that's buried almost as soon as it rises. Strong enough for Isabel to notice, but still protected enough by Voronov's natural barriers that she doesn't pick it up clearly. It helps that Isabel is nowadays always trying *not* to pick up on anything outside of her own head.

Whatever it is makes her watch him carefully, curious.

'These people . . . they tend to run in the same circles,' he says. 'The investigation team gathered enough intel from informants to convince them that he was the one running the Houses.'

'What are the Houses?' Isabel asks.

'That's what they call the underground business that Venâncio allegedly runs,' Voronov explains, 'they've never been able to fully track them. We know they're called the Houses because a woman who belonged to them managed to get free at some point. She gave the officers working the case as much information as she could,' Voronov goes on, 'but refused to testify. The force refused them witness protection.' And his mouth does that thing that tells Isabel exactly what he thinks of that decision. 'When we first learned about the circumstances of Marta's death, I mentioned a similar murder, remember? The dead body was found shortly after they spoke to the police.'

'I remember,' Isabel says. 'What about her? The girl who spoke to the police?'

'I don't know, best thing would be to disappear after we refused witness protection,' he says, tone grim. 'The person they found like Marta was a young man actually, mid-twenties. They found him in a back alley in Montijo. Neck nearly severed. No clothes, no ID. The fingerprints had been burned off and there was no blood at the scene – face was completely bloodied up. No way to identify him.'

Isabel doesn't remember this. 'Was it connected?'

'Yes. One of mine and Seles' informants actually. They came forward and aided the team in the investigation.'

Isabel gives a low whistle and swings side to side in her chair. 'Balls of steel.'

'He didn't do it out of the goodness of his heart, he needed something from us. He didn't tell us who had done what. Just that someone was missing and he . . . *thought* it might be related to the fadista.'

Isabel processes that and looks over at the board and the scrawled information on there. The looped orange letters blur in front of her.

'Marta was Gifted,' she says. 'She was a higher-level, wasn't she?'

'A seven,' Voronov confirms.

'It says the case is open but inactive now.'

Sofia, the manager at the youth centre, had said that Marta had been with them for five years. But like Voronov had said before, Madalena had told them that her sister would go missing from time to time.

She thinks about Mario saying that Alma was upset after Marta went missing. That she had come back with the same tattoo as her.

Had Marta still been associating with Ezequiel Venâncio? Is that what the tattoo meant? Had she tried to pull Alma into that world? She thinks of Marta's smiling picture and the uncle who had hated her guts. Working at a youth centre, a job everyone insists she loved, with kids she cared for just as much. How does someone like that end up as a person of interest in an investigation like the one on Venâncio?

Who were you, exactly? Isabel wonders.

This new information *does* give them a new line of inquiry though.

'Will we be stepping on any toes if we go and speak to this guy?' Isabel asks.

'Probably. But if the operation is inactive then there's not much they can do about us speaking to him, especially about a case that isn't in relation to what they were originally investigating.'

Isabel smiles. She likes it when Voronov shows his little rebellious streak.

'Chief Bautista will have to clear it first,' he says.

She hikes up a leg onto her chair. The hairband is sagging under the weight of her hair, so she tugs it off and ties it back again. 'What do you think?'

Voronov shakes his head. 'There's such a thing as too much coincidence,' he says, 'Marta's connection to Venâncio isn't something I think we should ignore.'

'All right. Let's see what the Chief says.'

'Monitoring left you alone?' Chief Bautista asks, letting them both into her office.

That takes the shine off of Isabel's high. 'They aren't here this morning, and they didn't come find me again after he rescued me.' She jerks a thumb at Voronov.

The Chief eyes him but, when his face stays perfectly blank, she doesn't say anything. 'If they come back to bother you,' she says to Isabel, 'I want you to let me know ASAP. I've put in a call to the prosecution team to ask what their problem is with our paperwork that they're sending Monitoring here to do their work for them.' She sits down, takes out a cigarette, lights it and settles in.

'Thanks, Chief,' Isabel says.

Chief Bautista brushes that aside and points her cigarette at them both. 'Tell me what you want.'

Isabel glances at Voronov and motions for him to take the floor.

Voronov outlines their case so far and their findings about Marta's previous connections. Isabel watches as the Chief becomes more alert, feels the sharp stab of apprehension that cuts through her when Voronov says Ezequiel Venâncio's name.

By the time he's finished, she's leaning forward, blowing out a stream of smoke that makes Isabel wince and lean back.

'That's a serious name you've got there.' She sighs and digs her thumb into her temple. 'And it's going to have people knocking on my door that I'd rather not have to deal with.'

Isabel waits.

'Tread carefully,' she tells them. She looks at Voronov. 'You've had some experience with how that side works. Maybe it would be convenient for this to pan out for you both, but I hope there isn't a connection there and this is just all . . .' She whirls the hand with the cigarette in the air, letting it speak for her.

'Coincidence?'

Chief Bautista scoffs and shakes her head. 'Sure.'

'Thanks, Chief,' Isabel says.

'Make sure you report back to me directly after you speak to him. And remember what I just said. Tread *carefully*. We've barely cleared one scandal. I'd like us to avoid getting involved in a second one.'

20

Given the green light from the Chief, they don't waste any time.

'Think we can walk it?' Isabel says.

'Sure,' Voronov says.

Isabel leads the way, though she's sure Voronov would know where to go. O Vermelho, the fado house in Baixa-Chiado owned by Venâncio, is about a twenty-five-minute walk from the precinct.

'What's the matter with you?' she asks.

Voronov is mostly quiet all the time, but there's usually a calmness to that quiet, an ease that Isabel has become familiar with. She finds it soothing. Not that she'd ever tell him that. That calmness though, is nowhere to be seen right now.

'Do I not seem okay?'

Isabel glances away, uncomfortable. 'Did you forget who you're talking to?' she asks.

Voronov looks curious where most people would be horrified. 'Are you reading me right now?'

'No,' she scratches uncomfortably at the side of her neck, 'but little things slip through sometimes. Like when you spoke about crossing paths with Venâncio earlier. I wasn't prying . . . but I felt something spike from you. And now.' She shrugs. 'Something just feels off. I rarely sense anything from you so it's unusual. That's all.'

He nods like he understands, and they walk on in silence for a while.

The streets are packed with the after-work rush, streams of people heading down the wide road, packed into the narrow pavements as they head to the busiest part of Lisbon. The wide-open expanse of the Praça do Comércio will be crawling with people, some heading to the trams, a lot heading for the Terreiro do Paço terminal to catch the boat that will take them across the river and into Setúbal.

Isabel feels like she and Voronov are being dragged along with the tide, mingling with the steady crowd all heading in the same direction. Some stop along the way to call into the open shops and cafés, dipping in and around the tourists to have a chat with the locals; some veer off into quieter streets.

There's a collective heavy tiredness that emanates from the crowd as they go and it's comforting in a way. Isabel recognises this feeling in them, she feels it herself, so it doesn't feel intrusive.

Is there such a thing as having a favourite feeling? This is one of them for her. Yes, people are tired, but their spirits are lifting a little as they head home after a long hard day. For the majority, they know they're heading toward comfort and rest, and that envelops Isabel in a soft glow of feeling that she doesn't want to shake just yet.

That isn't to say that as they walk, she doesn't get spikes of negativity. That's always there, like little holes worn into fabric, marring it but not quite ruining it completely. She's learning that she can't block everything. It costs her less energy to pick and choose what she does and doesn't let in.

'Hey.' She taps Voronov on the shoulder and tugs him off the main road, leading him until they end up on a much smaller and quieter street. A rock ballad is drifting out from high-up windows. The paint is flaking off the buildings and someone somewhere behind them is throwing a bucket of water onto the pavement. Someone else is yelling. There are shops on this street too, many of them closed, with apartments above.

'Quieter,' she explains.

The sun is still out, its warmth persistent despite the breeze picking up, carrying a sobering chill with it that makes Isabel glad she'd worn one of her warmer jackets. She wishes she'd grabbed her sunglasses from her car before leaving, but can't bring herself to care too much and finds herself tilting her head back so the sun can bathe her face in the soft heat. It's nothing like the intensity it will pack in the next few months.

She takes them up another turn-off and catches his slight frown as he realises they're not heading straight to Baixa-Chiado.

'Taking the scenic route,' she throws over her shoulder as they start up a hill, and they fall into companionable silence as they walk.

As they go, Isabel feels the tension that had been radiating from Voronov soften and release until he's taking in the view with appreciation.

Problem with taking the scenic route is that Miradouro da Senhora do Monte is a tourist magnet, especially on a bright day like today. When they get there, it's packed. Isabel stops to grab them two bottles of water from the nearest shop, and they walk across the churchyard, the highest point in this neighbourhood, and past the grass to the railings overlooking the spread of Lisbon. All the benches are taken but Isabel doesn't particularly feel like sitting down anyway.

She heads towards an emptier spot and hands Voronov one of the bottles before leaning on the railing and taking a drink.

'I jog here sometimes,' she says, 'from my place. It's quieter at night in winter and spring. But in the summer? Forget it. Packed all the time. Love it though.'

Voronov leans in next to her, bottle dangling from his hands. Definitely more relaxed now. 'Yes, I've been here a few times myself. Not as local to me as it is to you though.'

'Hmm.' It occurs to her that she doesn't actually know exactly where he lives. She's never thought to ask, and he's never shared. In the back of her mind is the polite invitation he made a few months back when they'd first started working together, that if she wants good vodka then the best place to get it is at his house. She doesn't doubt that he's right.

'So, we're here because . . .' he says.

'Because you've been wound up tight since we saw who Marta's name was tangled up with,' she says. 'But you said you weren't personally involved in the Ezequiel Venâncio case, so I wondered if there was more to it.'

Voronov's eyes look different when the sun hits them like that. They make Isabel think of cat eyes. Eerie but compelling. 'Yes and no.'

Isabel pins her eyes on the faraway river. People buzz around them. She has to concentrate harder here to hold their thoughts at bay. There is a fresh green excitement that is intrusive and rubs Isabel the wrong way, but there's also a softer crystal-like wonder that she doesn't mind as much.

She turns her back on the stunning view and leans against the railing, folding her arms, muscles relaxing under the sunlight soaking into her back, warming her jacket and the skin on the nape of her neck.

Voronov draws closer to her, straightening up, leaving a hand on the railing but turning to her, not much space between them. It means Isabel has to tilt her head back to look at him, but it also means that they can keep their voices low enough that no one near them catches their conversation.

'I don't like that he's cropped up,' he says.

Isabel is a little thrown by all this. 'I'm surprised I've never really heard of him.' And she is; from Voronov and the Chief's reaction, she would've thought that word about Ezequiel Venâncio would have travelled far.

'You definitely would've if you worked Vice. Otherwise, it's kept quiet. Despite the investigation, he's not showy.'

It makes sense, if he's the kind of man who has neighbours refusing to say a bad word about him. Baixa-Chiado has become a touristy place, but the Chiado District is an old town. It shows in the houses, and in the people who live there today, old mixed with young, generations that have been there for years and stayed through the hardest changes the city had undergone – financial blows, the fire that had torn through it in 1988 leaving the Chiado in ruins. Those kinds of people aren't hardened criminals. They're the nosy but well-meaning neighbours asking you if that young man you were walking with the other day was your new boyfriend, the kind of people who refer to anyone aged thirty and below as so-and-so's son or daughter, who come and knock on your door with slices of cake they made too much of.

If they're not reporting him then he's a darling to them.

'Why wouldn't they report him? What, just because he's nice?' She watches out of the corner of her eye as a young girl throws a handful of seeds onto the ground and then runs away shrieking with laughter as pigeons converge on the spot in a chorus of flapping wings.

'He's not just nice,' Voronov says and the smile he gives her is an unamused one, 'he's smart about what he does. He invests in local businesses, gives people a lending hand if they're struggling, attends morning mass every Saturday and is friends with the priest too.'

Isabel arches an eyebrow. 'Seriously? What, and they don't suspect what he does?'

Voronov shakes his head. 'The impression I get is that he's some kind of Robin Hood to them. In their eyes the authorities are just trying to bully someone who does something for the people.'

Unbelievable. If that's the narrative that is spread around about him, of course it would make those living in the area view him favourably.

It doesn't surprise her that people would rather believe in the perceived goodness of someone rather than actually care that maybe Gifted individuals are being abused by him.

People see what they want to see.

Isabel looks out at the spread of the city and sighs. She tucks a stray curl behind her ear. 'And these Houses. Where are they based? Did they ever figure it out?'

'Not as far as I know.'

'Do you think he'll talk to us?'

'I don't know.'

* * *

Ezequiel Venâncio's Fado house, O Vermelho, sits quiet at this time of day. As they reach it, it clicks into Isabel's memory, that vague sense of recognition that she'd felt when Voronov had mentioned it earlier. O Vermelho has a wide arching door painted an inky black and it's tucked behind a set of stairs that lead to a street higher up. Its sign, lit up with red light, stands out, even in the daylight.

The pavement narrows dangerously to a point right beneath its door. One side of the entrance's double door has been left open. From where they stand, Isabel can see far enough inside to glimpse a few steps leading down into the establishment.

She taps Voronov on the arm and waits until he meets her gaze. 'Do you want to play this a particular way?' she asks.

Up until now, despite their working well together, she has more or less directed their investigations. But Isabel's not stupid. If someone has more knowledge than her about a situation, she can take a step back. Well – depending on who that someone is.

'I think we'll be fine.' He looks up at the sign above the door. 'We're not accusing him of anything.' The 'yet' doesn't need to be spoken aloud.

'All right,' she says, and gestures for him to go ahead, 'after you.'

Voronov pushes the door the rest of the way open and has to duck his head as he goes in.

Though the place is open, Isabel doubts there will be many customers at this time of day. When she enters, the silence is as refreshing to her mind as the cool balm of air that washes over her face. A server appears immediately, peering around the open doorway into the entrance.

The lighting is low in here, most of the brightness coming in from the outside. She can smell the sweetness of alcohol in the air, faded but there. The interior is dark and feels heavy, notes of melancholy music filling the space around them. Directly opposite the entrance is a door with WC on it and two little figures representing the two sexes.

'Boa tarde,' the man greets them, smiling politely. He's dressed in a uniform and not a thing is out of place; his smile is warm and welcoming as he takes in both of them and asks if they'd like a table for lunch.

Isabel declines politely. 'Is Mr Venâncio in? We'd like to have a word with him.'

He looks startled. 'I'm afraid Mr Venâncio isn't expecting anyone. He won't be able to meet with you at this time.'

Isabel smiles, keeping it as nice as she can. 'I understand, but we're with the Polícia Judiciária.' She shows him her ID. 'If he could spare myself and my partner a moment, I'd appreciate it.'

Either he has his staff super well trained, or this guy has no idea that the PJ have reason to be watching this man and stepping in at any time. Isabel doesn't feel a flicker of apprehension or any nervousness from him. It's nice, actually, to not have to fight off someone else's emotions; but, in these circumstances, her edge relies on her being able to sense these things. It won't do her any good if she's not getting anything.

Or maybe my Gift is just broken, she thinks and swallows the bitter laugh that tries to rise.

'Certainly, Inspector,' he says, 'please wait here.'

Isabel agrees, and the server goes. Calm as anything. No rush in his step.

When she glances at Voronov in askance, he nods. 'He'll see us.'

Hmm.

Despite their earlier conversation, Isabel can feel the unease in him rising again. It makes her uncomfortable. It's odd. She's used to having to fend off the emotions and thoughts of others on a daily basis; she's stopped feeling bad about intruding because frankly, she doesn't have the energy to be trying to hold them off and feeling guilty about it at the same time. But with Voronov, even though the spillover is minor, it's not the same.

The feeling it leaves in her is familiar. It reminds her of when it started to go wrong for her and Michael. The way she'd just hear a thought or two and it would catch her off guard. Things she wasn't ready to hear. Things she didn't want to hear. It had left her in a constant state of uneasiness and turned her defensive about every little thing. Mostly, it'd left her feeling like she was the wrong one, unable to grant her partner even the most basic privacy. That defensiveness had eventually turned to resentment. It wasn't something she could have even had a go at him over. Because how can you argue with someone about their thoughts? He wasn't expressing them, only thinking them.

Although, that had been part of the issue too.

Because how can you trust and be yourself with someone who gives you sincere smiles and tells you everything is okay, but in their mind, there is a constant replay of all the things that they're sick of or don't want to deal with any more? And you can't even call them out on it because, well, you weren't supposed to be listening to their thoughts to begin with.

'If you'd like to come through.'

Isabel's head snaps up and she realises she's let herself get distracted. 'Right. Thank you.'

Voronov's look asks if she's okay and she waves it away.

The fado house is bigger than she expected. Though it's as narrow as the outside of the place suggests, the room is long, going deep into the building. The floor itself is packed with enough tables that Isabel wonders how servers get around without tripping up, and at the end of the room is a small stage, big enough to hold about five people. Just off to the side is a small corner bar and a door that she imagines probably leads to the kitchen.

There are only two occupied tables. A man and a woman are sitting together, a basket of bread and a little bowl of olives between them. They each have a small glass of wine, and their heads are bent together as they talk, voices low enough that the music covers them. Just a couple of tables down from them is an elderly man, white beard a little erratic, a cap on his head, newspaper held out in front of him, an empty plate, and a tiny glass of what was probably port on his table.

But there's a curling iron staircase in the middle of the room that leads up to the first floor. It looks like a long length of balcony, dotted with smaller tables in single file. It overlooks the whole downstairs with a good view of the stage.

Right at the end of that section sit two men. One is watching them. He's got his back to the wall and has a view of the whole lower floor. Isabel can't make out his features. The lighting is too low, designed to keep pockets of the place in shadow so that whoever is on the main ground-level floor stands out in stark relief.

The server gestures at the stairs.

'Please go ahead, Mr Venâncio will speak to you now. Would you like me to get you anything? Our lunchtime specials perhaps?' he asks.

Isabel's stomach says yes. Whatever it is that she can smell coming from the kitchen is amazing. But priorities.

'No,' she says, 'thank you for your help.'

The stairs creak a little alarmingly when Voronov starts up them.

'One day, we're going to get into an accident because of you,' she says. He gives her an unimpressed look. 'I'm serious,' she mutters and continues up. But the comment has eased something in him, although not distracted him; that tension is still there, bubbling up against whatever stopper he's using to keep a lid on it.

As they walk along the balcony, the man with his back to them stops talking, hooks an arm over the back of his chair and twists to watch them approach.

The two men at the table are remarkably alike.

'Which is which?' she asks.

Voronov keeps his voice low as he talks over his shoulder. 'The one who was watching us from upstairs is Ezequiel Venâncio. I haven't seen the other one before.'

'He looks like family,' Isabel says.

'It would make sense,' Voronov says. 'From what I recall, Venâncio isn't the type to bring new people in unless necessary.'

As they approach, the second man gets up. He says something to Venâncio and Venâncio nods and turns to speak to him.

The light falls on his left cheek and Isabel notices the bad scarring that starts just above his cheekbone and travels down onto his neck, tapering as it disappears into the collar of his white button-down.

Despite the scarred skin, he's obviously a handsome man. Sharp, strong bone structure and soft brown eyes. His hair is dark brown, and long; it falls in a sleek waterfall over his right shoulder and cuts off just above his hips. He could easily use it to hide the scar, but he doesn't. Isabel wonders what that means. If it's a statement of defiance, or a subtle threat to anyone who might be thinking of messing with him.

Isabel stops, leaving enough room in the narrow space for the other man to walk past them. When he gets closer, she thinks she was right about them being family. Same eye shape, same mouth. His jaw is wider, though, and his hair is short, neatly combed back from his face. His eyes, when they meet hers, are cold and when he walks past her, she gets nothing. It's like walking through a ghost.

The man gives Voronov a hostile look as he goes. There's no acknowledgement of Isabel at all.

'Please have a seat.' Venâncio brings their attention back to him, closes the folder in front of him and draws in closer to the table, at ease and waiting. He doesn't try to disguise the assessing once-over he gives them. He peers at her and tilts his head, curious.

'You have a new partner, Aleksandr?' he asks. 'I suppose Seles isn't too forgiving.'

That leaves her feeling wrong-footed. She hadn't expected the first-name terms. She resists the urge to give Voronov a look that would put him six feet under. So much for not working that case.

He'd recognised Voronov instantly.

'Ezequiel,' Voronov greets the other man. He sounds polite enough, no particular inflection in his voice.

Glancing away from them, Venâncio gestures to one of the tables behind them. 'I think we can fit another chair, if you wouldn't mind dragging one over for your new colleague.'

'His new colleague,' Isabel says, 'can get a chair for herself.' She suits action to word and sets one down in the tight space at the table.

When they're both seated, Venâncio looks her over, unsmiling. 'And you are?' He holds out a hand.

Fuck. She doesn't want to touch him. 'Inspector Reis,' she says. She braces herself and takes his hand, and gets – nothing. A firm, brief, shake. Through sheer will she keeps her astonishment from showing on her face.

The server below . . . there had been nothing. The guy who had just left – nothing. And now Venâncio. Thoughts, emotions. All silent.

It dawns on her that they're Gifted, maybe everyone in this place. Probably higher-level Gifted at that. Why had Voronov not said?

She pulls herself together. 'Did we interrupt?' she asks.

'Family business,' he says, 'my brother Tito.' He smiles then, revealing a sharp incisor, and looks at Voronov. 'I think this one is better suited to you. Seles liked keeping quiet. Too quiet. How is he?'

'In prison,' Voronov says dryly.

'Of course. And your sister?'

His sister? What?

Voronov doesn't offer a response and Venâncio seems content to carry on without one.

'Can't say we've missed your face around these parts,' Venâncio says. 'But you're not here to catch up and I appreciate you showing up during my quieter business hours for whatever this is. How can I help you both?'

This is a man completely at home. There's nothing from him that suggests that he's even the least bit worried about having them in here.

When someone is this confident it's either idiocy or well deserved. Considering that despite years of being under police watch, they still have nothing concrete that they can drag him in for, Isabel suspects the latter.

She gets the distinct impression that this is someone she doesn't want to mess with.

Voronov crosses his arms and sinks into his chair, cool blue eyes locked on Venâncio. 'We wanted to have a conversation about Marta Nunes. She used to work for you.'

There. Isabel just about keeps herself from cocking her head like a dog that's caught a sniff of something good. Gifted and with strong wards, but not impenetrable, she thinks.

But what she just felt isn't emotion, though. Nothing that stark. It was just more of a jolt.

'That's a name I haven't heard in a while.' He eases back in his chair, crossing his legs and sliding his hands into his pockets.

'Oh, no?' Isabel says. 'We were wondering if your paths had crossed recently.'

His expression stays polite, and she doesn't feel anything that suggests otherwise. 'And why would that be, Inspector Reis?'

'Marta Nunes has been found dead, Ezequiel,' Voronov says.

And there's a flicker there. Venâncio's eyelashes sweep down for a second and he closes his mouth. 'That's unfortunate. I haven't seen Miss Nunes since she left her job here. I believe she joined a youth centre in Setúbal shortly after her time with us.'

'What did she do here, exactly?' Isabel looks around at the place. 'Seems like an interesting jump from a place like this to a youth centre.'

'She managed my bookings. We host a fadista every night, and, as I'm sure Aleksandr will have told you, we cater to people who appreciate discretion and want to enjoy a relaxing night without having to worry about eyes on them. Her work was always flawless. She was a good worker and my clients liked her.'

Isabel arches an eyebrow at that and when he catches her expression his interest comes through.

'You don't believe me.'

'Your clients *liked* her. Is that a euphemism? Because my partner here has briefed me on your history with the force and I wasn't born yesterday.'

His eyes bore a hole through her head. 'You're suspicious of me.'

If the shoe fits.

'No,' he says, 'there is no euphemism.'

At first, she's so focused on his expression she doesn't realise it. A curiosity that isn't her own filters through her, the enquiring touch against her mind so delicate, like a fingertip skimming over a page.

He's a telepath. And right now, he's trying to take a peek inside her head. It makes the hairs on the back of her neck stand up.

Isabel shuts down so fast that he can't hide his reaction, surprise widening his eyes for a split second before he gets it under control.

'Definitely an improvement on Seles,' he murmurs. 'I'm surprised,' he goes on. 'It's rare seeing one like you walking around freely. No Monitoring dogging your steps.'

Beside her, another crack splinters through Voronov's normal steady shields and when she looks his way, something darker plumes around him like smoke. Though she can't pin down the emotion, it makes her uneasy.

It's deeper than the mild annoyance she's felt from him before, and it makes Isabel start to reassess him. Strangely though, she's not alarmed by it. Voronov has done enough for Isabel to trust him. But no one can be that naturally calm all of the time. She's been tempted to probe before. She can admit that to herself. To slide beneath the layers – they would be nothing to her if she really wanted to see what emotions roil inside him. But she's never crossed that line and she doesn't intend to. No matter how much she wants to see what lies beneath.

'Seems like I'm not the only one here who would be of interest to Monitoring.' She looks in the direction his brother had left in not that long ago. 'Your brother, Tito, did you say?' she asks. 'His shields were something. Like he isn't there at all. Yours aren't bad. I think his might be better. I take it Gifted blood runs in the family?'

Sure, she's trying to get a rise out of him now. It works. Something that she's said has pissed him off. She's not sure what but she feels it flare to life, a deep rose-red that makes Isabel think of a bitter red wine.

'Does that mouth get you into trouble often?' he says. 'Careful. I might like it a little too much.'

Voronov shifts and settles his elbows on the table. All of a sudden, he seems bigger. A little menacing even.

'I think it would be in your best interest not to like anything here a little too much, Ezequiel,' Voronov says. He uses the same courteous tone he always does, but it doesn't feel courteous at all.

Venâncio turns so his body is facing Voronov. 'Then let me help you wrap this up faster. I haven't seen her since she left. I'm sorry to hear that she's passed. I've got nothing more to offer you.'

Isabel stares at him. She can't feel any indication of a lie. But his wards *are* good. Still. Something here feels incomplete.

'Then we'll be on our way.' Voronov stands and turns away dismissively, and waits for Isabel to get up.

Venâncio sits back, narrowed eyes on her. 'I hope our paths cross again, Inspector Reis. This has been interesting.'

Interesting my arse. 'Thank you for your time,' she says instead.

As she turns to leave, though, Voronov settles a hand on the chair and addresses Venâncio once more. 'Marta was found with her throat cut. No clothes, no jewellery, nothing. Got tossed in the river,' he says. 'I thought it sounded familiar.'

Venâncio says nothing.

Voronov nods. 'Have a good day.'

21

The next day when Isabel gets into the office, there's a packet of doughnuts waiting for her on her desk. Voronov's jacket is thrown over his desk chair, but she can't see him.

The day before, they'd walked back to the precinct in silence. Isabel had let herself fall back, watching the wide expanse of Voronov's back as they went.

The meeting with Ezequiel Venâncio had left her with more questions than answers. And the questions she does have aren't all related to the case. She'd felt unsettled after Venâncio's attempt to read her thoughts. It had lingered. If there was a way for her to open up her head and scrub it clean, then she would have done it.

She'd never felt an attack like that.

Gabriel Bernardo had been . . . his form of attack had been different. Despite having a dual affinity, he hadn't attempted to get inside her head in the same way.

Isabel wonders if that's how Gabriel's girlfriend had felt. He'd essentially been mind-controlling her. That's what it boiled down to. He'd been in her head 24/7. Left a piece of himself there to keep a watch at all times.

When they'd reached the precinct, Carla and Daniel had been back and they'd gone over what still needed to be done and what had been covered so far.

Some of Marta's neighbours were still being questioned, though they'd cleared the ones on her floor. The man right next door worked shifts and long hours, so was rarely home for little more than sleeping and eating. During the times he *was* home, he said, he hadn't heard anything. The rest of the floor hadn't seen anything suspicious either. Getting around everyone on the other four floors in the building would take a little more time.

The toxicology results also came back in along with the coroner's report. No traces of any suspicious substances had been detected in Marta's system. If there had been any, they were either undetectable or they had worn off before she'd been killed.

Isabel had gone home in a funk and had stopped at Tia Simone's house to give her a quick hug and check in, lest she get told off again for doing nothing but focus on work. She ended up staying for a tea and the latest news and then left before her tia could start asking about when she was going to take the time to find herself a partner (*a nice young man or woman, you know I don't care about those things, Isabel*) because she's not getting any younger.

Isabel loves Tia Simone, she really does, but God those conversations make her want to bash her head on the wall a couple of times. Sebastião managed to dodge that bullet when he chose to become a man of faith.

Anyway, that had been followed by another night of shitty sleep, despite the fact that she'd left her side project alone for the night. At least the walk this morning with her dogs had left her feeling a bit more revived.

'Might want to go and rescue your partner.' Jacinta leans over the partition. She looks better.

'Hey.'

'You didn't even hear me coming,' Jacinta says, 'unusual for you. You all right?'

'Yeah. What's this about Aleks needing rescuing?' She seeks out his familiar form in the room. It's hard for a man of Voronov's size to actually hide. And since she can't see him, he's either in the case room or elsewhere.

'Your visit yesterday, to Ezequiel Venâncio.'

That grabs Isabel's attention. 'What about it? Did he make a complaint?'

'Nope.' Jacinta crosses her arm and looks over her shoulder. 'But it seems that operation that is currently inactive isn't as inactive as we thought. They're in the case room with him now.'

Isabel frowns and sets off for the case room. 'Where's the Chief?' she calls over as she goes.

'Meeting. Or that arsehole never would've got through,' Jacinta says.

Merda.

Isabel doesn't bother knocking on the door, just opens it and steps in, and hears the conversation cut off abruptly.

'Am I late?' she says, smoothing her hair back from her face.

Voronov is sitting leaning back from the table, arms folded, face like stone.

The guy attempting to tower over him – impossible, even with Voronov sitting down – is familiar but she can't quite place him. He's in a suit and his hands, which had been aggressively gesticulating, drop to his sides. A moment later he tucks them into his pockets.

'This is a private meeting,' he bites out. His moustache covers his top lip but can't hide the snarl to his mouth. He's tall himself but beefier than Voronov, older too. His tie is loosened around his neck and his brown suit jacket is wrinkled at the back. His hair is cropped short.

'If it were a private meeting then Inspector Voronov wouldn't be having it in our case room. Where work needs to be done,' she says, 'but as I've already been told that this is in regard to our visit to Ezequiel Venâncio yesterday then it definitely needs to include me.' As she nears them, she notices the tightness in Voronov's jaw. He's still staring up at the man opposite him, a muscle ticking in his jaw.

Yeah. He's pissed off.

'Who is this?' the man asks Voronov.

Isabel answers. 'Inspector Reis. I'm his partner.'

At that a sneer covers his mouth. 'Right. The Gifted partner.'

She narrows her eyes. 'Yes. That one.'

'Not very bright, are you? Considering what happened to the last one.'

'Chief,' Voronov stands, 'as I've already said. You'll need to take up your complaints with Chief Bautista. It was cleared with her before we set a foot in O Vermelho. Now if you don't mind, we have time-sensitive work that we need to be getting on with. Unless there's some information that the OF would like to share with us? I'm sure we can stay out of each other's way.'

It clicks into place then. Why he's familiar and why he's here attempting to breathe down Voronov's neck, even though he no longer has anything to do with him.

'Oh, she'll be hearing from me. That woman oversteps too often,' the man says, and then slams out of the room.

She sincerely hopes that he has the guts to say all of that to Chief Bautista's face. What a fucking mess.

Isabel lets out a loud breath. Luckily, he's taken his rage out of the room with him and it feels lighter without him in it. She rests her hands on her hips.

'What in the hell is going on?' she asks.

Voronov sits back down on the table, hands clenching on the edge. 'That was my old superior.'

'And he was here tearing you a new one. Why? How did he even find out we were there yesterday?'

Voronov links his hands together behind his neck and turns his eyes up to the ceiling. 'The case isn't as inactive as they'd like everyone to believe.'

Ah. Shit. 'Great.' She paces away from him. 'Okay, what was that about? We didn't ask any questions pertaining to their case and we weren't even there that long. We haven't compromised them.'

'No, but they're going to try to block us if we keep working the Ezequiel angle.'

Which is pure crap. They're not even sure he's a valid lead right now. There are vague connections, but they have nothing on him. They'd been fishing more than anything.

'And what about you?' she asks. She backs into the table, hitching herself onto it and looks him in the eye. 'What was that about yesterday?'

Voronov stays quiet.

'He greets you by your first name, knows about your partner. Even mentions your sister.' Isabel had thought about it when she'd got home. She knew Voronov has a sister. He'd mentioned it once. But only once. And even then, it had been brief; the way he'd changed the subject had left her thinking maybe their relationship wasn't all that close.

She hasn't pushed since.

'He knew,' Voronov says.

'About what?'

'About Seles. And what was happening. He has a lot of people in his pocket. We generally stayed out of his way but like I said before, we crossed paths a couple of times. Some of the meetings with informants happened at his place.'

Isabel frowns. 'Isn't that risky?'

He shrugs. 'It worked for everyone involved,' he says, 'Ezequiel Venâncio knows that information is valuable currency.' He looks at her. 'I'd say that more than the Houses, that's where his most important trade actually happens. O Vermelho ends up as a sort of safe house, almost, middle ground. He knows a lot about a lot of people just from allowing them to use his place to meet safely. You don't really talk about it outside of that.'

'And that's how he knows you?'

Voronov nods.

'And the jab about your sister—' She shakes her head. 'Never mind. Not my business.' She pushes off the desk, intending to just get started with her day.

'My sister and I aren't on speaking terms,' Voronov says, and Isabel stops, 'she stopped talking to me after Seles got put away.' And with that he walks past her and leaves the room.

Isabel stands there, still staring at the door.

Jesus. What a shit-show.

22

News quickly spreads through the precinct that Chief Bautista is in a mood after having caused another senior official to storm out earlier that day. The name of said official isn't being circulated, either because no one was able to get a good look at him, or because Chief Bautista has warned them off. She can tolerate gossip, but everyone knows not to take it too far.

Isabel doesn't pay it any mind because they finally get something from one of the neighbours in Marta Nunes' building. Isabel's hoping this is the kind of day where they'll get a break.

The neighbour is a young woman from the third floor. She reminds her a little of Mario from the other day. It's odd. Isabel hasn't seen anyone so obviously cheerful in a police station. When Isabel and Voronov walk into the room she's sitting upright, eyes sweeping the room around her, eating up every detail. She has pale, wavy blonde hair pulled into a thick braid and her brown eyes get even bigger when Isabel introduces herself.

'They told me you would be Gifted and might want to look at my memories,' she says. Her eagerness spills over with the same scent and colour as newly cut grass and Isabel struggles not to show her distaste.

Right. She'd forgotten about the flip side of the coin.

Just as there are people who can't stand Gifted and don't want to go anywhere near them, you have people like this. A little too into Gifted and what they can do, always eager for any contact they can get because of their fascination. Most people like this are harmless, but there have been a few creepier cases. Isabel really hopes this isn't one of them. She looks at the name that Laura on the front desk gave her. 'Ana?' she asks.

'Yes.'

Isabel slides behind the table and Voronov closes the door but doesn't sit. Isabel introduces them both. 'The officer you spoke to suggested you come in to see me because you saw something, is that right?'

'I mean, I'm not sure if it was something important. It was really brief, I was just coming in from work and I saw her, uh, Marta from downstairs. She was leaving but I thought it was odd – she was with a guy, and they left through the emergency exit, which we're always being told *not* to do.'

Voronov joins Isabel by the table. 'When was this?'

'On the second of Feb? Kind of late; I worked a later shift at the shop that day so I got home around eight in the evening. I was coming out of the car park,' she says.

Isabel needs to double-check but she's positive that's the same day as the shopping receipt that had been found in Marta's home.

Before she can say anything else, though, Ana is scooting to the edge of her chair and peering between Isabel and Voronov. 'The other officer said you'd want to take a look at my memories?' She obviously doesn't know who is who, but the way her gaze lingers on Voronov, Isabel has a good idea of who Ana would like peering into her head.

'If you would consent to that,' Isabel says, trying to keep the dryness out of her voice because really, they need this, 'it would be extremely helpful if you would allow me to take a look.'

'Oh.'

Wow. She doesn't even bother hiding her disappointment. Isabel refrains from any kind of facial expression that might make the girl take offence and rescind her offer. 'Would you be okay with that, Ana?' she asks.

Ana sags a little in her chair. 'Sure. I've heard it doesn't hurt?'

'It doesn't.' Isabel drags her chair around to Ana's side and holds out her hand. She doesn't need to, could easily slide in just sitting where she was, but it pays to keep up appearances.

Ana places her hand in hers. It's soft, and her nails neatly trimmed, painted in a mint green, and tapering into sharp points that Isabel knows she would never be able to function with herself. 'Now what?' she asks.

'Now Inspector Voronov here has to bear witness to you giving explicit consent, and then I take a look at your memories. It would help if you would think back to that night. It makes it easier for me to find the memory needed.'

The last time she'd done this had been with the young man who'd witnessed Gil dos Santos bashing his head into a train door. With him, the memory had been recent and traumatic enough that Isabel hadn't needed to search for a thing. It had just floated toward her.

Ana does as asked, consenting to allowing Isabel into her mind.

Isabel closes her mind and breathes.

Giving in and just doing what feels natural to her Gift is . . . a relief. She slips into it like slipping into a warm pool of water.

It takes her a little longer to follow the path that Ana's thoughts weave, to reach the memory, but Isabel sifts through, gently. It's a little disorientating. Entering someone else's mind always feels like entering foreign territory.

Maybe it's because the memory isn't as recent, but when she finds it, the colours as she settles behind Ana's viewpoint are more muted. Or maybe that's because it's night-time. The streetlights are few and far between, leaving slices of darkness in the spaces between the cars around her, and the memory is tainted with apprehension as Ana looks carefully around her, constantly checking over her shoulder as she hurries closer to her building.

It's a feeling Isabel is familiar with. The keys between her fingers are no doubt a last resort, but one that doesn't do much to help that familiar creep of hyperawareness.

Isabel feels Ana's fingers relax their grip a little when she reaches the side of the building. But then a noise startles her. The shock jolts her and Isabel jumps, heart racing. It's not her heart, it's Ana's, but to be honest Isabel would have felt the exact same way in her position. She focuses and waits patiently.

The wide sweep of her eyes catches a door at the rear end of the building swinging shut. A man and a woman walk away from it. He has his arm around her waist. They could be a couple. The woman's braids sweep all the way down her back as she keeps pace with the man.

Marta Nunes.

Isabel feels her arm – Ana's arm – lift and her mouth opens. Isabel feels the 'boa noite' forming in her mouth but after a moment, awkwardness flits through Ana and she drops her hand to her side. The couple pass under the spotlight of a streetlamp, heading towards the car park.

In the too-bright light, Isabel sees broad shoulders and dark hair, but from here the light renders them nothing but silhouettes. The man lifts his arm from Marta's waist to wrap around her shoulders instead and something winks in the light. Impossible to tell what. A ring? A watch? The weapon that would later be used to slash her throat?

Before Isabel can see any more, Ana is turning away, heading toward the front of the building as she slips her key into her pocket. Fear forgotten.

Isabel pulls out of the memory.

'Well?'

She blinks a couple of times and tries not to glare at Ana, whose thoughts and voice are both irritatingly loud. She struggles for a moment to put a barrier back up between them.

'That was the only thing you saw?' Isabel asks.

Ana pouts and she flicks a look at Voronov before giving Isabel an apologetic shrug. 'It was late and . . .'

Isabel sighs. 'No,' she says, 'it's fine. It was helpful.' She manages a tight-lipped smile. 'Thank for you for coming forward.'

Ana is only too happy to be shown out by Voronov. Isabel follows them to the door and watches them go. Arms crossed, she leans her shoulder against the door frame as she mulls over what she's just seen.

Fuck. Isabel lets out a heavy sigh. She wishes Ana had called out to them. Maybe then Isabel would have a face to put to all this. Or maybe Marta wouldn't have ended up in the river to begin with.

Marta hadn't been fighting the man off or calling out for help. Had she gone along willingly?

Had Marta known her murderer?

23

'This is why you love me,' Daniel says.

The door to the case room is closed and Isabel, Voronov, Carla and Jacinta have taken seats up close to the board where Daniel is standing. There's a frozen scene on it, in high resolution, of what Isabel recognises as the foyer in Marta's building.

Isabel had briefed them on the memory she'd taken a peek at from Ana.

While it was only a small glimpse, they know now that Marta was in that building. And that she'd gone out the back way with an unknown, white male. Ana had made it clear that building regulations were strict about using the emergency exit stairways and that there was a fine in place for anyone caught doing it, though she'd also added that naturally, teenagers did it all the time. It was unusual, however, for more mature residents to be seen doing it.

'These are the stills from the footage on the day that Marta went to the shop,' Daniel says and starts putting down A4-sized prints, clearly snapshots of time-stamped CCTV images.

He slides them across the table and Isabel pulls one close to her. There are several from the front of the supermarket and a few from inside the actual shop, different aisles, all showing Marta, on the second of February, with a shopping cart.

'And these,' Daniel says, 'are from the foyer in Marta's building.' And he separates them out.

There are more images from the foyer than there are from the supermarket. There are two angles, one camera facing out toward the entrance and the other toward the space directly in front of the postboxes.

Marta's face is familiar and obvious where the pictures focus on her, but she is only in two of the images.

'What are we looking at, Daniel?' Isabel says.

He gestures to the image on the board and they all still, a hush falling over the room as they wait for the image to respond to the click of the tiny remote in Daniel's hand.

The video plays.

It has no sound, so the quiet whirring of the overhead projector serves as the backdrop as they watch someone who is clearly Marta Nunes arriving at her apartment building on February second. Her hands are weighed down with shopping. She's wearing a thin white duster jacket that stands out against her skin.

Not what she'd been wearing when Ana had seen her later that evening.

Isabel takes note of the time stamp: 6.30 p.m.

On screen, Marta can clearly be seen through the glass doors of the building, shopping set at her feet so she can key in the code for the building. There's no one near her, though the camera doesn't capture as wide an area as Isabel would like. It focuses on people entering and leaving the foyer from the head up.

It takes Marta a few seconds, but she doesn't seem to be in any hurry or panicked. Doesn't mean she wasn't, but most likely she just hadn't realised that she was in danger. She picks up her shopping, goes in, the door shuts behind her and she walks out of sight of the camera. Daniel lets it continue to play out for a bit and no one comes near the door.

'So, code to get in,' Daniel's saying, 'she comes in alone. A few people come in after her over the next thirty to forty minutes.' He fast-forwards and keeps going. When he stops it again, the frame is from forty minutes later.

The speed of the video returns to normal and they watch another woman arrive. She's a speed walker, small bag on her shoulder and foot tapping impatiently as she puts the code in wrong and then has to do it again.

That time it works. She goes through and disappears from their screen.

A few seconds go by, the door slowly sliding closed.

Casual as anything, a man pushes the door back open before it can shut and lock.

He has on a baseball cap. He keeps his head down. He matches Ana's memory of the man walking away with Marta in height, breadth of shoulder – and Isabel glimpses a ring on his right hand when he splays it against the door to keep it from shutting.

The door swings shut behind him and he disappears.

For a moment they all stay quiet.

'He could be a resident,' Carla says, 'but he was the only one that we spotted who didn't walk in clearly with other people, but also didn't key in the code to the building.'

Daniel rewinds it to freeze the picture on him and Isabel shakes her head and leans forward to eye him more closely. They get a glimpse of his jawline and that's it. They can clearly see what he's wearing. That might help them a little if they ask the locals.

'Cameras on that street?' Isabel asks.

'None,' Daniel says.

Isabel mutters a curse. 'He matches the guy I saw walking away with Marta in Ana's memory.'

Daniel swears and goes to the laptop. 'There's more.'

'More?'

The screen goes blank while Daniel taps deftly. When it comes back, the time stamp on the video is 4.21 p.m. The foyer is brighter, lighting it up and making it easier to see the girl on screen.

Isabel glances at Voronov and he shrugs. What she sees takes her by surprise.

The girl is tiny. But her face is familiar.

Jacinta's phone goes off and she excuses herself, ducking out of the room and closing the door behind her.

Daniel clicks play and they see the girl in motion.

She's wearing an oversized purple jumper, skinny jeans, and chunky black lace-up boots. Her hair is pulled back into a high ponytail, leaving her face on the camera completely clear. There's a backpack on her back and she's got a bottle of water tucked into the crook of her elbow as she keys in the code and gets in smoothly.

She walks off the frame and Daniel pauses it.

Isabel twists in her chair. 'That's her, isn't it? That's Alma.'

Daniel's face is grim when he nods. 'Yeah.'

'What the hell was she doing there?'

'That's the thing,' Daniel says, 'I've gone through every inch of that footage and there's no sign of her at all. We don't see her leaving. At least not out the front.'

'The witness, Ana, she saw Marta come out of the fire exit. Could Alma have done the same?'

Isabel crosses her arms, chewing on the inside of her cheek as she mulls it over. 'It's possible. She had to leave somehow.' She could have been taken too, just like Marta. Without someone to have witnessed that too, they had no way to know for sure.

Then it comes to her, and she snaps back round to look at Voronov, eyes narrowed, excitement and dread building. 'The footprint. That could've been her.' The shoe size had been different to Marta's, that's what Jacinta had said.

Maybe Alma had been in Marta's apartment. And now she's missing and Marta turned up dead.

Jacinta opens the door and sticks her head inside.

'They've found Marta's car.'

Isabel rises out of her chair. There's no such thing as coincidence. 'Where?'

'Abandoned on a side street in Setúbal, reported by a local. I'm going there now.'

'All right,' Isabel says, 'I'll come with you to take a look.' She turns to Voronov. 'We're going to need to go round that whole building with a picture of Alma,' she says.

Voronov stands too. 'I'll take care of it. Call me if anything.'

'You too,' she tells Daniel, 'knew we kept you around for something.'

He gives her the finger and then, with one last look at Voronov, she leaves.

24

THEN

The clinking of the glasses blends in with the crack of the balls on the pool table as another game is started. It smells of fried bifana and beer and Isabel's stomach growls, a reminder that she hasn't had anything decent to eat since breakfast.

Pure adrenalin had got her through the rest of the day.

Isabel's face hurt from how hard she'd been grinning since they'd made the arrest a little earlier that day. Her first case as a full-fledged inspector – not a junior any more. The short but approving nod she'd got from Chief Inês Bautista, someone who barely cracked a smile for anyone, had sent pride rushing through her and Isabel had felt the first cementing of her confidence. She *can* do this. She's good at this and she's an asset to this team.

Now she's proven that.

An arm curls around her neck and jerks her back into a hug. 'Why didn't you say you'd finished your drink?'

Isabel rolls her eyes even as she clutches at Jacinta's arm to keep it from choking her. 'How many have *you* had?' She turns her head to look at her colleague.

Jacinta had entered the crime scene specialist unit around the same time Isabel had become a junior inspector. They'd shared some of the same training and had hit it off during their time sitting in the back row of the lecture room, listening to an old white man speaking in brain-numbing monotone about evidence logging and prosecution. It helped that Jacinta hadn't batted an eyelash when Isabel had told her she was Gifted.

'Calm down,' Jacinta says, slanting her a look, 'it's only my second.' She's out of her white lab coat and in a plain white T-shirt and slim-fitting black jeans. Her hair, currently in short shoulder-length braids, is gathered in a satin scrunchie at the back of her neck.

The bar is around the corner from their precinct in the Anjos area and right now, it's packed and buzzing with conversation as the day starts to slide into the post-work hours. People are spilling out into the outdoor space, most of the plastic tables and chairs taken; the sun remains strong, keeping the temperature at a solid 28° C.

Another person squeezes in on Isabel's other side and a rough hand messes up her short curls. Isabel yanks away, swearing. She scowls at Daniel's grinning face. Jacinta rolls her eyes and sticks a hand up in the air as she leans over the bar to try to get the attention of the bartender at the other end.

'You're such a pain,' Isabel says.

His grin widens. 'You both love me,' he says, reaching an arm around her to nudge Jacinta's shoulder.

Daniel had started at the Anjos precinct just a couple of months before Isabel and, like Isabel, had been spending way too long on minor offences and as a glorified secretary for the inspectors higher up when the Chief had paired him up with Isabel. Today had been as much of a success for him as it had been for Isabel and Jacinta.

If Isabel had been told a few years earlier that the two people in the force who would have her back, no matter what, would be two Regulars, she's not sure she would have believed them.

Jacinta manages to get the bartender's attention and orders them three beers, sliding a note over the counter. Turning to Isabel and Daniel, her full lips are curved in a proud smile. 'It was a pretty good day today, wasn't it?' She takes the beers with a *thank-you* and hands Isabel and Daniel one each. 'Here's to us nailing it every fucking time.'

Isabel takes the sweating bottle from her, the glass slick in her hand and so good against the heat surrounding them. 'Every time,' she agrees.

Daniel doesn't stop grinning, like the idiot he is, and they toast to it.

Isabel has just taken a drink when her phone rings. She fishes her phone out of her pocket and sees her brother's name on the screen.

'I'll be right back,' she says, 'have to take this.' She smacks Daniel's shoulder as she leaves. 'Order us some food, I'm starving.'

By the time she gets outside the phone has stopped ringing.

Isabel weaves her way past the tables to a spot where the narrow pavement is clear of them. She heads for one of the big tree planters and sits on its edge, taking another drink of her beer as she goes into her missed calls. There's a massive crack on her screen that has been there for a couple of months now. Sebastião keeps taking the piss because she's still walking around with it like this.

A shadow falls over her legs as she's about to call him back and she glances up, squinting as the sun hits her full in the face. She raises a hand to block it and focuses on the guy in front of her.

She doesn't know or recognise him. He's about her height with short brown hair and there's a hint of dimples as his mouth quirks in what could pass for a small smile. His eyes are either a very golden brown or a golden green; she can't quite make them out. He's nice to look at.

He's holding a drink too and, unlike her in her loose white vest, light blue jeans and beat-up trainers, he's dressed a bit formally; the sleeves of his dove-grey shirt are rolled up past his elbows, showing that the tan isn't just on his face and neck, and he's wearing black trousers, belted and with the shirt tucked in and everything. Proper shoes too.

Isabel arches an eyebrow from beneath her shielding hand. 'Can I help you?'

He turns and gestures towards the bar with his drink. 'Heard you guys inside, sounds like you're celebrating.'

'We are. Is eavesdropping normal for you?'

The quirk turns into a full-on smile. It lends a touch of mischief to his face. It also takes him from nice to look at to really good-looking.

'Something caught my eye,' he says with a shrug.

Isabel tilts her head to the side, traces the damp rim of her bottle with her thumb. 'Something, hmm?'

'Can I buy you a drink?'

She holds up her bottle with a pointed look and then takes a drink from it.

He laughs. 'Your *next* drink.'

Isabel can't help the reflexive smile that slips onto her face. Still. 'I'm Gifted,' she says. She's learned the hard way that it's best to put that out in the open.

He shrugs. 'I'd still like to buy you a drink.'

She eyes him for a moment longer. Then she holds out her hand. 'I'm Isabel.'

When he takes her hand, his is cool and slightly damp from the glass he's been holding. 'Michael.'

'Pleasure.'

25

Night has fallen by the time Isabel leaves the precinct.

She'd spent the rest of the afternoon in Setúbal with Jacinta, where they'd secured Marta's car, directing officers to canvass the nearby businesses and houses in case anyone had seen anything.

The car itself had been abandoned but from what Isabel had seen there wasn't any sign of foul play inside. She'd watched from further away as Jacinta and her team carefully went over the vehicle, then they'd driven back to the station together.

'Isabel?'

She's outside the precinct, lost in thoughts about the abandoned car and missing women. She turns in the direction of the call.

An older woman is standing there. She's wearing a canary-yellow knit cardigan over baggy dark-grey dungarees, and chunky boots. Her white hair is piled on top of her head in wisps that fall down the side of her face and tangled in her big green hoop earrings. Earrings that spark a memory. Isabel refocuses on the woman's face, and freezes.

It's been so many years since she's seen it but her face is exactly the same. Still kind, though now weathered by age. There are laughter lines bracketing her mouth and little crow's feet branching out from the corners of her eyes. Her skin looks softer too.

Rosario.

'Rosario . . .' she says out loud now, and then she's at a loss for words, caught off guard. She hadn't been prepared for this.

There's a reason why she hadn't been able to take the final steps that would get her close enough to press the doorbell and actually come face to face with Rosario.

There's no familiar smile on that face though. If anything, Rosario looks wary.

'If I hadn't seen you on TV, I don't think I would have recognised you,' the older woman says. 'Or maybe I would have, given how often you've been standing outside my house lately.'

Yeah. It would look bad wouldn't it. And Isabel wants to explain. She wants to. But now that the moment is here, the words won't come. It doesn't help that Isabel is acutely aware of the fact that they're standing in front of the precinct, a place where only a couple of days ago, Monitoring had come knocking for her.

The breeze is a little warmer than it has been, and she tilts her head up to it, letting it soothe her.

Finally, after a long moment where she's certain Rosario is just going to turn her back on Isabel and walk away with a warning for her to stop being a stalker, she's able to face her.

'I'm sorry,' she says, voice low, and steps closer, 'I know how it probably looked. You said you saw me on the news?'

Rosario folds her arms over her chest and nods. She casts a wary look at the building, obviously not feeling too comfortable here either. 'Yes. You and that partner of yours were all over the press after the Gabriel Bernardo case.'

Isabel laughs, the sound a little shaky.

The first time she'd met this woman her father had been right there with her, holding her hand. Rosario had been part of that weird time where Isabel's life had been changing irrevocably but hadn't yet turned into the complete nightmare that it would become after her dad died.

'Yes, well.' She seals her lips together and stares at the floor, tucking her hands into her back pockets and trying to find the courage to say what she needs to.

She'd gone out of her way to locate Rosario. Just as she'd been going out of her way to find the names and stories of other high-level Gifted like herself. And now that Rosario is here, her throat is constricting and she feels as if she's a child again, in that waiting room, clenching her dad's big hand tight and scared to death at what's about to come. Because she'd tried to find this woman based on the impression she'd created of her as a child – of someone safe, someone who was there to help. Isabel had trusted Rosario.

She hasn't trusted many people since.

Isabel isn't stupid. She's done her research on what Rosario has been doing since those times. Knows that she was pushed out of her job as a Guide because she'd been arrested one too many times, at Gifted-rights rallies and protesting against public figures on high-profile platforms. She'd been particularly vocal after the disappearance of a teenage girl who had levelled an entire section of Colombo, Lisbon's largest shopping centre. They'd taken her licence after that, and she'd slipped under the radar.

Not completely though, or Isabel wouldn't have been able to find her.

It was the events leading up to her dismissal that had given Isabel a small seed of hope that maybe this woman who had helped her when she was younger would still be a person Isabel could be able to go to and ask for help now.

Still. Placing her trust in someone who is essentially a stranger makes the palms of her hands sweaty.

She takes a deep breath. 'Do you mind if we go somewhere else? I . . .' She wraps her arms around herself. 'To be honest, I looked for you. I-I wanted to ask for your help with something.'

Rosario stares her down.

Isabel is expecting a no.

Then Rosario nods. She throws one last glance at the precinct and gestures for Isabel to follow her. 'I'd rather we weren't talking in front of this place either. Come on.'

The café is about a fifteen-minute walk from the precinct, far enough away that Isabel feels Rosario relax.

They sit in the outside area at the back of the café. The inside is packed with men watching a football game and their shouts and cheers are enough to make it difficult for anyone to eavesdrop on their conversation.

Isabel stirs the sugar into her carioca de limão. Her jacket hangs over the back of her chair and she lets her hair down.

The only good thing about a place like this is that with the entire crowd focused on a game, their charged-up thoughts and pent-up energy are almost one single voice. It makes it easier to keep at bay when it leaks past the doors separating the café from the outside area.

'Isabel?' Rosario is watching her as she takes a sip of her galão. The wariness is still there, but it's softer.

Isabel manages a small smile. 'Sorry.' She glances back at the inside of the café, then, 'This happens a lot when I'm in crowded places,' she admits.

Rosario pauses in the middle of taking a sip. 'What do you mean?' Then her eyes drop to Isabel's hands and when Isabel follows her gaze, she notices her hands are trembling.

Isabel laughs and puts her hands in her lap and clenches them into fists. She looks everywhere but at Rosario.

'Isabel,' Rosario says, holding her out hand as if trying to calm her, 'you came to me for a reason, didn't you? There's a reason why you came to find me.'

Isabel breathes in, lets her chest fill with air and then blows it out through her mouth, willing the shakiness to go with it. She's not like this. She's never like this. She doesn't know what to do with the ball of anxiety lodged in the centre of her chest.

When she finally calms again, she forces herself to meet Rosario's gaze.

Rosario gives her a slow nod. She picks her drink back up. 'I'm not in a rush,' she says, 'start from the beginning.'

So, Isabel does.

It doesn't come easy. The words fight against a defence mechanism that's been up for too long and that she can't just easily brush aside; but she gets it out. In a tone barely loud enough to be heard over the bursts of cheering from inside, Isabel tells her about how it started – going from reading emotions with her Gift to unwelcome thoughts slipping through her head. How those random wisps of thoughts had turned to loud voices, running commentaries, all of them amplified if someone touched her. She tells her about the pills, how they'd dialled it all back, and the headaches that she'd learned to function with.

Then, haltingly, she tells her of the night it all snapped and the pills stopped working and she woke up hearing everything, everyone, all the time.

She tells Rosario how it hasn't stopped once.

What Isabel doesn't tell her is what it's doing to her.

She doesn't need to.

After, Rosario doesn't speak right away.

She's on her second glass of galão. Isabel hasn't ordered anything else.

'Isabel,' she says, and her voice is kind but matter-of-fact, 'what classification are you now?'

It's funny. After spilling all that, Isabel can't make herself say it.

'Isabel, olha,' Rosario says and hitches her chair a little closer to the table, 'I'm not entirely sure what I can do for you here. But you know what I hear when you speak of your Gift, linda?'

Isabel waits.

'That it's a side of you that you don't want. That it's something that frightens you and that you reject.'

Isabel clenches her jaw, picks at a little carved line on the table with her thumbnail.

'You're never going to gain control and be at peace with something you reject to this extent. If you're not going to trust in your own abilities, who do you think will, Isabel?'

There's nothing in what she's saying that Isabel can refute. It's not until this moment that she realises some part of her had still been hoping for a quick fix.

'You're a smart woman. Strong too,' Rosario says, and settles back in her chair, picks up her galão again, 'I can't do it for you.

But Isabel?' She waits until Isabel looks up at her. 'I can help you along the way, hmm?' and she smiles, a smile Isabel remembers from sitting in her room when she was young, learning how to build up her shield with imaginary bricks.

Isabel's *thank-you* is almost too quiet to hear, but she knows Rosario does.

26

Marta's car didn't turn up anything of note. It had been wiped clean. Isabel had been hopeful that they would at least have found her clothes, her shoes, something. Anything. Jacinta's team had been thorough, but half of them were also still dealing with the aftermath of the freak pile-up that had taken place on the 25 de Abril a week ago.

The news had sent a chill through Isabel, too easily plucking at old wounds, and she'd been glad she hadn't been called in for it. She would have spent the entire time wondering if her father had been in the same shape as every person she saw.

Even the morgue, which normally catered just to the precinct, had been unusually run off its feet and unable to take any further bodies. Isabel had heard someone else in their department complaining about it and Chief Bautista had been in an awful mood, making everyone tiptoe around her to avoid getting their heads bitten off. Isabel and the rest of her team had taken advantage of having an assigned case room and they'd all holed up there.

So, Isabel didn't have the excuse of a fast-paced investigation to keep her from being exactly where she is right now: a small intimate restaurant in Montijo, surrounded mostly by people she doesn't give a crap about, and having to paste a smile on her face and make small talk, at the engagement party of her ex-boyfriend and her sister.

Isabel really doesn't know what she did to deserve this.

Her brother Sebastião had been stolen away by Rita to be introduced to some of her single friends. Sebastião had reminded her that, as a priest, he wouldn't exactly be able to rescue her friends from singlehood, but Rita had just pointed out that he could still flirt and that there was no harm in talking to people.

As for Isabel's mother. Well. They've both been doing an excellent job of avoiding one another.

Isabel glances around the room, sipping from her champagne flute as she takes in the couples in the centre, dancing to the kizomba playing from the speakers overhead. Tiny sips. She hates champagne. But every time she makes so much as a small dent in the glass, the server, who seems to have laser vision, zips over and tops her up despite her protests.

Isabel tells herself repeatedly that she's not allowed to punch the server and that, seeing as she's police, it would reflect even more poorly on her if she did.

She's turned her back on most of the room in a bid to not be seen and is bouncing her foot restlessly where it's crossed over the other leg. Her feet haven't started hurting in the heeled sandals yet and she counts that as a small blessing as she digs her phone out of her bag for the umpteenth time in the hopes that she'll have a message calling her back to work.

She'd made sure to give her team the address and made them double-check they had it several times. She'd ignored Jacinta's unimpressed look and the amusement on Voronov's face. He wouldn't be smirking if he'd been stuck here with her, the arsehole. Jacinta just hadn't understood why Isabel had agreed to come in the first place.

Truth is that Isabel hadn't wanted to. But the combined forces of her sister's puppy eyes and her tia's quiet requests and words about how in the end family is family, and surely that's more important than an idiot man, had made Isabel feel as if her back was up against a wall. It was the only reason why she'd ended up making an actual effort and turning up.

She can't remember the last time she'd touched mascara or a lipstick, but she'd managed to touch up her face without making herself look like a clown; and luckily, she'd had a dress – a small moment of indulgence because despite preferring to be comfortable in her everyday life, she does have a weak spot for pretty things. The simple pastel pink off-the-shoulder dress suits her, showing off her shoulders and capturing the dip of her waist, and following the line of her legs to cut off just below her knees. She'd even blow-dried her curls and in a moment of vanity slipped into the rose-gold sandals that tie neatly around her ankles.

Tia Simone had taught her how to clean up nice.

Isabel drags her thumb over the screen, scowling when no notifications come up.

'I've lost count of how many times I've seen you check your phone.'

Great. Just great. Her evening is complete. Screw not liking champagne; she takes a big gulp, ignoring the way the taste makes her entire face scrunch up.

'You've never liked champagne,' Michael says, amused, and drags out the chair next to hers. He doesn't ask if he can sit.

Why would he. It's his engagement party.

It irritates her that he looks good too, decked out in an expensive-looking navy suit, shirt buttoned up all the way and slim tie tucked into the waistcoat. He's neatly shaven, and his hazel eyes are warm as he looks at her.

'I'm checking my phone repeatedly,' she says, 'because I don't want to be here.' She gives him a closed-lip smile. 'I think your time would be better spent at my sister's side, Michael.'

The hint of a smile that had been on his face fades away. When his gaze falls on where Rita is standing, arm firmly locked around Sebastião's to keep him in place as they talk to her friends, he is quiet, eyes serious.

'She looks happy,' he says.

Despite hating the reason why she's here and still feeling resentful at everything that has led up to this moment, she can't help the softness she feels at the wide, dimpled smile on her sister's face. She looks beautiful in the yellow satin that moulds perfectly to her slim figure, setting off her naturally olive skin. He's right. She does look happy.

Not for the first time, Isabel wonders how long it will take her to get over this when it's so obviously what her sister wants. Isabel and Michael's relationship has been over for a long time now and it's not as if she wants a repeat of it.

There's a reason why they broke up.

Still.

She can't deny that the hurt is there. Maybe there's no way to really get over someone who has been such a big part of her life. He's tangled up in her past, in her hopes for normality. And he's tied up in her present. In her struggles. She hates it.

Isabel finishes the champagne and is grateful that she can finally put the flute down. She sets it on the floor though, just under her chair, lest the server notice that it's empty and come rushing over. Perversely though, without something to hold onto, she feels vulnerable. With nothing to do, nothing to focus on. Unless she picks up her phone again – and she doubts anyone has messaged her in the last five seconds.

She forces herself to answer Michael. 'She does look happy.' She hopes he sees how serious she is when she says, 'And I sincerely hope it stays that way.'

A complicated emotion flits over his face. It doesn't touch her, thank goodness; she's blocking as hard as she knows how to right now. Hopefully, something good that will come out of this whole night is that she'll be so exhausted from aggressively blocking people's thoughts all evening, when she finally gets into bed she'll just collapse.

He doesn't reply directly. Instead, he runs a frustrated hand through his hair and smiles at someone who calls out to him, making a joke. Isabel does her best to tune him out and hopes he'll just get up and go.

He doesn't.

Quietly, and sounding wistful, he says, 'You look lovely.'

Isabel picks up her bag and her phone and stands up. 'I'm going outside for a smoke.'

'You don't smoke,' he says, standing too, and now he's starting to get frustrated.

'New habit,' she says and walks toward the front entrance, weaving her way around the tables. She feels her mother's gaze on her as she goes, a cold weight between her shoulder blades that makes her want to tuck herself away from sight completely. It's only her tia's affectionate smile and her voice calling out to her as she goes, asking where she's going, that makes Isabel slap a smile on her face too. Without stopping, she gestures to indicate she's going outside to take a call.

She's half expecting Michael to follow her, has to physically stop her shoulders from bunching up at the thought of having to tell him to back off if he does. She really doesn't have the energy for a confrontation right now.

As if the universe is taking pity on her, as cool night air enfolds her her phone actually starts to ring. Now she can feel the points of her shoes, pinching her toes, starting to edge into discomfort, and she wants to slip them off to ease the strain on the arch of her feet. That's what happens when you rarely wear these things.

The road outside the restaurant is quiet, not many people around. It's behind an old, abandoned clothing production plant. Isabel can see the top of the large building from where she stands. White paint flecking off with time, graffiti over the blue and yellow walls that ring around it and back up into the street. Not the nice kind of graffiti either. The red lettering here and there is about strike action and in protest to pay cuts. Isabel thinks she remembers when that happened. Over fifteen years ago now? She was in her teens maybe.

Still, it's one of the things Isabel is repeatedly charmed by in this place she calls home. How little back alleys and no-name streets will house some of the most amazing tucked-away culinary gems you will ever find. Back when she hadn't been bombarded by people's thoughts and emotions everywhere she went, in the days when she would find herself with nothing to do, she would search out the most obscure ones and take herself out for a meal.

It's so peaceful sitting in a place by yourself, glass of wine in your hand, enjoying lovely food, no one's expectations there to stress you out.

She misses that.

Maybe, she thinks, recalling Rosario's offer of help, it's something she can get back.

Voronov's name on her phone screen makes her smile. She leans back against the wall of the restaurant, tilts her head up to the sky and answers.

The stars are out.

'Hey,' she says.

'You sound a little too happy to be getting a call from me on an evening off,' he says. He sounds like he's driving.

'No. I'll only be happy if you're about to give me an excuse to leave this party. If that's not what you're about to do then I won't be as nice,' she says. She watches a small grey and white cat on the other side of the road, steps dainty as it sniffs delicately at the base of a streetlamp and then jerks back. It blinks up at Isabel and then turns, walking along the wall until it turns the corner and it's out of sight.

Someone else comes out of the restaurant. An actual smoker. A small man who Isabel doesn't know. He gives her a small wave of acknowledgement with a hand that has a cigarette tucked between his forefinger and his middle finger and then walks a little closer to the road to light up. Maybe one of her sister's friends. Isabel doesn't know. She's tried her best to stay away from them all.

From inside comes a bundle of celebratory noise, glasses clinking, music and excited voices. It's odd to be so detached from it all despite how the festive mood fills the place, rising to the ceiling, shimmering.

'Okay. What do I get in return?'

'What?' She straightens. 'Are you serious?' she asks.

'Yes. Carla got an alert from another precinct. A worker for a hostel catering specifically to Gifted individuals in Moita. Called to say they had someone matching Alma's description.'

Isabel closes her eyes as she processes that, muttering a small *thank God*. Finally, *something*. 'Moita? That's at the other end of Setúbal, isn't it?'

'About half an hour by train from Bomfim,' he says, 'the worker was on reception. Says she arrived two days ago.'

'Where is she now?'

'We've picked her up. They're en route to the precinct right now.'

Ah, merda. She should've driven here herself. But then she'd expected to drink the night away just to get through it, so she'd come in with Sebastião. 'Um. Okay. I'll see if I can get my brother to give me a lift.' She's not relishing the disapproving looks she'll get from her tia and her sister, but she can't wait to leave, if she's honest.

'I'm already on my way over to you,' he says. 'Isn't that why you were force-feeding us where you'd be tonight?'

Isabel laughs. 'Okay. How long?'

'Another ten or fifteen minutes. No traffic at the moment.'

'Okay, I'll be waiting outside. It's the small street behind the production plant.'

'All right.'

They hang up and Isabel heads back inside, only realising how chilled she has become when the warmth envelops her as she steps back into the main floor of the restaurant. She looks around, trying to spot Rita and Sebastião. Maybe if she can avoid having to tell Tia it won't be too bad. She'll just get a telling-off some other time.

She spots Sebastião, still trapped with Rita's friends although Rita has disappeared off somewhere. When he realises Isabel is trying to get his attention, he takes the opportunity and quickly excuses himself.

He's making his way over to her when the now-familiar sensation creeps over her. Like a stirring at the nape of her neck, almost like the ghost of someone's breath there, but without the physical sensation, and her mind goes quiet.

She feels like her breath slows with it and even though she knows, she *knows* there will be nothing there, instinct and the need to protect herself from any vulnerabilities makes her turn and check behind her.

Again. Nothing.

Deus, is she losing her mind?

'Thank you, maninha,' Sebastião says and wraps an arm around her shoulder to pull her into a small hug. 'Not sure how many more times I was going to have to just nod and agree with whatever it was that they were saying. Rita left me with them.'

Isabel pastes a smile on her face. 'Yeah, I could see that.'

The amiable expression fades from his face. 'I saw Michael talking to you and you walking out.'

'It was nothing.'

'Hmm. I'm not the only one who noticed,' he says quietly.

Isabel glances up at him. 'You mean, Rita?'

'Yes. She covered it well, but I saw that she felt uncomfortable with it.'

Yeah. This is the kind of thing Isabel is worried about. She can't see her sister or Michael and she feels a stab of guilt. Even though she has nothing to be guilty about.

Her mum and her tia are sitting together at a bigger table near the doors leading out to the patio. The group on that table is a little older, dressed to the nines and having a good time, clearly.

Isabel sees the smile on her mother's face. A genuine thing, full of mirth that lights up her face as she talks and gestures, her hand on Tia Simone's arm.

It hurts to see that expression. She's never going to see it aimed at her again.

'That's between the two of them,' Isabel finally says. 'Look, I don't want to cause a fuss, but I have to go.' She holds up her phone. 'That was my partner, he's on his way over now. We've been waiting for a breakthrough on this, and it's finally happened, so I can't stay.'

Sebastião's whole body seems to sag with his sigh. 'Do you have to? You know Tia isn't going to be happy.'

'I can't help it,' she says, and crosses her arms. 'Besides. I'm here. I showed up and smiled when they needed me to smile, didn't I?'

'Yeah,' Sebastião says and gives her shoulder an affectionate squeeze, 'you did. Be careful though.'

'Of course.'

Sebastião offers to go by hers on his way home and check in on Branco and Tigre, which Isabel is grateful for. Then, as subtly as she can she leaves the room, collects her jacket from the restaurant cloakroom and heads back outside to wait for Voronov.

'Isabel.'

She turns and, this time, finds that Michael has followed her out. He takes in the floor-length black jacket she's now wearing.

'I have to go,' she says.

His mouth thins. 'Work.'

The disdain in that one word puts her back up. Is he serious?

Isabel just scoffs and shakes her head, doesn't even deign to reply. Maybe she's not the one who is losing the plot. How can someone be so out of touch with the nuances of this kind of situation?

'I'm serious. This is your family.'

Oh God. Isabel closes her eyes and prays for patience. 'Michael. Please. Shut up.'

Has he always been this way? So wilfully ignorant?

Suddenly, bright headlights hit her head-on and she twists her face away from the glare of them. It's brief and when she opens her eyes again, Voronov's car is rolling to a stop in front of her. He doesn't get out but leans on the steering wheel, peering out of the windscreen at her. When he knows he's got her attention, he nods at the passenger side.

'Enjoy the rest of your night,' she says to Michael.

She can hear what's going on in his head and that's enough.

Her heels are loud as she crosses in front of the car and to the passenger side.

Voronov has his head cocked and is still looking at Michael as Isabel slides into the car, as gracefully as she can manage given the dress and heels. She adjusts the skirt of the dress as she swings her legs into the car, and pulls the long trail of her jacket out of the way before pulling the door shut.

'Hey,' she says.

Voronov doesn't say anything right away, just looks at her. He does it for long enough that she shifts and looks away, her cheeks a little heated. She drags the seatbelt over her torso and clicks it into place.

'Shut up,' she says and shakes her head.

There's a touch of humour in Voronov's voice when he replies. 'I wasn't going to say anything.' He puts the car into gear. The headlights slide over Michael's form as he turns the car, which he shouldn't be doing here because it's a one-way street. 'You look nice.'

Isabel tries to put the clinging emotions of Michael's thoughts out of her mind. 'Thanks,' she says. Then she sighs and rolls her head to look over at him. 'And for picking me up. Thank you.'

'You're welcome.'

27

The only clothes Isabel has at the station are dirty gym things, so she makes do with swapping her heels for her pair of battered running trainers.

Voronov waits for her downstairs. Carla had said that Alma had been taken to one of the interrogation rooms downstairs. Isabel buttons up her long jacket and ties it closed with its belt. While it's not her chosen uniform, at least it's plain black, and hides the short dress beneath.

As she goes down the stairs, she pulls off her earrings and slides them into her pocket, then drags her hair into a small bun at the back of her neck. It will have to do.

When she walks into Room 1, Voronov is leaning against the windowsill, the light from the streetlamps outside filtering through. Carla is sitting next to the young woman, who is hunched in on herself. Isabel pauses inside the room, feeling like she's passing through a wall of tension that makes every single muscle in her body tighten up and leaves her feeling on edge.

Alma is dressed in a navy-blue hoodie zipped all the way up to her neck, the hood pulled over her head. Isabel thinks the skinny jeans and the black boots are the same as the ones they'd seen her wearing on the CCTV footage. Up close, Alma seems even smaller. Her hair is in a plait that falls over her shoulder. Her hands are clutched together between her thighs.

Her eyes, when she looks up at Isabel, are big and dark.

Carla gets up from her place at Alma's side and walks over to Isabel. When she speaks, she does so quietly, even though the room is too small for it not to carry.

'She had a bag of clothes on her and barely enough money to last her until the end of the week,' Carla says, 'and we found a laptop in her possession that we think belonged to Marta Nunes.'

'I didn't steal it,' Alma says. Her voice is surprisingly deep. She's staring at Isabel when she says it.

Carla sighs but doesn't reply. 'We also found the pair of trainers that match what we saw her wearing on camera the night of Marta's disappearance. Jacinta is already taking a look at them to see if they're the same as the print found on Marta's balcony.'

'And the laptop?'

'Daniel is on it.'

'Good,' Isabel breathes out, 'that's good. Thank you, Carla.'

Carla murmurs a *no problem* and then, with a pat to Alma's shoulder, she leaves the room.

Isabel doesn't go any further in. 'Your friends have been worried about you,' she says.

'What friends?'

'At the youth centre.'

'They're just people I hang out with.'

Isabel thinks Mario might feel a bit heartbroken if he hears that. She slides her hands into her pockets and rocks back on her heels, considering the young woman in front of her.

Like with Mario, Isabel isn't getting much feedback from her. She can sense her, sure, a prevailing sense of discomfort that hovers around Alma's small frame like grey smoke. Upon closer inspection, she notices that Alma's nose is red-tipped and the delicate skin around her eyes is puffy and bruised.

'Are you okay?'

Alma laughs. Then she sniffs. Roughly she scrubs at her nose with her sleeve-covered hand. When she stays silent, Isabel shares a look with Voronov and then goes over to take what had been Carla's seat a moment ago.

'You know Marta got hurt. Don't you?'

Alma bites into her lip. The veins on the backs of her hands stand out as she tightens her fists.

'We think you were there. When Marta was taken,' Isabel says. 'Is that why you ran?'

She shakes her head. 'I can't . . . I can't.'

'Can't what?'

'She's dead,' Alma says, 'she's dead because I left her.'

Isabel looks at Voronov. His expression has softened in sympathy.

When she turns back to Alma, she keeps her voice gentle. 'Did you see it happen, Alma?'

Alma shakes her head no. She digs her fingers tighter into her arms.

Isabel tries a different tactic. 'Mario told us you're a telepath.'

Her *yes* is so quiet Isabel almost doesn't hear it.

'Me too.'

That gets her attention, and she peers up at Isabel. Her eyes are bloodshot and sore. 'You are? And him?'

'No. Just me, Inspector Voronov, is my partner though,' Isabel gives her a small smile, 'he looks out for me.'

Alma's eyes linger on Voronov for a bit longer. Isabel can tell she's not convinced, but she doesn't seem intimidated by him either.

'Alma,' Isabel says, 'I think you're finding it hard to talk about what you saw. But what if you show me instead? We need this,' she goes on gently, 'we're trying to find out who did this to Marta. If you help us, then we get one step closer to finding out who did it. Did you see them?'

Alma just stares at her. Then, 'No.' She glances away, wipes at her eyes. 'No. But I was there. When she—'

She seals her lips together.

Isabel doesn't push.

And then, Alma reaches for Isabel's hand, and grabs onto Isabel's arm with her other hand.

Receiving memories from someone who is telepathic is . . . different. Everything is sharper, down to smell and touch, down to the panic that isn't Isabel's.

Marta's face fills Isabel's vision and she looks down to see what Marta is shoving into her hands. A laptop – Marta's laptop.

'Go,' Marta says, and her voice is so similar to Madalena's that it leaves Isabel feeling a bit sick. Or maybe those are Alma's own emotions.

'But—'

'Go. Now. They can't find you here, Alma.' She's hissing the words, her long fingers biting into Alma's upper arms, forcing her backward.

The laptop digs into her arms because Alma is clutching it so hard. She feels cold all over and can't understand what's happening. Marta had only just set her shopping down. She'd just been asking Alma what she wanted to have for dinner, showing her pictures of where they'd be going now that Marta is free to leave.

But then the knock on the door came. Alma hears the sharp intake of breath Marta makes when she peers through the door at who is on the other side. She sees Marta back away slowly from the door, as if expecting it to be thrown open. Fear rabbits up Alma's spine.

All warmth is gone from Marta's face as she turns. She grabs up Alma's backpack where it sits on the sofa, and forces her arms through the handles one by one and then pushes her back.

Alma's back hits the glass separating Marta's living room from the balcony and to Isabel's frustration, Alma's eyes stay glued to Marta's face, not looking anywhere else. From what Isabel can tell, whoever is at the front door is still outside. It's only Alma and Marta inside the apartment.

Marta stretches her arm past Alma, out of Isabel's field of vision, and she can hear the sound of a lock turning. A door squeaks open and then Marta is shoving her out. Isabel strains to isolate what other sounds Alma is listening to but can't hear anything, can only feel Alma's heart beating in her chest, beating so loudly that the sound of pounding blood fills her ears.

Marta's eyes are so wide the whites of them seem to fill Alma's vision. 'Go. It's not too high up. Jump over the balcony and run and hide. Okay?' Isabel feels Marta's hands as she presses them to Alma's cheeks and holds her face steady. Marta tries to smile but it doesn't work, and she stops trying. The panic is there, so alive Marta can't hide it. She squeezes Alma's face and gently pushes her back until Alma's standing on the balcony, the leaves of the potted plants to the side of her brushing against her ankles.

Marta pulls the door closed between them and all Alma can do is stand there.

Go, Marta mouths through the glass. She closes the door and then, muffled through the glass: 'Just a second,' she calls out, 'I'm coming.'

Adrenalin fires through Alma and she turns.

Her face is wet. Her lips taste like salt. Air whooshes in and out of her, and Isabel feels the frustration of observing and being able to do nothing. Even if she could, what she's seeing is already in the past.

Alma's hands are shaking as she sets the laptop down and, as quietly as she can, moves the pots out of the way so that the path is clear for her to brace herself on the balcony parapet to jump off. She picks the laptop back up and shoves it in her backpack as quickly as she can. The sound of a new voice from inside the apartment jacks her heart rate up even more. She slides the backpack on and starts to climb over the edge of the balcony.

Her foot knocks into a pot. It sends a knife of panic through her and before she can think better of it, she scrambles the rest of the way over, trainers scraping over the balcony wall. She forces herself to breathe slowly, arms straining with the effort of holding her weight as she lowers herself to arm's length until she's dangling. Then, she takes one deep breath and drops.

She lands, the impact hard, her teeth clacking together. She teeters and falls back. Her hands scrape over the rough ground. Isabel has a second to register the dull burning sensation before Alma is back up and taking off, bag slamming against her lower back as she runs around the side of the building.

She doesn't look back.

Gently, Isabel pulls away. The smell of coffee is the first thing she notices. There's a cup on the table where there hadn't been anything before. Under her hands, Alma is shaking. Her head is bowed, body hitching with her quiet sobs. Isabel can see the wet shine of tears on her round cheeks. Her fingers are clawed into the sleeves of Isabel's jacket, her eyes wide open, her eyes fixed on something that Isabel cannot see.

'They're from the Houses,' Alma whispers.

28

'Isabel, Voronov.'

Isabel and Voronov are standing by the entrance to the station, and they turn to find Daniel walking towards them. The police vehicle with Alma and Carla inside drives off down the narrow road, tail-lights briefly flashing red in the night. Isabel had called the Chief and she had agreed to authorise special accommodation. Alma's father was hardly going to protect her, and they had no way of knowing if the person who had taken Marta had checked to see if anyone else had been in the apartment with her.

After Isabel had seen her memories, she'd got her some water. Without once looking up again, Alma had recounted that it had started when she'd been scouted a while back. She had been hanging out at the youth centre after she'd finished school when a man had come there looking for Marta. She hasn't seen him before. She hadn't been in that day, but Alma had stayed until closing.

She said she couldn't pick up on his thoughts without touching him, but that even his emotions had been well guarded, beyond what a Regular could achieve if a telepath tried hard enough. Alma said that left her feeling on her guard. She told him she didn't know where Marta was. After that, everything is a blank until she wakes up in Marta's home with that mark on the back of her neck.

Marta had never explained what had happened. Only told Alma that she was safe now. She'd then asked her if she trusted her. Alma had said she did. That's when Marta had told them they would be leaving.

The question is, what happened between now and then that led to Marta's death?

The only thing they know for sure is that it's related to the Houses, whatever the Houses actually are. That's the other thing. How little they know about them. But . . . if it's related to the Houses, then it's definitely related to Venâncio.

'What is it?' Isabel asks Daniel. She tugs the lapels of her jacket up around her neck and holds them in place. The temperature has dropped, and goosebumps rise on her legs and arms. She's jealous of Voronov's wool sweater. He has his sleeves shoved up above his elbows and is in comfortable jeans and trainers.

'You need to come and see something.'

Voronov glances over at her and then motions for her to go ahead as Daniel leads the way back inside.

'You're not going to believe what's on that laptop,' Daniel says.

Isabel stares at the names on the screen.

The list is long, and the names are mostly female, though there is the odd male name, some of which crop up twice. Some of them have pictures and some of them don't. There are notes next to them, stating age, the level and affinity of each person's Gift, and they're followed by a either the number 1, 2 or 3 and a date. They date back to the time when Marta would have been working with Ezequiel Venâncio.

There is a two-and-a-half-year gap before the most recent names. Daniel has barely started cross-referencing the names with missing persons reports on the police system. The ones that he's managed to match up so far are registered as Gifted.

It takes Isabel a little while to understand what she's seeing.

'It looks like a log,' Jacinta says, looking incredulous. 'It almost looks like an audit checklist.'

There are no new entries for the years when Marta worked at the youth centre. Then it picks back up, with one name that they all recognise.

Alma Pontes. The date entered corresponds with when Mario told them Alma had gone missing the first time.

'What does this all mean?' Isabel asks, trying to make sense of what they are looking at.

'I think this is Operation Fado's wet dream,' Jacinta says.

A grim silence settles in the room.

The dates match up too cleanly with Marta's term of employment at O Vermelho. Whatever this list is, it is what Marta had really been working on during her time with Venâncio. Not dealing with guests and booking in fadistas.

This . . .

Isabel only realises she's clenching her fists when she registers the sting of her nails cutting into her mounds of her palms.

'You said Venâncio was being investigated over suspected trafficking, right?' she asks Voronov.

He gives a tight nod. The light from the laptop bathes his face in white. His eyes are locked on the information displayed on the screen.

She doesn't want to say it, it leaves a bad taste in her mouth. But they're not paid to find palatable answers. They're paid to find the truth.

Her eyes fall to the names. God. So many names. And young. Some of the ages on that list have Isabel taking a step back and rubbing her hands over her face to breathe and calm herself.

'This makes it look like Marta was actively recruiting,' she says.

29

Isabel's shed her jacket and pinned up her hair. The case room is warm enough and they'd managed to get their hands on coffee. The clock on the wall reads 11.00 p.m.

She stirs the sugar into her mug absently, stares at the pictures up on the board of Marta. Marta laughing and alive; Marta on a morgue table, leached of personality.

The woman on that board and the words of those who had known her don't match with the image that's emerging from their investigation.

Who are you really? Isabel wishes she could ask. Was Marta really a victim or had she been part of a system designed to exploit her own people?

Isabel steps back and glances at Daniel. 'Where are all of these girls now?' she asks.

Daniel is still hunched over Marta's laptop, where he's been since they went over the list. There was something else he'd been trying to get into, and he'd lapsed into silence, chewing on a wooden stirring stick as he tried to work it out.

Voronov had suggested they recommend Felipe and Sansão, the two junior inspectors who the Chief had assigned to take over their minor cases, to be part of the rotation they'd assigned to Carla. Isabel had been getting an irritated Chief Bautista on the phone to approve the move. Isabel agreed that the two officers were reliable. They'd done what Isabel and Voronov had asked of them without any questions and hadn't bitched once about having to wrap up all the admin. More importantly, never had they emitted any kind of thoughts or emotions that indicated unease in her presence. Nowadays, things like that went a long way to making Isabel appreciate someone.

'I haven't finished cross-checking all of them yet,' Daniel says, 'but there is one.' He touches the name on the whiteboard. It has a strike through it. 'He shows up on our system.'

Voronov narrows his eyes. 'Wait.' He motions Isabel over. 'Remember I told you about the witness, the one who got away?'

Isabel takes a good look at the name and the picture next to it. A gaunt face with deep-set eyes and a face that looks two shades too pale. He looks like a ghost. 'That's him?' she asks.

'I think so. Only way to verify it is if the OF let us access their case files or confirm it for us themselves.'

The problem they have on their hands now is that they've already had a Chief from another department kicking up a storm about them even sniffing around their operation, and Isabel doesn't think they'll be too keen on sharing their intel.

Voronov is standing with his back to the rest of the room and eyes on the information on display.

'Aleks.'

He glances over his shoulder. He looks sombre.

'What are the chances of the OF being willing to share information?'

His lips curve up but the lines around his eyes don't follow through with the suggestion of a smile. 'Unlikely.'

'Okay,' Daniel cuts in and blows out his breath, 'we have something else that might help with that.'

They turn to him.

'What?' Isabel asks.

Daniel fiddles with the projector set-up and flicks a look at the closed door before bending down to focus on the laptop again. A staticky sound crackles in the room as the speakers come alive before falling silent.

What's on the board disappears and is replaced by something else.

'This is actually what took me the longest,' Daniel talks down at the keys, 'it was a locked folder. Marta password-protected it but what she didn't realise was that the password was retained in a keystroke register.'

Isabel gets the basic concept, but the keystroke register bit goes over her head.

As they watch, the folder opens up to reveal a list of audio files. Each file has a date, followed usually by two or three letters, in some cases four. The list is long enough that Daniel has to scroll the page down for them to see the extent of it.

'I've listened to one,' Daniel says, and selects the top file. 'I think it's Marta speaking.'

He plays the file, and they listen.

At first the only sound that comes out is that odd way silence makes itself heard only when there's a recording happening. Then a woman's voice comes on. It sounds haggard and slow, like someone who is coming out of a long sleep and struggling to remember how to form words.

It sounds like her, it sounds like Marta. But the deadness of her voice is unsettling, like it's someone else speaking through her mouth.

The thought makes Isabel tense, and she has to shake off the apprehension.

They listen as she begins to describe a room and a person in the room. They can hear panting, and then her voice comes out even shakier. Then she says: 'This . . . this isn't too clear. I can't make out everything that is written on the page, the memory is too blurry.'

Isabel stands there, stunned. A memory? She's in someone else's memory?

A male voice interrupts, urging Marta calmly to concentrate and try a little harder, telling her that she can do it. And there's a jolt of recognition. Isabel snaps round to look at Voronov.

'Is that—?'

'It's him,' Voronov says, 'that's Venâncio.'

As they listen, Marta goes on to detail more, picking up what words she can from the document within the memory, though she can't quite get past the fuzziness of it. It sounds increasingly dodgy with each detail they hear her uncover. It sounds to Isabel like it's about plans for a piece of land and the conversation that takes place in the memory is about—

'They're talking about burning land,' she murmurs.

Daniel looks grim as he nods. 'To bring down the value of it.'

Isabel studies the letters on the recording. Initials? Marta in a room, reading someone's memory, and Venâncio is there questioning her, coaching her to give a clearer description of whatever she's seeing in that person's head. The list of recordings is substantial. Isabel eyes the initials. Do they stand for the person whose memory Marta is looking into?

'Marta was a telepath, a level five.' Isabel thinks it through aloud.

It's not unusual for a level 5 to be able to access memories; Isabel's own official classification is as a 5. But it's tough for a 5 to have enough control to manage a strong connection *and* examine a memory at the same time. Touch facilitates it. When Isabel's own Gift had been at a level 5, before it started to expand, that's exactly what she had needed to do. It wasn't long after that that she had started not to need the help of touch at all.

She remembers a conversation not so long ago, with Dr Alves, talking about how a mid-level Gifted could probably do a great many other things if only they'd taken the time to really learn how to wield and control their Gift.

'This explains it,' Voronov says, 'the consensus is that Venâncio has never been caught because he has too many friends in high places.'

Isabel remembers what Voronov had told her before. That Venâncio has a lot of high-profile people walking in through the doors of his fado house on a nightly basis.

'But maybe they're not friends like we thought,' Voronov says, 'maybe they're under his thumb. He's been using high-level Gifted to get information he can use against them.'

Blackmail.

If that's true, then this would mean that the list of names and the recordings they've found are an actual treasure chest for the OF. Unless . . . Voronov had said when they realised who they were dealing with that Venâncio had friends in high places, and that maybe that included people in the force.

Maybe the OF *does* have this information. Maybe they've just been prevented from using it.

If the list of names really is some kind of record of the women and men Venâncio has working under him, and the OF had these, then they would have been able to move against Venâncio a long time ago.

There's no way to know though, unless the OF agree to share intel.

Marta's murder took place about ten days ago. If the OF could provide some insight into any movement that Venâncio or any of his people had made around that night, it could tell them what to look for. *Where* to look. If they could release the details of the other deaths involved with the OF investigation, then that might also give them something. They still don't know where she was murdered.

That, or if they could talk to the witness who had come forward all those years ago. Except if he was smart, after being refused witness protection he would have cleared out.

Isabel sighs. 'How similar is Marta's murder to the ones that were related to the OF investigation, do we know?'

Daniel scratches at his head with both hands, eyes on the ceiling as he thinks it over. 'Voronov said the bodies were recovered from the water. There are two murders that he knows of but there could be more.' He looks at Voronov to check if he's on the right track and when Voronov nods, he continues. 'Both victims were severely beaten prior to being killed, and their faces weren't identifiable. Their throats were slit, and their fingerprints burned off. Found naked, no jewellery.'

'Tattoos?' Isabel asks.

Daniel shrugs and shakes his head. 'Not without being able to see the reports, and those are under the OF's investigation files.'

Voronov straightens up, working his shoulders as if trying to get rid of excess energy. There's a hard line to his mouth that has been there all day. All of this is pissing him off, she doesn't need her powers to tell her that.

'That's all you can remember?' she asks.

'Yes,' Voronov says, the word short and clipped.

Isabel sighs and reaches for him before she can think better of it, just a light touch to his shoulder. The frustration in him snaps at her and she barely keeps herself from flinching away. Instead, she keeps her eyes on his face. 'Hey. You said it yourself. You weren't on that case. What little you've been able to tell us has been helpful.'

He nods, but it's a jerky movement and he's not meeting her eyes. He moves out from under her touch. It's subtle enough that no one apart from her notices it, but she knows he's doing it because he'd seen her reaction to touching him.

She really must be slipping if he keeps catching her out this easily.

Nothing has come of the uncle, Lucas Pinto. The officers in Porto have looked into his whereabouts and his boss has confirmed that he had been on shifts every day of the week except Sundays. They'd checked the son and the wife too and they also hadn't left the city.

This being related to Venâncio, and the cryptic Houses, would explain why Marta had been in such a rush to leave Lisbon. Having worked for him, she would have known what Venâncio was capable of.

But why now? What prompted them to go after her now and not before?

'What if we offer an exchange of information?' she asks.

Voronov folds his arms. 'What are we offering them? The list and the recordings? They could have those already.'

'Maybe, but it's worth a try.' Isabel leans on the edge of the table and crosses her feet. She picks her coffee back up. It's gone a little cold.

'I agree,' Daniel says, and leans an arm on the projector – is he supposed to do that? Won't it break? – and glances between them. 'I think either way we have the upper hand here and we can use it. We have information that either they don't have, or they do but failed to make a move on. You could go as far as saying that Marta might be dead as a result of their inaction. If they want to save face, it's in their best interest to share what they know . . .'

And if that happens to leak . . .

The PJ ends up with a public outrage on their hands.

Isabel finishes her coffee and stands. 'All right, let's make sure we get the okay from the Chief, then.'

The Chief doesn't look happy to see them at her home at this time of night.

She stands at the door, robe wrapped around her frame, hair loose around her face and slippers on her feet. She barely even glances at Isabel and Voronov, just motions them in impatiently and shuts the door behind them.

The Chief's house is over the bridge and given the hour, they'd called ahead.

Their steps are loud in the quiet of the house. Isabel is surprised; she'd expected the Chief's home to stink of smoke, but it doesn't. There's the sound of a radio playing a golden oldie on low coming from a room somewhere, the song mellow, the bodyless voice singing about the still of the night.

The Chief's slippers slap-slap on the cork flooring. She leaves the sitting room mostly in shadow, only reaching to switch on a tall lamp next to the sofa. It lights up a small space. There's a round rug at the centre of the room, a coffee table on it with magazines stacked in its bottom shelf. A porcelain figurine of two dancers graces the top and next to it is a crystal ashtray that gleams in the light. A tall plant rises high up on the other side of the sofa, its leaves wound around a moss stick.

The Chief sits down smack in the middle of the sofa and gestures at the two armchairs. She stares from one of them to the other. There are bags under her eyes but, despite the dark of the apartment, she seems too alert to have been asleep before they arrived.

'Well?'

Isabel scoots forward. 'Sorry to come in like this, Chief. Daniel has confirmed that the laptop in Alma's possession belongs to Marta Nunes.' She takes a deep breath and then takes the Chief through what they have found on the laptop.

'There's still a possibility that these recordings could all be unrelated to Marta's death,' Voronov says, 'but the list of names found is making it look like Marta may have been in deeper with Venâncio than expected. The recordings though could explain how Venâncio has kept the PJ off his back for this long. The odds of Marta having her hands on both of these things, coupled with Alma's statement . . .' he spreads his hands, 'we do need to look at Ezequiel Venâncio a lot more closely.'

The Chief curses and, from her pocket, produces a packet of cigarettes and a lighter. She gets up and crosses the living room to one of the windows. The latch protests loudly as she opens it and the window swings in. It's big enough that she can comfortably lean out. She lights up and takes a drag, the point of the cigarette glowing a fiery orange in the muted light inside the room.

She twists her body so that she's still leaning against the window parapet, arm braced there but body mostly facing them. The streetlights outside paint her hair white. She's addressing Voronov when she speaks next.

'This might get a little hard on you, Voronov,' she says. Then she puts the cigarette to her lips again and takes another drag.

Isabel frowns and looks between the two of them. 'Because of that arsehole Chief that came barging in the other day?'

'Watch it, Reis, that's still your superior,' Chief Bautista says and takes another drag, but her expression seems to suggest that she doesn't really give a shit what Isabel says. Obviously, it would be a completely different story if Isabel had been talking about her. Which Isabel wouldn't do. She does value her job – and her life.

'If we can at least get the OF to share information on the historic murder victims and on any recent activity within Venâncio's operation, we might get somewhere with this case,' Isabel says.

'Okay. I'll sign off on what you need. You have my permission to approach Venâncio. I'll handle Chief Costa. Arsehole is bound to be difficult,' she says, 'it shouldn't be this way but that's how it is.' A couple more choice swear words follow that, muttered out the window as she finishes her cigarette with impressive speed.

They wait as she waves the smoke away. She shuts the window again and fixes the curtains until they're straightened out, leaving the outside visible only through the gauzy filter. Tucking her hands into her pockets, she walks back over and looks down at them both.

'Hold back on approaching Venâncio right away. Dig into Marta Nunes' information a bit deeper. Let me know what you have in the morning, and we'll go from there. Expect tomorrow to be a rough day.'

'Yes, Chief.'

30

The end of the case room table is littered with bottles of water, Coke bottles and empty cardboard cups. The smell of coffee has turned stale, and the stacked boxes of pizza are empty too, save for a few bits of pineapple that most of them had picked off after Daniel had insisted on at least two Hawaiians.

Isabel's lower back aches and her knees feel a little creakier from spending the night hunched over a computer. As the hour had crept closer to five in the morning, she'd had to look away and take more breaks, switching back to coffee after the bottles of Coke had run out.

She feels jittery, the caffeine in her system palpable, but her eyes are gritty and her body slower. She hates this feeling. The only consolation is that she isn't the only one.

Carla had been the last to arrive the previous night, after ensuring that Alma was okay and settled into the secure accommodation. They'd arranged for Felipe and Sansão to be on first watch. Isabel glances at her watch. It's a few minutes to 7 a.m., and the officers with the day shift will be arriving to make the swap soon. Felipe and Sansão are probably reporting to Carla right now.

Maybe they're going overboard.

Alma's accommodation isn't too far; in fact, it's only about half an hour away from Marta's house. Isabel's fairly sure that if someone had known Alma had seen anything, or had been looking for her at all, then they would have found her, and Alma would have been on her way out to sea herself. That's if they really were dealing with organised crime. As it was, she'd been fine all this time by herself.

Still. Isabel doesn't want to take chances, especially as so much of what they need relies on them having Alma safe and sound. And on top of that all, well, she's just a kid.

Isabel doesn't even want to think about the kind of fear Alma must have been living in since Marta had been taken. Or, she thinks as she takes in the notes they've written on the board, maybe even longer than that.

Beside her, Voronov pushes up off his chair and stretches. She hears the catch of his breath and the groan of discomfort that forces its way out as he works his muscles one by one.

Daniel is at the end of the table, chugging down a bottle of water. The skin under his eyes has taken on a green sheen. He's been at this a lot longer than they all have.

Jacinta is the only one who went home a little earlier. She's still splitting her time between Isabel's investigation and assisting with the accident on the bridge.

'Chief will be in soon,' Isabel says.

She thinks about going to the window and lifting the shutters, but doesn't feel like being blasted in the face by sunlight. Which is exactly what will happen – she can see the glow of it silhouetting the shutters.

She spins around in the chair – and that's a mistake, giving her this chair, she'd been spinning the stupid thing all night and Daniel had eventually thrown a marker at her to get her to stop. They've been scrawling the chart onto the board in green and red markers. The black had started fading halfway through.

They'd split the timeline based on the information Marta had noted down for each girl.

There was the pre-youth-centre timeline and the timeline that started from summer last year.

Small pictures the size of Isabel's palm accompany the names of those individuals they have been able to find on the PJ's missing persons database. But there are some pictures missing and every time Isabel looks at the squares drawn on in place of faces, a sick feeling unfurls in the pit of her stomach, and she glances away.

Those are the ones where no one has even noticed that they're gone.

They'd chosen to focus on those last five names leading up to Marta joining the youth centre and then the names falling under the summer timeline, which kicks off with Alma's disappearance. This was confirmed by Alma herself and corroborated by Mario's statement.

That's followed by five more names logged after Alma was taken, all of whom correspond with missing persons reports on record. Two of those names have a strike through them. They had come up as resolved cases.

Those women had both walked into a police station of their own volition. One in Faro and the other in Castelo Branco. The reports had been filed in the Lisbon and Greater Lisbon area; however, a little more digging revealed that neither of those women had returned to Lisbon.

Both were Gifted individuals. Their missing person reports had stated one was a level 5 and the other a level 6, both telepaths.

The whereabouts of the other three were still unknown; there had been missing reports for two of them. Same thing. All of them Gifted. Of the ones they have found reports for, one is classed as level 5 with the other classed as level 4. No details were found on the third. They've put in a request with Monitoring to verify all of them, though with only a name, Monitoring might not be able to accommodate the request.

Maybe before, Isabel would have been tempted to reach out to Dr Alves for some advice, but now . . . well. She doesn't want the woman near her or any of her investigations. If push came to shove, someone else on the team would have to make the request.

For every name on the list, there's a number that they think might refer to which 'House' each woman might have been placed in. Or may still reside in. They still don't know if 'Houses' refers to actual literal houses or some other physical building. It's frustrating that they still don't know enough about what exactly these 'Houses' are.

Marta's spreadsheet also had notes on sightings. So, she was at least in contact with someone who was giving her some kind of information. Operation Fado was technically inactive by this point, so it's safe to assume that they may not know any of this. Would the case stay that way if they saw Marta's notes?

Underpinning all of this is a third timeline, one that has nothing to do with the missing girls but that has to tie in with all of this somehow: the timeline for the recordings.

They hadn't even begun to make a dent in the recordings. Most of them had the same sound quality as the first and Daniel had commented after listening to a few more that, from the muffled quality of the voices, it was possible that Marta had been recording them secretly.

Maybe this had been her insurance.

The dates of the recordings all fall on the pre-youth centre timeline, before that two-and-a-half-year gap in information.

'You guys think this will get our foot in the door?' Isabel asks, staring at it.

Voronov has been combing through names from both timelines for hours, trying to make connections with missing persons reports. Carla has been going through Jane Doe cases. So far they haven't had a hit. But then, they might have washed out to sea. Or been buried somewhere no one will find them.

Isabel thinks of the picture of Marta, a smirk and cigarette smoke, life an inviting gleam in her eye, and then the shell of her, throat torn, skin stripped of its glow and patterned with scrapes.

She wonders if the two girls who made it out have the same tattoo as Marta and Alma.

'Carla,' she says, and leans back in her chair to look over at her, 'the most recent two, the case-closed girls. Contact those precincts and see if they have any idea where they might be, or a way to find out. If they have something on them, then I'd like you and Daniel to go over and speak to them. But get some sleep before heading out anywhere.' She looks at Daniel. 'Is that good with you?'

'Yeah,' he cracks his neck, 'sounds good. Are you two good speaking to the Chief?' he asks.

Voronov nods. 'Don't worry, we'll take care of it and keep you posted. Think we should take a break too,' he says, talking to Isabel, 'something to eat and some sleep as well. I have a feeling we'll be busy tonight.'

'Are you going to push for permission to speak to Venâncio?' Daniel asks.

Isabel tries to ignore the sense memory of that gentle nudge against her mind. 'I think so. Before the other team can tell us no. I'm hoping the Chief can arrange for a meeting with them, but hold off on it until tomorrow morning. Let us get another meeting in with Venâncio before the OF muddies the waters. I don't know how happy they'll be to let us go in alone and the more leverage we have the better.'

It's frustrating. Working a case like this is hard enough without having to try to outplay the people who are meant to be on your team.

But if this is the way it has to be then that's what she's going to do.

31

It doesn't go the way they want it to.

Isabel and Voronov brief Chief Bautista on what they've managed to unearth overnight, and she goes over the information, sharp-eyed and tight-lipped, nails clacking on her desk as she reads over it. Then she makes them wait outside like they're kids during the call with Chief Costa.

When they walk back in, Isabel can tell it wasn't a pleasant call. The energy leaking from the Chief is like that of a caged animal itching to tear someone into pieces.

Bautista doesn't lift her head from the papers in front of her and barely waits for Voronov to get the door shut. 'Well. You've got their attention. They'll be here for twelve noon. Whether they'll actually give you anything of use is a different story, so don't get your hopes up too much.'

'Foda-se.' Isabel rubs a hand over her temple, turning and staring at the door, praying for patience, and sealing her lips over all the other swear words trying to force their way out of her mouth.

Voronov is pissed too. 'What about Venâncio?'

Chief Bautista leans back in her chair and the expression on her face lets them know that they really should know better. 'You'll be talking to him, regardless of how the meeting with the OF goes,' she says. 'We're not accusing anyone of anything, we're not bringing him in. They can't stop us from going in on his turf.' She arches an eyebrow, distinctly unimpressed. 'Chief Costa is welcome to have that conversation with me if he has an issue.'

Isabel sighs, hands on her hips. 'At least we've got that and can still approach him' – she looks at Voronov – 'guess anything we get after this will be a bonus.'

* * *

Noon comes and with a lot of the rooms occupied, Isabel finds herself heading to the same room that Monitoring had used to corner her the other day.

When she walks in Chief Costa is there, with his lip-eating moustache, and two other men who clearly recognise Voronov when he, Isabel and Chief Bautista enter the room. They don't bother to hide their distaste and Isabel finds it odd, feeling that kind of attitude aimed at someone else when she's in the room. She suspects the only reason they don't spout some crap at Voronov that will make her want to punch them in the mouth is because the Chief is with them.

Chief Costa introduces them as Fonseca – clean-cut, a scar that cuts into his upper lip and small eyes – and Mauricio, short and stocky with a thick neck and shaved head.

Under Bautista's no-nonsense direction, everyone takes a seat. Isabel, Voronov and Chief Bautista sit on the same side of the table that Isabel had sat on the last time she was here, and Chief Costa and his two henchmen take the other side. The coincidence of once again feeling as if she's across from an adversary in the same room makes her lips twitch with humour. One of the other officers catches it and clearly takes exception to it, because the next glare is blatantly aimed right at her face.

This is going to be fun, she thinks.

'We're in the middle of a murder investigation,' Bautista says, 'and I'm sure you have things on your side that you're busy with too, so let's not waste time. Inspector Reis, why don't you bring these gentlemen up to date and explain what we need.'

'Thanks, Chief.'

Isabel details the circumstances of Marta's murder and how she had been found, eyes on Chief Costa the entire time.

'There are similarities,' Voronov adds, 'between how Marta was killed, and bodies found during the height of Operation Fado. Marta Nunes was also a person of interest for them.'

Isabel pushes forward a paper outlining their parameters. 'These dates are the ones we've isolated from the information we've received. We'd like to ask for your cooperation. Any intel you might have on Ezequiel Venâncio, anything unusual or heightened activity that you might have observed during this time.'

Chief Costa seems unimpressed. He doesn't lean forward or look and, in the end, one of his officers pulls the paper close and looks it over. His eyes flick up to Isabel and although his face gives nothing away, she feels the uptick of tension, like silver glinting in the dark.

Hmm. So, something on that page has pinged something that they know. Isabel stares at the officer and when he realises it, he shifts in his seat, trying to disguise his discomfort by staring ahead woodenly.

Although Isabel hadn't announced herself as a Gifted Inspector when they had come in, she hadn't needed to. Chief Costa had made it clear during his previous visit that they knew Voronov's new partner was Gifted; and anyway, they would have seen her classification if they'd looked her up.

'There's nothing in what you've told me that shows a clear connection between this murder and our investigation,' Chief Costa says.

Isabel's gaze snaps back to him. 'Weren't the murder victims Voronov mentioned also dumped in the river? Also stripped completely of their clothes and jewellery? Throats slit?' she asks. If looks could kill, she thinks.

'They also had their fingerprints burned off,' Chief Costa bites out. 'And those were never pinned to Ezequiel Venâncio.'

Chief Bautista cuts in. 'Chief Costa, let's not pretend here. You have at least one inspector in this room who was present in your department at the time, and who is aware of what was and was not being speculated at the time.'

'See the habit for snitching hasn't changed, eh, Aleksandr,' Fonseca says.

And yeah, Isabel really wants to shut him up. 'We have additional findings,' she says, 'and a possible witness.'

That does shut them up.

Okay, so maybe she's exaggerating a touch. But they don't need to know that. 'Of course, as this is in relation to our murder case, we'll be digging a little more into the evidence we have found among Miss Nunes' belongings as well as treating our potential witness with care. I'd imagine if this pans out, any information we might gain might be crucial to your investigation . . .' She lets her words trail off.

Chief Costa's cheeks mottle red around his moustache and he narrows his eyes before addressing Chief Bautista. 'If you have evidence pertaining to our investigation, it will have to be handed over to the OF.'

Bautista pulls out her pack of cigarettes and ignores the startled blinks from the two officers across from her. She pops a cigarette between her lips and lights it up.

Isabel is used to it by now, so she does nothing more than grimace as the smoke trails toward her. Voronov seems unbothered by it, but then he has a great poker face.

Chief Bautista points at Chief Costa, the cigarette between her fingers steady. 'Didn't *you* just say that what my inspectors have presented to you has no clear connection to Operation Fado?'

Chief Costa sits up straight, flattening his hands on the table and leaning forward, clearly intending to speak.

'So then,' Chief Bautista says before he can get a word out, 'why would my inspectors hand anything over? The evidence they have found pertains to a murder investigation. If there is no connection, it's best to keep such sensitive information in-house. We've seen in the past how easy it is for the press to get a hold of such things, haven't we?' She takes a deep drag of her cigarette.

When none of them speak, she stands. 'Well,' she says, 'it seems we won't be able to help each other at this point. My inspectors will be sure to be in touch if they find any *clear* connection between the two cases. Reis, Voronov, you have things to do, don't you? Get your arses in gear.'

She opens the door and waits for Isabel and Voronov to hurry through, then turns back to the men. 'Have a good day, gentlemen.'

32

Voronov and Isabel end up at Isabel's place, since it is a little closer to the precinct. Voronov always keeps a spare set of clothes in his car – typical – so they'd made the decision to shower and crash at hers for a few hours and then head out to speak to Ezequiel Venâncio later that evening, with Chief Bautista's permission.

She's glad of the company even as she feels a stab of guilt when they get to her apartment and she sees her dogs. Sebastião had had to take care of Tigre and Branco again the previous night.

Carla and Daniel had updated them both before they'd left the precinct. They'd been in touch with the police stations the missing women had walked into and had scored a hit with the one in Castelo Branco for a Ximena Antonio. They still didn't have anything on the other girl, Sylvia Camacho.

They would be making the trip later in the day, after they'd caught up on some sleep, to see if they could speak to Ximena, who was listed as having reported in there years ago. If they were lucky, the forwarding address provided by her would still be good for something.

The switch-over on surveillance for Alma had gone without a hitch and it seemed that she hadn't left the safe house since arriving. With her being legally an adult, they couldn't hold her if she didn't want to be held, but Carla had convinced her to stay. It wasn't hard; the girl was scared of being out there on her own again. But if she chooses to go wandering around, they can't stop her. So, they keep the officers watching her in place just in case that's what she decides to do.

Or, in case she's been lying to them and tries to make contact with someone else.

Isabel doubts the girl who had been in that room with her was lying, but it pays to be cautious.

The apartment is quiet when Isabel pads out of her bedroom, wincing as the light in the living room hits her in the face. Her hair isn't quite dry after her shower.

The clock reads 6.00 p.m. She's managed about three hours of sleep. If anything, her entire body feels heavier and slower now than it had done before she'd gone to sleep, but she'll snap out of it.

There's a slight sense of déjà vu as she takes in Voronov, stretched flat, face down on her sofa with his feet hanging off it, a blanket covering him and his head turned away from her. She has no idea how he managed to fall asleep in that position, and can't help feeling a small pinch of irritation that he'd refused to take the bed.

She'd been raised right. Guests get the bed. That's just how it goes.

Shaking her head, she goes into the kitchen, making sure to be as quiet as she possibly can as she roots through her cupboards to see what food she has. It's not all that long before Voronov fills the kitchen doorway.

He's in a navy-blue T-shirt and sweats. Unlike hers, his hair has dried completely, and it's taken on a slight wave, sticking up everywhere. He's running his hands through it, but it takes a few tries before it starts to obey him.

'I don't know how you managed to fall asleep on that thing,' she says, shaking her head. She goes back to peeling the onion. 'Don't have much in the house today, sorry. Omelette and toast are the best I can offer.'

Voronov hovers for a bit, as if unsure what to do with himself. 'You didn't have to do that. What can I help with?' he asks.

Isabel snorts. 'Please sit down. Won't be any room with you in here, you'll just slow me down.' She chops up the onion quickly, throws it in a bowl, cracks four eggs into it, adds the ham slices she's already cut into little pieces and the wilting coriander that she found squashed under a bag of tomatoes in the fridge tray.

The egg mixture sizzles as it hits the hot surface of the pan, pushing the melted butter outwards as it pools in. The heat seeping out of the oven warms her legs and she sticks the halves of day-old bread rolls inside to crisp and warm up.

'So,' she says, focusing on not burning the eggs in the pan and getting the mixture evenly spread, 'you can tell me to fuck off if you want.'

There's a stir that tickles her. It comes from the corner of the kitchen Voronov has settled himself in. Curiosity. Reservation.

'The sister thing,' she talks at the pan as she takes it off the heat, poking at it with a wooden spoon before flipping it, the sizzling somehow more satisfying this time around as it cooks the other side of the omelette.

'What about it?'

'There's juice and water in the fridge.'

'I'll have tap,' he says, 'what about her?'

Isabel slips the omelette onto a plate, then turns and sets it on the table. 'You don't have to tell me if you don't want to. But I think you've only mentioned her once before. In fact, you don't usually talk about family in general,' she says.

She takes the bread out of the oven, hissing as the hot rolls stick painfully to the pads of her fingers. She makes quick work of buttering the four halves, plates them and puts them on the table too. She grabs the jar of olives to set on the table – green olives stuffed with red peppers that she just usually sits on the sofa and eats out of their jar – and gets cutlery and napkins, then sits at the table.

'Why is that?'

She feels his eyes on her as she cuts the omelette down the middle and swaps it for two pieces of bread before sliding the plate over to him.

When she unscrews the jar of olives and scoops some onto her plate, he gets up, pours two glasses of water, and comes back to the table.

'I don't like to talk about it,' he says.

Isabel pauses and gives him the driest look she can muster. 'Really.'

There's a hint of amusement on his face at that and that makes her feel a little less bad about broaching the subject.

'Seriously though. I'm asking because I'm curious. But you don't have to talk to me about it if it's . . . uncomfortable.'

The scrape of cutlery on plates and quiet chewing fill the silence.

Laughter and loud shouting drift in through the living room window, punctuated by the sound of a basketball hitting concrete repeatedly. Seems like the kids are taking advantage of the decent evening weather to sneak up to the court and play a game or two. Soon, it'll be followed by the sounds of their mothers yelling at them to get their arses inside for dinner, shrill voices echoing loud enough for a good portion of the neighbourhood to hear.

'During the trial,' Voronov says.

Isabel glances up from the forkful of omelette she's stuffed into her mouth.

'My sister was living with me. Her and my nephew.'

Isabel sets her fork and knife down and waits, watching him.

'There was a break-in while I was on shift.'

Oh fuck. All of a sudden she regrets asking, is already bracing for whatever she's about to hear because she can feel it in him, that this is not a nice story, that it has its hooks in him deeply still. She can feel them herself, painfully sharp and tugging at her chest.

But she asked, so she's going to keep her mouth shut and listen.

'No charges were ever filed, and the investigation was closed. It was aimed at me, of course,' Voronov says, and he stops to drink down the entire glass of water. He sets it back down and twirls it carefully in his grip, blue eyes hooded as he watches the slow turn of the glass. 'Her injuries were minor. They slapped my sister around a bit. Tied her up. Wrote "snitch" on her forehead and left her like that for me to find. They didn't touch my nephew. Locked him in the bathroom.'

Isabel blinks fast and drops her eyes down to her hands. The handles of the knife and fork dig into the webbing of her thumbs and forefingers and she feels this twisted, sick sense of anger and relief. Anger because they'd dared to do that to a human being – worse, while her son was there. And relief. Relief that they hadn't done worse – the worst thing her mind had jumped to, that could only be trumped by death . . . although even that was debatable – and relief that they hadn't touched Voronov's nephew.

Not that it mattered. The boy must have heard everything. Damage was done to him, regardless of whether they put their actual hands on him or not.

And the way that Voronov is speaking . . .

'They were your colleagues.'

Voronov goes back to eating. 'No proof. She didn't see them. They wore masks. The investigation went nowhere.'

Or someone made sure the investigation went nowhere.

When he's cleared his plate, he sets his cutlery down and looks at her. 'My sister isn't stupid. She understood what had happened and why it had happened. She packed up and moved out and asked me to stay away. So, I did.'

Meu Deus. 'I'm sorry.'

Voronov smiles, small and sad. 'Me too.' He drops his eyes to the empty plate. 'Thank you for the food.'

Isabel's chest feels tight with emotion. Tentatively, she lowers her shield and reaches past it, gentle, just a brush, and the pain – it's so familiar. She snatches herself away from it and drops her gaze to her own food, a little cold now. She clears her throat. 'You're welcome.'

She finishes her omelette and stands to clear the table. He follows suit.

'Let me do it,' he says quietly, and takes the things out of her hands before she can say anything. 'You have coffee?' he asks, turning the tap and sticking the plates under the rush of water. 'I have a feeling we'll need it.'

But Isabel is still not over what he's told her, standing there with her arms crossed, frowning down at her feet.

'Isabel.'

For a moment they just watch each other. And there's something, in that stillness, and it doesn't feel awkward staring at each other like this. There's a shift in the feeling coming off him.

Isabel wonders, later, what he might have said but for the outside gate buzzer going off, breaking the moment.

'I'll be right back,' she says and turns, planting a hand on her chest and rubbing over it, trying to ease the fast pace of her heart.

She isn't expecting anyone. Unless it's Sebastião stopping in to check on her, except that Sebastião always texts or calls first.

When she picks up the intercom phone, she's surprised to hear Rita's upbeat voice asking her to let them in.

Still a little stumped, Isabel buzzes her through and goes over to the front door to wait for her.

Rita's smile is bright, making her dimples pop. She's clearly happy to see her sister. That twinge of guilt Isabel is still feeling at having left her engagement party flares a little. Except then it dies altogether when she sees what Rita meant by 'them'. Coming in just behind her sister and closing the door behind himself is Michael.

'Hi,' Rita says and drags Isabel in tight for a hug. 'I actually didn't think we'd catch you in, but I wasn't getting through on your phone.'

Fuck. She'd put it on silent earlier, arguing with herself that just for an hour or two it wouldn't kill her. Besides, Voronov was here too and if someone from their team tried to contact them, they would have got through to him at least.

And that reminds her that Voronov is actually in the house with her; and Isabel is suddenly and ridiculously conscious of the fact that she's standing here, looking like she's just rolled out of bed with her hair a mess of still-drying curls, in an oversized T-shirt and shorts.

Despite herself, she feels heat climbing up her neck and her cheeks, even though she has no reason to feel that way.

'The officer on reception said you'd headed out for a break, so I took a chance,' Rita says, easing back. She holds out a tub. Isabel reaches out automatically to take it and it takes her a moment to realise that it's cake. 'Since you didn't get to have any,' Rita says, 'I made sure to save you some.'

Isabel shoves her hair back from her face. 'Thanks,' she murmurs and realises that Rita is looking at her expectantly. Right. No choice. 'You want to come in? We're actually going to be heading back in a bit. We were on all night,' she says, leading them the short distance into the living room.

As if on cue Voronov comes out of the kitchen, wiping his hands on a dish towel.

Yeah.

This doesn't seem odd at all.

'Sorry,' Michael says, and he sounds stiff, like he's having trouble getting the words out, 'we didn't realise you had company.'

Rita's blinking at Voronov like she's never seen a man in her life and Isabel would rather just shove them both out of her place right now, but ingrained manners make her grit her teeth and make introductions.

'Aleks is my partner,' Isabel says, setting the cake on the coffee table and turning to face them all. 'This is my sister, Rita, and her fiancé Michael.'

Voronov reaches out a hand to Rita, kissing her on each cheek in greeting, calm as anything, and shakes Michael's hand, saying that it's nice to meet them both. Then he steps back and turns to Isabel. 'Do you want me to step out for a bit?'

Isabel shakes her head. 'No, no. Thanks. I was just telling them that we have to head out soon anyway.'

Rita's nodding her head so fast it's a wonder it stays attached to her neck, her cheeks have taken on a rosy tone, and she's laced her arm through Michael's. He has a face like stone and isn't looking at anyone in the room. 'I didn't know we would be interrupting,' Rita says, 'but it was only a quick stop anyway, to make sure you were okay and to give you an early happy birthday hug, I assumed you'd probably be working.'

Isabel nods and gives her sister a small smile. She hasn't mentioned her birthday. She never does. Besides, her plans remain the same as they are every year. 'Yeah, I'm okay. And thank you for the cake. And the early birthday hug.'

Rita's smile becomes a little more relaxed and it's only then that it occurs to Isabel that the ring of nervous energy that has been spinning in the back of her mind since opening the door isn't her own, but her sister's. She hadn't been sure of her welcome.

That makes Isabel's throat tighten up a bit and she reaches out and nudges her. 'Next time we can sit and talk for a little longer, okay?'

'All right.' Rita tightens her arm around Michael's. 'We'll let you get on with it.' She kisses Isabel on the cheek.

Michael is watching her, unsmiling. 'Have a good night,' he says.

'You too.'

She watches them walk out and when the door closes behind them, she finds Voronov watching her.

She sighs, picks up the cake to stick it in the fridge. 'Guess we should get going.'

He turns away and heads over to where he left his things. 'Yeah.'

Yeah.

33

The last time they had been here, the fado house had been quiet, the street itself mostly empty.

Now, it's as if the entire strip of street has come alive.

The windows of the old apartments that surround O Vermelho are open, washing lines packed with clothes, lights glowing from inside. But just as Isabel and Voronov can hear the music before they even turn on to the street, that same music is drifting up into the evening air, the sorrowful story sung in a throaty voice that Isabel feels on her very skin, climbing into the homes of those who have left the windows open for it to steal inside.

It's a night that carries with it a hint of summer, despite it being so far off still. The breeze is soft and has a warmth to it and the small cafés in the surrounding streets are packed to the brim, people unwinding with a little gossip and a little company after a work day; some still haven't yet gone home for dinner.

There's no queue to get into O Vermelho, but there is someone manning the door, dressed in a neat black suit; he's smiling and chatting with a couple before motioning them in and wishing them a good night.

He looks taken aback when Isabela and Voronov approach. They're on duty and not really dressed for a night out to dinner. 'Boa noite,' Isabel says with a smile and gets an automatic smile back.

'Boa noite,' he says, and steps back to let them through.

The atmosphere is completely different this time around.

There's that low buzz of conversations on top of conversations, the sound of clinking glasses. The music pauses for a second but when Isabel and Voronov enter the room, lit mostly by the candles on the tables, a woman is standing at the centre of the floor, tall, black dress and a black shawl around her shoulders, black hair streaming down her back. On the stage, one man under a spotlight, with an acoustic guitar.

As if she'd been waiting for them to come in, the woman starts to sing to the beat of his knuckles on the guitar, her voice filling the room.

The voices quiet down as people pause to listen.

Isabel and Voronov stand at the entrance and Isabel looks around, her gaze going up to the balcony tables. It's hard to see in this light and she squints, trying to spot if Ezequiel is there. There are three people up there, crowded around a table. She reaches out, fingers catching the sleeve of Voronov's jacket. 'Aleks,' she says. She can just about make out Ezequiel Venâncio. But it's not really him she's looking at. Her hand tightens on his sleeve. 'Is that who I think it is?' she asks.

Under her fingers, Voronov's arm goes rigid and that confirms it for her.

The other person, leaning in close to speak to Venâncio under the cover of the fadista, is arsehole officer number two, who had been glaring flames at Isabel throughout their entire meeting that morning.

'What the *fuck* is he doing here?' she bites out. And then it dawns on her. She swings round, mouth falling open. 'Is he here to give him a heads-up?'

Voronov's jaw is clenched tight, his eyes zeroed in on that table too.

'Inspector Reis and Inspector Voronov.'

Isabel turns.

The brother. Dressed to the nines and not even bothering to hide the hostility. 'As you can see, Ezequiel is busy. If I can help at all . . .' he asks and the way he rakes his eyes over Isabel makes her want to make him spit out a few teeth. 'Or pass on a message?'

'No.'

She feels Voronov step closer. 'We'll come back another time,' he says.

Isabel walks halfway up the staircase leading to the street above. 'Fuck.' Voronov follows her but stops on the first step. The security man at the door watches them curiously but keeps attending to the people waiting to go inside. Where there hadn't been a queue when they'd entered the fado house, now there's a short one, groups of people laughing in the warm air.

Isabel paces back and forth along the length of the step, anger building, climbing up her throat and forcing her hands into fists. Shoving her hair back from her face. 'What shit is this? What shit is *this*?'

Voronov is tense, shoulders tense and facing the doorway.

Isabel pauses. 'Aleks?'

It's like he doesn't hear her. She takes a step closer and touches his shoulder. 'Hey. Aleks—'

The leashed violence curls around her wrist and when she breathes it in, it's like a deep crimson spreading through her and into her lungs. Isabel sucks in a sharp breath and yanks her hand back. 'Aleks,' she snaps out, then smooths over her expression as a guy walking up the steps gives them a wide berth.

Voronov turns to look at her and drops his eyes to the hand she's let fall at her side. 'Sorry.'

Isabel takes a deep breath and starts to wave it off, but Voronov narrows his eyes. He's staring beyond her, over her shoulder. Isabel looks behind her but doesn't spot anything. 'What is it?'

Voronov starts around her. 'Come on.'

Isabel, confused, watches him walk up the steps for a second. A glance back over at the door to the fado house shows her Ezequiel's brother standing there, eyes on her.

Smug prick.

Isabel turns, hurrying to catch up with Voronov.

The stairs lead up to an even narrower street, less busy, not lit as well. Voronov is walking fast, steps eating up distance, and Isabel has to jog to reach him. 'Aleks,' she hisses, and almost reaches out to grab him again before she can help herself, 'where the hell are we going?' She gets to his side and keeps pace with him, cursing when he takes a sharp turn into another, quieter street.

There's only one other person here, walking at the same pace as Voronov, a bit further up ahead.

The guy from the steps just now.

Isabel shuts up and follows, allowing her Gift to unfurl, actively pushing it out toward the individual ahead of them.

Nervous energy and an undercurrent of fear. But he's not rushing to run away from them.

'You know him?' Isabel asks, quieter now.

'Cesario Monte,' Voronov says, 'he used to be one of my informants.'

Isabel looks at him sharply.

In front of them, Monte disappears into another turn.

Isabel checks behind them but there's no one else following. The street is mostly closed shops up for sale, their windows painted white with sales stickers on them. Other windows are blank and ghostly, reflecting their images back at them, all colour is leached from their mirrored counterparts.

When they take the same turn as Monte, Isabel finds that they're walking toward an underpass. The area beneath it is completely dark. She can see the bright yellow light on the other side of it and the suggestions of a few shapes tucked low on the floor and against the walls.

The underpass swallows them up as they enter it and Isabel feels that prickle of apprehension on the back of her neck, lets her senses dial up another notch and almost flinches back into her own head at the melancholy that drenches the space, thick and clinging, as if she's walking through thick oil trying to suck her in.

Emerging from beneath the underpass, Isabel can't see Monte, but Voronov continues without faltering so she figures wherever they're headed, it's a place that he is at least somewhat familiar with.

They come up to a wider road and a group of tall apartment blocks. Voronov leads them through a passageway into what must be the central recreational area for the surrounding apartments. The square is dotted with four tall trees in each corner; the centre is hemmed by benches.

There's a group of teenage boys spread over two benches on one side, playing music on their phones. Isabel feels their eyes on her as they cut their way across to the tree furthest away. Monte has stopped there and is half hidden behind the thick trunk. He's shifting on the balls of his feet as if he's going to take off if they don't reach him soon, but when they approach, he's still there.

He flicks a distrustful look at Isabel before focusing on Voronov.

'Então,' he says to Voronov, 'I didn't think you were around these parts any more, man.' His jeans are baggy, and he wears them with a hoodie and a black beanie hat. He seems to be in his late twenties, although Isabel can barely make out his features under all of that beard.

'I'm surprised you're still around.' Voronov folds his arms across his chest.

Monte hums and digs a crooked cigarette from his back pocket, lights up.

'I heard rumours the PJ was sniffing around Venâncio,' he says. 'I didn't think it would be you, man.'

Voronov waits.

'Saw you come in the other day, with your new friend'– he gives Isabel a little wave – 'then again today. The ones in there with him now though are a bit more familiar. Saw those ones with you back in the day. Are you back on their team or something?'

'No,' Voronov says. 'I'm not.'

'Oh,' Monte smokes for a while longer, not saying much, 'so you're not offering anything?' He glances around, eyes flitting quickly, seeking out all the points from where someone else could join them.

Voronov tilts his head. 'You have something worth making an offer for?'

Monte's grin bares crooked, yellowed teeth with a few glaring gaps, but it's a nervous grin, not completely sure of itself. That fear is there, souring the air between them, and Isabel wants to step away from it. But she stays put.

'Things have been bubbling around these parts for a while now,' Monte says.

'Don't mess around with me,' Voronov says and draws himself up to his full height, looking down his nose at him, 'you either have something or you don't. You know better than to waste my time.'

Monte's tongue flicks out to lick over his lips. He starts shifting on the balls of his feet again, cheeks hollowing out as he takes a last drag of his cigarette before chucking it on the floor and crushing it under the heel of his trainer.

'Okay, okay, why are you always an arsehole? Your partner always sweetened me up first, you know? He knew where to get the good stuff.' He still keeps checking around them and it's starting to make Isabel feel paranoid too.

'The question is why are you trying to get my attention so badly?' Voronov says. 'You sought me out. You heard I was around, and you found me. So, I'm here, tell me why.'

'Ahhhh,' Monte sticks his hands in his jeans, 'all right. Things have been quiet for a while, you know, but I heard about the girl in the river.'

Isabel narrows her eyes. 'How?'

His eyes dart to her and then shift away again as if she's about to do some damage. 'Is this your new one?'

'Who told you about the girl in the river?' Voronov says.

'You know how these things get around.'

No. Not unless it's someone on the inside. There had been no report released to anyone about Marta's death. Had it been the OF?

'There's been a rumour of a few disputes happening in the fadista's ranks, you know' – Monte shrugs – 'no clue what. A few big names showing up at the fadista's place like the old days.'

Isabel has no idea what any of this means, and she has to swallow back frustration and let Voronov handle this.

'Who's been coming in and out?' Voronov asks.

'I don't know. I've just heard,' he says.

'Right.'

Voronov crosses his arms. 'Last year, summertime. Was there anything going on then?'

Monte scrunches up his face and peers up at Voronov. 'Last summer? That's a while back. About what?'

'Any new additions to the Houses?' Voronov asks.

Monte shakes his head. 'We don't really talk about the Houses any more, you know. The fadista cracked down on a lot of that. People are more careful nowadays.'

'How about maybe you tell me why you're sharing all this?'

That same grin makes an appearance again. 'What do I get for it?'

Voronov takes a step closer, close enough that Monte's grin slides off his face as he's forced to tilt his head back to look at him.

'Okay, okay.' Monte licks his lips again, darts a look at Isabel, who is standing quietly, waiting. If he's looking for someone to intervene, it won't be her.

'They're saying the Houses are open again.'

34

Isabel sits in her car; she taps her fingers on the steering wheel and her foot bounces in the footwell. The temperature has dropped lower than it's been for a while and she reaches into the back for one of the old hoodies she'd tossed in there over winter. She pulls it on, and it drags her hair into her face, leaving strands clinging to her mouth that she has to pluck away.

Through the windscreen, Marta's building looms over her.

It's late evening now.

She'd gone home, taken Tigre and Branco for their run. They'd stopped by the water for a while, Monte's words playing over and over in her head. Eventually, two hours after trying to fall asleep on the sofa post-shower, the neighbour's thoughts slithering through the cracks and into her apartment despite the body-busting workout she'd pushed herself through, she'd got up, logged onto the work system, and started going through the information they'd collected so far.

It bothered her, this image that was forming of Marta. She knows that not everything is black and white and that just because a person did good things, it didn't mean they couldn't do bad things as well. But this person who had been hated by her own family for being Gifted, who went on to work with Gifted youth and provide a safe haven for them – this person didn't sound like someone who would go out there and lure Gifted into some sick business where they would be exploited and forced into even more suffering.

The bairro is busy. People have had time to wash off their day and are sneaking down to the cafés below for a quick drink after dinner. Children on scooters race each other while their parents sit at the outside tables with their coffees and snacks. There's an air of relaxation that is mostly attributable to the fact that it's a Saturday night and most people won't have to work the next day.

Isabel steps out of the car as a breeze picks up and makes her shiver.

Everyone else that she can see is out in short sleeves and shorts, or skirts, a few with a cardigan or a denim jacket on. No one seems to be particularly cold. Maybe it's just her. She tends to feel colder the more tired she is. She's been feeling tired a lot recently.

She should really let Voronov know she's here but if she's completely honest, she doesn't know what's brought her here exactly. She's not expecting to find anything new. But there's a little voice in the back of her head trying to convince her that if she just walks in Marta's shoes and gets a proper feel for the space she used to exist in, maybe something will click into place.

Drawing curious eyes as she crosses the street to where all the cafés are nestled beneath the bairro's apartments, Isabel makes sure she has the keys on her and double-checks that her phone is still on her too.

She doesn't cross paths with anyone on her way up to the apartment and it doesn't take her long to get there; it's only on the first floor.

The apartment, when she opens the door, is silent, which is to be expected, she supposes. But it's a different type of silence to the one that she used to come home to before she got her dogs. She flicks the lights on.

There's no smell this time. It feels like a husk, like a place that has been abandoned. There are wisps of emotions, and voices rise from below. She can hear the lively discussions of the people out for the evening, muted by the windows and the balcony doors, but audible.

Stepping inside, she closes the door carefully. She's not looking to alert any nosy neighbours to her presence. Her gaze lingers on the extra locks on the door and she can't help thinking about the amount of fear that would lead to someone going as far as adding lock after lock as if guarding against the devil himself.

'Was it Venâncio? Was he the one coming for you?' She says it out loud.

And if it was, then why? Marta had been out for some time, and he was roaming around free. Had she still been helping out behind the scenes and screwed up?

Something just isn't clicking here. Why all of this now?

Isabel turns back to look at the rest of the apartment. Whereas her first time here she saw nothing but the vestiges of someone's life and possible evidence, now the living room has a different meaning. She knows what this room is like with living people inside it – with *fearful* people inside it.

She sees Marta's frantic eyes as she shoves a laptop into Alma's arms and tells her to go. Here the echoes of their steps, frenzied and filled with chaotic energy as Alma gets pushed into the balcony and watches in mounting fear as Marta turns to face the music alone.

Isabel blinks and finds herself standing in front of the door to the balcony. The curtains that had been here shielding it from view, are gone. Probably still with Jacinta's team.

Jacinta's team hadn't found any traces of blood in here.

So, what happened after Alma jumped from the balcony? Did the man who the witness saw Marta leaving with through the emergency exit just calmly take her away? There had been no ransacking of Marta's home, no documents or cupboards that looked like they'd been rifled through.

Just a cold walk to her murder.

The shopping that had been on the kitchen table is gone. She wonders if Madalena has been here to take a look at what remains of her sister.

Isabel would like to say that she can't imagine that kind of loss but, unfortunately, she's felt it way too many times. Her own, and then as her Gift grew and changed, every person who she'd had to inform about the death of a loved one, their emotions seeping into her very pores and insisting that she feel it with them.

The photo of Marta and Madalena is still pinned up on the surface of the fridge and she can't help taking another look, staring hard at Marta's wide smile and the way she's beaming.

There's nothing for her here. She needs to leave and get a decent night's sleep. That's what she needs to do.

As she turns to leave, a torn bit of paper pinned up on the fridge catches her eye – she remembers it from the first time they were here. A little scrap of paper with an arrow doodled on it.

Except as she stares at it, she remembers being in the morgue – remembers the thick wrinkled skin of Marta's hands, and then a little bit higher than that, on her wrist . . .

A stylised arrow.

Isabel stares at the pencilled drawing. It's similar. Similar enough. The paper itself looks like a corner that's been torn off an A4 lined pad.

She plucks away the magnet holding it in place and turns it over.

When she sees a number there it feels like her heart stops. She tries to remember whether this number had been on the call logs, but there were too many, she wouldn't remember one. She yanks out her phone but then takes a quick look at the hour – it's nearing 10 p.m. Daniel won't be at the precinct at this time.

Tapping her nail on the screen of her phone, she thinks. This could be nothing. This could be absolutely nothing. With a sweep of her thumb, she unlocks her phone and, after hesitating for a second, keys in the number.

She stands in the empty kitchen and hears the sound of cheering coming from outside as the dial tone starts.

It rings around six times. She's about to put it down and bother Daniel to look into it tomorrow morning when someone picks up.

'Who is this?'

The sharp question takes her by surprise. It's a woman's voice, sounds young but it's hard to say for sure over the phone.

Before she can think better of it, Isabel responds. 'This is Inspector Isabel Reis with the PJ.'

Silence.

'I'm investigating Marta Nunes' murder.'

Silence.

Isabel turns around, eyes sweeping the kitchen, trying to work out how to play this. She paces over to the door. 'Listen,' she says, keeping her voice level, 'I'm just looking for someone who can help. Someone who maybe knew a bit more about her.' She stops, resting her hand on her hip as she tilts her head back and closes her eyes, praying for a break here. 'If you're someone that can do that, would you be willing to talk to me?'

She has this number now; they can break their backs trying to trace whoever this is if needed. And Isabel will make sure that they do because clearly, this isn't just anyone, not the way they've reacted to this call.

They're still on the line. Isabel can hear them breathing and, as she listens, what sounds like the faraway sound of cars. Maybe. Isabel can't be too sure.

'Can you help me?' she tries again.

Finally, the woman speaks again.

'Okay. I'll tell you where to go.'

35

'I'm ten minutes away.'

Voronov's voice fills the inside of the car as Isabel drives down and turns into what could loosely be called a parking spot near the Zeca Afonso Municipal Park in Baixa da Banheira. It had taken her about thirty minutes; there was hardly any traffic on the road at this time.

Isabel grabs her phone again, gets out and locks her car before taking the phone off speaker and putting it to her ear. 'She should be here soon; I don't want her to get spooked if she sees you.'

'It doesn't matter.' Voronov's voice on the phone is hard and she can tell he's not going to get over this so easily. 'You should've called me right away. I can wait a safe distance away. Do you get what could happen to you without me there to back you up?'

Isabel stops, standing behind her car and looking over to see if she can spot the woman who she's driven over to meet. She'd said her name was Lydia. 'Aleks—'

'Isabel, merda! *Don't* move until I get there.'

'Okay, *okay*. I'm not moving. I'll wait for you here.' She hangs up before he can say anything else.

She runs her hands through her hair, tugging it back from her face as she scans her surroundings. Despite the late hour, the park isn't empty by any means. It's a decently sized park with views of the river. There are groups of teenagers here and there, and people taking nightly walks. There's a guy and a girl on one of the benches a little further away from the exposure of the streetlights, oblivious to the world around them, wrapped in one another and not caring who is watching as they make out. Beyond that, sitting directly beneath the lights, are a group of boys, skateboards at their feet and a couple of bikes leaning against the back of the bench as they talk and laugh.

Others walk hand in hand through the winding paths. The sprinklers add to the rhythmic sound of crickets. The quieter waters surrounding the park reflect the night city and Isabel leans back against her car, stretching her arms up and breathing in deep. It's peaceful here.

She should bring Branco and Tigre.

She checks her phone for any calls. After telling Isabel where to meet her, Lydia had told her to wait for her call.

'Maybe she won't show . . .' Isabel murmurs, staring at the screen.

By the time Voronov arrives, the temperature has dropped a little more and she's back in the car, foot bouncing, checking her phone every few seconds.

Voronov gets out of his own car, a black cap on his head and jaw darkened with stubble. He's wearing a worn grey T-shirt beneath his jacket and his jeans are frayed at the knees. He comes to stand beside her when she gets out, looking around.

'She's not here yet?'

Isabel shuts the car door, shivering as a breeze ghosts over her. 'Not yet.' She taps her phone against her leg. Voronov's arrival has caught the attention of the group of teens and they've toned down their conversations, eyeing both Isabel and Voronov with interest. 'Maybe she won't show.' She flicks a look at him, then, grudgingly: 'Sorry I dragged you out. I thought about leaving this for tomorrow but . . .'

Voronov sighs. He goes back to his car and when he turns back around, he's holding out a hooded jacket to her. 'It's fine. I would've been pissed off if you hadn't called me for backup.'

When she doesn't immediately take the jacket, he gives her a pointed look.

'Jesus. Fine, thank you.' She shrugs it on and is a little thrown when his smell surrounds her.

Her phone lights up in the dark and starts vibrating in her hand. She looks at it and sees a message. It's the same number Isabel had called earlier on in the night. It reads:

The gazebo.

'It's her,' Isabel says.

She knows the park well enough to know there's a small gazebo near the water. The interior of the park isn't as well-lit as its outskirts, however. She glances up at Voronov. He's staring into the park as if trying to locate the woman with laser vision alone.

'All right' – she shoves her phone into her back pocket and pats him on the chest – 'stay here. I have my phone on me.'

He doesn't look happy about it. 'If you're not back in thirty minutes I'm following you.'

'Jesus, Aleks.' She frowns, starting off.

'You're lucky I didn't make it twenty minutes.'

Despite the apprehension she's feeling, Isabel scoffs and calls back over her shoulder, 'It's cute that you think you can tell me what to do.'

'Just be careful. I'll be here.'

She waves to show she's understood and heads into the park.

The gazebo is easy to spot if you know your way around. Isabel passes a few people on her way, more young lovers sneaking in a few kisses in the shadows of the fat palm trees dotted around the park, some friends on a late-night roller-skate.

There, at the point where the pier stretches out into the water, is the gazebo. In the shadows, Isabel spots the telltale glow of a cigarette and can just about make out the shadow of someone sitting on the bench inside it.

As she approaches, that shadow resolves itself into a short figure turned toward the river, taking a smoke. Isabel stops at the steps leading up to the gazebo. She's not sure what she was expecting but the woman in front of her takes her by surprise.

She looks like she's stepped out of presenting a prime-time TV show. Slim-fitting trousers and heeled black ankle boots. She's wearing a black blazer and a gauzy white top beneath. Short black hair styled into a neat wave that tucks into a low bun. When she looks at Isabel, her eyes are lined in black, and her lips are a matte red that exaggerates their fullness.

She eyes Isabel for a moment, seeming unimpressed, and flicks the butt of the cigarette with her thumbnail, shaking the little bit of ash free. 'You don't recognise me, do you?'

Isabel blinks, stumped. 'No. Should I?' She climbs the steps up to the gazebo and settles against one of its beams. 'Lydia, I take it.'

Lydia pops the cigarette back between her lips and nods as she finishes it off. 'Yes,' she says on the exhale. 'Lydia Tavares.'

'Where am I supposed to recognise you from?'

Lydia picks up the handbag that sits next to her on the bench. She turns so that she's facing Isabel as she digs inside it and comes out with another cigarette and a lighter.

'My face has been on TV a couple of times, some magazines too.' She says it matter-of-factly, no vanity to it. The smile she gives Isabel then isn't a nice one. For some reason, Isabel gets the impression of a woman who's fought many battles and always come out on top. 'Usually, I'm being interviewed about my hatred for the Regular population.'

She started hanging out with certain groups of people on these causes . . .

That's what Madalena Nunes had told them the first time they'd spoken to her about her sister's death.

'You're . . . some kind of activist?'

Lydia lights up the second cigarette. 'That's right. I'm with the Seta Group.'

Seta. The name is familiar. It is regularly in the news, stories about staging protests or suing someone or other over discrimination against Gifted, a thorn in the side of the government when it comes to Gifted rights – and now the arrow makes sense. 'Is that what the tattoo Marta had on her wrist is about?'

'That's right. Marta . . . she was with us for a long time.' Lydia turns to stare back at the water. That thread of iron that's been in her voice since Isabel arrived fades now.

Isabel tucks her hands into Voronov's jacket pockets. 'For her to have your number specifically, I'm guessing you worked closely together?'

'We did.'

Isabel sighs. 'Lydia, I need you to explain some things to me. I'm getting a conflicted image of Marta here. I'm sure you would've been aware of the rumours circulating about O Vermelho, both about the owner and the establishment. It seems like the kind of thing that would be on your radar. Why would someone like Marta be working there?'

Lydia snorts, still facing away from her. 'Yes, I know all about those. What? You think Marta was actually in there doing his bidding?'

Isabel narrows her eyes. 'Based on what we've found, that's what it's starting to look like.'

Lydia shakes her head and mutters under her breath, 'She should've stayed out.'

'What do you mean?'

Standing, Lydia begins to pace the length of the gazebo. 'Marta's dead because of him. I can guarantee you that.'

'Why do you say that?'

'Because she was there for *us*,' Lydia snaps out. She stops and looks Isabel dead in the eye. 'She was there working under that man for *years*. For. *Us*.' She laughs and shakes her head; then she points at Isabel with her cigarette. 'Because *you* people are in his pocket. The PJ has known for so long about him recruiting Gifted into his twisted shit-show, pimping them and their Gifts out to get the upper hand on all sorts of people in the city, and they did *no-thing*.' Cursing, she spins away and starts pacing again, her heels loud on the wooden floorboards.

Quietly, processing what she's just been told, Isabel tries again. 'What was she doing there? For you guys?'

Lydia halts her pacing. She sighs. Her shoulders slump. 'She started out as a waitress. Worked her way up to manager. Got close enough to earn Venâncio's trust. Until she was brought in to help manage his other businesses.'

'The Houses?'

Lydia nods and looks over her shoulder at Isabel. 'She helped us start getting them out. She would help them get out; we'd help them disappear. It worked for a while. But then . . .' she makes a restless motion with her hand, 'something changed. I don't know if they got too close, or started figuring out what she was really there for. Marta started acting strange, dropping communications. We started to get worried. We decided it would be better if she pulled out.'

'And Venâncio never noticed anything? No one ever suspected what she was doing?' That seemed unlikely. He didn't seem the type of man not to notice when something was going on right under his nose. Then again, Marta could have been very good at what she did.

Lydia scratches at her eyebrow with a thumbnail. 'He suspected *something*. Marta told us he did anyway, but there was something about the way she spoke about it . . . almost as if she was trying to find excuses for what he was doing. She started talking about what he did for the community, for other Gifted. Telling me about the fact that he cared too and' – she sounds dumbfounded – 'I couldn't believe what I was hearing. I told her she needed to pull out. We have more people in other places. We couldn't afford a fuck-up here.'

'And did she? Step down.'

'She didn't have a choice,' Lydia says grimly.

'Okay. What happens after that?'

Lydia seems to remember she has a second cigarette. She takes a drag. 'I think you know the rest. She stops working with us. She gets a job at the youth centre. And that was the last I heard of her until . . .'

Isabel waits.

'Until a couple of weeks ago.' She finishes that cigarette too and puts it out. 'She called asking for help. Said she needed help disappearing. We have safe houses scattered around Portugal and a few others around Europe.'

'And what happened?'

'Nothing. Nothing happened. I waited for her to call again so we could iron out details. I'd told her she'd need to find a place to lie low for a while until we sorted something out for her.'

She meets Isabel's eyes then and Isabel sees the sheen in them.

'Next thing I knew, she was dead.'

36

Isabel had arrived home in the early hours of the morning to gentle snuffles at her ankles, and had made it as far as stripping off her clothes and collapsing into bed. It had still taken her a surprisingly long time to fall asleep, which is why, after her morning jog and sitting on the floor for a while to play with her dogs before leaving, she slides on a pair of sunglasses to hide the redness of her eyes and the dark circles.

There's a small headache building in her right temple, but she's had a lot worse.

She gives Tigre and Branco a last affectionate rub. 'I won't be long today, I promise. Then we can go chill with Tio Sebastião later, hmm?'

Rosario had told her to meet her at Cais do Sodré and had instructed her to take public transport. That had been a strict rule.

You have to start acclimatising yourself. I know you don't believe me, but the more exposure, the better. It'll be overwhelming at first but it's something you need to get used to. Establish your baseline.

Sure. Baseline, Isabel thinks, as she steps out of her building and heads on. 'Easy for you to say,' she mumbles.

The tram is climbing up the street. It's quite empty, which isn't unusual for a Sunday morning. Even with tourists, things slow down quite a bit at this time. Isabel makes her way down the steep descent, sticking close to the houses on the left in case today is the day that she trips up and goes rolling down the hill. That's what she gets for choosing a place to live based mostly on the view she gets of the city. Idiot.

She almost doesn't hear the person calling her name over the sound of the tram bells.

Frowning, she looks over her shoulder and immediately feels herself lock up as she sees Dr Nazaré Alves hurrying after her, not seeming as worried about the sharp downturn of the street as Isabel is.

Isabel is tempted to turn her back on her and keeps going, but clearly it's not like Nazaré doesn't know where she lives as well as where she works. She shoves her hands into the pockets of her baggy trousers and waits. She's even more grateful for the shades on her face as Nazaré draws close.

Nazaré's cheeks are pink from her rush to catch up with Isabel and she's extremely casual today, in a cheerful yellow sundress and a bulky cardigan on top. Her bag is slung across her body and she's wearing chunky black boots.

Nazaré adjusts the round glasses perched on her nose. No smile in place today.

'Hi – sorry. I didn't want to ambush you outside your house.'

Isabel looks up past her to check if Coval is following close behind. 'So what, you're stalking me instead?'

Nazaré gives her an exasperated look. 'After the complaint your Chief filed against us, I shouldn't even be here.'

'Good. Then go away.' She turns to continue on her way.

'Wait, *wait*—' Nazaré grabs for her arm. 'I'm sorry, just please listen.'

Isabel brushes her hand aside. 'Let go.'

Nazaré clenches her hand in a fist. 'Look,' she glances around them and steps closer, lowering her voice, 'I didn't have a choice. It was a high-profile case, okay? There is no way Monitoring weren't going to take a closer look at it. And there are gaps in your statements. Yours *and* your partner's. You know that.'

The words get Isabel's back up and she draws herself up to her full height, squaring her shoulders. 'I've already told you—'

'I'm not here to ask you to tell me anything. I'm *not*. I'm on *your* side, here, okay?'

Right. Of course she is.

'I shouldn't even be here. Monitoring *is* watching you and it doesn't help that you pissed off Coval.' Nazaré takes a step away from her. 'That's all I came here to say. Be careful and watch your back.'

She holds Isabel's gaze and gives her one final nod before turning and making her way back up the hill.

Isabel sighs, tension bleeding out of her as quickly as it had built. The ache at her temple pulses, a little stronger now, and she digs her thumb into it.

Gritting her teeth and praying for the universe to just give her a break, she mentally prepares herself to deal with a metro full of people.

37

THEN

For a second, before Isabel puts the key in the lock, she almost expects it not to turn. It's been months since she last used it and that had been while her mum and sister had been away. She'd only come that time because Rita had asked her to check the post.

When the lock clicks and the door eases open, Isabel immediately feels like a trespasser and for a moment she's frozen by the conflicting emotions and thoughts that flood her. They scrape over her already taut nerves like nails on a blackboard and she has to steady herself as she steps inside.

It smells like lemongrass tea and there's a new plant catching the light that comes through the door. It's a tall devil's ivy planted in a new sturdy clay pot and Isabel says a quiet hello to the plant – Tia Simone had drilled it into her that plants like to be spoken to – and trails a gentle finger down a leaf.

The sound of steps coming from the kitchen has Isabel quickly shutting the door behind her, still uneasy. The sound of it closing echoes through the house. She can hear the sound of the TV and knows, considering the time, that her mum is probably getting ready to sit down for the evening news. But there's also the low sound of the radio playing from the kitchen.

'Isabel?' Rita's head pokes out from around the kitchen doorway. Her braid slips over her shoulder as she leans forward to look around the door frame at Isabel. 'What are you doing here?'

Isabel tucks the keys away and heads into the kitchen, ignores how the question makes her feel even more unwelcome, as if she hadn't grown up in this house and lived here with Rita. This house had been hers long before it was her sister's.

It's as if that fact has been erased from her sister's and her mother's minds.

'Hey,' she says, 'it's a quick stop. Just had some news.' She's itching to rub her hands on her jeans, get rid of the sensitivity that makes it feel as if her palms are prickling. She stops by the door to kiss her sister on both cheeks. She's got their mum's old apron on and is holding a sponge in her hand.

'Rita? Who is it?' Her mother's voice comes from the kitchen.

Rita turns back, making space for Isabel to slip inside the room too. 'It's Isabel, mãe.'

There's no response.

When Isabel steps into the kitchen her mother, Maria, is sitting on the furthest side of the table, facing the door, a mug in front of her and a small plate of ginguba next to it. Isabel's dad had always preferred peanuts this way, used to buy packets of them and toast them in a dry pan with the red skin on and then peel them while they were still hot, to eat with a cup of tea.

'Boa noite, mãe,' Isabel says.

Her mother stares at her, chin tilted up, unsmiling. It makes Isabel feel looked down upon. She's dressed all in black, as she has been ever since Isabel's dad died. The black cardigan and top make her seem even smaller than she is. Her thick black hair, which is streaked with a lot less white than someone her mother's age would normally have, is pulled into a tight knot.

'It's late, Isabel.'

It's about seven fifty and a glance at the stove shows that they haven't even had dinner yet. Right. She starts to feel stupid for coming here, but there's a part of her that thought that maybe—*maybe* . . .

'I won't stay long,' Isabel says, and stays where she is, by the door. 'I just had some good news today.' She feels as if someone else is saying the words, gets a sinking feeling as she starts to understand that this isn't going to play out how she'd thought – stupidly – for a moment it might.

Rita hovers in front of Isabel, not looking at her or her mother. The sponge in her hand is dripping but she doesn't seem to notice.

'I passed my exam,' Isabel says and swallows. Her throat is so dry, and she wishes she could stop and get some water. She sticks her hands in her pockets. 'Got a place with the precinct in Anjos as a junior inspector. It's just in minor offences for now but I'm hoping I'll be able to move up quick if I work hard.' Like her dad had.

The radio DJ announces a new song and the faster beat of semba comes on, cheerful and at odds with the dead silence in the room.

Without another word, her mother drops her gaze to the ginguba, picking up a few and rubbing the skins until they come off. She continues eating. 'Maybe now you can start paying your aunt for all the time you spent there, living off her money.'

The words hit Isabel like a blow, and she's surprised she doesn't physically rock back from them. Her jaw tightens, teeth clenching as she feels the hurt swell in her chest and rob her of her breath.

The quiet remains, filled by the radio, until Rita sets the sponge on the counter and wipes her hands on her apron, her movements awkward. She shuffles closer to Isabel. 'Congratulations, Isa, that's really cool.' With tentative hands, she pulls Isabel into a gentle hug.

Over her shoulder Isabel watches as her mother continues eating, not once looking up again.

Isabel shuts her eyes against her blatant rejection and hugs her sister tight.

'Thank you, maninha.'

38

Alma is sitting on the front steps of the safe house when Isabel steps past the gate, the hinges protesting loudly.

Isabel had left the precinct a little earlier, having briefed the rest of the team and Voronov on the developments with Lydia Tavares and Monte's intel on rumours that the Houses were reopening.

Before leaving, Isabel had pulled the photos from the historic crime scenes that had similarities to Marta's. They had been treated as homicides unattached to the investigation on Ezequiel Venâncio, though of course there were strong suspicions that they were related to his operation, so they weren't locked by OF.

Voronov had been right, of course. The similarities couldn't be denied. The crimes had been a lot more gruesome though. Both bodies were severely beaten to the point of disfigurement, stripped and their throats slit. But the killers hadn't stopped there. The pads of their fingers had been burned, distorting their fingerprints, and – Isabel had to take a moment after reading the accompanying notes – their teeth had been pulled out. There had been nothing left in their mouths. Even Voronov hadn't been aware of that part.

She'd had to stare ahead at the wall in front of her for a good while until the wave of nausea passed.

The victims of those attacks remained unidentified.

Marta's murder had been vicious, but the older murders had a different level of brutality to them.

Which meant that either Marta's death was unrelated or perhaps her previous association with them had granted her some . . . leniency.

Daniel and Carla had managed to get a hit yesterday when they'd gone to Castelo Branco, but when they'd arrived at the address of the girl who had reported herself to police there, she had already moved on. But the wonderful thing about nosy neighbours is that they often know useful things. It took them a good two extra hours but eventually they managed to find out where Ximena Antonio had moved to. Turns out she hadn't gone all that far.

After they'd spoken to her, the Castelo Branco police had put them up overnight. They'll be heading straight into the station as soon as their train gets in to Lisbon. Alma glances up as Isabel latches the gate closed behind her.

The house is on the same street as a primary school and the laughter and shrieks from the children, currently on their break time, carries all the way down to the house. The watch shift for Alma has already switched again and the car sits in front of the gate.

'Expecting me to run or something?' Alma asks. She tips her head back to look at Isabel and has to shield her eyes from the glare of the sun.

'No,' Isabel says and eases herself down into the small space beside her. 'But I thought it would be good to check in on you. Why? Would you prefer Carla?'

Alma shrugs. She has her phone in her hands and is playing with it, flipping it and throwing it from hand to hand, unlocking the screen and swiping down. No notifications show up on the screen and she locks it, twirls it again as she frowns straight ahead.

'Are you expecting to hear from someone?' Isabel asks.

'As if,' Alma mutters. 'Carla told me you guys went and spoke to my dad.'

Isabel shifts until her back is to the wall, pulling her leg up and wrapping her arm around it. 'Not me personally.'

'But you know he's a piece of shit.'

Isabel raises an eyebrow at that. 'Yeah. I know he's a piece of shit.'

'There you go then. No one to call me.'

'Your friends might.'

This time, Alma isn't as quick to denounce friendships. She swallows heavily and runs her thumbs over and over the back of her phone.

'You don't want to speak to them?'

Alma clears her throat. 'It's dangerous.'

Ah.

Alma scuffs the heels of her trainers over the steps. She's wearing bright red Converse today. The laces aren't white any more and one of them is trailing over the steps, but it doesn't seem to bother her.

'What did they do to her?' Alma asks.

It doesn't take a genius to know who she means.

The sky is a wash of blue, the kind of blue where it's so bright that it hurts to look at, even if you avoid looking towards the sun. Isabel stares at it, feeling her eyes water.

'They wouldn't tell me,' Alma says, voice quieter now. She sounds more like a scared kid when she speaks like this. Isabel supposes that's exactly what she is.

'You know she died,' Isabel says, 'do you really need to know how?' The warm breeze has stayed overnight, and it sweeps over them now. Isabel tilts her head back a little bit more, letting her eyes close.

'It's bad isn't it. They hurt her really badly, didn't they?' Alma's trying to keep a brave face on but it's crumbling.

Isabel's intention in coming here this morning hadn't just been to check in on her. It had been to push. To see if Alma would be willing to let Isabel poke around her head and see if she could find what the girl says she does not remember.

But looking at her now, stubborn jaw clenched and wet eyes that she refuses to acknowledge in any way, a tremble to her mouth even as she tries to stare Isabel down, Isabel can feel it, how brittle all of it is; she's barely keeping the fear from eating into her and Isabel isn't sure how long it's going to last.

And she really doesn't want a broken teenager on her hands.

Yes, Isabel wants to solve this. But Marta is already dead. There's no saving her.

That's not true for the teenager sitting in front of her.

She can't lie to her either.

'Yes,' Isabel says.

Alma's chest rises as her mouth opens and she sucks in a breath, her eyes going wide, and she twists away from Isabel. She clenches the phone in her hand hard and gulps in deep breaths as she stares unseeingly at the patterned mosaic that makes up the small pathway leading up from the gate.

Isabel steels herself. She reaches out and lays a hand on Alma's shoulder. When Alma doesn't shake off her touch, she leaves it there and stays sitting in quiet support as the teenager tries so hard not to fall to pieces.

Finally, after she's cried out, Alma uses the sleeves of her hoodie to wipe at her eyes.

'I really want to go to her funeral. Can you guys take me?'

'All right.'

39

‘She was in one of the Houses,’ Carla says.

‘She’s sure?’ Isabel asks.

‘Yes,’ Carla says.

True to their word, Carla and Daniel had come straight to the station. Isabel doesn’t think she’s ever seen Carla this rumpled. She’s thrown her blazer over the back of a chair and her shirt is creased all along the sleeves. Her hair, always perfectly in place even when she wears it loose, has today taken on a slightly oily sheen, probably from her brushing her fingers through it one time too many overnight.

As for Daniel, he always looks like his alarm didn’t go off and he had to run out of the house in a hurry, so there isn’t much of a change there. Isabel had told him so when they had walked into the room, and he’d given her the finger.

‘Was she able to give a location?’

Daniel shakes his head and Isabel figures that would’ve been too good to be true. ‘She doesn’t remember much but she knows there was another girl being kept with her. She says they made her take enhancers, strong ones.’

Enhancers.

It isn’t the first time that the subject of enhancers has come up. Enhancers had been created as a counterpart to the suppressors that the government had rolled out years ago for Gifted. Suppressors had been made illegal, though, after concerns that Gifted were using them to downplay their Gift levels during testing. The worry being that higher-level Gifted people were walking around without being appropriately monitored and able to do what they wanted.

Well, Isabel thinks, they hadn't been entirely wrong. She had done it herself.

But enhancers had never been rolled out. They'd been created but held back. Conspiracy theories posited that these had been created for the government to take advantage of Gifted and their abilities, use them for less than innocent means.

There are a lot of conspiracy theories where Gifted are concerned.

'So, someone who can definitely get access to illegal drugs then,' Isabel says.

'Like someone with friends in high places,' Carla says.

Exactly like someone with friends in high places. 'What were the enhancers for?'

'It might have something to do with what they were using the girls for.'

What follows makes Isabel press a hand to her mouth and stare fixedly at three pockmarks on the table where someone has twirled a pen point into the surface over and over until it left a mark.

The Gifted were given to clients.

The people running the Houses would let the Gifted into the room after the client was settled, ready and waiting, and their job was to use their Gift to create a false sense of euphoria that lasted for however long the client had paid for. They weren't allowed more than two clients per day – creating and pushing artificial emotion like that into someone else had taken it out of them.

According to Ximena, she was one of the lucky ones. She belonged to what she had referred to as the First House.

The statement she'd given to Daniel and Carla had said she remembered being well fed; the room she'd stayed in when not working had even been comfortable. But they had used blindfolds when moving them to the client rooms and the enhancers had made her feel sick, so she'd suffered more than the other girl, or so she thought.

The Gifted assigned to the Third House had had to provide a different kind of service. When Carla had probed a little more, she'd confirmed that the Gifted there had been required to use their powers to get their clients off – people with a taste for the unique, she'd said.

'Jesus,' Isabel says and drops her face into her palms. It's so beyond what she'd thought she would hear. 'And Marta got her out?'

'Yes,' Daniel says.

'So, she did know where the Houses were. This matches up with what Lydia Tavares has told us.'

'It seems like it.'

That just makes the question of how Marta had survived this long even more pertinent. She'd clearly known too much and rebelled. So why now?

There is a three-year gap where no new names were added to Marta's list, and there are no new recordings even after new names were added. It all starts up again when Alma is taken. Why?

'Ximena doesn't want to be involved with this. She doesn't want them remembering she exists.'

Yeah. Isabel doesn't blame her.

There's a quick rap on the door.

Daniel switches off the projector and the board goes blank.

Voronov walks over to the door to Laura, who apologises for interrupting but then leans a little closer to murmur to Voronov. Isabel is temporarily amused by the way Voronov has to stoop to be able to catch her words. She knows Laura is doing it for their benefit; the people on the other side of their room who love to keep ears out for what's going on are probably trying their hardest to listen.

The way Voronov looks at her, incredulous, piques her curiosity. Isabel stands. 'Aleks?'

Voronov thanks Laura and shuts the door again. Then he says, 'Ezequiel Venâncio is here to talk to us.'

Ezequiel Venâncio looks as at home in their small interrogation room as he had in his own fado house.

'Boa tarde, Inspectors,' he says, and Isabel gets the distinct impression that they're walking into his domain.

She almost feels amused, but remembering Daniel and Carla's report of what Ximena had been through kills it pretty quickly. 'Mr Venâncio,' she says.

He's dressed a lot more casually today, in a black crewneck jumper and jeans. His hair is caught in a ponytail, leaving his facial scars on full display. A black jacket is folded over the back of his chair and he has one arm hooked over the back of it. He holds a small black lighter in his other hand, which rests on the table, and he's flipping it in his grip, over and over again.

'I heard you stopped by to see me yesterday but saw that I was busy,' he says. 'I wanted to be helpful.'

'Were you being helpful to the officers you were speaking to yesterday?' Isabel asks. She's not in the mood to mince words and any intention she had not to step on any toes had disappeared the second she'd walked into the fado house and seen fellow officers sitting at this man's table.

It doesn't seem to faze him though; he just inclines his head. 'Of course. But since you weren't there for the same reason, I thought I would drop by. I'm assuming you wanted to talk to me in regard to Marta's death.' He puts his lighter away, sits up and rests both his hands on the table. 'It doesn't look good for me if I have police enforcement making repeated visits to my establishment, and I don't need rumours spreading that might have a negative effect on my business. Ask what you need to ask. I really don't want either of you, or your colleagues, to return.'

'All right,' Voronov says and pulls the folder he's brought in with him into view.

Isabel settles back, deepening her breath to prepare herself, allowing herself to reach out. She doesn't try to read him. She just spreads her awareness, ready to receive the slightest shift in emotion, ready to catch any thoughts that might slip the strong barrier he'd displayed with such ease the first time they'd spoken.

Voronov takes out three pictures, blown up to A4 size. Two are images of the murders that had taken place years ago that were suspected of being linked to Venâncio. Isabel can't afford to be distracted here and just the memory of what those pictures show is enough to make her feel ill, so she keeps her eyes up and on Venâncio, whose expression she really wants to see.

Venâncio flicks his gaze over them, face impassive, not so much as a twitch. Isabel gets nothing off him. He lifts his gaze back up to Voronov, his expression clearly asking why he's being shown these.

That is one impressive poker face.

Voronov slides the third one next to the other two.

This time when Venâncio looks, his gaze lingers. There's a split second there, a snap of emotion not unlike what she'd briefly sensed the last time they'd met, when she'd brought up Marta. It's there and gone in the same time that it takes for his eyelashes to sweep down and shield his gaze before he's back to staring drolly at them.

'I'd rather not have seen that. Aren't you supposed to warn people?' he asks.

Voronov makes no move to collect the photos, just flips the folder closed and sets it aside. 'Why? Are you upset?'

'Anyone would find it upsetting.'

'You know there's an ongoing investigation against you. That's not news to you,' Voronov says, 'isn't that why you were paid a visit by them yesterday?' Voronov indicates the first two photos. 'These two pictures are from murders committed three years ago, and your involvement is suspected. But you already know this.'

'Yes.'

'Good, so do me a favour,' Voronov says, 'and look closely. I'm sure if you examine them carefully, you'll see the similarities.'

'No thank you,' Venâncio says and turns to Isabel. 'And what is your role here? Are you trying to read me? And without notifying me of your classification, no less? Isn't that grounds for dismissal?'

Yeah. And Isabel has been there recently enough and would rather not repeat the experience. 'Oh? But I did inform you,' she says, 'at our first meeting. You must not have heard. I apologise.'

'Oh really?' he says.

'Besides,' Isabel says, 'if one of us were to accuse the other of poking around in their head, I'd say the one who should be worried about that is me, wouldn't you say? Considering that's exactly what you attempted to do last time.'

'Did I?' His tone is as insincere as hers. 'If I did, it was done unconsciously.'

Bullshit.

'Ezequiel,' Voronov says, 'I think it would be in your best interest to cooperate with us.'

Venâncio turns back to him. He's still unconcerned. He's also, Isabel notes, very carefully avoiding looking at the photos. 'Why? You know better than this. The PJ has nothing on me, Aleksandr. This is getting tiring, and I want to run my business in peace.'

'Which business exactly? The Houses? Where were you on the evening of the second of February, Ezequiel?'

'At O Vermelho.' The words are clipped, his expression closed off. He's clearly done playing around. 'You can talk to my staff if you like.'

Yeah. After they've been given a heads-up.

'We've heard you have a lot of wealthy friends,' Isabel says.

The change in subject gets her a sidelong glance from him. 'I do. And?'

'How does someone like you make friends in such high places, Mr Venâncio?'

'They're my patrons. They like the services I provide.'

'Services.' Isabel smiles. 'Interesting choice of words. What services *do* you provide? Through the Houses?'

'A comfortable and welcoming place to spend an evening, good food, good drink and fine music. At O Vermelho.'

'And that's all?'

He spreads his hands. 'It's not my only business, no. I do well for myself. I have other business ventures. They're all above board.'

'Right.' Isabel reaches forward and taps Marta's picture. 'I didn't know her. But since we started this investigation, I've come to understand that Marta was an extremely intelligent and resourceful woman, probably with a lot more guts than most people. Was she involved in all of those "above board" business ventures too?'

She pushes Marta's photo until it's on top of the other two.

'You don't have a problem with the other two pictures. Why are you having one with hers?' Isabel asks.

He still doesn't look, but what he does do is gather all three pictures and politely push them back to the centre of the table. 'I dislike seeing women being harmed. It makes me uncomfortable.'

'Hmm.'

'We'll be speaking to your staff,' Voronov says and stands up, 'and this is a waste of time. But something you should keep in mind, Ezequiel.' Voronov tucks the pictures back into the folder. 'I'm not in anyone's pocket. And Chief Costa's people don't know everything that we know.'

Venâncio stands. He takes his time shrugging into his jacket, scooping his hair out from beneath the collar, and tilts his head at Isabel in goodbye. As he passes Voronov, he pats his shoulder. 'You've always been too straight-laced for your own good. Good day, Inspectors. Here's to hoping we don't run into each other again so soon.'

Isabel blows out a breath, frustrated.

Voronov looks at her askance. 'Did you sense anything when we showed him the photos?'

She shakes her head. 'He's good, Aleks,' she says, 'not a thing slipped past his shield. Nothing big enough.'

'But he refused to look at her picture.'

Yeah. Peculiar. 'Not so much as a blink with the other photos,' she murmurs. 'There's a flash of . . .' She mulls it over, frustrated.

She'd caught it again, just like last time, that snippet of a reaction, but it feels abstract in her hands, the shape of it familiar but gone too quickly for her to properly understand it.

They need more, and they need it without revealing their hand.

Alma.

'I didn't want to push her,' Isabel sighs.

'Alma?'

'Yeah.'

'I think you're going to have to.

Isabel sinks back into her chair. 'Yeah. I think so too.'

40

The irony is that Isabel's dad had hated cemeteries.

He'd never been able to explain why. Sebastião had told her that when their grandmother had passed away, their dad had only been there for the church service and then the procession to the cemetery. He hadn't been able to go past the gates for the burial.

With the oncoming of evening, the air has cooled a little. Her steps crunch on the path as she walks along, sunflowers in one hand and a bag containing her dad's favourite brand of cognac in the other, two small glasses tucked alongside it, and a few other things.

Carla had gone to check in on Alma today and they all needed a bit of a longer break from the case. The Chief had kicked them out anyway, so Isabel is a little earlier than she'd planned to be, which is nice. Means she won't have to rush; there's an hour or so until the cemetery gates are due to shut and visitors will have to make their way home.

There aren't that many people. She passes a total of two. Most prefer to come in the morning.

The air smells of flowers. They dot the gravestones, some with their blooms still fresh and bright, lending colour to the graves. A card here. Some balloons there.

It makes her think of Jacinta's dislike of flowers. She says they remind her of funerals. Isabel can kind of see why. They see too many deaths in what they do, even if they're not usually present when their victims are put in the ground. Though with Marta this will be different, for the first time in a long time. She had promised Alma that they would go.

Truth is that Isabel's not a fan of cemeteries herself.

Not because of any kind of superstition or anything like that. But being here always puts her back in that day, the day she'd had to say goodbye to her dad. It's weird, because every year, it's where she spends a slice of her birthday.

Dad's grave, when she reaches it, is clean. Every time Isabel comes here it's like this. She knows her mother comes religiously, washing the headstone, clearing out old flowers, replacing them with new. Rita had mentioned it once to Isabel, how she comes twice a month without fail, even if she's not feeling well.

Isabel doesn't know what to do with that. Can't reconcile that version of her mother, who can love so deeply and feel so much sorrow over the loss of someone so many years on, with the person who can't even be in a room with her own daughter – for doing nothing more than being different from her.

Isabel stops in front of his grave.

Paulo Ernesto Reis.

Just seeing his name causes an ache. She runs her fingers over it, tracing the carvings with the pad of her thumb.

'Sorry it's been a while.' She sets the bouquet of sunflowers down. She knows nothing about the meaning of flowers, what symbolises life or friendship or devotion or whatever. Sunflowers though have always been her favourite, and there's no way she can see them now and not be drawn into them. They're like little suns grown from earth and when she sees them, she feels a softer version of what she'd felt like under her dad's affection.

So, she always brings him sunflowers. She hopes he doesn't mind.

'Another year, hmm?' She pats the headstone and sits.

Quietly, she takes out the cognac and the two glasses and the small figurine of a lion striped in white and green.

'I don't want to jinx it yet,' she says as she tucks it against the headstone, 'but I think they may actually win this year. Don't get your hopes up though.'

She pours a splash of the cognac into one glass and another

splash into the other, and sets it closer to the lion, before curling her fingers around her own glass.

If anyone walks past, she'll probably get a dirty look. But the few people she'd seen didn't look likely to come this way and she doubts anyone new will arrive at this time.

It's quiet, quiet. Refreshingly so. Isabel tips up the collar of her jacket. The temperature has dropped a bit and the back of her neck feels vulnerable.

'Happy birthday to me,' she says and toasts the grave. She sips it and it's smooth up until it hits the back of her throat and has her squeezing her eyes shut against the potency, rubbing her tongue along the roof of her mouth to get rid of it. She actually hates cognac. She's had this bottle for years, had got it as a present from Chief Bautista.

It's the one she always brings with her and only because it's something that he likes.

'I don't know if you know. Mãe probably told you. Rita's getting married.' She laughs as she tilts the glass, watching the way the liquid follows the turn and settles accordingly. She thinks about it for a second. 'I . . . don't think you'd like him' – She laughs – 'okay. Maybe you would have liked him before, but he's been a dick and now he's with Rita.' The brief burst of amusement disappears. She tucks her hair back off her face. 'It's my fault, you know.'

The hardest thing about the situation with Michael is that it hadn't been all him.

She could have tried harder to explain. She could have tried harder to trust that he would understand and help. He's proven enough times that he's there for her. He always helps, always. Has never once said no to her.

But it's like—

It doesn't make her feel looked after or cared for. It makes her feel indebted. And that's on her. She knows that. But it had come across, despite his best intentions. During an argument or a period of distance, his resentment, sitting, rusted over, and growing between the two of them.

'Pai . . .' She sighs, 'you know, I don't love him.' She'd come close, she thinks. Maybe if her Gift hadn't changed – then maybe. Maybe. 'I really wanted something normal though.'

At the centre of it all, though, is the feeling that whatever it is Rita and Michael have between them is too one-sided. Just like it had been for Isabel and Michael. In the long run, it won't work. What Isabel sees is her sister stuck in a marriage that she refuses to leave, because Rita doesn't let go of things she wants and which she believes can make her happy. Even when they don't.

Isabel hopes she's wrong.

She cradles the glass in both hands, hunched over it. 'Pai. I really, really hope you're watching over us.'

She's not sure how much time passes but a while later, she hears footsteps behind her and turns her face away, swiping a thumb under her eye.

The hands on her shoulders don't startle her because she'd felt her brother's emotions clear as day before he'd even got near her.

'Good conversation?' he asks and then settles down next to her, crossing his legs. He's not smiling but she can see the touch of dimples on his cheeks, like he's about to.

She shrugs. 'A little one-sided, but you know.' She finishes her drink, knocking it back and regretting it almost immediately when it makes her face scrunch up like a prune. 'Fogo.' She glares at the glass like it's to blame. 'I'll never know what he liked about this stuff.'

She looks at Sebastião, who is taking in the sunflowers and the little lion. 'Don't get his hopes up, Isa,' he says, 'you know what happens every time we get too excited about winning.'

'You mean when *you* get too excited about winning, I only check the scores now and then for you guys.'

He taps the miniature lion on the head and then reaches for the other glass.

Isabel raises her eyebrows as he knocks it back.

'That wasn't meant for you, you know,' she says, 'and should you be doing that when you're, you know, in uniform?'

'He wouldn't want it going to waste,' he says, 'and besides, I'll repent.'

Isabel chokes out a laugh. 'You're so terrible.'

'You're the only one who says so, everyone else loves me. Come on. Dad's had you long enough.' He stands up and reaches down a hand for her, 'you have people waiting for you.'

She gives him her hand without thinking and lets him pull her to her feet, then watches, bemused, as he packs away the bottle, glasses clinking as he puts everything back in the bag. 'What?'

Wrapping an arm around her shoulders, he leads her back onto the main path.

'You're getting old, maninha, can't let it pass without celebrating.'

Isabel shoves him, laughing again. 'Shut up. Don't want to hear it from you, idiot. Old my arse.'

She lets him guide her away, talking more bullshit as they go.

When they get to her place, she's greeted by her dogs, Tia Simone and then, inside, Voronov, Jacinta, Daniel and Carla, smug as can be, under the cheesiest birthday banner she's ever seen, and she really can't stop laughing then.

It's nice, she thinks as she's ushered in and a birthday hat strapped to her head, it's like sunflowers filling her home.

41

Madalena Nunes cuts a lonely figure where she stands near the priest as he reads over Marta Nunes' coffin. Already small, she seems even smaller today in her simple black dress with its bell sleeves, and flat shoes. Her jacket is folded and held in front of her. Her eyes are forward and Isabel wonders if she's actually seeing anything in front of her or if she's checked out. Isabel wouldn't blame her.

The sun isn't out, like it has been so often in the past few weeks. The sky is thick with clouds, an eerie glow behind them where they refuse to let the light through.

Isabel is surprised to see a fairly good turnout.

She hadn't expected any family other than Madalena to turn up and, looking around, she sees she had been right. But aside from Madalena there are at least twenty people in attendance.

Isabel is wearing a black suit out of respect, as is Voronov, and between the both of them is Alma, in black jeans and a hoodie, hands shoved into the big pocket at the front and her eyes on the ground. They're standing far away from the main group and the hole in the ground, under the trees.

Isabel had explained to Madalena without giving too much detail about who Alma was and Madalena had agreed without hesitation to let her attend.

And in the group surrounding the grave, Isabel spots a few familiar faces. Marta's old boss at the youth centre and other staff members she and Voronov had seen when they'd gone there for the first time.

The priest's voice drones on, laying an added blanket of heaviness on the grief seeping into the ground around them.

It lasts about thirty minutes. Isabel is surprised by how quick it feels, mostly because the only funeral she has ever been to before this is crystalised in her memory and lasts for ever.

It's surreal, seeing this happening and hearing the birds chirping, the sounds acute.

As the service begins to wrap up, Isabel turns to Alma beside her. 'You want me to come with you so you can lay the flowers down?'

They'd stopped at the little shack at the entrance to the cemetery, bursting with blooms and other gifts that loved ones might want to lay at the graves of those they are visiting. Alma had chosen a bunch of white lilies.

'No, it's okay. I can go on my own.' But she waits until anyone she recognises from the youth centre has paid their respects to Madalena and walked away before making her way over to the grave.

Isabel senses the shift in Voronov without even having to turn and look at him. His energy changes. Where it had been a lulling, pacifying calm, it knifes up. 'What is it?' she asks, tensing, ready to go and drag Alma back if she needs to.

The officers assigned to keep an eye on Alma aren't too far away. Stationed outside at the cemetery gates waiting for them. If they had seen anything unusual, they would have let them know.

Isabel catches sight of it then.

Two men, coming from the other direction.

She easily recognises Ezequiel Venâncio and his brother. They're both in sharp black suits. The brother carries a bunch of white flowers that Isabel thinks might be the same as those Alma is holding. Isabel feels every bit of her ramp up and throws her Gift out. Shit. What are they doing here? And what if Ezequiel recognises Alma?

'I'll get her,' Voronov murmurs and strides quickly to Alma.

But Ezequiel and his brother aren't focused on who is standing by the grave. As Isabel watches, they head for Madalena Nunes.

Isabel is too far away to hear what they say, but not so far that her Gift doesn't pick up on the emotions and thoughts whirling around Madalena. Not if she tries hard. And she is. She pushes, feels her Gift thinning to reach out, and is frustrated when she captures only Madalena's grief and confusion as Ezequiel bends his head to speak to her while his brother hangs back.

Isabel stays rooted to the spot during the exchange, which she doesn't think lasts for more than a minute. What she gets is clear. Madalena has no idea who this is, and she's baffled by what he's said. An offer? Her thoughts are too jumbled right now, too much happening at once, and Madalena's just trying to understand who he is and how he knew Marta.

Then Ezequiel is giving Madalena a last bow of his head, taking the flowers from his brother's hand and walking over to the casket, where he places them down with care.

'Isabel,' Voronov says in the tone of someone who has said it more than once.

'What?' She flinches back when he presses something to her nose, before she realises what he's doing.

Merda. She hadn't even realised. She mutters 'thanks' and wipes carefully at the blood that she can feel now, thick and wet, on her upper lip.

'Alma, do you recognise that man?' she asks.

Alma, who had been staring at Isabel, wide-eyed, seems to take a moment to properly process the question before following Isabel's gaze to Ezequiel. She squints. Her eyes are red-rimmed. Isabel doubts she got any sleep the previous night.

'No, I don't.' She looks confused. 'I don't know. I don't remember him.' But she's frowning and she shrinks back, a bit closer to Voronov. 'But there's something . . . I don't know. Isabel, there's something familiar I can—' She licks her lips and her eyes flit over to Voronov, unsure, before forging on: 'I can sense it.'

Yeah. They need to get her out of here.

'Aleks,' Isabel murmurs, 'we should head back.'

Except, of course, that's when Ezequiel notices the three of them standing there.

'Take her back to the car,' Isabel says. She needs Ezequiel not to focus on Alma. 'I'll be right there.'

'Isabel,' Voronov says, tone sharp.

Isabel gives him a tight smile. 'Wait for me there. I'll be fine.' She wipes at her nose again and hopes there's no traces of blood left, then folds the handkerchief and stuffs it into her pocket. Trust Voronov to carry an honest-to-God handkerchief with him.

Ezequiel waits patiently for her to join him.

A quick assessment lets Isabel see that his brother has stayed put, standing on the outskirts of the dwindling ceremony, apparently happy to wait for his brother.

'I'm surprised to see you here,' Isabel says.

Surprisingly, he smiles. 'The PJ stakes out funerals now, does it?'

Isabel resists the urge to check that Voronov and Alma are out of sight.

'Aleksandr didn't want to greet me?'

Isabel tilts her head. 'Were you under the impression that Aleks likes you or something?'

'Not at all.'

Isabel drops the chit-chat. 'What are you doing here?'

'She was my employee, Inspector, and I'm not a monster.'

Debatable. Maybe they just have different definitions of a monster. 'You came to, what, pay your respects? For someone you haven't seen in over three years?'

'Not unusual.'

'This isn't a usual circumstance.'

Ezequiel tilts his head up, peering up at the sky. 'It'll start raining soon, Inspector. I should head back.' With that he bids her a good day with a nod of his head and walks back over to his brother, though he stops once again to say something to Madalena before walking off.

Isabel watches him go and then is about to turn to head off herself when she hears Madalena call out for her.

'Inspector Reis,' she says, 'I saw that man talking to you. Who is he?'

Isabel looks at the direction in which Ezequiel disappeared. 'From what we've gathered he used to be Marta's old employer, before she worked at the youth centre. He told me he came to pay his respects.'

Madalena runs a hand over her face. There's a small tremble to it. 'Right. He said something like that but . . . my head's just . . . I haven't really been processing things properly.'

Isabel waits, sees Madalena's thoughts lining up, like a trail of crumbs leading to what she wants to say next.

'But it's still weird.'

'What is?'

'He offered to pay for all the funeral costs.'

Isabel blinks. He what? 'Did he say why?'

Madalena lifts her shoulders helplessly. 'No. And it's not like I can accept it, anyway, just told him thank you but there was no need. But if he was just an old employer then why go that far? Do you know if they were still in touch?'

Yeah. That's the question Isabel would like an answer to herself.

'No. I'm sorry, Madalena. Did he say anything else?'

Madalena dips her head and reaches into the pocket of the jacket she's been carrying all throughout the ceremony. She pulls out a black business card. The gleaming red lettering on it is familiar.

'He gave me this and told me to call him if I ever needed help. I just – I don't even know him.'

There's nothing Isabel can say.

She's as confused by the whole thing as Madalena is.

42

Alma is withdrawn as they drive back.

Isabel's sitting in the back with her, and she's turned completely away. In the reflection of the passenger window, Isabel can see her eyes are closed, though she's definitely not sleeping.

As if the sky itself was also under Ezequiel's command, soft rain had begun spitting down as they'd driven away from the cemetery, dotting the windscreen and windows, and it had stayed that way.

Alma had been waiting in the car when Isabel had caught up with them again. She'd agreed to return to the secure accommodation but had asked if they could take her instead. Isabel had acquiesced.

Isabel feels claustrophobic in the back of the car. She's in such close proximity to Alma and whatever inbuilt protection the girl has for her Gift, it's in pieces at her feet, not a thing in place to protect her thoughts or her emotions. Isabel is stunned that everything pouring off her isn't manifesting in a physical way. No tears, no shaking, nothing. She's so still.

In the rear-view mirror, Isabel glimpses Voronov's blue eyes as they flick up to check on them.

'Do we have to go straight back?'

Isabel turns to Alma. She's still facing the window but now Isabel can see she's opened her eyes and is staring out. 'Why?' Isabel asks, keeping her voice light. 'Do you have somewhere you need to be?'

Alma lets her head drop, her forehead thumping against the window. 'No. I just . . .'

'Maybe we need a little distraction.' Isabel meets Voronov's eyes in the mirror again, posing a question of her own, and catches his slight nod.

'All right. Inspector Voronov,' she says, and wonders what the hell she's doing playing babysitter, but she can't not, not when Alma looks ready to curl into herself and never lift her head up again, 'are you good with us making a quick stop?'

After the impromptu stop at Isabel's house, they head to Ribeira das Naus and walk along the steps, Tigre and Branco running around and chasing the lapping water and Alma and Isabel walking side by side.

The rain hasn't let up but, like them, some people are undeterred, still walking alongside the water and stopping to soak up the stunning view.

Voronov has opted to stay a little behind them, keeping an eye out just in case.

Even Isabel feels the heavier emotions draining from her as she's surrounded by the smell of the water. She doesn't even mind the soft, soft rain that settles deceptively light on her shoulders and hair. They'll all be completely soaked by the time they head back. Tigre and Branco, naturally, don't care. They love this spot and do the same thing every time Isabel brings them on her runs. She always makes sure to stop here, slow to a stroll even when it's pitch black out and the streetlights barely reach far enough to illuminate the water.

Being here always brings with it a sense of calm.

'I wish I hadn't seen her,' Alma says. 'I always read that when someone is put in a casket it looks like they're sleeping. Maybe seeing Marta that way would have helped.'

Isabel encourages her to go on with a hum, eyes tracking her two dogs all the time, their presence a balm for the bruised colours wrapped tight around Alma.

'She didn't look like that,' Alma says, 'she looked wrong. It just looked – so wrong. There was nothing in her.' She stops and turns to face Isabel, hand reaching out to stay her. 'You know what I mean, don't you?'

Isabel lets loose a quick whistle to get her dogs to stop and pay attention. When they see that she's stopped they start running back, darting in and out of the waves as they do.

Isabel folds her arms. 'Yes. I know what you mean.'

Alma's breathing starts hitching.

Behind her, Isabel can see that Voronov has stopped too, and he must understand what's about to happen because he climbs up the wide steps and then sits down, calm as anything, and stares out at the river. He doesn't even blink when Tigre and Branco run up to him, shaking the water off and no doubt getting it all over him.

'Like—' Alma's breathing gets shallower, 'I'm alone. She's really gone. They killed her. And I've got no one.' She starts whispering. 'What am I going to do? I don't know what I'm going to do. We were going to look after each other. She promised. She said w-w—'

Isabel hates not having words, not being able to have at hand what she knows will alleviate this type of pain. No one has that. And she can't bring herself to utter little lies, promising everything will be okay. More than not having the right words, she hates making promises she can't keep.

All she can do is weather it, and wait as Alma struggles for control, rain gathering on her face and mixing with tears until it runs in rivulets down her cheek. Two girls run past them, squealing, jackets over their heads. Alma turns away from them and wipes roughly at her face.

'Is it the same for you?' she asks. Her voice comes out hoarse. 'You said you didn't meet my dad, but that you knew. Is it the same for you?' When she turns back, she looks over Isabel's shoulder. 'Your partner. He's not one of us. But he doesn't seem to hate you.'

'That's because he doesn't,' Isabel says. She thinks carefully about it and then steps closer to Alma. 'In a way, yes, it's the same for me.' She thinks of her mum. 'But there are people, like him,' she nods her head in Voronov's direction, 'and the rest of my team, and my boss. I still have people. Someone very close to me didn't – still doesn't – want me. But I have people.'

She takes Alma's shoulders gently in her hands. 'You have people too. Your friend Mario, who misses you. And I'm here, aren't I?' she says. 'And Voronov. And Carla. We're here. It doesn't seem like it right now, but it's a start, okay?'

Alma doesn't say anything, just wipes at her face again.

'Come on. We'll all get sick if we stay here in the rain. And you're going to help me dry my dogs too, don't want my house stinking of wet dog.' Isabel lets go and steps away.

Alma's fingers are wet and chilled, but the strength in her grip as she grabs Isabel's hand is surprising. Isabel notices Voronov rising up out of his seat fast and the dogs barking even as she turns.

'What—'

She's going to throw up. She feels it in the back of her throat, bitter and spreading. She's surprised at how strong Alma is. The memory is distorted as it's pushed into Isabel's mind's eye.

Fingers squeezing her wrists tight, forcing her hands – Alma's hands – to seal her palms to someone's temple. Crying, crying, the heaviness a near-physical thing, the pressure spanning the space between her shoulder blades and her chest. The hands holding onto her wrists are large, a man's hands. It hurts. It feels like those hands will grind her wrists to nothing, the ring on his finger digging into bone.

There are words. Someone is talking to her, telling Alma what to do, but all she can focus on are her trapped hands touching the sleeping man's face. The voice – the person talking to her is forcing her to do this. He's telling her to concentrate.

Isabel shakes off the surprise of having the memory forced on her and takes control. Really trying to see through Alma's eyes and to understand what's happening.

Everything around her feels unsteady and the room is dark. Isabel pushes through the nausea and tries to focus, but it's tough. The Alma in the memory is too distraught and it's affecting her senses. It's the kind of dark that makes Isabel think of spas or massage parlours. The room shadowed, but with a soft glow of light. There's a window to the side – blue, the sky? – it's in her peripheral vision but Alma doesn't look that way, doesn't notice it, too busy trying to peel her hands away even as the person is telling her to calm down and focus, to do as she's told. There's a rushing sound, beneath the voice that is too distorted by Alma's rejection of it, a rushing sound she can't pin down. And on the back of her neck is a sore pain, like the aftermath of a minor burn, her skin feeling stretched and oversensitive, but it's buried under the layers and layers of dazed panic.

Then it all cuts off.

Isabel stumbles before she catches herself. Her face is completely wet, rain dripping from her chin. She feels scratches on her legs and when she glances down Tigre and Branco are attempting to jump up at her and whining, distressed sounds, thin and pitiful.

'It's okay, I'm okay,' she says, dazed, and reaches a hand down to them, still a bit unsteady, petting them.

When she looks up, Voronov is standing there, kneeling next to a sobbing Alma.

As she watches Alma break down, Isabel almost wishes she hadn't seen.

43

THEN

The candyfloss disappears on Isabel's tongue, leaving only the taste of sweetness and the after-impression of a shrinking sticky mouthful. She goes right back for another bite though.

Around her, the funfair is glittering with lights and happy screams from the rides spinning the fair-goers in the air, friends running to queue up and children begging their parents for more coins for the games dotted around, huge teddy bears and giant lions on display.

She's waiting with Sebastião in front of the bumper cars. She can see her dad, hunched into the small car seat, Rita at his side, head back and laughing so hard. Her small hands cling to the sides as their dad drives the car around the floor, swerving and then coming to abrupt stops as other cars ride up against it.

Sebastião has already finished his candyfloss and is watching their dad and Rita too, smiling a bit and laughing every time they get hit.

The Feira Popular in Lisbon is packed even though it's a weekday, families crowding into the eateries dotting the amusement park and piling onto the rides.

Normally they wouldn't be here either, but Dad had finished his shift early.

When he'd got home, he'd seemed tired but happy to be back; but then things changed when he asked Isabel how her session with Rosario had gone and Isabel had admitted she hadn't gone. Her mother hadn't wanted to take her. She hadn't said that part.

She hadn't had to.

Her dad had patted her on the head and walked through the house, his gait changing, his emotions shifting from honey-clear and mellow to something acidic, and Isabel had snuck off to call Sebastião. *They're going to argue about me again.*

Isabel had quickly learned that after an argument, things went a lot better if her mother didn't see her. It upset her dad when she did it, but every time the argument started, she would call Sebastião and he would come and get her. Sometimes Rita would go with them, sometimes Rita wanted to stay with Mum because she was crying.

Today, after her mother's yells had stopped and the house had fallen silent, her dad had found her sitting on the front steps of the house.

He'd sighed when he'd seen her, then lowered himself to sit beside her with a groan. Rita had hurried out and squeezed herself onto his other side.

Outside, the neighbour's twins were playing football in front of their house, arguing every now and then when the ball bounced off a car. Isabel's dad told them to be careful and they quickly picked up their ball and rushed off.

Wrapping an arm each around Isabel and Rita, he'd tugged them a bit closer to him. He was smiling at them but there was something wrong with it, like he had to force it.

'Is your brother on his way?'

Isabel had nodded.

'All right. Well, since I don't have to go back to work, when Sebastião gets here, we'll go eat out. How about that?'

'We have school tomorrow,' Isabel had said, staring down at her hands. She couldn't tell her dad how sad he felt and how that was making her want to cry.

'I know.' Her dad kissed her head and then did the same to Rita. 'Don't worry about that. It's just for today.'

Now, as she watches her dad smiling for real and listens to Rita giggling like crazy, she feels happier and she's glad that they've come here.

Sebastião glances down at her as she finishes her candyfloss. 'You've been quiet, maninha.'

Isabel rubs her fingers on the napkin the lady had given her earlier, frowns when the lingering stickiness of the candyfloss makes it stick to her skin.

'Isabel?' Sebastião nudges her and although he's tall, he's also skinny and the point of his elbow against her shoulder hurts a bit. She nudges him back a lot harder and glares at him.

She huffs and turns back to look at their dad and sister.

'Do you think Tia Simone would let me live with you and her?' She blinks her eyes, doesn't want to rub them. Doesn't want Sebastião to see that she's almost crying. It's not because he'll make fun of her, because he never does. He always gives her a hug and stays with her until she stops, even when he has to go to his part-time job and staying will make him late, even when he has to finish his homework or he'll get in trouble.

'Why did they argue this time?' he finally asks.

'Mum didn't take me to see Rosario today.'

Sebastião spits out a word he would never say in front of Dad or Tia Simone. 'Why?'

Isabel picks at the napkin, tearing it into little strips. 'She said it won't change anything.'

'Isa, Tia Maria is just stressed out, she doesn't know what she's saying—'

Isabel rubs angrily at her eyes. 'I'm not dumb. She doesn't want me any more.'

When Sebastião doesn't say anything, it takes Isabel a moment to realise that there's someone standing in front of them.

She looks up.

Rita is staring at her, confused. Her dad is looking at Isabel too and all of that sadness that Isabel had felt from him earlier is on his face as well now.

Isabel hadn't realised they'd finished in the bumper cars and hadn't noticed them making their way back over to them.

Ashamed and scared of what her dad will say, she doesn't say anything else.

Then, her dad gives Sebastião's head an affectionate rub and holds out a hand to Isabel. 'Come on, we need some dinner.'

Tentatively, Isabel takes his hand and when her dad gives hers a reassuring squeeze, drops her eyes to the floor. Sebastião takes Isabel's other hand and they set off in silence, listening to the loud music from the rides and the conversations all around them as they go to find a place to eat.

44

'She's doing okay, has started talking to her friend Mario again,' Carla says, 'still quiet but looking better.'

After their visit to Ribeira das Naus, Alma had fallen ill. The doctor had said it was a mixture of exhaustion and stress that, coupled with being soaked to the bone, had culminated in fatigue and a low-grade fever for a day or two. Both Carla and Isabel had been by to check in on her. Alma clearly feels more comfortable around the two of them. Whether it's because they are women or because they are Gifted, Isabel hasn't been able to tell.

Isabel blows out a breath and takes the hot mug of coffee Daniel passes over to her. 'Thanks.'

Alma isn't the only one who had felt a bit off after that day. The memory left Isabel chilled. She tries not to go near it. 'What time are they coming?' she asks.

With Lydia Tavares' information, Ezequiel Venâncio's appearance at the funeral and what Isabel has seen in Alma's memory, as much as they would prefer to get to the bottom of this without the OF, they need them.

There are three names on Marta's list that have not been accounted for. Isabel needs to know if they are three more dead women. Or if they're trapped. Like Alma had been. Like the woman from Castelo Branco had been. They need to find them.

Their whole team had sat down with Chief Bautista and gone over what they had. She'd been surprised when they'd asked her to try again with Chief Costa's team. They have no information on Venâncio's assets. If the OF could just share their intel on monitored properties, accounts – anywhere they could look for evidence of some kind of movement – then maybe they'd find out what had happened to the missing Gifted.

None of them were happy about it, including Jacinta, who is finally back with them full-time. She still looks a little tired, but alert and ready to go.

None of them had been happy but everyone had been in agreement: if this thing is to move forward, they need what the OF have. So, they'd baited them by offering access to the voice recordings they'd secured from Marta's laptop.

That had been hours of listening. Even after splitting them apart.

It had confirmed their suspicions.

Whatever role Marta had played in Ezequiel's organisation, it had been a significant one. He'd used her to steal into memories of people in various positions of power, in politics, yes, but not only politics. It seems Ezequiel had found someone from every corner and got Marta to peer into all of them and extract what she could. It had taken them a while to realise that not all the recordings were of different people. Though the dates in the titles of the individual recordings always changed, the letters didn't. This lent weight to the theory that they were people's initials and information had been extracted over several sessions.

It's unlikely, though, that the people Venâncio had targeted would put themselves in a vulnerable position willingly, certainly not multiple times.

That's where their theory comes in.

The witness in Castelo Branco had referred to the Houses as the First House and the Third House, catering to different things. The First House, where Marta had been based, was a slightly lesser evil. Any 'client' who got caught there at any point could still talk their way out of it. But anyone caught in the Third House . . . well. There's no getting out of sexually abusing someone. Not even if that person happened to be Gifted. That would be enough blackmail material. No need for any other recordings.

That brings them to the Second House. The recordings. That's where Venâncio fills his treasure trove of insider information. Based on what Isabel had witnessed in Alma's memory after Marta's funeral, she thinks that that's where those happened. That's where Alma was that day. They get the Gifted to put their targets under and then comb through their minds for the information they're looking for.

Yes. Isabel is sure this is how Venâncio has stayed at the top for so long.

O Vermelho is the lure, where he networks, how he identifies who has something worth taking. From there, she thinks he allocates them to whichever House will be most lucrative in the long run. Politicians, prosecutors . . . law enforcement – he gains an advantage if he gets them to the Second or Third House. Then for people with less authority but with money to waste, it would be an easy thing for him to get them hooked on the First House. And who's to say he doesn't extract information from clients there too? After these customers are put into a state of euphoria would they even know what was happening around them? Who was coming in and out of a room? Would they really notice if the person tending to them changed from pushing manufactured emotions into them to browsing their head for incriminating information buried in their memories?

A perfect trifecta that guarantees him protection from the law and keeps money feeding into his business.

The amount of dirt he holds on the highest people in Lisbon right now must be insane.

The key thing here is finding out the location of the three Houses, getting the remainder of those Gifted out safely, and then using all the information that Marta had been in possession of to nail him for her murder.

Marta was the only one outside of his control. The only one who could incriminate him sufficiently if she'd just found the right people in the PJ to talk to.

'They should be here soon,' Carla says, checking her watch.

'I bet after the Chief's call they were drooling,' Jacinta says. 'I really hope they have something of note. If we're giving them all of this' – she gestures at the information they have up about the case in general – 'and they're useless . . . well. It's not like we can do anything about it, but the Chief will definitely rip them a new one.'

'We're not giving them everything,' Isabel says, 'we're not giving them Alma. I don't trust them not to fuck us over as far as she's concerned.' They've managed to keep Alma's presence hushed up. The guys on her watch are the same two groups, night and day, and are always on standby. Sure, they're bored as fuck, but they've been doing as they're told.

'It's a shame,' Jacinta says, going through the printed version of Marta's notes. 'If she had just given us a little more detail.'

'Like a map to the Houses,' Isabel mutters into her coffee. 'I do wonder why she didn't. She was already doing the unthinkable. Just the recordings being found would've probably been considered reason enough to have her disappear.'

The truth is more likely to be that Marta had honestly never planned on sharing this with anyone. When she'd been on the inside, she'd probably kept her head down, done what was asked and not drawn too much attention to herself. Then after that, not having Seta's backing any more, it would have been too risky for her to keep trying to help.

Isabel wonders how she'd even got those girls out. There are a lot of names not crossed out in the first timeline – those who Marta had got out. She'd probably helped each Gifted as the opportunity arose, one by one, choosing those who she could trust wouldn't point the finger at her. Even if Marta had come across a miracle situation where she could have let them go all at once, she wouldn't have taken it. It would've been like signing her own death warrant.

Turns out that, somehow, Marta had managed to do that anyway.

Isabel closes her eyes and rubs at them, pausing when she feels it – like the current of air that slips inside as a front door opens.

And as always, that sensation of feeling watched settles. That sensation that makes her feel hunted.

She keeps her eyes closed a moment longer, forcing down the instinct to turn around and check behind her because she knows there's nothing there.

'Isabel?'

'Yeah,' she snaps her eyes back open, shaking it off, 'let's get prepped then.'

Mauricio and Fonseca, the two OF officers who they had dealt with before, look as happy to be in a room with them again as Isabel is to be in a room with *them*.

It's like a line has been drawn down the middle of their case room, with OF on one side and Isabel's team on the other.

Chief Costa hasn't joined them, which is probably a relief for everyone involved.

The rain that had started up the day of Marta's funeral has persisted. It pitter-patters on the windows and Isabel thinks how soothing the sound would have been if she were on her sofa under some blankets with her dogs at her feet.

She needs a break.

Mauricio, the shorter one, starts them off. 'First things first,' he says, and Isabel hadn't noticed it during the first meeting because he hadn't spoken, but his accent is Alentejano. It's softer though, rounded out probably by a chunk of lifetime spent in Lisbon. 'Your Chief gave ours a licking over us being at O Vermelho that night. And something has been misunderstood.'

'What was misunderstood?' Voronov asks.

'It was a routine meeting. Look, the fadista knows we keep an eye on him, all right? It pays to be friendly.'

'Yes,' Isabel says, 'and that's fine, but it depends on *how* friendly and how much it pays. Has the same ring to it as *bribery*, doesn't it?'

The scar that cuts into Fonseca's upper lip gives the impression of a permanent sneer on his face. Or maybe he really just does have a permanent sneer on his face. 'Yeah, we know what you're thinking but we don't turn our backs on our own.' And the look he sends Voronov's way surprises no one.

'Show some respect,' Isabel snaps. 'You're here because you need the information we have and unfortunately for us, we need your intel to try and solve this murder. If you make one more reference to Inspector Voronov's past testimony against a *criminal*, I *will* be filing a complaint against you *and* your bloody Chief for obstruction.'

Immediately Fonseca makes to open his mouth, puffing up in the most ridiculous way, and Isabel is really willing him to give her an excuse right now because she hates these kinds of people. She doesn't have to say anything more though; Mauricio throws out a hand to keep his partner in place.

Seconds tick by as the tension lingers. Then Isabel works her shoulders and does her best to shake it off. 'You got the recording that we sent you?' she asks.

They'd sent them only one, for now. They'd promised access to the rest if OF agreed to the exchange of information.

'Yes,' Mauricio says, 'to be honest, it's the sort of thing we've been trying to get our hands on for years.' He sighs and, all of a sudden, the exhaustion shows on his face. It's not something Isabel envies. She's been on cases that are never-ending before, cases where they get nowhere; eventually, although they're still open, they have to be shelved until a new piece of evidence turns up or someone decides to come forward. Not every case she gets ends up solved. It's one of the most frustrating things about her job and sometimes, especially when she's being forced to accept that there are no more ways to move forward, she goes home and it eats at her and all she can do is try to run it off, hang out with her tia and her brother and distract herself from the sense of failure.

This operation has been ongoing for more than six years. Imagine being onto someone for that long, being certain that they are to blame for the crimes you're investigating but never having enough to corroborate your theory?

Still. It's not an excuse to be dicks about it.

Mauricio gestures at Fonseca and Fonseca stands up and pulls a handful of files out of the backpack he'd come in with and hands them out.

'We'll take you through everything, so bear with us,' Mauricio says, 'this might take a while though.'

The file they've prepared for them is extensive and, true to their word, they take them through every single piece of information. It's a lot to unpack.

The OF task force started six years ago, originally with a team of seven. This has now dwindled to a team of four: Fonseca, Mauricio and two others, who work surveillance.

Ezequiel Venâncio and his younger brother Tiago 'Tito' Venâncio had a more tragic beginning than some. Born in Lisbon, they were aged nine and four respectively when they lost their parents in a house fire. Tiago comes out of the fire with minor smoke inhalation; Ezequiel is in the house for longer and has severe burns and is hospitalised. They are then taken in by their aunt on their mother's side, a widow with no children of her own, and inherit her estate. Ezequiel Venâncio tests as a low-level Gifted – Isabel carefully keeps her face expressionless as she sees his classification in print – and his brother tests as Regular. There is a history of Gifted individuals running through their father's line, none on their mother's side. From then on, they lead a pretty simple life, nothing that raises any eyebrows. They go to university, earn their degree and eventually open up O Vermelho.

The Operation Fado team is put together three years after O Vermelho is opened by Ezequiel Venâncio. Informants drew attention to Ezequiel Venâncio with talk of two established Houses, where apparently clients with a lot of money were being catered to by Gifted women. They suspected human trafficking and forced prostitution. They began monitoring and trying to find dirt on Ezequiel but were never able to pin anything on him, especially as the first body turns up one year after the OF is established, followed by the second two years later. The first was one of the early informants on the case.

The escaped girl – Isabel remembers Voronov telling her about this – came in during the third year of the investigation. She refused to testify and left the country.

They have been searching for the Houses for some time but have never been able to pin down the locations and suspect that they are moved periodically so as to avoid detection.

At the top you have Ezequiel Venâncio, next you have his brother Tiago Venâncio and right behind them is Marta Nunes. She was there from the start of the investigation and handled most of the client-facing work. According to their investigation, their surveillance shows that she wasn't just someone who took bookings and managed things over at O Vermelho. She did work on bookings, yes. But not in relation to the fado singers.

She was also seen going in and out of Ezequiel's residence with his brother Tiago on multiple occasions, sometimes with the clients.

They'd wire-tapped Marta's home at the time, as well as O Vermelho. They also kept a close eye on O Vermelho's wealthier patrons, tracking them and their activities. They'd noticed a correlation between the type of clients and the spread of Ezequiel's influence in certain markets. In the last year before Marta stepped back, Ezequiel bought a significant amount of land on the outskirts of Lisbon – a chunk of which had been protected land. How he got permits has a lot to do with one of the names of the suspected clients on the OF's list.

He'd amassed a lot of influence in a very short period of time. His rise seemed to coincide with the number of big names being spotted in O Vermelho.

'The content of the recordings,' Mauricio continues, reaching to pour himself some water, 'explains a large chunk of his quick rise in society and how he began to gain power.' He shakes his head. 'I think this will only be confirmed the more of the recordings we listen to but, just by looking at the initials for each one, it's easy to link them up to people on our watch list.'

So they *were* initials.

'And what then?' Isabel says.

Mauricio blows out a breath. 'Well. It would have been easier for us if Marta were still alive, but the recordings will be a nice touch, might finally get us the warrant we need to get inside O Vermelho.'

'You've never managed one before?'

Mauricio shakes his head. 'We always get shut down.'

'Connections?' Voronov asks. 'You think he has someone in on it at the force?'

Mauricio sends him a sharp look. 'We take care with those kinds of accusations.'

An interesting way to say that yes, they suspect they do but won't call them out because they'll probably get their arses handed to them if they do.

If they have enough evidence of a mole within the force, they can always hand it over to Internal Affairs – but then again, everyone will know who exactly it was that did so. No matter what, Mauricio and Fonseca and Chief Costa will have their names attached to that. And considering the way they're still speaking to Voronov, it's clear what they think of people who turn on their colleagues.

One could say they're loyal, yes. But like Voronov, Isabel just thinks their priorities are messed up and the force would be better off without them.

'Speaking to that witness of yours would help.'

'No,' Isabel flips the file closed, 'I've told you that's not going to happen. I've already relayed to you what our witness knows, and you are well known as being associated with Operation Fado by Ezequiel. Having you accidentally leak our witness's whereabouts or even that they exist is not something we're willing to risk. We've given you plenty.' She rests her arms on top of the file. 'What we need from you now is for you to give us information going back at least two weeks to the second of February and in the week directly following, and any intel you have surrounding Ezequiel during the summer of last year.'

'There hasn't been any.'

Next to her, Voronov shifts. 'That's not what we've heard,' he says.

Fonseca draws himself up. 'Really? Stop talking shit, Voronov. You have no idea about this investigation.'

Voronov remains as he is, sitting back in his chair, hands tucked into his pockets and watching them both calmly. 'Two days ago, an informant reported to me that Venâncio has been on edge. There are rumours that someone close to him has double-crossed him. They're saying he's putting distance between himself and everyone else. They're even talking about a power struggle.'

Isabel waits to see their reactions.

'As you can see, we're not a bunch of fucking idiots,' she says. 'We have a murder on our hands, and we have three women on our list still unlocated. Isn't it funny that Marta Nunes, someone who was actually participating in whatever Ezequiel's scheme is, did more to rescue his victims than the entire OF team has?' She tilts her head. 'And ended up dead for her trouble. That sits right with you, yes?'

'Our witness was taken the summer of last year. We think this is what might have set off the chain of events for our murder victim,' Voronov says. 'So, what do you know?'

Mauricio and Fonseca look at each other, Fonseca's scarred lip twitching up into that snarl as he obviously struggles to keep his temper down. It's not working very well. Isabel can feel it free-flowing like lava into the room.

Someone clearly doesn't like to be wrong or get called out on their bullshit.

'All right. But it's not much, might as well be nothing,' Mauricio says. 'Yes, there was a new burst of activity around O Vermelho that time in the summer, similar to the renewed activity on the fourth. The problem is, whatever was taking place was off our radar. We only picked up on it because we have ears out on the Chiado for anything that seems unusual. There was nothing on the phones, nothing with their listed associates. They were saying the Houses were operating again but we didn't find any evidence of it. Now, Marta had left by this time, so there was a possibility that they had started operating differently or brought in someone else to handle the Gifted aspect. But we were never able to find out who. Whatever they were doing, they were keeping it well underground.'

'What about the Houses themselves?' Isabel asks.

'We've gone through all their listed property records and checked out each one. Nothing found.'

Isabel sighs, frustrated. 'Well. Maybe now is the time to dig a little deeper.'

45

Old man Dias' café is packed, everyone and their grandfather out to enjoy the nice evening warmth that has settled in the few hours since the rain finally stopped coming down.

The five of them have squeezed round a table outside. Isabel almost begged off and went home when she saw how busy it was, but then she remembered Rosario's advice. She can't afford to be scared of her own Gift. Accept it and face it head on. That's what she needs to do.

So, she's here, between Jacinta and Daniel, Voronov and Carla completing the circle of chairs they've pulled up around the little round aluminium table. Other café customers sit at their own tables, most people just with a cake or small plates of petiscos.

Isabel has a small bowl of moelas in front of her and is dipping the fresh bread to soak it in the sauce and then popping a moela on top with a fork before taking a bite and letting its flavour burst into her mouth. She's been snacking all day and hasn't had proper food since that morning, despite Voronov sneaking her yoghurt drinks and God knows what else. It's like he's her dealer sometimes.

Not that she's complaining. She never says no to food.

Carla has followed suit with the moelas but everyone else is working their way through a plate of olives and pasteis de bacalhau. Voronov is settled back and at ease with his bica and Daniel and Jacinta are drinking from sweating bottles of beer.

'You guys think we'll find anything?' Jacinta asks.

They'd split from Fonseca and Mauricio with a little more civility than Isabel had expected, with the aim of renewing efforts at locating the Houses.

'They've been doing this a very long time,' Voronov says, 'and if it weren't for Marta, we wouldn't have found what we did. It'll be hard turning up new connections.'

It's a hard pill to swallow but Voronov isn't wrong.

'Still,' Isabel swallows, then spears another moela with her fork, 'Venâncio has gone to a lot of trouble to get control of a lot of people in power. The Houses would only be where he can control the situation. It has to be on land he owns, or anything else that he owns.'

'Or one of his clients?'

Isabel doesn't think so. 'That brings a third party into it, more chance of something going wrong.'

'Yes,' Voronov says, 'he's not the type of man to leave something like that to chance.'

Hmm.

They put a self-imposed ban on talking about the case for the remainder of their meal and Jacinta instead tells them about the aftermath of the pile-up. Isabel listens as Jacinta works through it, reminding herself that this is a completely different incident, not related to what happened to her dad. Besides, as Jacinta's colleague – friend – the least she can do is listen. Sometimes that's all someone needs to get through a night with fewer nightmares.

Isabel finishes her food and sits back, arms wrapped around herself, says yes to a carioca de limão. When old man Dias' daughter stops by to ask if anyone wants anything else, she does as Rosario suggested, lets her mind relax. She doesn't lower her wards, keeps them as high as she can; but she has to start small right? If she can at least learn to relax in mildly crowded places, then it's a start.

She settles and watches and listens and lets herself be as her team talk around her, and notices when she feels a collective sense of easing at their table. She hadn't realised how tightly wound they had all been, not truly, until she'd allowed herself to ease off herself.

Eventually they all get up, chairs scraping over the rough ground as they head inside to pay. There's a tilt then, an adjustment she makes, recalibrating as she steps into the interior of the café, where it's packed. The volume in her head ticks up but she keeps it at bay as they banter with old man Dias a bit and then bid him goodnight and head back outside.

Isabel gets in her car, tired, and starts that short drive to her place, for a moment thinking that it would've been nice to walk it.

She's on the road, paused at a traffic light, one hand on the wheel and the other out the car window, letting the night air in. The radio is low in the background, and she listens absently to the evening's news report. She's about five minutes from her house when her phone starts going off and she glances over, expecting to see Sebastião's name on the screen. But when she recognises the number as belonging to the team watching over Alma, her heart slams up into her throat.

Jerking her head up, she scans the road and then, gritting her teeth, she quickly manoeuvres her car off to the side. It sends her phone flying into the footwell and sets off a chain of swerving, honking and swearing.

She unhooks her seat belt, swearing as she stretches, hand scrabbling at the bottom of the footwell, until her fingers close around the still-vibrating phone and she answers.

'Reis here, what is it?'

Rasping breaths fill the line and Isabel feels herself ice over. 'Inspector Reis, you need to get over to the safe house. We were attacked.'

'Where's Alma?' she demands, even as she shoves herself back upright. She drags the seatbelt back over her chest so fast she feels the friction burn of it through her clothes.

'I have her. We called an ambulance. It doesn't look good.'

46

The ambulance is there when Isabel skids to a stop in front of the house.

Only one of the inspectors is visible: Felipe. He's sitting on the front step where Isabel had sat with Alma herself not that long ago, a paramedic hovering over him. She looks over at the car he and his partner had been using and her gut turns over as she sees the shattered windscreen and dented bonnet. Then she zeroes in on the hole.

She threads through the medical personnel littering the scene. The entire house is lit up by the ambulance's flashing lights. Neighbours are at their windows, peering out from behind their curtains; others, not as subtle, have come out to stand on the street to see what's happening.

Isabel has to flash her ID at them so she can get to the officer on the front step. The door is wide open behind him, and she can hear the people inside. One of Felipe's trouser legs has been cut off at the knee and his leg is in an emergency splint. His face has a yellow cast to it. He cuts off from the argument he'd been having with the paramedic.

'What happened?' she asks.

'Crashed into us. We were parked, just settling into our shift. Came out of nowhere. Then he fired two shots. Hit Sansão, the other one got me in the arm. I was knocked out. Woke up and came into the house. The girl . . . the girl was on the floor and bleeding out. Called the ambulance, called the precinct and called you.'

Fuck. *Fuck.*

'Did you see who?'

Felipe starts to shake his head but freezes, face twisting up in pain. 'No, sorry, Inspector.'

'Inspector,' the paramedic standing over Felipe says, 'we need to get him to a hospital. The leg is bad, and I'm concerned about the impact on his neck and shoulder wound. He was refusing to cooperate until someone else got here.'

Isabel stands and drags her hands through her hair, stares at the window. 'Of course,' she says, 'take him. Don't worry Felipe, I'll take it from here. What's the status on his partner?' she asks.

The paramedic starts to help Felipe up and when they glance back up, his expression is grim. 'Critical, but stabilised.'

'And the girl?' she asks.

'They're trying to stabilise her so she can be transferred to the hospital, but it's not looking good, Inspector.'

Isabel bites into her lower lip and gives a sharp nod.

She hears another car pulling in and a glance over her shoulder shows Carla and Daniel jumping out.

She gives Felipe a gentle touch on the shoulder and manages not to flinch back as the pain latches onto her almost as if it wants to drag someone else into it. She manages a softer expression. 'Do as they say. We've got this.'

With that she moves around him and goes into the house. She's careful, conscious that medics have already contaminated whatever evidence there is.

She doesn't have to go far.

Alma is in the kitchen. She's lying on the floor, spreadeagled and still, surrounded by paramedics calling out sharply to each other. She'd been dressed for bed. The T-shirt that she's wearing comes down to mid-thigh and Isabel finds herself noting that it was yellow before all the blood soaked into it.

You have people too.

The stench of blood. Deus. Isabel breathes in sharply, punched in the gut by how much of it is all over the floor, all over the cabinets.

And I'm here, aren't I?

There's a ringing in her ears.

Isabel slowly backs out of the room and goes to the living room, staring at the open door. Slowly, and just as carefully, she makes her way back out to the front of the house.

Carla is on the top step and stops in her tracks at Isabel's face.

'They're trying to revive her,' Isabel says, and her voice is calm. She feels as if someone else is saying the words. 'Call Jacinta. Don't let anyone else in until the forensics team arrives.'

'Isabel?' Carla says and there's an odd note to her voice.

'Secure the scene. Is Voronov on his way?' she asks. She hasn't stopped walking. She's in front of her car now.

'Yes, he's on his way – Isabel, where are you going?'

But Isabel's already sliding into the car and slamming the door behind her.

'Call me as soon as you get an update on Alma, I'm going to see Venâncio.'

She doesn't hear anything else that Carla tries to say. The tyres screech as she peels away from the scene.

47

O Vermelho has a queue tonight.

There are people loitering outside, smoking, and chatting, drinks in hand from the café a little further down the street.

Isabel doesn't stop as she strides past the people waiting and shoves past the guy at the door. She ignores his yell and shakes off the hand he gets around her arm. She spins around and he stops in his tracks, staring at her like he's seen something that spooks him.

She doesn't stop to analyse it, just heads inside.

This time the fadista isn't alone on the main floor among the diners; the two musicians accompanying her with their guitars are right on the floor with her. She has a crown of red flowers around her head, arm sweeping in front of her as she sings, her voice rising to the ceiling and her black dress following her movements.

He's there. As he has been each time she's come in here. Except this time, he's alone at his table and his chair is to the wall, his eyes on the fadista below. He's dressed much the same way as when Isabel first saw him. And just like the first time, there's a moment when he seems to sense something, and then he turns his head and his gaze meets hers.

Isabel doesn't wait. There's a commotion behind her but she doesn't pay attention to it, just cuts through the ground floor and up the stairs, weaves her way until she reaches Ezequiel's table.

She grabs a chair and drags it over to where he's sitting. The legs hit the floor with a slam, drawing the eyes of nearby customers.

He doesn't say a word until she's sitting down and staring him in the face.

His hair is loose today and it's the first time that the scarred cheek isn't immediately visible.

'Looking to cause a stir tonight, Inspector Reis?' he says. The only thing on the table is what she thinks is red wine, in a small glass. The kind that she remembers her father having after dinner.

Isabel leans in close. 'You must think I'm like those idiots that come crawling over to you every time you snap your fingers. Not every team is in someone's pocket,' she hisses, 'and mine won't be paid off or bought.'

His expression remains placid and like before, there's no ripple of any emotion breaking the surface.

'I want to know who talked to you. You must've seen her at the funeral, hmm?' Isabel says. 'Who in the PJ do you have in your pocket?' She leans closer. 'Don't worry. I'm coming for you too, you piece of shit.'

He sits up. 'People with more weight behind them than you have tried, Inspector. But let me help you this one time.' His hair falls to brush over the edge of the table as he gets closer to her. 'I don't know what you're talking about.'

Alma's blood-speckled ankles, bare feet limp, snapped-out words from the paramedics, the fast activity to keep her tied to life. It all rises up, washing over Isabel, hazing her vision in red.

The fadista's voice echoes in the room, holding the note on a precipice.

He doesn't see it coming.

She knifes into his mind.

It's not like with Gabriel. There's no desperation. She never knew anger could feel so clean, like wrapping herself in a cold, cold sheet that lends clarity as she rips through his layers of protection and dives right for the centre.

She feels the violence in herself – but that expression on his face, of knowing, knowing that he will win again. And Alma's lifeless body on the hard kitchen floor, in the house where she was meant to be protected.

He's quick to try to push her out, a testament to how strong his ability is. He too, is not the classification that he's legally recorded as. He's not fast enough. And he doesn't have her brute force behind him. He pulls up the equivalent of concrete walls to block her and it takes her a moment to gather up her strength – and then she smashes and smashes.

What she sees clears the haze of anger, leaves her stunned.

That split second of distraction is enough.

The fadista's voice floods back in a crescendo and seems to hang there for ever as Isabel blinks, dazed, then focuses.

Ezequiel's face is almost a mirror of her own. He's got a hand pressed to his head, breathing hard, staring up at her, incredulous.

The fadista's voice cuts off and a loud pulse of applause and cheers and whistles floods the room.

And it dawns on her. What she's just done. Not in self-defence. Not out of desperation.

She rises up from the chair so fast it falls back with a clack. It barely registers over the noise of the applause.

She has to get out of here.

There's a wet heat on her lip and she wipes at it. Doesn't even glance at the streak of red that smears across her hand as she grabs at the chairs in her way, ignoring the indignant looks she gets as she staggers towards the stairs. As she rushes down them, she's bombarded by the thoughts around her, suddenly overwhelmed and exposed, caught unprotected.

Ezequiel is standing, hands gripping the railing and jaw clenched tight, eyes locked on her.

She rushes out. The fresh air hits her like a balm and she sucks at it greedily. Everyone is looking at her and the guy at the door is cursing her out, but she doesn't register it. Just starts walking. She keeps going. Shivers settle in. Which is ridiculous. It's not cold. But it feels as if she's vibrating with it.

She'd seen Marta.

It hadn't been a glazed eyes Marta, or a Marta with her throat slashed, or a Marta being tossed, naked, into a river.

No. This Marta had been wrapped in white sheets that contrasted with her dark skin, a hand on her cheek, a thumb tracing her sweet smile as her fingers played with long black strands. And the memory had been wrapped completely in gut-wrenching grief.

What?

She stops, leans against the side of a house. It's quieter here. She closes her eyes and breathes. Tries to get herself under control.

There'd been something before that – something else. Something intertwined with that memory—

Her eyes fly open.

A couple walk by, side-eyeing her, murmuring to each other as they turn away from the little street.

Some of the rage in that memory, she'd been so immersed in it because it had been hers. But not all of it. It had been Ezequiel's brother, spitting out her name – *believe her over m—*

Isabel scratches at her head. The informant. Cesario Monte. He'd said infighting. The rumours that were flying around. Ezequiel had been isolating everyone. And Operation Fado had clearly said, Ezequiel, Tiago and Marta. He'd known what Marta had been doing. He'd let her go.

Ezequiel had let her go.

It's then that she registers that it's not her shivering. The vibrating is coming from her pocket. Her hand is still trembling when she digs her phone out.

Voronov.

'Are you insane?' his voice snaps out, not giving her a chance to speak. 'What did you think you were doing? Where are you right now?'

She doesn't think she's ever heard him so furious. 'Aleks – it's not Ezequiel – *Tia*—'

That's as far as she gets. Maybe it's because she's all over the place, her Gift scrambled. She senses nothing. She just hears the scrape of a step right behind her. When she turns, pain slams up the side of her head. Then nothing.

48

Her whole head is suffused with pain and Isabel lies very still.

There's a tightness stretched across her front, her chest pushed forward and an ache in her shoulders that almost doesn't register because the pain in her head is so bad. She doesn't want to move. She doesn't even want to open her eyes, knows that the second she does, the pain will multiply.

She's in a car, she realises as the sounds around her finally filter in, and when she takes her next breath, she has to fight down panic as fabric gets sucked against her lips from her indrawn breath. It sends a shock through her that forces her to try to see.

Almost immediately she has to shut her eyes again. The pain radiates from the right side of her face to the centre of her forehead, and she feels sick. Gritting her teeth, she presses her forehead hard to the giving surface of what's probably one of the passenger seats and forces air out in as controlled a way as possible.

There's a bag over her head, its material soft. When she finds the will to push past the pain, she opens her eyes again. Some light filters in through the material but it comes and goes rhythmically. She can't see anything else.

Her hands are tied behind her back. Rope. It feels like rope. It's chafing at her skin. The hum of the wheels over asphalt is the only thing she can hear.

God, she feels sick. She has to swallow back a groan at the queasiness in her stomach.

She needs to focus, knows that she needs to ground herself and take in the turns of the car, try to figure out a way to check for any transport points they might be passing. But it's hard to get her thoughts in order.

She's definitely in the back of the car, she can tell that much. Though her cheek is pressed to the seat, she can feel the hard surface of the door against the top of her head and as she tentatively stretches out her feet, they touch against the other end. She can't straighten them out entirely.

Swallowing back panic, she forces herself to relax. If she can calm herself for long enough then she can try reaching out with her Gift to whoever has her in here. She'll have to be careful because they must be driving. She lets the motions of the car rock her back a little more until her fingers brush against the back of the seats. She starts rotating her wrists back and forth, careful not to draw too much attention to her movements or to jostle herself too much. The less she moves her head, the better.

They'd knocked her out so badly that even her Gift feels out of kilter. There's nothing. She can't feel anything, not even a touch of an emotional impression. Normally she'd get at least that. At least her feet aren't tied. That's something. Might be the thing that gives her a chance whenever they come to a stop. And if she can use her Gift to stun them, then that gives her decent odds. If she can actually walk or run in a straight line when it comes to it. The logical voice in the back of her head is telling her she's concussed and the most she might be able to manage right now is a crawl.

She thinks back. She'd lost her shit and gone to see Ezequiel Venâncio. And then she'd done the one thing she wasn't supposed to do: forced her way into his mind.

Merda, merda, *Isabel, you fucking idiot.*

Voronov.

She'd been on the phone to Voronov. He'd been yelling at her for being stupid and she'd been about to tell him—

Rest. She needs to stay alert but conserve her strength. She'll deal with the rest when—

Suddenly the terrain beneath the car changes and the smooth ride turns bumpy; she can hear the crunch of gravel beneath rubber. It rocks her body side to side. The motion sends that same mind-numbing pain radiating down the back of her neck.

The car stops.

Fuck. She's not ready. She can barely think straight. She hears water. As if to make matters worse, the sensation of being watched returns. She feels the sensation ripple through her the same way it always does, registering even despite the state of her.

She doesn't have a chance to think about it because the car door opens and shuts, rocking the whole vehicle. She hears them walking around the car. Hears them stop outside her door. Her heart is beating so hard, her mouth so dry. She fights to remain calm. She has to be ready.

She gathers herself as much as possible. Not even thinking about how she'll get rid of the bag that's over her head when it's time to run.

Hands hook into her armpits and drag her out of the car and set her on her feet.

Isabel takes a deep breath and throws her Gift out. It hits nothing. It's the same feeling as if she'd leaned on glass, thinking it was there only to fall right through it into thin air.

Which is impossible. They're standing right in front of her, hands on her arms now – which, if anything, should have made this easier.

She tries again and the same thing happens, like she's pushing her Gift through a sieve and all that's on the other side is emptiness. Nothing. There's nothing for her to latch on to here.

'You might as well stop trying.'

She recognises that voice.

The bag is pulled off her head and even though it's dark it takes her a moment to be able to adjust and focus, though she thinks that has little to do with being able to see properly and more to do with the blow to the head.

When she focuses, Tiago Venâncio stands in front of her.

49

'She burned herself out the same way,' he says and slams the car door shut behind her. He tugs on her arm, forcing her to follow him. A silver ring glints on his middle finger.

Isabel looks around them.

The terrain here is rough, mountainous. Her vision is blurry as she tries to make out something that will indicate where they are. He's parked the car on what's basically just a dirt track interspersed with dry weeds and spurts of tall brown grass that bends under the taunt of the breeze. The road that brought them here is one of those that always makes her nervous, way too narrow and with no wall to keep cars from veering off the road and driving straight down the side of the hill. There's a set of steep steps leading down to water.

Through her spotty vision, she sees the sky. It's completely black, only the wide glow of the moon lighting up the night. And in the far-off distance she can see a touch of purple, hinting at dawn.

How long has she been out?

He steadies her as they go down the stairs, not saying much.

There's a yacht at a faraway point. It's illuminated by the moonlight.

The steps lead down to a narrow boardwalk and she sees a speedboat at the bottom. There's someone there too, a dark shape she can't identify.

'Who?' Isabel asks.

Tiago glances over at her before going back to minding his step.

Briefly, Isabel considers shoving him. That would be one way to get free. Except the odds of him either dragging her down with him, or her losing her balance and joining him anyway, are both too high for her to consider that option.

'Marta. She thought she'd try one of the mind tricks you telepathic Gifted are so fond of. Kept trying to get into my head until the end. Couldn't understand why it wasn't working. She should have known better, but she kept trying. She burned herself out completely.'

The coroner's words from what seems like a very long time ago. Fried. Shorted out. That's what the coroner had said. Isabel wonders if she had meant it quite so literally.

As they go on, Isabel feels more and more unsteady. It's like the strength is leaking out of her legs. It forces Tiago to take a firmer grip on her and slow down.

'Why?' Isabel manages. Is she slurring? The slant of her mouth feels abnormal.

'Why what?'

'Why can't we get into your head?'

He smiles and for a split second she sees the resemblance to his brother, the hint of charm, before it disappears completely.

She remembers the first time she'd passed him and felt absolutely nothing. It had been the time she'd gone to O Vermelho with Voronov. She'd thought he'd just had a better grasp of his shields than Ezequiel, better than anyone else she had ever come across.

But now, she remembers Fonseca taking them through their information. Tiago tested as a Regular.

But in the face of what Isabel knows, does that even mean anything?

'You're Gifted.'

'No,' he says, answer short and clipped, 'are you thinking I fudged the tests like my brother? Although,' he gives her a sidelong look, 'I have to give it to you. Your attack feels stronger than theirs. Marta's and my brother's. You must be quite high up.' He frowns. 'What a waste.'

Isabel isn't sure if it's because she's too busy putting one foot in front of the other that his words don't incite the fear that they should. She supposes she'd known from the moment he'd taken the hood off her head. No one shows their face if they're planning to let somebody live.

They reach the bottom and head for the speedboat.

'Then what?' she asks. And yes. She's definitely having to feel her way around her words. She's tired and she wants to just let her eyes close. Except she's sure if she lets that happen Voronov is going to kill her when he finds her. It'll probably be too late but – well.

'I'm just a Regular but,' he raps his knuckles on the side of his head, 'no one's ever been able to get in here. Odd, isn't it? Ezequiel always calls me o impenetrável. He's never once managed to get inside my head.'

The person in the speedboat climbs out and the smell that clogs up her nose is a familiar one. It forces Isabel to lift her gaze and she is suddenly aware that she has been hanging her head.

The bearded face and the beanie hat. Exactly the same as before.

Cesario Monte can barely meet her eyes as he helps Tiago get her into the speedboat.

It's all falling into place, a little too late.

The rumours of infighting. Operation Fado noting the renewed activity but the differences that meant they couldn't get a read on it. It's because this time it hadn't been Ezequiel. And Tiago had been at the funeral too. Ezequiel hadn't been lying. She'd been in his head long enough to see he hadn't so much as laid eyes on Alma.

The speed of the boat pushes Isabel back against the seat as it jets toward the yacht sitting like a ghost in the water.

Her eyes glance over the name scrawled in black on the side of it. A Sirena, it says. She's so close to shutting her eyes, can feel the way her body is so loose, jostled by the boat. She feels like a lifeless doll but the pain in her head feels like it's sinking deep, sinking deeper, and burying itself in her brain like roots burying into deep, dark soil.

They have to lift her out of the speedboat. The yacht is huge and looms over them, casting a shadow as it blocks out the moon.

Exhaustion weighs her down.

The interior of the yacht is in darkness and the sounds of the water flows through the interior as they guide her through. It's luxurious inside. They pass through a section with the kind of seats that look so soft that you'd sink down into them and never get up. There's a bar opposite. Lights are strung up but they're not on.

When they finally stop, she's pulled into a room with a sprawling bed and a window that provides a view of the sea outside. There's a sense of déjà vu. But then she's being helped into a huge bathtub and her hands are being untied and this should be it, this should be when she makes some kind of break for it, but her head feels like lead.

'I don't get it,' she murmurs, frowning.

Tiago doesn't say anything as he works, re-tying her hands. This time he loops the rope around the tap, ties it tight enough that she feels it cutting into her skin. Monte is no longer with them. Isabel doesn't know when he left.

'She was out,' Isabel swallows, trying to wet her dry throat, 'why attack Marta?'

He flicks a look up at her as he rises and settles his hands on his hips. 'My brother stopped the business. Because of her.'

'That's it?' Isabel asks and sinks further into the tub. The cool of it feels soothing against the back of her head.

'We'd been moving steadily up the ladder and then that stopped. I wanted her help one last time. One tiny thing,' he says, and even now, she can hear the bitterness in his voice. 'I asked her to do it for me. Just three people. That's all it would have taken. They used to be House regulars, I just needed her to root around their brains a little for me. She refused, so I baited her. She had a very promising mentee working under her.'

Alma.

'I just needed enough to get Ezequiel to hand the business over to me. He didn't want it anyway. Not as it was. I forced her hand,

and she gave me what I wanted. All those recordings, every secret he'd used her to get. Now I can get things back on track, get back what he pissed away because of a fucking woman.' He smiles. 'My brother isn't a forgiving man. I couldn't have him finding out.' The smile fades. 'But she was going to tell him. She couldn't keep her trap shut. I would've left her alone.'

Isabel remembers Marta's face and the soft touch tracing the edge of her smile.

He shakes his head, a little stunned. 'What are the odds she'd wash up' – he sounds incredulous – 'but she did. It was an easy solve. He wouldn't have known.' Then his eyes drop to hers. 'And then you broke the rules.' He kneels by the tub and looks at her. 'Hasn't anyone told you it's illegal to go into someone else's head without their permission, Inspector Reis?'

Isabel stares him down; she's struggling to keep her grip on consciousness.

'And you saw what you needed to see in there.' He stands. 'It's done now. The girl is dead. You and what remains of the Houses are the only things left that can give me away. I've taken care of the rest. We fix that and there's barely any evidence left. The police will think it's all over. And it keeps you from blabbing to my brother about my plans for the business and what I did to his precious Marta. It buys me enough time to fully take over. Start anew, everything properly under my control. That way that joke of a police operation won't have any clue. It'll be outside of anything they've had their noses in. That's all I need, just a little more time. Then it will all be done.'

Isabel closes her eyes. There's something in the back of her head, something foreign that doesn't belong there. It's pushing her to open her eyes again.

But she can't.

50

Isabel jerks forward and coughs.

Her head feels like it's wrapped in bubble wrap and she's gone a few rounds with a professional boxer. She's arched back, arms stretched above her head and hands tied to the tap.

She looks around her, trying to blink away the dizziness, can just about lift her head to peer above the lip of the tub although it puts an uncomfortable strain on her shoulders and neck.

The dawn light makes the bathroom almost magical, adding a rosy touch to the luxury she finds herself surrounded by.

The tub she's lying in is wide enough to comfortably hold two people. It's like something out of a high-end hotel suite bathroom. Sleek in glass and gleaming white and gold.

Fuck.

Her hands are numb. She spreads her fingers and can feel the tightness of her skin, the blood flow being harshly restricted.

She coughs again. And again. And the smell registers.

And she gets it. Why they've left her here.

They've set the yacht alight. The smoke is slipping in, insidious and serpentine as it finds the crack beneath the door. Isabel laughs aloud, the sound a touch hysterical. What she wouldn't give for a little bit of telekinesis right now.

She's going to burn alive in the middle of the sea.

Who would even think of that?

She's breathing too fast, can feel it building in her chest, a trapped feeling that leaves her sitting there, stunned and out of her depth.

Then she pictures Alma on the kitchen floor.

And that fucker getting away with it all. Because, like he said, it will all be buried.

She eyes up the knots around her hands. They're tied tightly enough that all she'll do if she tries to wriggle them free is tear up her skin.

Grimly, she levers herself up.

She's still foggy, misjudges; her mouth knocks against the tap and she gasps, the metallic taste of blood flooding her mouth almost instantly. She ignores it and goes slower this time, more focused, stretching her neck and arching her head back, grunting at the effort as she looks at the knots upside down. She uses the leverage of being anchored to the tap to drag herself back enough for her mouth to line up with the knots.

The rope is rough, and it chafes at the corners of her mouth. She twists her wrists as much as she can in their bindings. The rope burns and doesn't loosen, but she keeps working at it.

She doesn't know how long she tries but after a while, teeth aching, mouth feeling rubbed raw, wrists burning, she sinks back down against the tub and gasps in breaths. She coughs. The smoke is rising.

Jesus.

The rope is too tight.

The thought that she won't get her wrists loose sinks in. Okay. Okay. Okay.

She drags in another deep breath, pulls herself back and up and tries again.

She ignores the rising smoke and keeps tugging, digging her teeth in and pulling. Has to remind herself to keep twisting her wrists.

When she falls back again to rest, she doesn't open her eyes.

The smell is getting worse. She can't measure how long she's been working on the rope. The time feels so slow and too fast all at the same time. Her face is wet. She doesn't know from what. Tears, sweat, saliva. She grunts. Tries again.

Desperation is clawing at her, sharp nails digging into her gut. The rope is becoming stained with reddish brown. She can taste it. She keeps going. Ignores her sobbing breaths, muffled by the rope, and keeps tugging.

She's about to drop her head back again, exhausted, when she feels it.

A tiny bit of give.

She freezes, eyes flying open. Her chest is heaving from her efforts. Did she imagine that? Tentatively, she shifts her wrists again, hissing at the pain.

No.

It's loosened.

She throws herself back into it so fast that her mouth clacks against the tap again, but she pushes past the pain and tugs with renewed energy. Starts laugh-crying as it slips again. And then the rope starts to gape.

She falls back and works her wrists.

'Come on, Isabel,' she mutters, over and over.

And then her wrists are free.

She pushes up off the tub. Her hands, wrists and mouth throb and she staggers but manages to catch herself before she falls over. Despite the impulse to just throw herself into getting the hell out of there, she forces herself to slow down and go carefully.

Her breath is shaking out of her when she stops by the door, her hand unsteady as she touches the back of her hand to the handle.

It's warm, but not burning.

Isabel stands back and quickly strips off her jacket. She yanks her T-shirt off and wraps it around her face, a makeshift mask, before shrugging her jacket back on and zipping it over her skin. She feels too naked beneath it. She ignores thoughts of the flames on her vulnerable body and opens the door.

Heat bathes her face like she's opened an oven door and been hit with a wall of hot pressured air. She opens her mouth, gasping in as much as she can.

Isabel pushes off, sweat pebbling on her brow, and goes into the room. The bed is familiar; she has a vague memory of being guided past it. The door is wide open.

Flames lick into the air ahead but the room is not completely closed off. Maybe if she wets her clothes she can get across—

That's when she hears it. Banging. Like someone's pounding on a door with their fists.

What?

Isabel edges further toward the flames, trying to listen over the loud sound of her own breathing, trying to pinpoint where the noise is coming from.

Her failed attempt at using her ability to attack Tiago earlier rises up to the surface as she considers using her Gift. But there's no time. She can't second-guess herself right now.

If you're not going to trust in your own abilities, who do you think will, Isabel?

Shakily, wary eyes on the flames as they climb up toward the ceiling and paint it black, she thinks past the throbbing of her injuries and extends herself, like splaying a net and trying to catch something in it.

It doesn't take long. It's almost as if whoever is there is projecting themselves as much as they can. They notice and it's like they grab on as tightly as possible.

The T-shirt she's tied around her face feels suffocating and her coughing intensifies. She's getting short of breath and her head is getting worse. She inches forward a bit at a time. Has to cut past the flames, feels the heat bathing her face and tenses, waiting for the burn. She can see the way out from here, can see the pink of the sunrise on the water. The floorboards there are slick though and flames flicker along the surface.

They must have doused it in petrol.

Fuck. Fuck.

She spots, across the room, the steps leading to a deeper part of the yacht, and before she can second-guess herself – she can feel the need for flight burning in her bones – she dashes for it. She almost skids down the three steps when she gets there and now, she can hear the banging.

'I'm here,' she yells as she rushes down into the small passageway. There are two doors, but she can see one shaking under the thumping of the fists on its other side.

'It's locked, we can't open it! We're locked in. Please!' It's a woman. She can hear other voices too, also women.

Helpless, Isabel stares at the handle. She has no key. Thinks they're probably in the pocket of the piece of filth who left them here to burn.

The last of the Houses.

That's what he'd meant. The women on the other side are what's left of the Houses.

Bastard.

The sound of the flames is crackling in the air, like whips of heat.

'Hold on,' Isabel says, even though the women's panic and fear are leaking out from behind the door, 'hold on, I-I—' She's looking down the passageway and then back up to the upper deck, 'hang on, I need to find something to get this open with. Just be careful, stand back from the door and stay low. I'm coming back, I promise.'

'Please hurry, please hurry.' The words are distorted by sobs.

Isabel tries the other door. It flies open with the force of her hand, slamming back against the wall, but there's nothing there.

What are you going to do, Isabel, what are you going to do?

Something heavy. Something to smash the handle in.

Like what? Fuck, like what?!

The cockpit – maybe the cockpit. She dashes back up the stairs, skidding to a stop at the top as she sees the flames eating into the panelling.

Where are the emergency supplies?

She makes a run back outside and the relief of cold air floods her lungs. She sucks it in, greedily, knees weak.

There's another level to the yacht. The trek up those stairs feels harder than it should be, but eventually she reaches another bar area. There's a bright red box and a fire blanket by the bar and she hurries over and scrabbles at it.

There's a fire extinguisher too and she lets out another hysterical laugh because this – this isn't even going to touch what's happening below.

She turns on the spot, hands dragging through her hair, trying to think of something, anything.

Maybe it won't work on the fire, but she could use it to hold back—

She turns back around and tentatively reaches out for it. It's weighty in her hand.

Her dash down the stairs sends her flying and the extinguisher catches her ankle; she cries out as she hits the deck. She scrabbles to grab it back and pushes herself to her knees, wraps the fire blanket around her as well as she can.

She becomes aware of a loud rumbling noise, but she's too busy staring at the flames blocking her way back into the lower area to think about it. They've fanned out, grown bigger. She drags the blanket up higher, so it covers her hair. She clutches the extinguisher to her and tugs the T-shirt back up around her face and dives back in.

The heat is different now. It's like walking into a furnace and she hurries, limping.

Behind the door, they're screaming.

'I'm here, I'm here. Stand—' she breaks off, coughs, 'stand back. Stand back!'

Then, half afraid the thing will burst in her face, she smashes the fire extinguisher against the door handle. A crack forms around it. She smashes it again. And again, and again. The handle gives, the crack around it deepening and caving in. Isabel sets the extinguisher down, grits her teeth and smashes her weight into the door.

The door breaks open and there are screams of alarm. Isabel lands on her hands and knees, fire blanket flying to the floor.

Hands rush to drag her up.

They're young. The face staring at her, naked fear etched into it, is so, so young.

Isabel swallows. She can't think of Alma. Not right now. 'Let's go, it's really bad.' She shoves the blanket at them, even though it'll just about cover one of them. She forces a tremulous smile onto her face. 'We may get a little singed. Push through, understand me? Push through.'

They nod and follow her back out into the hall. They're barefoot, dressed in flimsy, sheer black robes that hide nothing, but Isabel can't let herself focus on that right now.

'All right,' she says, 'grab each other's hands.' She grabs one woman and waits until they're all holding onto each other. 'Whatever you do, you don't stop, and if someone falls, you drag their arse back up, understand?'

Once they've all nodded, she rushes forward, dragging them all up the steps with her.

The heat – God the heat; she rushes through it, death grip on the hand she's holding, and keeps moving even as she feels it catch onto her. Feels it singe her face.

The whole thing is going up. She can hear the women yelling in pain behind her. The distance had seemed so short before, but now—

They burst out into the fresh air but there's only a narrow space left with no flames. They're too far from shore.

'We're going to have to—'

'Isabel!'

She snaps her head round.

The rumbling noise earlier. She stares, incredulous, at Voronov, sure for a moment that she is hallucinating. His shirt is plastered to his wet body as the rescue boat speeds toward them.

'Into the water,' she snaps, 'now. Go.'

She doesn't know how they do it, can't even feel the pain now, something else entirely pumping through her veins as they run round the edges of the deck and toward the stairs at the back, and then the sea is closing over her, icy and numbing, closing over her head. She hears the sound of bodies hitting water and opens her eyes.

Through the prism of water she sees the gauzy black robes floating up like something out of a dream and legs and arms cutting through it to propel themselves up.

Isabel breaks the surface.

The sky is aflame with the sun.

51

She sits shivering in the back of Voronov's car, wrapped in a blanket, hair stringy from the salt water, sipping from a bottle of water a paramedic has pushed into her hand.

Out in the distance, emergency vessels litter the water.

Her wrists are wrapped up and her ankle has been wrapped too. Her mouth stings. She'll have to get an X-ray, but they think it's bruising, nothing else. Her hair is singed and there's a burn on the back of her left shoulder where the flames caught and stayed, but all in all, she's not too bad. She still has to go to hospital to get her head checked though.

The three women have already been taken away by the ambulance and Daniel and Carla will be there to greet them when they arrive, to take statements and to make sure they're safe, that no one else gets in to see them while they wrap everything up.

Voronov breaks away from the other officers on the scene, who will be investigating what they can take from the wreckage of the yacht, and walks toward her. She watches him approach. His jacket is nowhere to be seen and his hair is a complete mess. His blue eyes are alive with barely restrained anger.

She knows 50 per cent of that is aimed at her. She can't blame him.

When he stops in front of her, she doesn't say anything. Just waits.

'Do that again,' he says, 'and you can find yourself a new partner.'

She glances away, mouth working tightly, even though she knows he has every right.

'Isabel.'

'Don't talk to me like I'm a child, Voronov,' she snaps. Then winces. Then swears.

She hears him swear too and pace away, hands fisted at his sides.

She takes another sip. Can't seem to get enough, her throat still feeling so dry.

'Sorry.'

He stops, back still to her.

'I'm sorry,' she says again.

'What were you thinking?' he asks, quieter, calmer, closer.

'He killed her,' she says, 'and I'd made her a promise I shouldn't have. I lost it.' And it's not good enough.

It isn't. But it's the truth.

'She's not dead, Isabel.'

It takes her a beat to register his words. 'What?'

'It's still bad, they're not sure she'll make it, but she's not dead.'

She sags with the relief. Then she looks up at him. 'Have they found Tiago yet?'

Sighing, he walks over and leans on the side of the car. His sleeves are still soaked to the upper arms from where he'd helped reach down and pull them out of the water. 'Not yet. But they found Cesario Monte.'

'And is he talking?'

'He's dead.'

Of course. Monte would have been another loose end.

'We've got eyes out for him. We'll get him,' Voronov says.

He straightens up and goes around to the front of the car. Isabel doesn't bother moving from where she is. Doesn't want to move at all for a long while. Gingerly, she rests her head back and lets her eyes fall closed. He starts the car.

'Aleks.'

'What is it?'

'How did you know where we were?'

When he doesn't say anything, she lifts her head and meets his eyes in the rear-view mirror. She can't interpret the look he's giving her and she's too tired to try to parse it with her Gift.

'Let's get you checked out first,' he says, 'there's someone who wants to speak to you. It will help explain everything.'

Isabel stares at him but he doesn't say anything else, just pulls the car out and gets them onto the dirt track.

She finds she can't close her eyes again. Instead she watches as the morning settles into itself, the water a completely different sight in the light of day.

52

Voronov waits with her until she's cleared to leave the hospital. He tells her he's barely held her brother at bay and that Sebastião had agreed to wait for her at her place. Isabel hadn't wanted to speak to him on the phone. She hadn't wanted him to hear even the slightest hint of emotion in her voice, because she knows that would have sent him flying to her side and she's not quite sure she could take that.

After she's spent a solid ten minutes on the phone reassuring Sebastião that she's fine and that she'll be home soon and practically begging him to stay put, Voronov drives her back quietly, with her once again in the passenger seat. The normal way of things.

Seeing the doctors go through her injuries, she'd felt Voronov thawing out of concern, before edging back towards anger all over again because they were the result of her being reckless to begin with. And somewhere in those streams of thought that he wasn't even trying to hold back was guilt, deep-seated, that he hadn't been there to stop it happening.

Isabel doesn't call him out on it. There's nothing she can do other than apologise, but when she worked up her courage to say it again, he just waved it off.

She's curious though, her good leg bouncing with nervous energy as he drives them to a café close to the Torre de Belem.

She expects the café to be packed with tourists when they walk in and she's not disappointed. She feels too raw really to be in a place like this right now, but Voronov hasn't said anything else about who they're here to see and she wants to know how in the hell they figured out where they were when so many years of the OF turning over every stone hadn't got them close.

A lot of people are eagerly chomping down on pasteis de nata, children using a tiny spoon to scoop out the sweet custard, flakes of pastry scattered over the tables. A mixture of languages blends together and drowns out the radio playing in the background.

A portly man half-rises out of his seat when he spots them. He's wearing a suit that doesn't close around his middle and round glasses that lend his full face a touch of kindness.

'Inspector Voronov,' he says and reaches out a hand, 'I appreciate this favour.' Then he turns to Isabel and holds out his hand. 'Inspector Reis, I'm glad you're all right.'

Isabel takes his hand slowly, looking between him and Voronov. Who is this man and why the hell are they meeting here? She's cleaned up as best as she can and is wearing a jumper that Voronov pulled from somewhere in his car. It swamps her. But despite having managed to get most of the soot off her face and out of her hair in a hospital bathroom, she's sure she still looks as grubby and exhausted as she feels. Her body aches all over and she just wants to go home and rest.

'I'm Rui Carrilho. I'm Gabriel Bernardo's lawyer.'

Isabel freezes. 'I'm going to need you to explain.'

He nods rapidly, pushing his glasses further up his nose, and asks her to take a seat. 'I was woken up in the early hours by a call,' he says, and there's a flush to his cheeks, a nervous energy leaking out into the space around him.

'Gabriel had persuaded the person on duty to allow him to use the phone. Apparently, they took a lot of convincing.'

'I still don't understand what this has to do with me,' she says, 'and to be honest I'm not sure I should be meeting with you, Mr Carrilho. The prosecution team are already not happy with the fact that your client has been writing to me.'

Mr Carrilho holds out a hand, a plea for her to listen. 'In that call, Gabriel asked me to contact your partner Inspector Voronov and give him a message.'

Isabel blinks. She huffs out a laugh. 'What?' She shakes her head. 'What message?'

'Isabel,' Voronov says, and she looks at him, hoping he's about to somehow get this all to make sense. 'Mr Carrilho got through to me at four fifty in the morning. You'd been missing for four hours. The message Gabriel asked him to deliver – he told his lawyer to tell me you were on a boat called A Sirena.'

Isabel stares. 'That's – that's impossible.'

How could he have known?

'That makes no sense. That makes *no* sense—' she says.

And then she thinks back to the letters, how they'd contained information on the names that she'd been searching for. She thinks of all the times she's sat on her own and felt as if someone was watching.

She thinks about Gabriel Bernardo's ex-girlfriend, thinks about her standing there in her living room all those months ago, telling Isabel and Voronov that Gabriel was in her head.

'Isabel. Isabel.'

Voronov's grabbing onto her shoulders and she turns to him, not really seeing him. 'Aleks . . .' and she feels it, the horror blanketing her, drowning her.

'I need you to calm down. You need to calm down.' His eyes dart around them, reminding her that they are in a public place.

Isabel looks at Mr Carrilho, who is sitting there, not making eye contact with her, shoulders hunched in.

'I need to see him,' she hears herself say.

Mr Carrilho takes a deep breath and then lets it out slowly. Isabel gets the distinct impression that she doesn't want to hear what he has to say next.

'Your partner here also wanted the same thing. And I was happy to try to oblige him. Which is why I was shocked when I arrived at the facility where he was being held and was told that custody of Mr Bernardo has been transferred. He is no longer there.'

What? He hasn't even had his trial.

'When I tried to get information about who authorised his transfer or to find out what facility he's been moved to, I was blocked. I've been trying for the past three hours to find a trace of Gabriel Bernardo and where he's been taken. Inspector Reis, I can't find even a crumb.'

This can't be happening.

'He's gone.'

53

A week to the day, Alma wakes up and Tiago's car is located.

But Tiago himself is nowhere to be found.

Conscious that Voronov will probably tear her a new one, Isabel almost doesn't do it. But in the end, she needs to know. She picks a nice public spot and gets in touch with Ezequiel.

She's still a little surprised when he joins her, quietly sliding into place beside her and facing out to the view of the city. 'Didn't think you'd show,' she says.

'And risk you showing up at my place of business again, Inspector Reis?'

There's no grief on his face. Nothing that hints at any inner turmoil.

'I owe you an apology,' she says.

'It was a very interesting thing that you did,' he says. He turns his back on the view and watches her. He's not dressed to go into work; he's in similar casual clothes to those he wore when he showed up at the precinct.

Conveniently, with his brother's disappearance and the girls in the First House having been kept there by Tiago himself, it has so far been easy for Ezequiel to sidestep any blame. He has a team of fantastic lawyers, not to mention plenty of people in the system who Isabel suspects have a healthy wariness about moving against him. There's no telling when Ezequiel could turn on them. Despite everything, it seems Ezequiel is still untouchable.

'It was a violation of your privacy. And the law.' And it sticks in her throat that she did it. 'I won't blame you if you report it.'

There's a hard edge to his face as he regards her. 'My brother tried to burn you alive, Inspector.'

'That was your brother.'

He huffs a laugh. 'That it was.'

'We've found his car.'

He glances at her. 'Have you?'

'When we were there, on the yacht, he told me you weren't a very forgiving man.'

'I like to think I'm as forgiving as any other person.'

Which is to say, some things are beyond forgiveness. Backstabbing your brother. Killing someone said brother cared deeply about.

'Is he dead?' Isabel asks.

Ezequiel leans closer, close enough that his hair swings forward and brushes against her arm. 'Why don't you take another peek inside my head and find out?'

She doesn't, of course, just waits, the bustle of the tourists around them and the squeals from children a sharp contrast to their conversation.

Eventually, he eases away from her. 'He's dead to me,' he says.

Isabel nods and pushes away from the railing. The image flashes in her mind's eye, bullet-fast. Gruesome and dripping with misery and murderous intent. She sees Tiago's throat gaping open, head nearly severed. And the hand holding the knife looks so much like the hand that had touched Marta's smile.

Isabel closes her eyes and breathes.

'There's still plenty of evidence against you,' she says. 'I think they'll be coming for you this time.'

When he doesn't speak, Isabel turns to look at him.

He's watching her, a sombre expression on his face. 'You remind me of her, you know. Of Marta. She wasn't afraid of anything.'

Isabel looks back out at the spread of the city. 'You're wrong. She was afraid of everything.'

Later, after she's walked her dogs – can't run with them, her ankle is still too sore – and paid a visit to Alma, she falls onto her sofa, clicking through the TV channels in hopes of finding something mindless to just stop her from thinking.

Sleeping hasn't been going too well for her. She dreams either of sinking to the bottom of the sea and never making it back up, or of the flames finding her in that tub and leaving her a burnt husk.

She curls into a corner, Tigre and Branco jumping up and curling up beside her. The sun is setting outside and the sounds of kids at the basketball court drift in, soothing.

Despite herself, she starts to slide into a doze.

And on the very cusp of sleep, a voice whispers . . .

Isabel.

THE END